SWISS
VENDETTA

SWISS
VENDETTA

TRACEE de HAHN

MINOTAUR BOOKS

NEW YORK

SWISS VENDETTA. Copyright © 2017 by Tracee de Hahn. All rights reserved. Printed in the United States of America. For information, address St. Martin's Press, 175 Fifth Avenue, New York, N.Y. 10010.

www.minotaurbooks.com

Library of Congress Cataloging-in-Publication Data
is available from the Library of Congress

ISBN 978-1-250-10999-6 (hardcover)
ISBN 978-1-250-11000-8 (e-book)

Our books may be purchased in bulk for promotional, educational, or business use. Please contact your local bookseller or the Macmillan Corporate and Premium Sales Department at 1-800-221-7945, extension 5442, or by e-mail at MacmillanSpecialMarkets@macmillan.com.

First Edition: February 2017

10 9 8 7 6 5 4 3 2 1

For Henri

Acknowledgments

I would like to thank my editor, Elizabeth Lacks, and the entire team at St. Martin's/Minotaur for their help bringing this story to life. Also, many thanks to my agent, Paula Munier, for all of her hard work on my behalf.

Many people have provided support and encouragement throughout this process: Hugh Bromma, Stacy Cannon, Judy Hoffman, Brooks Horsley, Lois Kelly, Bette Morgan, Patty Morse and Mary Rordam kept me motivated; Daniel Bardy, David Bieri, and Anja Haelg Bieri answered cultural questions (all interpretations and errors are my own); Kathi Good, Stacia Momburg, Mindy Quigley, and Julia Smyth-Pinney read drafts (over and over); everyone I met at the Algonkian Writers Conference in NYC, most particularly Christine Stewart (aka The Real Writer Editing Services), nudged me toward the final draft; Cassie Carter and Chip Visci provided unflagging support outside the world of writing; and my sisters Kathryn Balch and Amber Willis had great ideas at critical moments and know how to support even the biggest dreams. Finally, a special thank you to Vacherin, for inspiration and a shared love of travel.

In an entirely separate category are my parents, Janet and Lynn Leigh, who define unconditional love and support. It was my mother who taught me how to read and my father who taught me how to write; they can dispute which task required more patience. Finally, deepest love and appreciation to my husband, Henri de Hahn, who always believed, and who introduced me to Switzerland, his country.

What is history but a fable agreed upon?
—Napoleon

DAY ONE

Château Vallotton, Switzerland

Felicity Cowell fled, her bare feet slapping the cold stone of the corridor. She tried to soften the sound, but her heart said run and she followed her heart until the corridor turned, ending abruptly at a steep flight of stairs. She stopped short, teetering on the top step. This path led to a ground-level door and the lawn. Another miscalculation. She needed a different escape.

It had started two weeks ago. "Welcome to our home," the old biddy had said in her quiet voice that first day. Her polite and perfect English twisted by a French accent, the hospitality of the greeting so nuanced with insult that Felicity nearly left, for it was what she had expected. To call this place—this mass of stone and land and art—a *home* screamed privilege and arrogance.

The idea had been enchanting: a few weeks' work evaluating art in the spectacular Château Vallotton on the shore of Lac Léman. Even that was a lie. Instead of the promised perfection of Switzerland, the days had been gray and wet, the château chilly enough to satisfy a Scotsman. She had known from the first greeting that the trip was a mistake.

Now she had proof. Everything she feared was coming true. She stood at the top of the narrow flight of stairs, trembling in a thin evening dress. She hurried down, her hands trailing the walls for balance. At the bottom, in the narrow back entry hall, she huddled out of sight, seeking solitude. She wrapped her arms around herself, silently cursing everyone she had ever known. The pressure in her chest was overwhelming, her lungs wouldn't expand and oxygen couldn't reach her brain. Questions. She couldn't face their questions. Her anger returned, transformed into rage. She belonged here. This could be her home, her possessions, her life. She thought about them—all of them—and remembered what would happen if they knew the truth about her. She shuddered. It was the end of a dream.

Voices neared, no longer echoes but distinct words, and she smacked the wall in frustration. Countless rooms in the château and she had backed herself into a corner with nowhere to go but outside. She pressed her stinging palm to her face and choked back tears, wadding the folds of the borrowed evening gown in her fists. How had it come to this? How had she lost control of her life? She straightened, refusing to be trapped. Whatever happened would be on her terms.

She grabbed the handiest pair of boots and a coat, shoving arms and feet into their proper places before pulling the door open. She looked out at the frozen landscape in wonder. The afternoon rainstorm had transformed into a monster of ice. Wind whistled, racing off Lac Léman and slicing down the stone blocks of the château's outer walls. She nearly slammed the door shut, but the consequences of staying were too great. Instead, she stepped outside. She knew a warm place where she could gather her thoughts unseen. The château's Orangerie. Normally only a two-minute walk, she was certain she could make it. She had done hard things before, impossible things, and knew she could do this.

The force of the storm pummeled her, pushing into the down jacket and whipping her long skirt into a frenzied tail. She leaned forward, shoulders hunched, and eyes nearly closed against the onslaught. The rubber-soled boots were too big, but they cut through the ice that crusted the normally lush green lawn and she angled away from the château, her jacket hood pulled so low she could only see a slice of ground. Halfway there, she stumbled and fell.

She scrambled to her feet, frightened. She'd lost her bearings. Wind howled like the roar of a waterfall and the air was so dense with ice that she couldn't see. She couldn't tell which direction she was going. She concentrated on avoiding the lake, hoping to find her way back to the château. Damn the consequences.

When she reached a small grove of trees she leaned against a trunk, her body in revolt, muscles shaking. She lurched forward, falling more than sitting on a bench. She was scared and relieved in equal measure. At least she knew where she was. Parts of her were numb—legs, hands, nose—but she was beyond caring. She bent over, hunched against the wind, disbelief filling her mind.

Twenty-eight years and much to show for it: salary, respect, position. All legitimate, but not enough. Never enough.

The cold sank into her bones and her ears burned. At least here no one could ask questions. Maybe it was for the best. First numbness, then nothing. Easier than living with grinding worry and indecision. She sagged: a test of surrender. The wind slipped by in sharp needles. She was incapable of moving. Of reacting. For the first time in weeks her mind was calm. No more lies. An end to everything.

Unexpectedly something hit her like a hard slap on the back. She slipped from the bench and her hands flew out in front of her. She fell, striking the hard cold ground. The pain wasn't in her cheekbone or even the wrist that twisted awkwardly under her torso; the pain was in her chest and down her arms. She was confused. Her cheek was pressed to the ice and it was too great an effort to push herself up; the cold ground contrasted with the strange warmth spreading inside her, like a coating.

With great clarity she thought of what might have been. She had allowed the past to confuse her. She could no longer judge time and it didn't matter. She shook uncontrollably and her vision clouded. She whispered: "I was wrong, I don't want to die."

One

"I thought you'd left."

The offices of the newly formed violent crimes division of the *sûreté* were unusually quiet for late afternoon and the voice startled Agnes Lüthi. She looked at the perfectly coiffed redhead in front of her desk and shut her drawer like a child caught with a hand in the cookie jar. Involuntarily both women glanced over the desk and shelves. The brushed aluminum and white surfaces gleamed. Not a photograph remained of the dozen that the staff had so carefully placed after moving Agnes's belongings from her old office at financial crimes, and what had been a tribute to a loving family was now a sterile workspace. Files, reference books, and procedure manuals were all in place, but no trace of her husband or her three sons remained.

Agnes met the other woman's gaze and said nothing. She saw a flicker of uncertainty followed by sadness as her colleague's eyes skimmed her disheveled hair and tweed suit.

"Monsieur Carnet was sorry to lose you, but change is good." The redhead paused. "If you need anything, let me know."

"Thank you," Agnes mumbled, startled by the mention of Robert Carnet. The invitation to transfer from his division into violent crimes couldn't have come at a better time. She tugged the hem of her jacket self-consciously, no longer optimistic about losing the ten pounds that seemed to come with her brand of grief.

"We're happy to have you with us," the other woman said. "Chief Bardy should have been here today to get you sorted out. It's all new, this group he has in mind. Even the offices are new." She shrugged slightly and leaned forward. "He's a bit distant and if you need . . . well, if you need more time off just let me know and I'll handle him. We've talked about it"—she glanced around—"and we can cover for you. Anytime. Monsieur Carnet said you might need . . . he said your boys might need you."

Anger flashed through Agnes and it was difficult to speak. Pity and concern were bitter medicine; she wanted anonymity. "Carnet has no idea what my boys need. None whatsoever." She ran a hand through her short hair, instantly regretting it. Wondering if she looked like a porcupine had landed on her head.

"I really came to say welcome and to let you know they're sending everyone home. All nonessentials." The woman rolled her eyes with a smile. "Be thankful you're still nonessential. A bit early in my view, but the news on Espace 2 has announced that this will be the storm of the century. The rain is turning to ice, and if you don't leave now you may be stuck for the weekend."

She gave a cheery wave and turned, but not before Agnes saw the uncertainty on her face. No one knew how to treat her, what to do with her. She was certain there was an abundance of euphemisms for her situation. She had heard the whispered exchanges. "Grieving." "Still in shock." Each in some way an accurate expression. It was the other unsaid thoughts that angered her, although it was to be expected. Even her place in Bardy's group was undefined. The invitation to join violent crimes as part of a special team he was assembling held promise. Unfortunately, she had been so desperate for change she hadn't listened to the details. Different work, new colleagues, new environment, that's all that had mattered. Now she considered her options. Iced-in all weekend away from home. A welcome reprieve.

She opened the desk drawer again and looked at her husband's smiling face. The photograph was only six months old. It was taken the day she won a first at the shooting match in Bienne. He had looked so happy. Not just his usual geniality but genuinely happy. Exuberant.

She slammed the drawer. Nonessential. That's what she was.

She was reaching for her coat when the phone on her desk rang. The voice over the receiver was crisp. "Inspector Lüthi, the *gendarmerie* at Ville-sur-Lac telephoned the chief. A woman has died. He's on his way and wants you to join him there." The voice added other essential details then paused and continued in a different tone: a human element inserted into police business. "Of course, if you don't want to . . . I mean, with the weather I could explain—"

Agnes interrupted. "No, I'll go. I'm leaving now." Although the child of American parents, she'd lived in Switzerland her entire life and wasn't going to let a winter storm stop her. Everything she had wanted, and now it was happening. She slipped her arms into her coat, relief flooding her. It wasn't yet time to go home.

Ten minutes later she had second thoughts about her decision. Her Citroën C1 handled well, but tonight it felt like a flimsy cocoon of heat as she moved through the storm. She turned on the radio and fiddled with the dial until she found Espace 2. It only took a few minutes to comprehend that she should have paid attention to the earlier warnings. The announcer's voice intoned disaster: roads closing, accidents on the highway, and the promise of more to come as the storm gained power with every minute. Farther west, in Geneva, Cointrin was closed and all flights were grounded. The temperature was dropping and the wind accelerating. A dangerous mix.

Agnes switched the radio off, eliminating the distraction. She wished Bardy had chosen to locate their new offices in the city center and not on the outskirts. Nervous, she gripped the steering wheel firmly and concentrated. The Citroën's headlights cut across the wind, barely illuminating a few meters of roadway, and she constructed the view from memory: the long gentle slope separating the highway from the lake, the famous view of Lac Léman and in the distance the French Alps. Normally, train tracks were visible between the road and the lake, however, tonight all she could see were a thousand shards of white falling from the sky.

Slowly, she looped through central Lausanne, the city a glow of lights. It was Wednesday and passing Place St. François she could practically taste the roasted chestnuts and mulled wine of the city market, a favorite childhood memory, a ritual unchanged in her nearly forty years. She turned the car onto the Avenue du Théâtre, then angled right to descend the Avenue Villamont to the Avenue de la Gare, before turning left onto the Avenue d'Ouchy. The road was steep and slick and she slowed her pace and leaned forward, white-knuckled. Reaching level ground at Ouchy, she skirted the luxurious Beau-Rivage Palace hotel on the left, the yellow awnings quickly fading from sight. Here, near the lake, the full force of the storm was in evidence. A clear line of white marked the advancing edge of ice where the wind blew moisture off the lake's surface, adding to what was descending from the clouds and freezing instantly. Immediately, she knew that she was in a race to reach the château before the road was impassable.

Her hand strayed to her mobile phone. It was still possible to call the station and say she couldn't make it, but the thought of going home prevented her. That, and a need to prove herself to Bardy. If he sidelined her, she would lose the cornerstone of her sanity. Her sons might need her, but she needed this.

The road veered inland at the Tour Haldimand and slipped behind lakeside homes. Here there was less ice and she hoped the road would provide more traction. Minutes passed in silent terror of losing control of the car. Near the village of Cully the storm allowed only a few glimpses of the vine-covered hills and terraced walls. Where the road aimed for the lake before turning to follow the curve of the shore, she strained to see her destination. Château Vallotton was across the water off the point. Tonight it wasn't visible. Or perhaps it was—that slightly brighter glow of lights through the whiteout. It was impossible to tell.

After passing a small port filled with ice-coated sailing yachts, worry turned to near panic. The few other cars were stopped at awkward angles and she didn't have any illusions that her own driving skills were superior. There were no more towns on the lake road until Ville-sur-Lac and road crews would not have gone beyond this point. She shifted into a lower gear. She touched the brake, then the gas pedal, undecided about continuing. This stretch of road was isolated. She turned on the radio again and frowned at the news. The storm's impact was unprecedented: a state of emergency across three *cantons*.

Ahead, the road narrowed. On each side were high stone walls and she knew she should not have started this trip. There was no way to turn back now, no place to stop. She owed her boys safety and security. If she died they would be orphans.

Twenty minutes later, the lane crested on the cliff and the wall on the lakeside fell away. Wind struck the car and it slid sideways, pushed inland. At that moment, just when she thought she wouldn't make it, the car slipped into the shelter of the village.

Agnes relaxed and took a deep breath, blinking moisture from her eyes. She unclenched her hands from the steering wheel, feeling her stress dissipate. She remembered passing through Ville-sur-Lac years before. The buildings of the tiny village were ancient stone and they shouldered together against the road, leaving only a narrow strip of pavement for cars to maneuver. Tonight, hers was the only vehicle battling the elements and she kept to the center of the street. The green pharmacy sign flashed through the white blur and she could imagine each business as clearly as if it was broad daylight: butcher, *confiserie*, hotel. Somewhere was the *gendarmerie* where the small local police force was likely worried about storm damage. She glided to an uneasy stop where the lane to the château sloped down precipitously. Farther up the main street she could make out the rear of a large tourist bus. Shadowy forms filed off and scurried into a building. The village hotel, she presumed, absently thinking it unlikely they had enough rooms to accommodate an unexpected busload of guests. At that moment her mobile phone rang. She glanced at the caller ID and remembered why she was anxious to take this assignment.

A few minutes later she interrupted. "It's an honor, working with Étienne Bardy." She'd said these same words to her mother-in-law a hundred times since she had decided to return to work. "This may be an important case." The white lie slipped out easily.

Through the darkness she could make out the roofline of the château on the shallow peninsula below the cliff and, to give her mother-in-law time to complain, she plucked facts about the historic property from memory. Every schoolchild knew the basics: the oldest part was a hulking round tower nearly a thousand years old. Perched on the edge of the lake, it was a well-known icon gracing generations of artists' sketches and postcards.

"More important than your sons?" Sybille's voice cut through her reverie. "Working when a mother should be home. I know your parents had different customs—"

It was an old refrain, one Agnes had long ago decided to ignore. In Sybille's mind *American* and *uncultured interloper* were equivalent terms. Knowing a response wasn't required, Agnes focused on the château and probed her memory. In addition to the original tower, there were three others, all joined by long arms to create the final square fortress. She peered out the side window of her car, squinting into the white blur of the night. Years ago she had read about the smaller towers and a wall along the top of the cliff where the village now stood. The whole arrangement was unusual: the family constructing a fortress to control lake trade and then adding protection high above.

Why not build on the cliff in the first place? The wall remnants were long destroyed or incorporated into the village; Agnes couldn't make out a trace of them.

"I'm at Château Vallotton," she blurted out, mentally excusing herself for the slight exaggeration. The silence over the phone spoke volumes. She added a few details about the reason she was away from her family on a stormy night and in the pause could sense Sybille's mental tug-of-war. No one they knew had ever been invited to the château. And, although not a social call, it would be the nearest any of Sybille's friends came to visiting the property. Agnes knew that she was tempted to be curious.

While her mother-in-law chewed on this dilemma, Agnes made out a few lights glimmering through windows high in the nearest tower. She was familiar with the château from trips on Lac Léman and tried to reconcile what was in her mind with the narrow illuminated slits in front of her.

"If the dead woman is outside then you're unlikely to go in," Sybille finally said, cruelty winning out over curiosity. "They'll keep you standing in the freezing rain and send you home to do your reports."

Agnes didn't argue.

Sybille's voice was raised. "None of my friends have daughters who work at night in a storm. The worst storm of my lifetime. Who knows what is going to happen, and you're thinking of yourself and not of your family—"

The line went dead. Startled, Agnes tapped the mobile phone screen. Call failed. At least she hadn't hung up accidentally. She tried to connect a few times before slipping the useless device into her handbag. Just then, the blurred glow of the village went black. With the light went any sign of the buildings and all that was left was a white haze fading into darkness. If power was out because of the storm, tonight's job just got harder, and would take longer. She lowered her forehead to the steering wheel in dismay. After a moment she smiled in satisfaction. She knew why the château was dramatically altered from this angle: the more familiar lakeside façades had newer, larger windows cut into them. She dredged up another morsel from her tiny store of knowledge about architecture: the windows facing the lake were in the Renaissance style, larger than the earlier narrow defensive arrow slits. She laughed under her breath. It made sense. Of course the Vallotton family had renovated over the centuries. Larger windows once they didn't need a fortified residence, and, likely, modern plumbing and electricity.

She pulled herself nearer the windshield and peered down the hill through the eerie white night, the nearer trees glistening in her headlights. What kind of people lived in a place like this? Her curiosity was aroused by Sybille's reaction more than she would admit. The phone call reminded her of the first time she met George's parents. They were intimidating with their politeness, their hesitant questions drawing attention to her own upbringing and reminding her how her parents had worn a veneer of Swiss-ness in public, while keeping to their own customs at home. George's parents' house had been her dream: the perfect wooden chalet with balconies running on the upper floors and flowers cut into the old-fashioned wood shutters. She frowned. If George's family home was at one end of Swiss domestic perfection then Château Vallotton was at the other, and she hoped she would have a chance to go inside. That would be something to tell her boys. Given the family's prominence, it was no wonder Bardy had been called.

Bardy. His name was like a dose of cold water. The drive from Lausanne had already taken too long and now she had delayed unnecessarily. She nosed her car closer to the edge of the lane. It was impossible to see the pavement that cut down the steep hill. She glanced around one last time as if Bardy might be parked nearby, perhaps ready to suggest they manage the situation from the comfort of the *gendarmerie*. But the street was empty and she was expected below.

Gripping the wheel, she touched the gas. Instantly she knew it was a mistake.

Two

The Citroën struck something, rolled a bit farther, then shuddered to a stop. "Inspector Lüthi, indeed," Agnes said, appalled by her own poor judgment. She loosened her hands from the steering wheel and rested her forehead on the cold plastic, shaking with relief. Glancing up at the looming wall of the château, she turned off the car's headlights, noting one had shattered on impact, and hoped no one had witnessed her calamitous descent. She decided not to dwell on the damage done to the driver's-side door by the branches she'd careened into, or the dent in the hood created by whatever hard object she'd struck at the base of the hill. At least it had stopped her sliding into the château itself.

Shaking off the shock of the crash, she stepped out of the car. Immediately she regretted her thin pantyhose and sensible pumps, wishing she had worn sturdy boots and heavy stockings. She had on her winter coat, but the severity of the storm was unexpected and she had left in a hurry that morning without scarf, hat, or gloves. To compensate, she fished a thin plastic rain cap from under the seat of her car. Ridiculous but necessary as the sleet fell in sharp streams.

A flash of light erupted to her left and she knew that was where the others were gathered. She acclimated to the cold and got her bearings: château in front of her blocking wind off the lake, cliff and village to the rear, with the long, flat peninsula on either side. Wander too far in three directions and the lake was waiting, a treacherous death trap.

Walking as quickly as she dared on the ice, she kept close to the outer wall of the château, hand clasped around the flashlight she kept in the car for emergencies.

Reaching the far side of the east tower she felt the punch of the storm full-on. She gasped and braced herself. In the distance, a beam of light filtered through the branches of a small stand of trees. She ran her own flashlight beam across the frozen lawn, sliding forward carefully to avoid falling, leaning to counter the wind. Overhead, milky ice, thicker than a finger, encapsulated every tree limb. Her plastic rain hat whipped off and disappeared and she wanted to turn back, her earlier enthusiasm for the job no match for these conditions. The temperature was bitter and her fingers, ears, and nose hurt.

She reached her destination and a man wearing a bright blue police coat with reflective striping stood in the glow from the electric lantern by his feet. He secured a second flashlight under his arm. It darted across Agnes's face, startling her.

"We're all probably gonna die out here," the policeman shouted over the wind. He pulled a long section of canvas taut and struck a hard blow on a metal stake. "Wanted to safeguard the area and the wind shifted."

The line tightened and the fabric pulled up and into position, creating a semi-protected corner; instinctively Agnes stepped near. They huddled together, shielded from the sleet.

The officer introduced himself as from the *gendarmerie* at the top of the hill. André Petit, he said. Agnes angled her head up to look at him, thinking of course that was his name. He was at least a foot taller than her five feet four inches. Beneath his cap his eyes bulged out of their sockets, giving him a startled look. He edged closer to her, uncomfortably close.

"I've never been this cold or seen so much ice," he said. "What are we supposed to call it? Global warming? More like a new ice age. Looks like pictures of Siberia."

Petit stomped his feet to warm them and Agnes eyed his heavy boots. He was dressed for the cold and yet was clearly uncomfortable. She doubted she would last fifteen minutes before being frostbitten.

"We called your Chef de Brigade Bardy," he said. "Standard instructions for anything at the château. Call Monsieur Bardy no matter what the trouble." Petit gestured to the square of canvas covering a mound that reached to their knees. "Monsieur Vallotton found her out here. Thinks she fell and hit her head. She's frozen to the ground. I sent him inside and covered her as best I could." He stomped again. "You took your time getting here."

"Bardy will be here soon," Agnes said.

"They need me in the village. It's going to be a long night getting everybody off the roads and indoors. I suspect power's out up and down the lake and the cold will set in. Don't know what will be worse, the old people living in the hills or the rich along the water. My boss is usually solid as a rock, but this is going to be bad and he's set to retire next week. Scared of a last-minute blemish on his record. Figures more people may die. He's counting on me."

Agnes doubted Petit could make it up the hill but she didn't waste her breath speaking. She moved her hands over her ears, then her nose, then back under her armpits to restore feeling in her fingertips. It wasn't enough. She tried to remember the first signs of frostbite, certain she was well on her way.

Petit leaned near, favoring a leg. "What's it like working for him? Monsieur Bardy? I've heard the rumors. He's brilliant but he is a little crazy, isn't he? I'm planning to apply for the cantonal police." He spoke directly into her ear and Agnes wanted to swat him away like a flea. She couldn't feel her legs anymore and her shoulders were shaking. She covered her ears with her hands, causing Petit to shift and look into her face, as if she could lip-read.

"How'd you get in with them? With Bardy."

"Mathematics." Her teeth started to chatter. "I was in financial crimes. I'm good with numbers." Where was her boss? Realizing that any movement was better than freezing to death in place, she knelt. The ice burned her knees and she rocked onto her heels before pulling back the canvas. Cracking the thin layer of ice that had formed on it she hoped she looked experienced. One glance was enough to tell her that death didn't need to be bloody to make the heart race.

The woman lay prone in front of a stone bench. The sleet had left its mark, coating her torso so that it blended with the surrounding ground, making the details hard to see. Her face was pressed against the earth and only half of her features were visible. Snow and ice had blown up against her, sealing both her flesh and her opened eye. Startled, Agnes dropped the canvas back in place knowing it would refreeze to the ground in a matter of seconds. She tried to make out the château in the distance, but there were no visible lights and suddenly she felt very alone and inexperienced.

She stood, knowing that they had to go inside, but before she could make a suggestion there was a shout from the darkness. Bobbing lights cut through the storm and the outlines of three men came into view. She didn't recognize the first two, however, through the icy haze the third looked familiar despite being encased in a heavy snow jacket. She frowned. "Not Robert, today anyone but Robert Carnet," she murmured through chapped lips. It had never occurred to her that he would be here. Why would financial crimes send someone? Like a child she turned away as if refusing to look at her former boss, not seeing him, would make him go away; the man whom she most associated with those horrible minutes after her husband died.

When the men reached the protective wedge of canvas she forced herself to look. Definitely Carnet, his irregular chiseled features at odds with the ridiculous puff of an old-fashioned down coat. A cold pit formed in her stomach. Maybe her parents were right: she should quit, leave Switzerland, and move to Florida. She could hear her mother: "Come live with us, it's warm! It's friendly! We'll take care of the boys!" Her mother always speaking in declarative sentences with no thought of the implications.

Her parents had given up everything to move to Switzerland as a young couple, leaving their families and friends to create a new life among strangers, eventually building up a business and prospering. All for the children! Yet the moment the children were grown the parents had returned to America.

Cold and miserable, Agnes knew that if her mother called at this moment—this exact moment—she would leave. All the hard work of getting a place on the police force, of establishing herself, of thinking maybe, just maybe, she had a role and that her thoughts added value; today, in this miserable weather, having to face this man's pity, she would toss it all in a second.

A blast of wind swept off the lake and she struggled to keep her footing. Ice cracked and shattered in the unsettling darkness and a long dagger landed on the ground nearby.

The larger of the two men accompanying Carnet dropped to his knees and pulled the canvas away from the dead woman. It was absurd that they were out here, any of them. Despite living in Switzerland her entire life Agnes hadn't been inside any of the grand estates that dotted the shore from Vevey down to Geneva, but she knew they were filled with diplomats, industrialists, movie stars, and rock icons. If a society woman had wandered out in the storm and keeled over they should have called an ambulance and removed her to the morgue. Probably too much to drink, or drugs. Tumbled and fell, hit her head, and died in the cold. Agnes slapped her hands together to warm them, and wished that she hadn't left her fur hat at home. Then she wished she was at home with the hat. Thinking about her boys and what fun they must be having, knowing tomorrow there would be an unexpected school holiday. She was thankful she had spoken with Sybille. At least the boys knew she was safe and not trapped on the highway somewhere.

Carnet put his head close to Petit's and spoke briefly before moving to stand next to Agnes. Squinting into the wind she watched Petit thump his waist then turn around with his eyes on the ground, like a dog circling to find a place to bed down.

"Came from the local *gendarmerie*." Carnet's voice was deep and cut through the wind. "They've been trying to raise Petit on his radio. Looks like he lost it somewhere." Petit wandered into the darkness, his flashlight beam sweeping back and forth, illuminating shards of ice. Carnet shrugged and blew into his cupped gloves, reflecting heat back onto his face. He shifted slightly to block the wind from striking Agnes full-on and she was grateful. Her teeth were no longer chattering, although that was possibly because she was too numb to feel the cold anymore.

"Bardy called me when he realized he couldn't make it—he knows I drive this way to go home—but I ran my car into a ditch a kilometer above the village. Had to walk the rest of the way or I would have been here sooner." He tugged at his sleeve. "Good thing this old coat was in the trunk or I would have frozen."

Despite the circumstances Agnes stifled a smile. Carnet had always been particular about his clothing and she imagined he had spent a long second weighing usefulness versus appearance. Shielded by his bulk she felt some feeling return to her face. Her skin stung.

"I went for a hot drink before coming down," Carnet continued, "and found Doctor Blanchard in the hotel bar. Thought you would need a medical man unless the coroner already made it. Didn't quite know what to expect here. 'Body outside' was all Bardy told me before the phones failed. They didn't know more at the *gendarmerie*. Well, they did tell me that Petit was all they could spare and that they didn't know how I'd make it down without breaking a leg. I'm surprised Doctor Blanchard was willing to try."

Agnes glanced at the man kneeling by the corpse. He wore oiled coveralls partially covered by a heavy Loden coat. With his wind-burned ruddy complexion he looked more like a farmer than her idea of a doctor. He was kneeling on a fur pelt.

"Blanchard raises rabbits," said Carnet, "and was at the butcher when the storm hit. The roads are closed and he was planning to stay the night. The other man is Estanguet. Frédéric Estanguet." Estanguet hung back from their circle, and Agnes gave him a nod, setting his age at sixty-five or so. She noted that the men were all dressed warmly and had the sense not to drive down from the village. Wind burned her legs and she wondered why she hadn't dressed warmly like any sensible Swiss person. Perhaps her mother-in-law was right. Maybe she didn't belong here. She quickly blew on her fingers then shoved them back under her armpits.

"Estanguet was having *un verre* at the bar," Carnet continued, "and overheard us wondering how to get down the hill. He knows the place. He found crampons and hooked us up to a rope. Still hard going, but at least we didn't hit a tree." Agnes grimaced and Carnet smiled at her. "Now, I suppose I can say I've been mountaineering."

He continued talking and she focused on his every word and expression, wishing she could read his mind. He had agreed willingly, eagerly even, when she requested a transfer from financial crimes. Now she wasn't sure: maybe he hadn't agreed out of kindness or relief. What if she was a failure in her new job, would Bardy insist she return to her old one? She had done good work for Carnet and maybe this was his way of maneuvering her return. Three months ago she would have laughed at the idea, but after her husband's death nothing seemed certain. How could she trust her instincts about others when she was so wrong about the man closest to her?

She turned her attention back to the men. The doctor had removed several items from the heavy bag Estanguet carried, including a spare pair of work gloves, which he handed to her. They were fur-lined and she felt the relief immediately. She pressed the soft leather against her face, blocking the wind.

"She's not really frozen, the body I mean," Blanchard shouted to them. "It's the ice around her. The wind was strong here, hundred kilometers an hour they said on the radio, and that froze her clothes despite her body heat. I'd say she's been out here at least three hours, more likely five or six and probably no more than eight, although it's hard to say right now. Body temperature's unreliable because of the wind and cold. Both are unstable."

Estanguet edged closer. "This is a woman? How could this be a woman?"

Agnes glanced at the mound of ice, biting her tongue. It was unwise to share her opinion that it was probably a doped-up society girl. "Definitely a woman. I saw her face."

Blanchard used a small tool, first measuring the thickness of the ice, then cracking the hood back from the woman's head. Ice scattered in the wind. He ran his hand across her skull and neck.

Estanguet looked so ill he distracted Agnes from her pre-occupation with Carnet and the cold. They should have taken the doctor's bag from the man and sent him indoors to get warm. He didn't need to see this. She took his elbow and pressed her flashlight into his hand, indicating the direction of the château. He shook his head, seemingly unwilling to leave until there were answers, and she sympathized. For a novice there was something both horrible and fascinating in the scene: the dead body both an object and a human. Very different from her years with financial crimes.

Petit emerged from the whiteout and Agnes noticed that he was still absently patting at his coat and waist. That boded ill for the missing radio, and with the phones dead any communication with the outside world. She glanced around. They were isolated on this node of land below the cliff. She should have opted to go home when she had the chance. The weather put even Sybille's company in a pleasant light.

Blanchard spoke over his shoulder, squinting into the wind. "No evidence of a head injury. You can see how she fell away from the bench, not against it." He brushed falling sleet from the body. "Face forward. Damage to her cheekbone probably from the fall and not before, broken bone but no bruising. The blood wasn't flowing anymore. Maybe she had a seizure or some other medical condition? I can't see anything else until we get more of this ice off her." He rubbed his hands together and put his gloves back on. "*Merde,* it's cold out here. Too early to tell if she died of natural causes. Who did you say found her? She's not familiar to me. Does anyone know her?"

Petit spoke up. "Julien Vallotton stumbled on her and called us. He gave us her name, she's not local."

"No matter. How do you want to handle it?"

They all turned to her and Agnes wanted a cigarette more

than she wanted to breathe: wishing Carnet wasn't here, and furious that the road to the village was impassable, although if she made it to the top of the cliff the highways would be closed by now. No phone, no way out, and no way to consult with Bardy. She didn't need this on her first day on his team. Why hadn't he made it here? She moved nearer the protection of the canvas walls, willing herself to focus, remembering a snowstorm early in her marriage. The joy of two days trapped at home together with George. Happier days that should have lasted forever.

"Completely frozen to the ground," Blanchard called over his shoulder. "That's one way to establish time of death. Take a few of this," he motioned to Carnet, who was using his camera phone to document the scene.

Agnes turned to Petit and gestured to Estanguet. "Take him inside." For a moment she was tempted to use the excuse of impending frostbite to join them and leave Carnet in charge. Only the memory of George stopped her. He'd been her biggest supporter from the day she applied to the police force, insisting she had good instincts and they'd be lucky to have her. She wouldn't let him down, even now.

"I'll look at the storm pattern," Blanchard said. "We'll do better to get her up and out of here quickly. Sad to think she might have taken a tumble and died, although probably not the only one tonight."

He chipped away at the ice, uncovering first the dead woman's face, then her coat-clad torso. When he reached the legs, Agnes shivered again. The long thin skirt had fallen to the side and the woman's bare legs, incongruous with the boots, looked cold. She wished they would hurry and cover the body again, but she didn't say anything, knowing that the woman was beyond feeling just as her husband had been.

It had been cool that day, a cloudy gray day typical of Lausanne in autumn. The ambulance driver had covered George before she could look, angering her and later making her grateful. There had been so many people around, watching and judging. Later she understood the sand on the road was there to absorb blood. That day she had seen only the outline of her husband's covered form, the flash of emergency lights, and the chatter of horrified pedestrians. It had started to drizzle and Carnet was there, encouraging her to leave. Other officers pulled her toward a waiting car, asking if her children were with her; could they call someone to come for her; was her purse still in the café? They had talked and talked, to her and over her head, and all she wanted was to see George for herself, to remember every detail. She remembered tiny things like the rip down the sleeve of his jacket where his arm wasn't quite covered by the sheet. A shame, for he loved that coat. It was the same today. The body was clad in a beautiful dress irreparably damaged by the ice, the coat torn. She looked up.

"Her coat wouldn't have torn like that when she fell." She stooped near the doctor and Carnet joined her. Together they shielded the body. The wind had shifted again and ice seemed to arrive from all sides.

"You've got good eyes," Carnet said. "The slit looks new, made by something sharp, a knife maybe, doesn't look like a snag on a nail. Could have been cut before she put it on."

"The fabric's not frayed." Agnes held the flashlight, curiosity making her forget the cold. She gestured for Carnet to sweep the remnants of ice away from the area.

"If you want to see underneath you'd better cut it away," Blanchard said. "The whole bit's frozen solid, moisture in and on the fabric, and you won't get it off her any other way. I'm going to keep her cold until we can get her somewhere to do a proper autopsy. I don't have many medical tools with me, mostly my . . . farm tools."

Carnet cut a large piece of the dead woman's jacket away, careful to keep his blade far from the incision they were studying. Agnes focused her attention. She wasn't thinking clearly. She had allowed the place and the weather to numb her to the possibility that this was a crime. When Carnet tried to lift the material it wouldn't move. Carefully he touched one edge of the fabric with his knife, lifting it slightly. It pulled away and they crouched nearer, trying to protect the area from the storm. Blanchard pulled the bottom of the fabric away, shining his light on it. There was a dark frozen mass concealed between the body and jacket.

"Not natural causes, I suspect," he muttered, running his hand under the fabric and separating it from the frozen blood. When the material of the jacket lifted away, Blanchard removed the layer of red ice and slipped it into a plastic container taken from his satchel. Beneath lay white flesh marked by the slit of a blade.

Agnes knew before Blanchard spoke that this was the reason they were here. This woman had been stabbed. She felt a thrill. *This was violent crimes.*

Three

A half hour later Agnes and Carnet stood in the cavernous entrance hall of the château, feet wet and coats tossed to the side, having decided to begin interviewing the household while Petit and Blanchard attended to the body. They had quickly settled into their former way of working, and while their old habits reestablished themselves, she knew there was a difference. Carnet watched her carefully when he thought she wasn't looking, and she could see the pity and curiosity in his eyes. It was maddening.

Despite the thickness of the château's stone walls, she could hear the storm howling and was struck by a sense of foreboding. All around them the walls were fitted with a collection of medieval weapons. High overhead dozens of fat candles burned low in an iron chandelier and the light glinted off the weapons, casting shadows. Agnes's confidence slipped another notch and she hoped the darkness concealed her concern. She wanted to take the lead in the investigation; she needed to in order to start a new life without George. She took a deep breath, wished for a cigarette, and tugged at her waistband. She had stopped smoking at home but kept a pack in her car for emergencies, and there were always emergencies.

Behind her, Estanguet emerged from the shadows. "The Vallottons will be up those stairs," he said, pointing into the darkness. "Officer Petit said they're gathering in the marquise's sitting room. That's the door on the left."

"You're familiar with the château? You know the family?" Agnes asked. Estanguet had guided them from the small side door to the front hall with a confidence that spoke of familiarity and she was again thankful he had helped Carnet and the doctor navigate the icy road down from the village. If he hadn't, she would be totally reliant on Petit. Not an adequate substitute for Bardy.

"I use the library." Estanguet mopped his forehead with a handkerchief. His coat was open and his shirt damp. "I know the place."

Before Agnes could ask more questions Estanguet stumbled, catching himself on the corner of an iron-banded leather trunk. His color was poor yet he was sweating, and she wondered if he didn't have hypothermia. The last thing they needed was for their Good Samaritan to take ill.

"You need to warm up by a fire. Have a hot tea or something stronger. Perhaps *une eau-de-vie?*"

"She was really dead, the lady outside?" he asked.

Agnes regretted allowing him to watch the police at their work. A situation Bardy would surely have handled differently. She exchanged a glance with Carnet and he took Estanguet's elbow and guided him into the darkness. Agnes went in the other direction, up the broad stairs that were fitted inside the north tower off the entrance hall. She slowed after the first steps. The household was likely in a state of shock. It was a mistake to let Carnet leave. She was too close to her own grief to wade unaided through the sentiment in others. Moreover, Carnet knew what questions to ask. People found him sympathetic. In unguarded moments at the station some of the men snickered behind his back and said it was a trait—like dressing well— that came with his lifestyle. She knew it was simply because he chose to listen.

He had listened to her that terrible day George died. His hand gripping hers. Tears forming in his eyes. Her confidence ebbed. There wasn't anything to lift her up. She needed her boys. To at least hear their voices. She gripped the carved balustrade, recalling the earlier phone conversation with her mother-in-law. Sybille, who had never liked her, who blamed her for the death of her only son. Every word, every greeting, laced with anger until the barest perfunctory exchange was charged with emotion. That was the atmosphere that would be waiting up these stairs. People angered, perhaps blaming one another. She took another step, wishing she had dry shoes and that her feet weren't so cold. Then she remembered that among those waiting, someone was possibly experiencing a very different emotion. Someone happy. Satisfied. A murderer.

In the distance a door opened and shut. Startled out of her reverie, Agnes trod the final stairs. The light at the top was stronger. The wide corridor was illuminated by candles fitted into wall sconces and candelabras. Glimpsing the paintings and tapestries lining the walls, she pursed her lips. A fortune in things; a museum where people lived. She felt the thickness of the carpet beneath her feet, quite a difference from the hard stone of the entrance hall.

Pausing at the door where the family was waiting, she took stock of her appearance. Her short hair was practically standing on end. Her suit was a damp mess and her stockings had runs in both knees from kneeling beside the body. She took a deep breath and swept into the room. Once across the threshold she stopped abruptly, realizing she was at a disadvantage. She should have arranged for a place less them and more her.

The room was large, divided into three seating areas. Near one stone hearth, cards were laid atop a marquetry table as if a game had been interrupted. Throughout the room a collection of antique clocks was scattered on various surfaces. Fabricated from bronze, gold, and porcelain, each ticked away the minutes creating a nearly musical sound together. Collected on a table was an arrangement of pocket watches with cases ranging from ornate to the simplest elegance, and throughout the room there was a carelessness in the placement of all the objects, as if they were of great value but also touched and admired. A Great Dane lay in front of the far fireplace. He raised his head briefly then laid it back on his paws.

An elderly woman was seated in front of the nearer fireplace on a low, broad chair upholstered in pale green fabric. All around her flickering candlelight was exaggerated by large mirrors on the walls and over the mantels. She was dressed in a slim wool dress so deeply red it went black in the questionable light, handmade leather pumps on her feet. Despite the roaring fires the room was chilly and across her shoulders she wore a silver fox stole that almost, but not quite, hid the strands of Indian rubies, some large as quail's eggs, that dangled from her neck. Her white hair was neatly rolled low on the back of her head.

Agnes swallowed. If she wasn't the marquise, she should be. A matching chair was opposite, separated by a small table. The arms and legs of the chairs glistened, and Agnes stifled a gasp.

"We are fortunate these were not melted for coin," the marquise said, introducing herself as Antoinette Vallotton de Tornay. "I brought the pair to Switzerland after the death of my husband. We hid them throughout the war, not their first. I think it remarkable that such things were made; on the other hand, what better use for wealth before banking: to form the metal into something usable."

Silver, Agnes thought, wanting to ask if the chairs' frames were solid and somehow knowing they must be.

"You are here to speak to us about the deceased," the marquise continued, motioning for Agnes to be seated. "I'm afraid we know very little about her."

Agnes pulled out her notebook, pleased not to face the entire family at once. The matriarch was intimidating enough. "Could you tell me who is at the château tonight?"

"I have no idea." The older woman's voice was calm and polite. A void stretched between them and Agnes realized that the marquise was a rare person who welcomed silence.

"Officer Petit said I should speak with you first. You must know who else lives here?" The old woman didn't look senile although it was possible.

"That's not what you asked. You asked who is here tonight. Certainly I know who lives here. We are a small household." She listed names, speaking rapidly. Agnes took notes.

"And who is here now?" she asked, when the marquise finished.

"I've said: I have no idea. According to Officer Petit, my nephew discovered Mademoiselle Cowell. That means he has arrived from London. Personally, I've been in my suite of rooms since luncheon and have only seen my maid, Marie-José. She brought tea."

Agnes changed tacks. "Could you clarify Felicity Cowell's role in the household? She's not local, I take it."

The marquise fingered her chains of rubies. "My brother's testament outlined the sale of certain pieces of art, the proceeds to be given to organizations he was fond of. My nephew is organizing details of the sale and Mademoiselle Cowell works for the auction house he has a relationship with in London. That is why he is here this weekend, to observe her progress. You will have to ask him about the specifics."

"Monsieur Julien Vallotton arranged for her to organize the auction?" Agnes recalled what Petit had said about the man who discovered the body. Vallotton lived in London. That was a rule of violent crime she did know: the one closest to the victim was often the culprit. Convenient that Vallotton arranged for her to be here, arrived the day she was killed, and was the one to discover her.

"You phrase that interestingly," the marquise said. "I doubt he arranged for her, certainly he engaged the firm, but my brother purchased many items through them over the years."

"Do you know why Mademoiselle Cowell was outside this afternoon?"

"We have lovely grounds. People often go outdoors to walk along the lake."

"In a winter storm?"

The marquise didn't respond.

"She was wearing clothing unsuited to the outdoors," Agnes added. "It leads to questions."

"Unsuited?" the marquise said. "There are many ways one can dress unsuitably. I'm afraid you will have to be more specific, although the few times I saw Mademoiselle Cowell she appeared well-groomed enough."

"You saw her only a few times?"

"My housekeeper had prepared a room, however Mademoiselle Cowell declined to stay here. The pretty little yellow room next to the west tower. It is not in the family wing, and she would have had her privacy and the adjacent room to do her business. One would hope she might have been more considerate."

Agnes was surprised anyone would turn down an invitation to stay at the château. Her colleagues had accepted the housekeeper's invitation to stay the night quickly enough. Of course that was also because it was impossible to make the climb up to the village. Carnet had shared details of their descent and even with Estanguet's expert guidance, wearing crampons borrowed from villagers, and clinging to a rope Estanguet strung for them, he and the doctor were fortunate they hadn't broken their necks.

"Mademoiselle Cowell was wearing an evening dress when she died," Agnes said. "With a man's overcoat and heavy boots. They were too large. Not hers."

The marquise's clear gaze didn't waver. "Fascinating, and definitely inappropriate, but I have no idea why. She was a very pretty girl, but insecure. I am not certain she was entirely as she appeared to be."

Agnes wondered if this was a subtle way of shifting focus from the household onto the victim. Or was the marquise trying to be helpful? She was surprised by the lack of a pretense of sorrow or anger or any emotion. "What do you mean? Not as she appeared to be?"

"Nothing particular. Simply an observation."

"When did Mademoiselle Cowell arrive? Officer Petit lives in the village and remembers seeing her last week."

The marquise rose and crossed to stand nearer the fireplace, warming her hands in front of the blaze. Before Agnes could repeat her question the door opened and a man entered. At a glance Agnes knew who he was: Julien Vallotton, the château's owner, and the marquise's nephew. Petit had described him as good-looking, early forties, tall. Good-looking was an understatement. He had a masculine version of his aunt's fine bone structure with a thick head of nearly black hair slightly brushed with gray at the temples. But it was his eyes—a cold piercing blue—that arrested her attention. He kissed his aunt on both cheeks then held out his hand to Agnes in greeting.

"Julien, dear, could you see if the others are coming?" the marquise said. "We don't want to keep the inspector waiting. I'm sure the police have other duties tonight with the storm."

Agnes hoped the nephew was more forthcoming. "Madame la marquise was confirming the date Felicity Cowell arrived."

"A fortnight ago, it must have been," Vallotton said. "We spoke the day before she traveled."

"It was her first trip here?"

"To our home, yes, but Switzerland? I don't know. Our conversation was brief, centered wholly on the auction." He paused. "She was British. Or I assumed she was. We were both in London when I called, and her schoolgirl French was competent but the accent—" He stopped in mid-sentence. "I did ask where she was from, but she didn't say, and I didn't care to inquire again."

Agnes turned a page in her notebook. "What was your general impression of her?"

Before he could answer, the door to the corridor opened and a young man entered. He had clearly come straight from out-of-doors, his face was red with cold despite his healthy tan, and he had bits of snow and ice in his hair. He moved quickly, straight to the fireplace, shedding layers as he went, a few scarves, gloves, coat. His hawkish features were tempered by a thick swath of dark blond hair that fell over one eye, and her first impression was of energy. At a second glance, he seemed brittle. Using the shadows, Agnes moved unobtrusively away, mentally running through the list of names the marquise had mentioned, assigning a label. The woman's godson, she guessed.

"I can't believe someone would be murdered here," the man exclaimed. "Christ, you would think we were safe enough. Someone needs to think about security—"

The marquise interrupted him, quickly introducing her nephew to Ralph Mulholland, using the old pronunciation, *Rafe*, adding that Vallotton surely remembered her godson. For her part, Agnes was pleased to have guessed correctly. She was also surprised by his accent. The young man was British. Another geographic connection to the victim.

Mulholland headed to a cabinet where he poured light brown liquid into a delicate glass. He gulped it down with a flick of his wrist and poured another, pressing his other hand to his chest as if to still his heart.

"I saw the cops, the lights. They were huddled over someone." He shivered, then walked to the marquise and bussed her cheeks with a kiss. "Don't you worry, no one would lift a hand to hurt you." Finally he noticed Agnes in the shadows. He lifted an eyebrow and shoved his hands in his pockets. "Didn't realize we have guests."

"Inspector Lüthi is questioning us," said the marquise.

Mulholland's face drained to white. "I shouldn't have made sport of it." He hesitated, then stepped forward, quickly recovering his poise and offering to get a drink for anyone in need. Agnes doubted there would be any takers since she could see into the open cabinet and there was only sherry and champagne, and this was definitely not the moment for the latter.

"Blasted cold outside," Mulholland said. "Inspector, you don't look like you are from the little station on the hill. I have always wanted to stop in and see the operation. It seems charming."

"What led you to believe the victim was murdered? I think that is what you said? Murdered?" Agnes asked.

Mulholland gulped his drink down and turned to set the glass on a table. Agnes had never seen so young a man drink sherry with such fervent appreciation.

"Have you questioned everyone else? I'm afraid I won't have anything to add. I just saw the police."

Agnes glanced at the marquise and found that the woman's expression was a mask of polite convention. It struck Agnes that Mulholland didn't ask who was killed. An interesting lack of curiosity or a lazy display of knowledge he shouldn't have. It also struck her that Mulholland had seemed genuinely worried when he first entered the room. Panicked even.

"It was Mademoiselle Cowell," the marquise said in a level tone.

Agnes watched the expression on Mulholland's face carefully: relief, surprise, horror, dismay. The emotions were so fleeting it was difficult to determine their order or even swear positively to their appearance. Mulholland started to pour another drink, but the slim decanter was nearly empty and he stopped and smiled thinly at Agnes. "I apologize. I'm afraid the police remind me of when my parents died. I overreacted, and badly. One does in these situations. You asked me a question."

"You seemed to think it was murder and not an accident. I wonder why?"

"Certainly you don't think I did it and confessed so easily. My fancy education taught me more than that." Mulholland changed tone. "During a storm like tonight, one of the local boys could have taken care of an accident or a suicide. Instead they've called in the troops." He arched an eyebrow. "Or am I wrong? You're not local."

"No, your reasoning is correct. The young woman was deliberately killed. Did you know her?"

"Of course, she was here every day, all day, for the last week or so. Two weeks. She arrived the night before the party. And had dinner with us then. I saw her a few times more. Seemed a nice girl, common but amusing and very clever."

"Did you see her today?"

"You mean before—" Mulholland gripped the edge of the sofa. "No, although I wouldn't have. I had a late night and rose 'round about noon. Went for a walk and paid a visit to our neighbor."

"Neighbor?" Agnes asked.

"Our resident oligarch."

"Ralph," interrupted the marquise. She shifted to face Agnes, fingers twined in the chains of rubies. "Monsieur Arsov has let a house from us, a villa built for my great-great-grandmother. We are quite isolated below the village and it is a comfort that the other property is no longer vacant. You should have a tour; it is a lovely example of neoclassical architecture, and Monsieur Arsov has complemented the furnishings with his own very interesting collection."

Agnes nearly swore. She'd been focused on the storm and the château and had forgotten the neighboring mansion. With the power outage it was a black hole in the night. Invisible. Sorting through mental images from trips on the lake, her memory offered the excuse that the mansion was a neoclassical gem overshadowed by the hulking château like a delicate piece of porcelain next to a mountain. She calculated that the grove of trees where they discovered the body was about midway between the two properties.

"We will interview the other household," she said. "For now, Monsieur Mulholland, if you could be more precise about your movements this afternoon. When you crossed the lawn to Monsieur Arsov's, did you take a path or the drive? Those kinds of details. It will help us establish a timeline."

"I'm very vague about it all. As I said, I'd been up late,

really till dawn and was still a bit under the weather when—" Mulholland was interrupted by a loud crash as the door flung open, the knob hitting an armoire against the wall. The marquise shuddered.

"*Merde*," a man's voice exclaimed.

The entire party turned and Vallotton rose, almost stepped forward then stopped. Agnes tried to fade into the background. This must be the brother, Daniel Vallotton. Petit hadn't told her he was in a wheelchair. One glance was enough to see he had recently suffered a severe injury. His right arm was weighted by a plaster cast while his right leg was propped stiffly in front of him, partially covered by a blanket.

"Can't believe you let me sleep through all the excitement," Daniel Vallotton said, struggling to turn a wheel with his one good arm. From behind him, still in the dark shadows of the hall, a woman's voice echoed, "You've caught my scarf. Wait, no, I've got it." And the wheelchair lurched into the room.

The dynamic of the room changed, but whether as a result of the startling beauty of the woman or simply pent-up nerves it was impossible to tell. Agnes surmised the woman was Daniel Vallotton's wife, Marie-Chantal. She nearly had to shake her head to stop staring. Marie-Chantal Vallotton was a living piece of art, not heavily made-up or the creation of a plastic surgeon, but a simple natural beauty.

Daniel wheeled himself awkwardly to his brother and offered his unbroken left hand. "Didn't think you'd turn up. MC, give your brother-in-law a kiss."

Marie-Chantal didn't move. "We've already said hello. Earlier, downstairs."

Julien Vallotton stepped away from the door. He moved to the cabinet where Mulholland had poured a drink and glanced at the bottles. Agnes watched the marquise give him a nearly imperceptible shrug.

"Inspector . . . is it Inspector?" Daniel said. "My wife told me we were being gathered. I feel positively left out of the excitement. Presumptuous to think a cripple like me wouldn't want to be involved in the speculation."

Agnes approached to greet husband and wife formally. The blanket had shifted and she noted the man's leg was held together with dozens of thin metal rods protruding through his calf. Despite his injuries, Daniel Vallotton looked the picture of health. Weeks of inactivity hadn't softened his physique or detracted from his charms. He wore casual trousers with one leg cut away below the knee to accommodate his injury and the arm of his sweater was slit and rolled up above his elbow. The trousers were of a fabric and cut from the orient, the V-necked sweater was gray cashmere. After exchanging greetings, Marie-Chantal rolled the wheelchair in front of the nearest fireplace and turned Daniel toward the room. She pulled an upholstered stool close by and sat, long legs extended in front of her, with an arm on the edge of her husband's chair. A bit incongruously she also wore a long scarf and small hand-knit hat as if unsure about the temperature indoors. In the flickering candlelight she resembled a fairy from a long-past age: delicate and almost too beautiful for earth. The diamond of her engagement ring reflected filaments of light from the fire onto the walls. The pattern was like a scattered constellation. Silently the Great Dane moved to sit near her, head lowered, waiting to be petted, and Agnes watched Julien Vallotton. He looked resentful.

"With the police here I will come clean and admit I took a tranquilizer after lunch," Daniel said. "Paid a visit to the surgeon this morning and the doctors pushed and probed so much my leg was killing me. I slept through the whole afternoon—"

"And would have slept through tonight if I hadn't made him get up," Marie-Chantal said, running a finger along the stiff line of the cast on his arm. While Marie-Chantal continued to talk, Agnes watched the assembled group. The atmosphere of the room had changed. It had electrified. As they arranged themselves it occurred to her that a photograph would tell a different story than the moving picture in front of her. A still shot would capture the cozy intimacy of the Vallotton couple, their faces and figures striking in their perfection; the marquise distinguished on her silver chair in the center of the room; Ralph Mulholland crossing between her and the bottle of sherry; and Julien Vallotton sitting apart, not needing the comfort of a companion to feel at home. That was what a still shot would capture. Ease, comfort, and beauty.

The moving reality was different. The motion of Marie-Chantal's hand on her husband's arm took on an edge of nervous tic, Ralph Mulholland's attention to the pouring of drinks was overdone, and the marquise's silence was so studied it was loud. Julien Vallotton tried to fade into the background and only the marquise appeared at ease. Agnes considered the two brothers and saw a family resemblance, the younger brother easygoing, the elder more careworn; the resemblance extended to their aunt. A handsome family. When Julien Vallotton glanced at her, Agnes couldn't help but think that with those looks and that fortune she was surprised he wasn't married.

Four

"Murder?" Vladimir Arsov's butler released his grip on her coat and Agnes neatly caught the wool garment by the collar, thinking she should have phrased the situation more delicately. Clearly, the dark trek from the château to the neighboring mansion had chilled the part of her brain that dealt with social niceties.

A credit to his profession, the man recovered quickly, plucking her coat away and indicating that she should remain in the reception hall while he spoke with his master. He disappeared into the dark shadows of the mansion and Agnes regretted having slipped her flashlight into her coat pocket. There were a few lit candles on a far table, but the oval hall was large and therefore mostly bathed in shadow. She waited, glad to have a moment before she questioned the household. The storm had abated and she had made the walk alone despite Carnet's admonition that she could fall and Petit's fear that she would run into the murderer. In her absence they would finish cordoning off the rooms used by Felicity Cowell and question the remainder of the household.

The palest flicker of light shone through a wide doorway across the hall and she listened carefully but couldn't make out any sounds. She was quite alone. Quickly, she slipped her shoes off, hoping the Oriental rug would be a relief from the saturated leather. It was. Her toes warmed until they had feeling. She flexed them, glancing around, pleased that the Arsov mansion lived up to expectation. The exterior of the nineteenth-century stone residence was constructed along clean, elegant lines with long rows of doors and windows uncluttered by towers or crenellations. To her delight the interior was a combination of perfect proportion and decorative splendor. Baseboards, window and door frames—essentially every piece of wood used in construction—were gilded, and all glowed in the candlelight. Along the perimeter of the oval room a series of six hand-painted porcelain urns towered over her. She was peering closely at the design of the nearest one when the butler returned.

Slipping on her shoes, she followed his long, thin shadow into an enormous salon, halting when she saw the uniformed staff arrayed in a line. A very old man in a wheelchair was addressing them. Vladimir Arsov, she presumed, feeling she'd stepped into the second act of a not-very-modern play.

Her overall impression of the household didn't change over the next two hours. She sat as close as possible to the lit fireplace in the small sitting room assigned to her, carefully working her way through interviews with Arsov's staff. First was the somber butler, followed by three young female maids, who in turn were followed by a slew of male servants and, finally, of all things, a laundress. By that time she needed to stand and stretch her legs. The butler, now wearing gloves and a scarf over his black tailcoat, appeared from the dark hall with a tray bearing steaming coffee in a delicate porcelain cup. He stood over her while she drank, conveying that the gardening staff did not live on the premises. In a slightly stiff tone he shared that the chauffeur was also absent. When Agnes finished her coffee and retook her seat, the butler ushered in the last of the resident staff: a chef trailing his assistants, each wearing tall pleated hats and pristine white aprons.

When finished with them, Agnes reread her notes and wondered if it occurred to anyone in the household that they were essentially locked in under surveillance all day. The outer doors were bolted and alarmed at all times, and the butler monitored comings and goings like a hawk studying his prey. And while at work, they worked. Cleaning, polishing, cooking, serving. Never alone. Never unsupervised. During the critical hours when Felicity Cowell was killed there were so many corroborating alibis it sounded straight from a television script. Now, glancing at her watch, she saw that it was after midnight. Thankful that the Vallottons had graciously invited everyone who was trapped by the ice to stay the night at the château, she wanted nothing more than to return there and collapse exhausted into bed even if it was likely the killer was lurking within the walls. Surely her bedroom door would have a lock.

Unfortunately, there were still three people on her list: Vladimir Arsov himself; his private nurse, Madame Brighton; and Mimi, a six-year-old girl. None of them were suspects: Arsov not physically able to strike down a young woman, the nurse never out of his sight during the hours in question, and the six-year-old whom Agnes ruled out based on age. Cold and fatigue ran bone deep and these last interviews were nearly too much to face, but it had to be done. Arsov was master of the household and had already insisted she speak with his staff first. He couldn't be made to wait until morning.

She held her feet to the fire until the soles of her shoes nearly cracked, then, physically ready, she rang the old-fashioned bellpull for the butler. He led the way, lighting the floor in front of them with his flashlight. Entering the room where she had first met Arsov and his staff, Agnes wished she'd chosen to return to the château and a warm bed. Thirty or forty candles had been lit; however, in the vastness of the space they only highlighted the darkness of the corners and ceiling. She felt the same chill she had experienced when crossing the empty lawn. There was no telling what lurked in the distance.

The old man turned when she entered but didn't speak and she confirmed her earlier impression that Vladimir Arsov was not a handsome man. She wasn't sure he had ever been, although it was hard to tell now that old age had collapsed his face into crevices. He snorted through nubs that extended from the plastic tube running from an oxygen tank, and, peering out from behind his large black-framed glasses, he looked like an ancient child. The man's suit was too large for his diminished form, but even to the untrained eye, it was obviously hand-tailored of fine fabric. For a moment she wondered if Arsov was ill or merely old, for during their brief conversation earlier, the sparkle she had noticed in his eyes conflicted with the decay of his body, and the smell she usually associated with old people was absent, disguised by a faintly odd mix of cologne and medicine.

"She's sleeping soundly," Agnes remarked as she approached. The little girl, Mimi, lay curled up on a long silk sofa, covered by a thick blanket. A stuffed elephant lay wrapped under her arm.

"I asked Monsieur Vallotton to allow Mimi to remain here," said the nurse. "She was traumatized and out in the cold too long. I want to keep an eye on her."

"Shouldn't she be with her parents?" Agnes asked.

"She lives with the Vallottons." The nurse moved the blanket higher up the girl's shoulders and touched her forehead as if checking for fever. "Adopted by old Monsieur Vallotton when her parents died."

"She's fine. Cognac cures most things," Arsov said.

Agnes noted the empty chocolate pot and cup nearby and her gut hollowed. She had used the same technique on her boys the night she told them their father died. The familiar soothing chocolate concealing the sleep-inducing cognac. She buried the memory and sat across from the old man in a wide, deeply cushioned chair. The arms were gilded and she was reminded of the marquise's silver chair earlier in the evening. The rich certainly liked their precious metals on display.

Under the watchful eye of the butler, who now wore earmuffs in addition to his gloves and scarf, a stream of servants brought in more candles to expand the circle of light. Beck-and-call parade, it looked like to her, yet somehow different than what she had experienced at the Vallottons'. The marquise gave the impression of austere control, whereas Arsov's staff appeared as more of a stage piece, with everyone playing their part until they exited behind the curtain. Brighter now, even the salon resembled a stage set more than a living space. Agnes wouldn't have blinked if Napoleon and Josephine had walked in trailing their court.

Satisfied that Mimi was resting peacefully, Nurse Brighton draped a blanket over Arsov's shoulders in addition to the one he normally kept over his legs. The blankets gave him bulk and it was possible to imagine him as a younger, more power-fully built man, while the trick of candlelight made his wheel-chair fade into obscurity. He flipped the oxygen cord onto the top of his head and removed a richly carved gold lighter from his pocket. The nurse sighed in exasperation and snatched the entire apparatus away, dragging the small tank across the room and away from the open flame. Arsov took a long drag on his cigarette and closed his eyes as he exhaled, then he coughed like it was his last breath. Nurse Brighton murmured some-thing about being unable to recharge the oxygen tank without electricity but she didn't move to stop him smoking.

Agnes peered into the corners of the room, wanting to re-member the details to tell her boys. And Sybille. The wall-paper was cut velvet and matched the burgundy curtains, and the paintings were palatial: life-sized portraits and great battle scenes. Ten pairs of glass-paned doors filled the wall overlook-ing the lake, and groupings of chairs and sofas and tables ex-tended across the parquet floor. She estimated the room was large enough to house a tennis court. Truly amazing. The nurse drew a chair close to the fire, extending her white-clad legs and feet near the flames.

"Scared you, didn't it? The woman dead out there," Arsov said. "You think about the cold and what it can do. You think this will keep me inside now?" He took a deep draw on his cigarette and blew out a cloud of smoke. Agnes resisted the urge to shift nearer and inhale. "You think it's cold tonight? You haven't felt cold until you have lived through a Russian winter. We used to wake up with frost on our blankets every morning from October till April."

The nurse made a disparaging sound and Arsov laughed. "You imagine I exaggerate? Find someone who grew up in the country eighty years ago and they will tell the same tales. Cold, real cold, hurts. It reaches into your lungs and burns with each breath. It dries your eyes and numbs your ears. Winter in Russia is a hard lesson."

A log crashed in the fireplace and the flames blazed. Agnes felt the added warmth and realized that her back was growing cold as the room lost the last of its electric heat. Reaching for a blanket from the stack left by the servants she was struck by the idea that she was seeing the room as it was originally experienced: a world lit only by fire.

"Tell me what happened tonight," she said. "Julien Vallotton came here to telephone the police?" She had already asked Arsov if he knew the dead woman. He didn't. Hadn't seen her. Didn't recognize her name.

The old man took another long drag on his cigarette and closed his eyes as he exhaled, enjoyment in the lines of his face. He fingered the fabric of his striped cravat. "The others, they have spoken with you. They are good people. Hardworking."

"Yes, but you were the one who saw Monsieur Vallotton arrive." Agnes had heard the same story from each member of the staff with varying degrees of detail. The discovery of the body went as follows: Julien Vallotton had pounded on a French door leading from the salon to the lawn. Hearing him, the nurse and Arsov had rushed into the room, unlocking and opening the door. Opening the door had triggered an alarm and others arrived at a run, entering the salon in the minutes after Vallotton was admitted. The butler had silenced the alarm; still, the remainder of the household knew what had happened second- or third-hand.

"They will exaggerate. We live by routine and this will excite some into creating little details. Misremembering to make their viewpoint important."

"I think they've been accurate enough," she said. The house ran like clockwork, no one alone at any time as they cooked and cleaned and served. Their impressions coincided. "Monsieur Vallotton arrived at that door?" She pointed toward the farthest of the sets of doors facing the lake.

"He pounded and we heard."

"We ran," interjected the nurse. "As I told you, Inspector Lüthi, we were in the smaller salon, the room next to this, working on correspondence, and heard fists on the glass. And a man's voice shouting."

"She can run." Arsov grinned. "Pushed me in here like a battalion was in pursuit. Unlocked the door and Julien ran in. I thought he was in London."

"Mimi was with him?" Agnes glanced at the child asleep on the long sofa.

"Yes, yes, she was with him. They saw the woman and ran here because we are closer than returning to the château. They were frightened."

"What had you heard earlier in the afternoon? Had you seen anything unusual?"

"What do you know unusual? How can we pick out what detail you must know to find your killer?"

"There might have been something, someone. A sound."

"You want me to tell you of a man with a weapon skulking around my lawn and say, yes, that was him? This unusual man is the killer and I will direct you to this evil. Is this how you think you will find your murderer? Inspector Lüthi, I will tell you that evil hides its face until the last minute. Evil hides in the ordinary. You will not find it with these questions."

Nearby, the nurse shifted. Her old-fashioned winged hat cast long flickering shadows. The woman looked tired, yet unable to go to bed while Arsov was awake. They were all tired and Agnes was prepared to tell Arsov she would come back in the morning when he surprised her.

"You have not seen murder before," he said, jabbing the air with his cigarette, trailing smoke in a lazy arc. "Do not argue. This is a truth. You were nervous when you arrived tonight, the thought of crossing near where the woman died was disturbing. Ghosts were in your mind. But you have courage. You made the journey alone. I know this because I remember the first time I saw murder. I was not seventeen. And this is how I know that evil can come out of the ordinary." Arsov grimaced. It was not a pleasing sight, and for a moment he looked every one of his ninety years.

"You are shocked that she was killed in our safe surroundings. I, too, found murder where I felt safest. In my village we knew of war, but as a distant idea. When it came, it came swiftly. It came with the Fritzes. When they invited us to a field at the edge of the woods. To collect data they said, and we believed them. We were deep in the heart of Russia and some of the children had never seen Roman letters before. They were excited. I remember how they begged to see the list with their names."

The nurse stood and without a word left the room, shielding a candle before her.

"When my family crossed the top of the hill we saw that the ditch was dug. The pit deep enough to hide a man and ten meters long, gutted into the hard cold ground. Easier for us. The walk wasn't far and the surroundings were familiar, so we hadn't time to worry. We had only a few minutes. Two . . . maybe three. Not enough time. Too much time."

Agnes wanted him to stop; he was veering too far from what she needed to know, but she couldn't speak. He was Russian and of a certain age. She knew what had happened in the last World War. The mass murders.

"In my life there are entire weeks that I don't recall; that day I remember each fraction of time. It is as if I lived it once and then saw it every day after. Do you know this feeling?" he asked.

She swallowed, remembering George's death. The distant scream that only later she knew was his. How the rain started to fall. The exact temperature of the air. The sound of traffic. All ordinary and yet all now part of that day in a way that made her pulse quicken and her mouth taste of adrenaline.

"I can tell you how the air tasted heavy with fir," Arsov continued, "and the smell of cow dung mixed with fresh earth. The air was dry and cold. Truly cold, so that our lungs hurt while we walked and so dry you could draw a spark merely by rubbing against someone." He tapped his cigarette ash and it fell to the floor and singed the antique carpet. Transfixed, Agnes watched the silk threads char.

"The sun touched the tops of the trees and the pit was in shadow. It took us a few extra seconds to understand. To see. Those who came before had laid their shovels at the edge of the ditch and were waiting. Not running or threatening or begging, but waiting. Disbelief on their faces. You know what is about to happen but your mind says—impossible."

Yes, impossible, she wanted to scream. Impossible that he was dead. That he had *killed* himself. That he deliberately left her and their sons. She reached for a glass of water and it shook, sloshing liquid onto her lips and down her suit jacket.

"I held my mother's hand and helped her climb across the uneven ground. My baby sister, my Anya, clung to my other hand and behind us I could feel the touch of the others bracing so they wouldn't stumble as we pressed together. We didn't want to humiliate ourselves. Can you imagine the state of someone's mind to ignore the men with guns pointed at them, the harsh commands of a tongue few understood, and the obvious threat of that ditch, and yet be concerned about falling? About loss of dignity?"

Agnes glanced up at the light of a candelabra to stop the tears from forming. Why? she had wanted to scream every day since George's death. Why?

Arsov smoked and watched the fire. "The Germans are an efficient people. It took only a few minutes for us to be in place and another few for the job to be over. I had never heard gunfire like that. The report of a rifle I had known from infancy, but not the thunder of a machine gun, and it sounded like the end of the world. In a way it was. My mother and sisters turned to me, they clung to me in desperation and that is how they saved my life. When the guns sounded I fell with my family, pushed down the embankment as they collapsed. The bastards shot into the ditch. My father taught me languages and I could understand the orders and heard them pointing out survivors.

'There! In the blue cap!' 'There, the woman with the crying baby!' You can't imagine what these words meant to me. My friend in the blue cap he hated but that his grandmother made for him. My older sister and the crying baby, her daughter."

Outside there was a loud crack followed by a thundering boom. Agnes half rose. Branches, even entire trees, were snapping under the weight of the ice, bringing down more power lines and blocking roads across the region. Arsov ignored everything and she sat down awkwardly.

"Few died instantly. I could feel them move and whimper. Blood from my mother and sister drained onto my face and into my mouth and eyes but I couldn't wipe it away; I was pinned by their bodies. I held my baby sister's hand as she died and felt her struggle to breathe with a bullet in her lung. I lay there from the time the sun hit the tops of the trees until it had disappeared and the sky was filled with stars."

Agnes remembered the blood on the ground beside George, how they had tried to cover it, but she saw. And the edge of his hand when it slipped off the gurney. Later she wished she'd been allowed to touch it, to touch him while he still had the vestiges of human warmth.

Arsov motioned toward Mimi. "She is Anya's age, almost. They can't last long in the cold at that age, they are so frail. Anya's fingers were those of a musician, long and thin and frostbite would have taken them even if she lived. I held her hand and felt it grow cold. All around me the cries turned to rasping gurgles and low moans, then they stopped. First Anya, then my mother. My older sister and her baby. All around me was death and still the Germans toyed with us. Then night fell, the wind rose, and the temperature dropped. Like tonight.

"When the Germans left, I couldn't believe it. They had their beautiful coats and gloves and boots, but they were too cold to stand over us and watch us die. They were too cold to finish the job. I waited until the moon was halfway across the sky, but not one of the bastards returned and so I pulled my-self out from under my dead family and childhood friends and crawled out of the pit and started walking away from my village into the night. I had survived and swore I would cut down these weak men who hid behind bullets but ran from the cold."

Agnes pictured the dead woman outside, and the ice and wind, and felt despair.

Five

It was the middle of the night and Agnes thanked the Vallotton housekeeper once again for offering the hospitality of the château in such strange circumstances, telling Madame Puguet she could find her own way to her bedroom. Over the past hours they had done all they could, although it hadn't felt like enough. Theft of money was a terrible crime, but this, stealing a life, weighed more. Now, walking the corridor to the bedroom wing she followed the directions she'd been given, clutching a small leather bag under her arm. Pleased that she had remembered the emergency "stop-over" kit George had put together years ago. She had laughed at his Swiss-ness when he showed it to her. Nothing left to chance. Always prepared. Just a few toothbrushes and other toiletries, he had said, before putting it in the car and most likely forgetting about it. Now it was a talisman of his thoughtfulness. How he'd taken care of her . . . of all of them, really. She wondered if she had appreciated him enough. She was certain she had. He must have known how she felt. But then, why? Why had he taken his life? No note, no explanation, but a dozen witnesses who saw him carefully climb the railing and step off the Pont Bessières. A deliberate choice.

She turned a corner and found the marquise staring down a flight of stairs. Backlit by flickering torches set in the walls, her profile was strong and beautiful despite her age. Her candelabra dripped white wax on the floor and Agnes liked the imagery and suspected the other woman knew the effect she had. According to Petit, the marquise had been widowed young. That meant that the vast majority of her years had been spent in this place where centuries of her ancestors had lived before, walking these same steps illuminated only by candlelight. Agnes clicked off her flashlight.

The marquise acknowledged Agnes with a nod, before glancing down the staircase to the door leading to the lawn. Agnes knew it was likely the victim walked—or ran?—through that door to her death.

"She has nothing to do with us," the marquise said. "Or perhaps it is that we had nothing to do with her. Not in a way that would lead to her death."

"She died here; there will be a connection. We'll find it."

"She seemed a smart sort of person, but not altogether truthful." The marquise glanced at Agnes. "Don't mind me, I am judging too harshly. She was young and the young always have their secrets. I have been reading Diogenes and have become too immersed in his theories." She turned as if she could see all the way down the stairs and across the lawn to the bench. "To fall and die like that; it is a feeble generation."

"I suspect feebleness had little to do with her death." Agnes stifled a yawn. They stood shoulder to shoulder in silence.

"My nephew tells me Mademoiselle Cowell was wearing the coronation gown."

"Her gown was white, with stones on the bodice, if that's the one he means."

"It is distinctive, white pleated silk with a spray of diamonds. It was worn by one of my ancestresses to Napoleon's coronation. Julien is quite sure that is what Mademoiselle Cowell was wearing."

"Stolen?" Agnes willed the word back as soon as she'd said it.

"How could it be stolen when it was on our property?" The marquise smiled coolly. "Mademoiselle Cowell had leave to look at our possessions as part of her work on the auction."

"I understood it was only art for sale?"

"Clothing can be art." Before Agnes could respond the marquise continued, "No, it was not part of the auction but perhaps what she called staging. Unnecessary in my mind, although that is Julien's concern and I told her as much. I only point out the gown as a matter of interest and to suggest that you will find her own clothing in the fur vault where she may have changed. Perhaps there you will also find . . . a clue. That is what you are looking for, isn't it? The reason you and your colleagues must stay the night. The reason for these questions."

"You could call it that, a clue."

"There are others who stay as part of this interrogation. The man who found a way down from the village for your colleagues, Monsieur Estanguet? I met him in the corridor a moment ago. It is like living in a hotel, strangers walking into and out of bedrooms." The marquise fingered her rubies. "He was distressed, nearly incoherent."

Agnes wished she had asked the doctor to attend to Estanguet. "He saw the body. I'm sure he'll feel better in the morning. It is the shock and the cold. We were outside too long."

"Death is a shock, and the death of a young person is a double tragedy." The marquise searched Agnes's face. "Do you have children, Inspector Lüthi?"

"Three boys."

"To have a child die would be a terrible thing. What parent would be satisfied with an explanation? What sibling would understand? My brother was a very old man when he left us, a century of living. But with a child there would be no talk of having lived a full life. You want a child to live forever, or at least to die after you, so the illusion of living forever is complete."

Agnes understood. What if one of her sons had died instead of George? Could she have survived that horror? Even for the other boys? Or would she have been only two-thirds of a person forever? This was the first time she'd been away from home in the evening since George's death and a thousand worries crowded her head. Were the boys safe? How could she know without seeing them herself? How could she have returned to work knowing there would be nights like this? Sybille was right: she should be with them.

"The bond between a parent and child," the marquise continued. "Permanent, yet an intangible connection. I wonder, would you recognize your boys if you hadn't seen them since they were young? Two or three years old maybe, not fully formed. Would you know them after years? Decades even? Is the bond that strong?"

Agnes forced her mind to send the message that her boys were safe and well and that she shouldn't worry. Their grand-parents loved them and would care for them. "Yes," she managed, "because I would recognize myself or my husband in their faces."

"I had not thought of that. Of course recognizing a family characteristic would make it simpler. A physical bond." The marquise turned away from her. "Mademoiselle Cowell's parents will be devastated. Their loss will be hard."

The dismissal was firm and Agnes said good night and clicked her flashlight on again. The Great Dane appeared from the shadows, and she was pleased. Winston was a comfort, not merely his size but his calmness. This was his territory and he had no fear. She laughed out loud; fatigue was making her fanciful.

At the top of yet another long flight of winding stairs, she found Petit dozing in a hard-backed chair in the hallway. She swept her flashlight down the wall of the corridor and counted the doors, looking for the eighth. Knowing that the other rooms were quite possibly occupied, she counted the doors twice. Winston's nails clicked as he turned to leave. Finally she looked at Petit, wishing he had disappeared while her back was turned.

"We've got her tucked away nice and tidy," he said.

Agnes motioned for him to continue, too tired to ask questions, yet knowing she needed to let him report so they could both go to bed.

"In a kind of old ice house. Doctor Blanchard wants her kept cold and decided it would suit. And we've walked the perimeter and finished blocking off all the rooms the victim used. I think Monsieur Bardy would be pleased."

"Felicity Cowell," Agnes said automatically. "Not the victim. She had a name. She is a person."

"Absolutely, Mademoiselle Cowell." Petit took a step forward, wincing. He ducked to bring his face near hers. "I took pictures of everything. On my camera phone, but the resolution is good."

"You're in pain, what happened?"

"Slipped coming down the hill, from the bruise on my leg I guess that my radio fell off and I landed on it. Couldn't see my own hand in front of my face and didn't know it at the time. Radio's gone for good, I think." He edged closer to her. "You won't mention this to Bardy?"

"He won't care about your radio. It's more important that we sleep and be fresh for tomorrow. In daylight we'll look at the crime scene again."

"Not another word. I'm Officer Petit reporting to sleep duty as of now." He started to leave. "I never thought in all my life that I'd get a chance to stay here. Most exciting thing that's ever happened to me."

Agnes crossed the threshold of her assigned bedroom, wondering how it was that her eyes were still open and her brain functioning. An oil lamp was burning, giving off just enough light for her to see the general outline of the space even before she ran her flashlight beam around. The wallpaper pattern was of vines laced with yellow flowers and the heavy curtains and upholstery, even the spread on the bed, matched it. The double bed was topped by a high dome of material stretched over a wood frame, and the effect caused Agnes to smile despite her weariness. No wonder Petit was looking forward to his night here.

She slipped off her ruined shoes and saw an old-fashioned linen nightgown folded on her pillow. The sight of it made her uncomfortable. The Vallottons and their servants saw to everything; they would have no problem creating a story out of whole cloth for the police if they wanted. Standing beside the bed, silently debating the ethics of wearing a nightgown possibly provided by the killer, she was startled when a light rap on her door was followed by Carnet's soft *"Vous êtes là?"*

Shaking her head to wake herself, she plucked her notebook from her handbag and slipped on her damp shoes before stepping into the wide corridor. "Everyone is settled for the night," Carnet said when she emerged. "I wanted to talk to you about a few things."

"Of course, I was just going over my notes." There was a small table a few feet away, and she pulled a chair over. Her flashlight provided enough light to read by, and Carnet picked up another chair and joined her. He rubbed his temple as if countering a headache.

"I had better luck getting straight stories out of the Arsov household," Agnes said. "I made a mistake and should have spoken to the Vallottons individually. Instead they were vague and probably not entirely truthful. Someone has to have known her better than they admit."

"Tomorrow will be time enough." Carnet rubbed his forehead again.

"To have their stories straight."

"Agnes, I doubt this is the work of the household as a group. They're not conspiring against us as we sleep. They're anxious and worried. No matter how carefully someone constructs a story there will be holes. Tomorrow will do."

"Did you talk to the rest of the household? The ones who aren't family?"

"Each and every one of them."

"There aren't as many as I'd think in a place this large. Not as many as next door."

Carnet nodded. "You interviewed the marquise, the Vallotton brothers, and Marie-Chantal Vallotton?"

"And the marquise's godson, Ralph Mulholland. As Petit said, Julien Vallotton technically owns the property since his father died two years ago, but he lives mostly in London. His brother lives here with his wife. Mulholland is visiting, although I get the idea that it is an extended visit with no end in sight. He's British, although he doesn't admit to knowing Felicity Cowell before."

Carnet nodded. "I spoke with the housekeeper, Madame Puguet. There's only a couple of maids here now. The others, including a nanny for the little girl, were out, stranded by the storm. The cook is here. And another man—an American college student—called Nick Graves is doing research in the library. He's been here for a few weeks. Part of a fellowship from his university sponsored by the Vallottons. Across the lot of them a great deal of trying to remember where they were. Conflicting stories. Nothing of real importance. Yet."

"Are you sure we can discount Julien Vallotton?"

"Bardy said as much when he called me. It was the first thing he did when he heard from the *gendarmerie*. Called

Cointrin's ground security and checked the time Vallotton's flight arrived. They noted when his car left the tarmac."

"How'd he know it was a crime?"

"Habit of experience. Imagine the worst. Anyway, he said it was impossible for Julien Vallotton to be involved with the woman's death. Those were literally Bardy's last words to me before the phone cut out. The ice that covered her came in the first wave of the storm before Vallotton arrived."

Agnes ran her eyes down the list of notes she had taken earlier. "Arsov has a large staff; all accounted for." She fidgeted with her waistband. "We have nothing."

"Tomorrow we start again. No one is leaving. And in daylight people are more cooperative."

"A killer is out there." Agnes glanced at Carnet. "Granted, probably not wandering the countryside killing randomly, and the property is not just private, it is hard to reach. Is it possible to go along the shore past the neighbor's and not have to climb up the hill? Maybe it was someone from the outside, someone on drugs, or simply crazy." She glanced at Carnet and saw that he found that scenario as unlikely as she did. "If not, at least we can rule it out."

"Agnes—"

"We need to know more about the victim, then we can see the connection to this place or the others, or if one even exists. Why would someone want to kill her? And why kill her here?"

"Jealousy, hate, greed, fear," said Carnet. "We have our choice of reasons."

"The Vallottons don't seem like killers."

"Few people do. Probably any one of us can kill if the reason is strong enough. Crimes of passion. Revenge."

"What she was wearing bothers me. My impression is that Felicity Cowell dressed carefully. Too carefully, the marquise seemed to think. Probably wanted to present herself well. She was a young professional." Agnes flipped through the pages of her notebook. "You remember that laundering scheme two years ago? How the auction types were all dressed to the nines, reeking money to impress their clients? I think Felicity Cowell was the same. The marquise likely doesn't have a concept of needing to impress since she had that mastered at birth. But dressing well usually doesn't mean overdressing. It means being absolutely appropriate. Felicity Cowell was wearing an evening gown in the middle of the afternoon, with a man's boots and coat. Forget that she was outside in that garb, why was she wearing it in the first place in the middle of a workday? She would have looked absurd. If the coat is supposed to have been taken from the armoire in the small hall by the door, well, I checked and there are other coats there. More-appropriate coats. Women's coats. A fur even. Why did she pick that one?"

Carnet sighed and rubbed the bridge of his nose. They sat in silence. Agnes ran her pen down her notes, wondering where to begin in the morning.

"Agnes, we need to talk about George." Her head snapped up, eyes wide in astonishment. "I know he's on your mind and having me here, having us work together, doesn't make it easier. You wanted a clean break and to return to work with different colleagues, a different office, and I thought it was a good idea. Anything to help you forget."

"What is there to talk about? He's dead." She felt tears rise easily to the surface. She didn't want to talk about her husband. He was already too present in her mind tonight and her family life had always been separate from work. That was all that allowed her to continue in the aftermath of tragedy.

"He was a good man, and he loved his sons. Remember that. And he was so proud of you."

"Don't say things to make me feel better. I won't have it."

"He *was* proud of you."

"You didn't even know George." Her voice quavered. She remembered Carnet arriving at the scene seconds after her: taking charge, making sure she was away before she learned more of the horrific details of the drop from the bridge onto the road; before hysteria could settle in.

"You've forgotten that I met George at Bienne just before the match. I came to see you shoot and you took a first."

She had forgotten, but now remembered seeing the two men talking. She'd been thrilled to show off in front of her boss; certain her husband was proud. Vigorously she rubbed a tear off her cheek.

There were footsteps down the hall. Agnes stood and turned her flashlight toward the noise. A match flared and a candle illuminated. In the arc of light they saw a young woman cup her hand around the flame. Agnes looked at Carnet who mouthed, "One of the maids, Marie-José." The woman approached and asked if Agnes was the inspector in charge. With a brief glance at Carnet, Agnes said yes, she was.

"May I speak with you privately? No disrespect to monsieur."

"Was there something else?" Agnes asked Carnet. He shook his head no and she said good night before leading Marie-José into her room.

In the corridor the young woman had appeared self-assured,

but once inside the bedroom she was nervous and Agnes gave her a moment to collect herself. Thin and pretty in a quiet way, Marie-José had brown hair and eyes and good teeth. She rounded out her appearance with jeans and a heavy sweater. Pouring her guest a glass of water from a carafe, Agnes wondered if the girl wore a uniform when on duty. Marie-José took a few sips before setting the glass on the small table near the bed. She opened her mouth a few times as if to speak, but didn't make a sound.

Agnes waited through a few tries, then took pity on the woman. "Is there something you didn't want to share earlier?"

"I was afraid of being misunderstood."

Agnes recollected that according to Carnet, Marie-José had contributed no more than basic facts about herself and a lack of knowledge about anyone's movements during the hours in question. "You've remembered something?"

"Yes, that's it." Marie-José looked so relieved Agnes wanted to scold her. "I remembered that I didn't hear Monsieur Graves when I was cleaning the library. That's harder than remembering something you did hear, isn't it?" She paused. "He was in the library when I started dusting but he wasn't there the entire afternoon. I'm sure of it."

"And he said he was?"

"Yes. And it may have been long enough to. Well, you know. Go outside."

After they had covered the timing of Nick Graves's coming and going as clearly as Marie-José could remember, Agnes had another question. "Did you notice him interested in Felicity Cowell?"

"We all were." Marie-José stopped herself. "Not in the way

that you mean, but she was interesting. And beautiful. Plus she was British. I loved to hear her talk. Not that she did much, and never to me." She laughed awkwardly. "She was mysterious and beautiful." She studied her fingernails as if inspecting a new manicure. "He was flustered around her. When I saw them together, I mean."

She stood. Agnes didn't stop her and, after apologizing for her earlier reticence, Marie-José excused herself.

Agnes locked her bedroom door, thinking about Nick Graves and wondering how many other lies were told during the evening. She changed into the borrowed nightgown, lowering the flame in the oil lamp near the bed. At least now she had a real lead. And a suspect.

DAY TWO

Six

Agnes dressed at dawn, thankful daylight meant she could at least pretend to work. She had slept poorly, her dreams filled with images of George, a somber George whom she had married but hadn't really known. Now, facing the morning with the same clothes and damp shoes, her mood worsened. She finished washing up and ran a hand through her flattened hair. After slipping a small bottle of hand lotion from George's emergency kit into her pocket, she exited the bedroom and trudged through the dark corridors. Relieved to find the morning meal had been laid out as promised, she helped herself to a croissant and cup of coffee before starting on a self-guided tour. She wanted to work, needed to work.

Last night she had made a sketch of the château, just enough to study the general layout. Now she was interested in what she might have missed the previous evening. Lacking electricity, the spaces were an uneven mix of dark and light. She felt a shiver of apprehension and wished the cell towers were repaired and that her phone worked.

Too many rooms and too much silence. She traced the route from the outside door by the kitchen—glad to hear voices at work—to the victim's workroom at the opposite side of the château, then to the room called the fur vault, before backtracking to the door near the kitchen which led to the lawn, wondering if that was the way Felicity had exited. Standing on her tiptoes she peered through the small window set high in the heavy door. The storm had resumed for several hours in the night and no footprints could have survived the frozen mess of blowing ice. Obtaining evidence at the crime scene was unlikely before, and nearly impossible now.

Her mind wandered down the halls and through various scenarios before locking on the obvious. They had no fixed points for the hours before Felicity reached the bench and was struck down. No one claimed to have seen or heard her and the sheer size of the estate lent the claims credibility. She could have been in her workroom—as expected and evidenced by a cold cup of tea—but why was she wearing an evening gown? Did she leave on her own or did someone lure her away? Was the cold tea left from the night before, meaning she hadn't returned to her workroom the day of her death and they could eliminate that room from their inquiry?

Agnes pondered the questions. Too many questions. Was the bench Felicity's destination, or was she on her way somewhere else? Was she there by choice, chance, or design? With no answers, she studied her sketch of the château again. Remarkably, there were only two exterior exits or, perhaps more important, entrances. On the principal level, there were doors that opened onto the interior courtyard; however, from there everyone still had to pass under the heavy iron portcullis and through the main gate. The other outside access was this small door near the kitchen leading down through the foundation to the lawn. Two points of entry or exit.

Agnes returned to the entrance hall and felt a weight press on her. There were dozens of ways to travel through the château unnoticed and the more she walked the more she felt the profundity of the silence. She worked her way up the various flights of stairs until she emerged to stand on the walkway at the top of the northeast wall. The morning was cold but clear and she pulled a pack of cigarettes from her pocket. Lighting one, she took a drag, edging closer to the parapet for shelter from the slight wind. The covered open walkway ran the circumference of the château's ramparts and linked the turrets. The outer wall was crenellated, while the inner wall intersected with the roof overhead. Despite this, ice had driven under the roof to almost completely coat the walls and floor. Everywhere she looked—as far as the eye could see—ordinary forms were outlined in ice, creating a surreal landscape.

"Hope you aren't contemplating jumping."

The man's voice startled her. Annoyance followed swiftly.

Julien Vallotton emerged from a narrow, low door. "I was going to leave these by your bedroom door, but one of the maids said you were already up here. She was impressed that you were at work so early; I think her way of criticizing the rest of us." Vallotton held out a wool hat and a pair of fleece-lined winter boots. "She also said that she offered you boots last night and you refused." He glanced at her thin damp shoes. "Understandable that you were uncertain about accepting help from the suspects—maybe the lining is poisoned—but I thought you might change your mind. Selfish really, I'm trying to keep out of prison for murder and don't want to find you frozen in a lonely corner. A second victim."

"Are you bird-watching?" Agnes nodded to the binoculars hanging from a leather strap around his neck. "I'd think all the birds outside today are frozen."

He grinned. "I'm glad Bardy sent you."

Agnes took the boots and after a moment's hesitation eased her cold feet into them, jumping back in surprise. "They're hot."

"They shouldn't be. Mine were only warm." Vallotton reached for one and she stopped him, embarrassed. Of course they warmed their boots before putting them on. Who would put on cold boots when there were servants to prevent such things? Her toes were so chilled the heat felt like boiling water. She waved him off and tried not to sigh with pleasure as the temperature evened out. She added the thick hat, mashing her hair flat.

"I think you aren't going to prison," she said, remembering what Carnet had told her about the timing of Julien Vallotton's arrival.

"Comforting. But someone is. Or should." Vallotton raised his binoculars. "I wanted to see the damage. Of course, I could be checking to see that I hid all the evidence of my criminal behavior yesterday." He lowered the lenses to look at the ground beneath them. "Yes, snowmobile tracks from the airport eradicated completely."

Over his shoulder she saw a shadow in the distance. A man. Ralph Mulholland turned quickly and headed around the corner to the far tower. She studied his disappearing back, wondering if it was her overactive imagination that made him appear to scuttle. Perhaps he was simply cold and in a hurry to return inside.

Vallotton held his binoculars out. She shook her head, more interested in the activity directly below. Carnet and Petit had emerged from the château onto the lawn, Petit peeling off toward the drive in search of his missing radio, while Carnet started a grid search, setting out small wooden stakes near where they found the body.

Squinting to see in the glare of sun on ice, Agnes located the canvas walls used to shelter Felicity Cowell the night before. They had blown into a tangled heap against the trees before being encased in several inches of ice. Carnet's efforts to find a weapon were likely in vain.

He called up to her, holding one hand to his ear with a questioning look. She shook her head: no cell service. For a few minutes she watched him slip and stumble as he went about his work. Just seeing the others had changed the morning. Normal human activity continued. She had had to remind herself of that every day for three months, and she wondered if it would ever end, this need to be prompted to engage with the world. Behind her, Vallotton cursed under his breath and she turned to see him slide against the wall. He was walking the length of the east wing and she followed, thankful for her new boots and hat.

Near the south turret they had a clear view of the entire lake. Remembering the predictions on the radio the evening before, she understood that this astonishing sight was what the meteorologists had expected. The wind had blown spray off the water and it had frozen along the shore in dramatic horizontal patterns, ice clinging to every surface: trees, hand-rails, benches. The façade of the château was coated in three inches of ice dappled by the force of the wind. Near the water's edge, the summer pavilion was encased in ice so thick it looked like a solid form.

She lit another cigarette, this one to enjoy. Across the lake, the French Alps gleamed white. Agnes could practically hear tourists cooing excitedly with their noses pressed to the windows of cozy hotel breakfast rooms, trusting to their hosts to find a way to heat and light the chambers while they took vacation photographs to post later on social media. From this vantage point the aftermath of the storm looked both awe-inspiring and chaotic. In every direction, fallen trees covered the normally ordered landscape and the road leading up to the village was a tangle of overlapping branches that created a barrier five meters high. She was fortunate Estanguet had helped the others down when he did. A few more hours and it would have been impassible. Now the ice would have to thaw before anyone could manage the steep slope, and even then a sharp ax would be needed to hack a way through. In the other direction, beyond the ice-encrusted shoreline, the activity on Lac Léman was altered with the ferries stopped, leaving the cold water empty. It would take days, if not weeks, to restore even basic services.

She leaned against the ice-covered stone of the parapet and closed her eyes. Mentally she reviewed the names of the château's inhabitants, wondering who was a killer. It was a shocking idea despite seeing the body: someone among them a killer. Suddenly she was exhausted in a way that not even a cigarette helped dispel.

"If I'm not going to prison, who is?" Vallotton was standing beside her, cool blue gaze studying her thoughtfully. He looked prepared to steady her with his hand.

"Slept badly," she mumbled.

"I should think so. Forced to stay in the house where the crime happened. Probably not the usual routine."

He was frowning at her cigarette and she didn't want to tell him that she had never been part of this routine and didn't know what was usual. "How well do you know the American staying here?" she asked. "Nick Graves."

"The fellowship student? Not at all. I think he was cordoned off in the library last evening. I steered clear of all but my family." He paused. "He's the, what do you call it, prime suspect? My aunt will be thrilled. She's convinced I did it. Coming from London, proximity to the dead woman. Probably she thinks I am most likely to slither out of an arrest—she can't imagine you would imprison my father's son." He raised his binoculars again. "She's a bit old-fashioned. I'm certain you would love nothing more than to put me in cuffs and have done with it."

"Fortunately your plane arrived after Felicity Cowell died."

They stood side by side for a moment watching the activity of her colleagues below, Agnes aware of Vallotton's height and elegance compared with her own disheveled appearance.

"I merely wondered if you knew him." Last night she was prepared to take Marie-José's story at face value. In the strong light of day she would question all motives.

"Bardy and my father were lifelong friends. Fellow stamp collectors." Vallotton turned to face her. "I'm glad he sent you. We must seem callous; certainly there were no tears last night.

I've often wondered what an outsider would think of my family and never had the chance to ask."

"I'm hardly the usual outsider."

"What does usual mean? We never meet anyone new— truly new. My aunt has possibly not met anyone new since the last world war."

"Impossible." Agnes crushed the remains of her cigarette under her heel then self-consciously picked it up and tucked it in her pocket. She couldn't tell if Vallotton was amused or contemptuous. Either way, much as she wanted not to like him, she did. "You were introduced to Ralph Mulholland last night."

"I've met him before, years ago. Anyway, he is my aunt's godson, not really someone new, is he? She's known him his whole life, he is like family to her. I mean someone new. Someone not tied to us in a way that we can pigeonhole immediately. We know exactly how far to trust someone, what to say and not say. Even the maids are the daughters of old maids. Plus we probably own the houses they grew up in."

"You don't know the American, that means he's new."

"Nick Graves? I haven't met him, and haven't any plans to." Agnes frowned and Vallotton shrugged. "The people I know are troublesome enough. The last thing I need to do is add others, full of unknown quantities and expectations, to the list."

"Not very trusting, are you?"

"Based on your time here, should I be?"

She leaned nearer the edge of the parapet to check Carnet's progress. For a moment she had a sense of vertigo. She felt the pull of the ground. The sense of inevitability. This was how it felt in that final second before George fell. Vallotton gripped her arm and pulled her back.

"You're ill."

"No." Embarrassed, she couldn't explain. She leaned near the edge again, this time prepared for the heady sense of tipping. She pointed down the ice-coated wall. "Are we above the door from the back hall, the one near the kitchen?"

Vallotton motioned for her to follow him. He stopped three-quarters of the way around the east turret and pointed down. Agnes gripped the wall and leaned over. Sighting the door, she studied the path Felicity might have walked from door to bench.

"Why was she sitting there?" She bit her lip, wishing she hadn't spoken out loud.

"Normally the lawn is appealing, and there's a promenade along the lake." When she didn't comment, Vallotton laughed, blue eyes flashing. "You're going to need me if you want the rest of my family, and the servants for that matter, to cooperate. They'll answer your questions, but you need more. I'm not very trusting and it's a family characteristic. But I trust you. I trust Bardy and he sent you."

Agnes admitted that what Vallotton said was at least partially true. This was an unusual situation and she might need someone from the family to smooth things over. Bardy's claim that there was no possibility Julien Vallotton was involved in the crime had better be right. She was about to stake her reputation on it.

"The appealing view is what I mean," she said. "Who would sit on a hard bench fifty meters from the shore, surrounded by a clump of trees, when they could sit in a pavilion near the shore under a beautiful roof?" Although the pavilion was encased with ice, the outline of the octagonal structure was clear.

"You aren't seeing the grove at its best," Vallotton said. "Although I think its best is now a thing of the past. Before the storm it was a pleasant place. Arsov is wheeled out there most days. Marie-Chantal likes to set up an easel in the shade. When you live on a lake it can lose its appeal."

Agnes glanced toward Carnet again. Beyond him was Petit. She angled her head and farther away saw a much smaller figure staring up the frozen hill. Mulholland again. Although it was impossible to be certain at a distance. The form appeared to be a man's, but it could be a tall woman well bundled against the cold with a heavy coat, hat, and scarf. She pictured Felicity Cowell's clothing. The thin evening dress and a man's coat. An unlikely combination in an unlikely place.

There had been unlikely combinations in financial crimes. They were the prompt, the literal thing that drew attention and started an investigation. Investigations that often led to ugliness far beyond stolen wealth to human trafficking, drugs, lives destroyed. Violent crimes appeared to be the opposite. The thing that drew attention was seemingly the worst on offer—the taking of a human life. Instinctively Agnes knew it wasn't the worst on offer and that ultimately they would find the dark and spoiled thing that led to Felicity Cowell's death. That was what she was looking for. The root of evil. Vladimir Arsov understood. He also knew that evil knew how to hide.

"Last night your aunt said that Monsieur Mulholland lives here, but you don't know him well?"

"He's visited over the years but I was always away myself.

And I've lived mostly in London for some time. I think Mulholland's on an extended visit now. It's kind of him, really. Antoinette is very much alone since my father died. Only our housekeeper, cook, chauffeur, and a few maids live here. Antoinette doesn't count the students who rotate through from university, although I suppose they are introduced to her upon arrival. And of course Mimi lives here with her nanny." He lifted a hand to shield his eyes against the glare. "I hope the poor woman wasn't trapped on a road when the storm hit. I'm certain my chauffeur is enjoying himself at the hotel in the village, drinking on my tab."

"Your brother and his wife also live here."

"Stuck here is more accurate." Vallotton moved into shadow. "Daniel was heli-skiing—jumping from a damn helicopter onto the top of a godforsaken inaccessible slope—when he hurt himself. He and MC don't really live anywhere. They wander around the world while Daniel searches for adventure. They'll stay here until he heals, then if ski season is over they'll head to Rio or somewhere exotic."

Agnes resisted commenting on the Vallottons' way of life and turned to leave, needing to see the bench and grove up close in the light of day.

"I don't suppose Mademoiselle Cowell could have been killed by someone we don't know?" Vallotton asked as he held a door open and turned on his flashlight. It was a different staircase from the one Agnes had used to come up, and very dark. The spiral was tight and so narrow it was dizzying, like walking down a vertical tunnel.

"Not likely, but we're looking." They reached the bottom

step and exited into an elegantly furnished sitting room. When shut behind them, the door to the stair appeared to vanish into the woodwork.

Vallotton noted her expression. "You must have come up the original stairs."

They emerged into the corridor and Agnes wondered how they were to piece together where everyone was at what time the day before. How many concealed passages were there? Or stairways? She would check the walls of her bedroom carefully before sleeping there another night.

"You spoke with Officer Petit about finding the body, but I wouldn't mind hearing what happened for myself." She started to reach for another cigarette but distracted herself by pulling out her notebook.

"Little to tell. My driver dropped me at the top of the hill and I put him up in the Croix Blanche. He didn't want to risk the walk down, and he was right. I nearly killed myself. Slid halfway down on the ice, and it's a miracle I didn't break a leg. That's why I assumed Mademoiselle Cowell had fallen and hit her head."

"Why were you so far away from the château in that weather?"

"Our housekeeper, Madame Puguet, was waiting when I came in the front door. She told me Mimi was pulling one of her disappearing acts. Usually that means she's at Arsov's since he lets her have the run of the place. I set off to retrieve her and that's when I practically fell over the body. Did literally fall and see her there, frozen. It was clear she was dead and didn't need a doctor. It never occurred to me, or to any of us, that she had been killed."

Vallotton pushed open a heavy door and clicked off his flashlight. These rooms were flooded with daylight. "It happened quickly. One minute I was worried about falling, and the next was in a panic to find what scared Mimi so badly. Then I slipped and saw what had. We ran straight to Arsov's—it was closer—and called the *gendarmerie*."

"Mimi was frightened? She found the body before you?" Agnes's hand fluttered to her pocket for a cigarette, but she stilled it. How had they missed that the girl discovered the body? "Tell me exactly what happened."

"I was on my way to Arsov's to see if Mimi was there. It's faster to cut across the lawn and I angled up through the grove, mainly for protection from the wind. The storm was in a lull but it was still intense."

"Why didn't you call them and ask?"

Vallotton grimaced. "I offered to go. I was trying to delay seeing my family and I'd already been out in the weather, a few more minutes wouldn't hurt. Expected to find Mimi cajoling one more cup of hot chocolate and planned to share a bottle of wine with Arsov. He has a case of—" He stopped before she could interrupt him. "Back to the point. I had my head down against the wind. I didn't see Mimi until she ran into me. She was crying. Hysterical. She pulled me along, deeper into the grove than I would have gone otherwise, and I slipped on the ice. That's when I saw Mademoiselle Cowell. I fell and she was there, on the ground in front of me. Not two feet away. Her face was icy." He glanced around as if to erase the image. "But I recognized her, or thought I knew who she had to be. A bit of face and the top of her dress was visible. It was enough."

Agnes remembered that this was at least an hour before she

arrived and therefore before the body was completely encased in ice.

"That's when I understood that Mimi had already seen her," Vallotton said. "Who wouldn't be frightened given what she saw? We ran to Arsov's. It was closer and I knew his nurse was there. I thought Mimi might need medical attention."

For a moment Agnes wanted to strangle Petit. He should have learned these details right away, when he first spoke with Vallotton upon arriving at the château. Then she remembered the ferocity of the storm and calmed herself.

"What precisely did Mimi see?" she asked.

"Felicity Co—" Vallotton stopped. He looked at Agnes for a long moment. "I see what you mean. I assumed she saw what I had. That she happened upon the body, perhaps slipped and saw her."

Agnes took a deep breath. There was a chance the girl had seen the killer. A slim chance. More likely Vallotton was right and she had only seen what he had.

"I'll talk to her this morning." Agnes calculated quickly. She would still speak with Nick Graves first, no need to wake a sleeping child.

Seven

Agnes wound her way toward the château's kitchen, following an airborne trail of rich aromas. Stepping through a stone archway into a large space with a high vaulted ceiling, she knew that the scent of baking bread, sugar, and roasting meat hadn't led her astray. This was the working center of the château.

"Hello?" she called out, her voice echoing. "Is anyone here?" She walked toward a door at the far end of the room. It led to a secondary corridor where the absence of decoration was pronounced.

"Marie-José, hold your breath, I'm coming." A large woman wrapped in a flour-covered apron backed into the hall. "You've no reason to. Oh—" She stopped when she saw Agnes.

"I'm Inspector Lüthi, sorry to intrude."

"Come to question me?" The cook smiled to show she meant no harm and indicated Agnes should return with her to the main kitchen. She set an oblong pâté mold on the table before dusting her hands on her apron.

"Not so much question as see what you might have remembered since last night," Agnes said, glancing around. She wasn't much for kitchens but this was a marvel, a perfect blend of modern need with ancient practice. The overhead vaults were not plastered; neither were the stone walls. Sunshine streamed in through high windows and glanced off copper pans and stainless steel utensils.

"When the old Monsieur was alive we'd have parties that made me want double the space," the cook said.

A pile of logs burned in a fireplace large enough for a dozen men to stand in. Meat was threaded onto spits and grease dripped and sizzled. A long, scarred wooden table commanded the center of the room and the sink on the far wall was as long as a bathtub.

"The old Monsieur would bring live game in like when he was a boy and we'd pluck and dry it back there." The cook waved a thick arm toward the secondary corridor. "An entire wild boar one time. Made our own jams and bread and most other things. He kept to the old ways. Liked things just so and was willing to keep the staff to make it right. Madame barely eats and likes a"—she paused—"a more modern lifestyle. Modern. Ha. Like not having staff means she's living like everyone else."

There were modern touches: a twelve-burner gas stove, four wall ovens, and bevy of high-tech Swedish-designed dishwashers. Agnes noted the handle on a door leading to a refrigeration room. Although her mother-in-law's kitchen was well-appointed, this was in an entirely different category. Sybille would swoon with jealousy.

"But that's not why you're here," the cook said, unmolding the pâté in one deft motion and placing it on a shelf for later.

"I know you've spoken with my colleague, Monsieur Carnet," Agnes said. "However, I wanted to see if you've remembered anything. Any detail out of the ordinary yesterday?"

"Nothing, and don't think I haven't tossed and turned all night wondering what I might have missed. That young woman must have passed right outside my door, or near enough, if she went down those steps. And I didn't hear a thing. I didn't even hear her. Of course the wind was howling all afternoon. I could hear it inside; it was that loud. Like demons were screaming at us. And then the power went out, right in the middle of preparing the dinner for Monsieur Julien's homecoming. Good thing they didn't want a hot meal after all." The cook caught herself and started to apologize.

"I understand," Agnes broke in. "Today, I think everyone will appreciate a hot meal to keep the cold at bay."

"That I can do easy enough. We never got rid of the old equipment when the modern came. I'll keep hot food on the table until it runs out . . . and that won't be for weeks. I keep a pantry ready for any emergency. The things people used to ask for when we had large parties. Kept me on my toes and I'd like to think I've not dropped my standards."

Agnes shifted to stand nearer the fire, enjoying the heat. Without pausing for breath the cook poured cups of coffee for them both and slipped a plate of pastries alongside. Agnes hesitated, then took one, biting into the almond filling. The cook nodded approvingly at her expression. "It's happened before, although not so bad," she said.

"An ice storm?" Agnes said. "I grew up near Lausanne and don't remember anything like this."

"There's never been an ice storm like this but we've had

wind. I'm a good deal older than you and I remember a time when I was a girl. Was a proper kitchen maid here, then under cook and finally head cook. One spring the *Foehn* knocked out the power and enough trees to trap us for a day or two."

Agnes had lived through the strong warm African winds that blew through Switzerland periodically, but she couldn't remember one doing that kind of damage.

The cook set a pan of hot madeleines on the table and nudged them forward. Agnes took a small sample, tasting butter and lemon.

"Can't remember the exact year but the electric lights were already here, and the phone line." The cook shot Agnes a glance. "They didn't put electric power in the château until late, just before the boys were born. I remember early on when the lines would get blown down in a storm, and it would be a few hours until everything was working again."

Agnes knew the rich were different but this was remarkable. Why not have modern conveniences if you could afford them?

The cook ran her hand across her face. "The radio. I'd forgotten. It's not having a butler that does it. When the old Monsieur died our butler retired and Madame didn't care to replace him. He kept the radio ready in case of emergency. We gave him grief about it, especially after everyone had a mobile phone, but he was old-fashioned and never took to having one himself."

She motioned for Agnes to follow and led the way out of the kitchen and down the main corridor away from the stairs. There she pulled out a set of keys and opened a door. "Habit, keeping it locked. Only room in the whole place I need a key for. Keep the account books here for the food and such. The silver room is through here as well, although it's only for the special banquet silver. The everyday is kept near the family dining room." She fussed through a cabinet. "It is here somewhere. Yes."

She turned with a flourish, a heavy two-way radio clasped in her fist. Agnes took it, trying not to laugh. It had the look and feel of World War II. "You're sure it works?"

"He tested it regular as clockwork on the first Monday of the new year."

"Then the last test was two years ago?"

The cook frowned. "It always worked. You press this button, don't touch the dial, it's set to the right channel. The *gendarmerie* will hear you. They'll be listening for us in an emergency."

Agnes looked from woman to radio and back again. "It's been a while."

"We've only missed two years testing the radio out of fifty." The cook crossed her arms over her broad chest as if fending off an attack on the integrity of the household and its practices.

Agnes pressed the button as instructed, thinking that this was a heavy-duty version of the small walkie-talkies her sons played with on the farm, calling each other from distant fields in an extended, technologically enhanced game of hide-and-seek. She spoke, feeling like an idiot, and released the button.

"Do it again. They don't sit around and wait for us. You need to give them a minute to realize you're calling and they'll get back to you. That's why we did it at the same time every year, to skip the waiting."

Agnes didn't comment. Not exactly an emergency test. The officers at the *gendarmerie* probably turned on the equipment once a year rather than argue with the Vallottons, then forgot about it the other 364 days.

"*Allo?* You are coming in," a voice echoed through the small speaker, the sound broken by static.

Agnes keyed the microphone with a level of excitement she didn't know possible. Contact with the outside world. She could reach Bardy and her boys.

The next response was so full of static that she couldn't make out the words at all. The cook pushed her out the door. "Sometimes you have to go outside," she hissed. "The stone walls are too thick for reception."

Agnes yelled this into the microphone, hoping they would hear her and wait. She ducked into the hall and raced down the stairs to the outside, ignoring the blast of frigid air, thankful she had not taken her coat off. Once outside she held the button and spoke, then waited. The transmission was still unclear, like a modern-day mobile phone in a weak service area. Quickly she moved toward the corner of the château, aiming for closer proximity to the station up the cliff.

"Yes, we are all well," she said in response to what she thought the officer asked. "We have the deceased in a controlled location," she added in case he had forgotten why she was at the base of the hill in the first place. "Otherwise we are fine."

Rounding the corner she nearly ran into Petit. She waved him off and focused on the voice coming through the radio speaker.

"You're lucky," the man said, finally clear, his excitement evident. "The village is stacked with people. Couple of busloads of tourists were stranded and it was market day for the locals. We are the epicenter. Government's sending us into the hills to check on households one at a time and make sure they have supplies to see them through."

Agnes let the man talk for a moment, realizing that in their isolation there was a need to share experiences. She watched Petit join Doctor Blanchard. Together they entered a door set in a small building dug halfway into the ground: the disused ice house where they had stored the body. She'd noted the roof from the height of the château's walls. Glancing past it toward the grove where they had discovered Felicity Cowell, she glimpsed a figure standing behind the bench where the body was found. She recognized Frédéric Estanguet by the distinctive color of his scarf. He was probably pondering how one good deed had resulted in his being trapped here.

"And tell Petit that his wife went to the hospital last night to have her baby," the officer said. "He'll want to know—"

Silence.

"Know what?" Agnes clicked the microphone button but nothing happened. No static, nothing. Batteries? she wondered, wishing she had interrupted the man earlier.

Petit approached, stopping within inches of her.

Agnes looked from the dead radio to him. "Your wife is having her baby." She hoped this was good news.

His face fell. "Early."

"How many weeks is she?"

He rolled his eyes up, concentrating, and took a step nearer. "Thirty-eight."

Agnes touched his arm. "That's not too early. She's probably ready to deliver."

"Early and alone?" His face screwed up in anger, his eyes bulging. "The dead woman might not be an emergency but this is. They have to get me out of here."

Agnes didn't need to ask if this was his first child; she recognized the particular kind of anxiety. "There is no *they*. We're part of emergency services and Bardy would never approve our calling in an evacuation helicopter for you to meet your wife at the hospital. I know it seems unfair, this is an important day for you both, but there are larger matters. They need those helicopters to save people who are in actual danger of losing their lives."

Petit took a deep gasping breath. "Just because no one cared about death enough to help us, doesn't mean they shouldn't care about life. My wife needs me. I promised her I would be there."

Agnes knew enough to not argue. He deserved the chance to be angry. "She's not alone. She made it to the hospital."

Petit scowled, then stomped off, turning toward the steep hill. Agnes hoped he'd work off his anger trying to walk up the slope. Without mountain climbing gear there was no chance he'd make it farther than a half dozen meters.

After he disappeared around the bend in the drive she ducked her head beneath the low beam of the door to the ice house. Doctor Blanchard was standing over a canvas-covered table. She could tell by the outline that it held the body.

"Felt wrong to leave her out here unattended, poor girl," Blanchard said. "The door was locked," he added as an afterthought. "No windows and the only way in."

The room was empty except for two rough tables, a chair, and a heap of old flour sacks piled in a corner. There were no windows and the doctor had set oil lanterns around for light. They cut through the dark better than a flashlight beam. A low door leading to the underground ice storage was set in the opposite wall. Despite its lack of use the room was clean and thankfully free of cobwebs. Agnes stepped nearer the table.

"Last night I did everything I could without cutting," the doctor said. "I was looking for other injuries. I usually get flu, cold, skiing breaks. Farm accidents. People in my village die of old age. I wondered what I should look for and even tried to call a friend, but couldn't get a call out, so I did the best a country doctor can do and made complete notes for the coroner. Came back this morning with a few more lamps, wondering if there were other cuts, or something that indicated she might have struggled. Maybe she was tied up and escaped?"

Agnes didn't want to dampen his enthusiasm by asking if he watched as many American television series as she did.

"She appears to have been a healthy young woman," the doctor continued. "No signs of drug use—again this is what I could see with the naked eye, no toxicology." Agnes nodded encouragingly. "A bit thin, but too many of them are at her age. Late twenties I guessed, but you knew that."

She shifted the canvas away from the body. Beneath it, Blanchard had used Mylar thermal blankets as a makeshift body bag. She glanced nearby and noted that the white evening gown Felicity Cowell had died in was neatly folded next to a clear plastic sack.

"Hardly ideal, but I didn't want to lose any evidence that hasn't already been destroyed," Blanchard said. "Petit took photographs of the clothes on her first."

"Do you have another of these?" She indicated the Mylar

blanket. Blanchard pulled one from his satchel and spread it on the ground. Agnes laid the coronation gown out on it, carefully spreading the delicate fabric of the skirt and arms. Beside it she laid the heavy coat and boots. Underwear occupied a final tiny heap.

"Quite something," Blanchard said, nodding to the dress.

Agnes had to agree. The white silk was delicately pleated from a high waistline. Stones—diamonds, she corrected herself—were embroidered into a floral pattern across the bodice and down the skirt.

"What is that?" she said, pointing to a flaw in the fabric.

"What you didn't see last night." Blanchard motioned for her to join him beside the body. He pulled the foil covering down to expose the chest area. It didn't take a medical degree to see the small incision below her breast.

Agnes glanced from the dress on the floor to the woman in front of her. "She was stabbed twice? In the back and chest?"

"No," Blanchard said. "This is the exit from the injury to her back." He pulled surgical gloves from his satchel and handed a pair to Agnes, then grasped the corpse by the shoulder and motioned for her to assist him. Together they rolled Felicity Cowell onto her side to expose her back. Suddenly Agnes wished she hadn't walked into this room.

"The edges of both entry and exit are clean," Blanchard said. "Something about seven inches long. We have a deep, precise wound. A thin sharp blade that entered from the back here"—he used his free hand to indicate the wound they had observed the night before—"and passed through the chest cavity before reaching the chest wall, which it pierced."

Agnes nodded, stifling a shudder. She'd seen enough. Gently they returned the corpse to its back.

Blanchard pulled his gloves off and brushed the hair from his forehead. "Her attacker struck with force, either through strength or fury. The location of the wounds combined with the lack of blood and other presentation that I observed indicate rapid cessation of heart function. Near-immediate death."

"Someone who is an expert at wielding a knife?"

"Not necessarily. Force and luck may play a role equal to expertise. An expert might strike carefully to be assured the blade would slip through the ribs. Fury could do the same job, driving the blade against the ribs, forcing it to slide past."

Agnes stepped away from the table and Blanchard re-covered the body with the foil blanket, then the canvas.

"You said that she was seated when struck."

"Technically she may have been standing," he said. "Although the angle of the blade was a clean stroke down. If she was standing, her assailant would have to be much taller than her."

"Like Petit?"

"Taller even than him."

"Or standing on something." Agnes paused. "Like a bench?"

"Not on that bench, at least in my opinion. She fell too near it. And the position of her legs makes it appear that she was seated and pushed forward."

Agnes sat on a nearby chair. "She was sitting like this? And shoved forward?"

Blanchard considered. "I don't know how near the front edge she was sitting, or what her posture was."

Agnes tried to imagine what it would feel like to be pushed. Different than falling since a natural collapse happened from the shoulders down. She tried it. Head and shoulders settling in on themselves toward the chest. Arms in and finally toppling forward headfirst. She straightened.

"She didn't strike her head?"

"I see what you are getting at and no, not what I believe you mean by the head. She didn't roll forward and hit the top of her skull. She landed on the side of her face in the lower quadrant. The cheekbone and below."

"And her wrist was broken under her? Broken because she fell on it?"

The doctor nodded. Agnes considered the sequence of injuries. Head erect, not tucked down, propulsion forward, not a collapse down. She hunched her shoulders and relaxed. "Give me a push."

Blanchard touched her between the shoulders.

"Not there, push where the blade entered. I need the direction of motion."

She sensed Blanchard eyeing her, judging where to strike and hesitating.

"I'm ready for you. And you don't have a knife. You won't hurt me."

He pushed forward with his knuckles and Agnes knew that wasn't what Felicity Cowell felt, but it did propel her forward and she gave in to the motion. As she slid from the chair instinct kicked in. She stumbled to her feet. Dissatisfied, she glanced around until settling on the mound of cloth sacks in the corner. She moved them to the floor in front of the chair.

"Do it again."

This time Blanchard was firmer and she was mentally prepared to not resist. She fell forward, catching herself on her palms just before her face struck the bags. She was dusting herself off when the door to the outside opened. Carnet entered. "The good doctor decided to strike you down?"

"An experiment," Agnes said. "We believe Felicity had her head tucked down when she was thrust forward. She didn't have time to get her hands under her although she tried to. That's why she broke a wrist. I landed on my knees. I think my legs would have shot back and extended under the chair if I'd passed out. Hers might have caught on the stone legs of the bench."

"We can check the photographs," Carnet said.

"She died so quickly she didn't have time to stir," said Blanchard.

"She was not expecting a blow," said Agnes.

"Either she was alone or comfortable with whoever was with her," Carnet said. "Comfortable enough to let them walk behind her."

Agnes thanked the doctor and motioned Carnet outside.

"Petit and I finished walking the entire place. Every room," he said.

Agnes raised an eyebrow.

"Every room we could find," he said. "I'm sure we missed a stair here or there. It's impossible to figure the place out. Stairs tucked away. Corridors that end abruptly."

"I could have helped."

"No, I'm working for you. You're in charge and I am—"

"The experience?"

"The legs. The housekeeper says a knife is missing," he added.

"There are probably a half dozen missing in my house, doesn't mean they're murder weapons. Julien Vallotton just told me the six-year-old discovered the body, and he only came along later. I don't think anyone gave it a thought; just sent her to bed with hot chocolate and never considered she might be a material witness." Agnes took a deep breath. "To be fair they left her with the nurse. But they certainly didn't say anything to me about it last night."

"Not surprising. How can anyone be normal living the way they do? They're trapped in another century and not even the last one." Carnet glanced up at the château. "You may have missing knives; here they count the silver every night and one is missing from yesterday's tea tray. A tray taken to the library."

"Where we find Nick Graves," said Agnes. "It couldn't be this easy. What kind of knife?"

"A pear knife, whatever that is. I'm going to have Madame Puguet show one like it to Blanchard. If we're lucky it will match the entry wound."

"It's time I talk to Graves, then the child."

Walking away she hazarded a smile. It felt good to be in charge.

Eight

"I'm sure your embassy would also love to hear from you, but the phones aren't working."

Agnes had taken the measure of the American college student, Nick Graves, and found him lacking. He was just a kid, a tall muscular kid full of bluster. With his khaki pants and button-down blue-striped shirt she could have guessed his nationality from twenty meters. His attitude didn't alter her first impression. In the vast space of the Vallotton library, he ranted and raved against the police, swearing his first call would no longer be to the embassy but to his congressman. While he paced around a table she kept her features expressionless, not admitting she knew what a congressman was. She pondered the dichotomy that had made her an American in Switzerland and a Swiss in America. She was positive that everyone else in the household suspected her American connection at first meeting, whereas Graves seemed to have no hint of her parentage.

Sitting astride two cultures had bothered her more since George's death than at any other time in her life.

Admiring the library in daylight, it was more remarkable than she remembered from her hurried tour the night before. Occupying the length of one wing of the fortress, the double-height space was lined with heavily carved bookshelves picked out in fine gilding. At regular intervals the bookcases turned toward the exterior wall of the château to create deep niches in front of the tall windows overlooking the lake. Partially enclosed twin spiral staircases at each end of the room led to the narrow walkway at the second level. From there the bookcases extended to the carved and painted ceiling high overhead. The central space of the room was occupied by four long tables covered with antique globes and other artifacts. Nick Graves had appropriated one of the tables, spreading books and papers across the surface, and this was where Agnes had found him.

He rounded the table a final time, abruptly flopping onto an upholstered chair, long legs extended, trying to look relaxed and at home.

"It's routine," she repeated, feeling a bit malicious that she didn't switch to English. Graves's French was good enough to be serviceable, although the accent was straight off-the-boat American, but that wasn't the reason. She wanted to keep him off guard. "We need to know where everyone was yesterday afternoon. I'm only confirming what you told Monsieur Carnet last night. I like to hear things for myself."

He had just mumbled something about not spending his day staring at his watch, when from all corners of the library clocks drummed nine. "I can see how it would be difficult to track time here," Agnes said, privately wondering how the family stood the constant reminder that the hours were passing. "Try guessing," she said. "You were in the library until . . ."

"I might have left," he said. "I like to pace. I went to the next room to walk a bit. Came back in and then left."

"This was before or after tea was served?"

He paused briefly. "Both, I suppose."

"You were out of the library more than in?"

"Yeah, just in the next rooms, like I said."

"It's surprising that you left." She took a deliberate look around. "Most people would find this space large enough to accommodate the need to stretch their legs."

He stared at her glumly. "Ice and wind were hitting the windows and driving me nuts. I needed to get out."

She made a note in her book. "You knew Mademoiselle Cowell before arriving?"

He frowned, his handsome face suddenly that of a sullen child. "I suppose not. No." Agnes cast him a quick look but didn't interrupt. "I met Felicity Cowell when she came here. She worked in the library for a few days. Afterward she mostly stayed in her workroom."

"Which is reached by the small stair in the next corridor?"

"That's one way, but she used the other stair mostly. The one from the outside, near the portcullis. I never went up there. She liked to be left alone."

"Did you leave her alone?"

"You think I harassed her?"

"No, I meant more of a friendly visit. Perhaps you got to know her, some personal details that would help us in our investigation. Right now we're having trouble contacting her family or place of employment. Networks are down and we're not a priority call according to those making the decisions." She paused. "You felt someone was harassing her?"

"No, I meant that you . . . never mind. Yeah, I tried to talk to Felicity but she wasn't interested. Why would I kill her?"

"You've already said why—she wasn't interested in you. Of course, we may be wrong about that. The victim isn't necessarily perfect. Maybe she was preying on you or knew something she shouldn't have."

"That's rich. She was what—stalking me—and I couldn't put an end to it without using a knife? You do know she'd only been here a few days? Hardly long enough for an annoyance to develop to the point of murder."

"Two weeks. You've been here only a month longer. And I don't think time alone moves people to kill."

"Good god, I think I may need an attorney." He tapped the table with his fingertips. "Forget I said that. Go on." He crossed his arms. "She just looked like—well, she looked like someone I would know and she wasn't. I don't know what her game was and you're right, she told me to get lost."

"You mean she looked familiar?"

"Yeah, but I didn't know Felicity Cowell before she was introduced to me here."

"You arrived six weeks ago. Your first trip to Europe?"

"Yes."

"Unusual, isn't it, that a graduate student would be given such a prestigious fellowship if they hadn't traveled before?"

"I've traveled alright. Asia, South America, lots of places, and this would let me continue that research in Europe. Made sense to my advisors."

Agnes didn't think it mattered why he was here. "You know

that she was killed in an evening dress?" It was impossible to keep details secret in such close quarters. "Do you have any idea why she would have been dressed so extravagantly in the middle of the day?"

He shrugged. "She liked pretty things. Don't most women?"

Agnes wondered if he had hit upon a truth. Could Felicity Cowell simply have been playing dress-up in the world's best closet? Not very professional but a secret passion fulfilled? The secret passion of a woman who loved antique things? Not unrealistic. She frowned. That didn't explain why Felicity left the room wearing a historic dress worth a fortune, or why she wandered out into a killing cold with a borrowed coat and boots.

"Is that all?" Graves asked and Agnes nodded. He left the library like he was being released from prison.

A glance at her mobile phone confirmed what she already knew: still no signal and the battery was slowly dying. She turned it off and wished the château had a generator; she would have traded the faulty two-way radio for a power source now that the indoor temperature had fallen close to that of outdoors. The fires at either end of the library were lit, but did little to warm more than a few feet beyond their hearths. Agnes wiggled her toes thankfully in the borrowed boots; she'd be frozen without them.

Moving near a fireplace she poured herself a cup of excellent coffee from a silver pot before walking the length of the library. Sixty paces. It would be impossible for anyone to say if the room was empty. The window niches were too deep and the upstairs walkway was completely obscured by shadow even in daylight. Perhaps Marie-José was wrong and Nick Graves was there most of the time, only stepping out for a few brief seconds as he claimed? Agnes studied the bookcases, swiftly calculating the number of volumes. Twenty thousand? Thirty? Each shelf was faced by finely worked metal covered with glass. She lifted a handle and had a soft leather volume in her hand when the door at the far end of the room opened. Frédéric Estanguet entered.

Earlier in the morning she had seen their Good Samaritan from a distance. Up close Estanguet's face was tinged gray with fatigue. Evidently they had both slept poorly. Handing him a cup of coffee she thanked him again for helping Carnet and Blanchard down the hill. It would probably be the last time he offered to do the police a favor.

"I wish we had a way to get you home," she said, knowing it was impossible.

"I can't leave, not yet."

Her face registered surprise and he shook his head. "I don't know what I'll find there. The damage will be the same everywhere. Roofs crushed by trees, water pipes frozen." He shrugged, "And like here, I would have no electricity."

Agnes pictured a small, dark, cold apartment. The château was cold but there were other amenities. She glanced at her hot coffee and the plate of pastries.

"And I live in Estavayer-le-Lac. It would be impossible to travel so far."

"You don't live in Ville-sur-Lac?"

Estanguet refilled his coffee cup. His color was improving. "I was in the village for a drink on my way home. It was wrong," he continued. "She had her whole life in front of her. Dead where she didn't belong. It's all wrong. She shouldn't have been out in the storm."

Agnes was in agreement: Felicity Cowell deserved a chance at a long, productive future. She let Estanguet talk about the unfairness of life, her mind drifting to her own parents. She almost smiled. Her father would shrink from any mention of a violent death, while her mother would use it as an excuse to visit each of her friends. The story would guarantee she was the center of attention for a month. Agnes started to take a pastry from the tray then remembered the two she'd had earlier in the kitchen and checked the fit of her waistband. As a substitute she sipped her coffee, appreciating the warmth.

Finally Estanguet stopped talking, sat back in his chair, and sighed. Agnes reached over to pat his hand, hoping that he would one day forget the sight of the frozen body, although she knew she wouldn't.

"You said that you don't know the family but you do know the château. That's curious."

"I like the library, and they let people use it. A retirement project."

"Were you a teacher?"

"Nothing of the sort. Started off as a guide. Hikes. Did some steep hills but not mountain climbing. That's how I know we are stranded here. People think they can out-anger or out-think any obstacle but it's not so. Mother Nature has a way of beating you down. She likes to fool you."

Agnes remembered him staring at the bench earlier that morning. "Mademoiselle Cowell didn't seem like a person to be outdoors in a storm. You said you didn't know her?"

"I didn't know her to recognize her, maybe I'd heard her name."

"She'd been at the château for two weeks, and you are here often. I'm surprised. She used the library some."

"I've been away for nearly a month myself. Vacation."

Agnes had to smile at a vacation from retirement. "Not a good time to return, in the middle of a storm."

"I'd picked my date and here I was. Didn't think it would be a storm like what came. As I said, Mother Nature can be tricky. Saw your man, Carnet, and knew he wasn't fit to walk down, not like he was planning to. People think they can sit and slide. They don't realize that the ice will take you, hurl you off the edge. He needed something to hang on to, no different than mountain climbing. And crampons. Something to grip."

"You got them down the hill safely."

"She ought to have had more respect for the storm and stayed inside."

"It must be a change to retire from an outdoor life and sit in a library and do research."

"I left working as a guide long ago, when I was still nearly a boy. Met a man on one of my tours who liked what I could do with a needle. Fixed his tent and he talked me into apprenticing as a tailor. Took over from him when he passed and sewed my way through a lifetime."

"What led you to do research here? I wouldn't have known it was possible."

"Fate." He sat forward in his chair. "I was having a drink at the hotel in the village—they have nice views—and there was a caravan of trucks passing by and going down the hill. It was summer, and we could see them from the terrace. The waitress knew the village gossip and told me who was moving in." He paused. "Vladimir Arsov."

"Recently? I thought he'd lived here forever."

"Last summer. The day before the Fête Nationale. Trucks and trucks of things they brought. The day of the Fête they have tours here, and I came down out of curiosity to see what kind of man had so many belongings. Someone told me the château library was open to research by the public." He set his cup down. "It seems like so long ago."

She knew that most of the furnishings and larger paintings at Arsov's belonged to the Vallottons and were already in place when the old man arrived with his truckloads. Estanguet would be truly amazed if he saw the inside of the mansion.

"You must like history."

"What? Yes, I do."

"Do you have a topic, something special you are interested in?"

"This and that. There's lots to read and see here."

Agnes thought about her retired parents and understood the need to feel like you belonged and could still be productive. Estanguet likely puttered about most days.

"You hadn't met Felicity Cowell. You must know Nick Graves, though?"

"He's been here since the new year. About six weeks. I know all the fellowship winners who come through. I'm a help to them, know my way around the organization of the books. Know where the maps are kept." He thumped his leg. "She shouldn't have been outdoors on a day like that. The young are foolish. But foolish doesn't mean you deserve to die."

Agnes wondered how it was that her boys stayed safe. They

did foolish things. How did anyone manage to stay safe? She sat back and took another sip of coffee and made an effort to shake off melancholy. Despite the tragedy and the gloomy atmosphere, they were at one of the few places in the region used to doing without modern conveniences. And the food was excellent.

Nine

Carnet brought news to the library, and Agnes followed him to where Blanchard was waiting. They instructed her to lean near the wall of the corridor. She did, quickly stepping back, grimacing. "You're sure it's hers?" The acrid smell of vomit was offensive at a close distance.

Blanchard slapped one hand against the other. "Deductions are what we're making until we can get her to a morgue, but I think we've hit on something important."

"Walk me through it again," Agnes said, suspecting that the doctor was enjoying himself. He looked better than he had earlier in the ice house.

"The maid"—Carnet glanced at his notebook—"Marie-José, found the mess while sweeping. She's a smart girl and didn't clean anything."

"She assumed it was Mademoiselle Cowell's?" Agnes asked.

"Said a family member would have called for her to clean up right away. Had to be someone," Carnet hesitated, "'inconsiderate' is the word she used; I'd say embarrassed."

"I didn't notice any odor or residue in her mouth," said Blanchard, "and I did look for obvious signs of obstruction. But the cold would have tempered the smell. Now I'll give her another look. Of course, the lab will swab when we get her there."

"Look at these fingerprints on the wall."

Agnes leaned in where Carnet indicated.

"It looks like they belong to whoever vomited," he said. "We can test for a match. If they were hers it appears that she crouched down and rested on her fingertips pretty hard, then moved them a few inches. As if she was keeping her balance. Fortunately, the stone held the oils. I think she'd put lotion on recently and the surface worked nearly as well as glass. Can't imagine why anyone would crouch over like this if they weren't sick."

"Why was she ill?" Agnes said.

"Stomach virus," said Blanchard, "ate something that didn't agree with her. Saw something? Could have simply been in pain. High-level pain causes vomiting, and a heart attack in women is often signaled by vomiting. Won't know until the autopsy. It's unusual to have heart attack in someone so young, but not impossible."

"She looked healthy to me, apart from the injuries." Agnes studied the surrounding area. There were a few chairs against the wall and farther along was a heavy chest. It was possible there had been a struggle, but nothing appeared disturbed. "Could she have been stabbed here, vomited because of the pain, and made her way outside?"

"Inspector Lüthi, where is the blood?" Blanchard said. "She

was stabbed where she fell. That I can tell you. It is just as we worked out earlier."

"You mentioned food poisoning. What about regular poisoning? Could she have been poisoned and then died of the knife wound?"

Blanchard closed his eyes for a moment. "Of course she could have been poisoned. That might cause vomiting. I still say she died as a result of the knife wound, not poisoned then stabbed . . . An autopsy will clarify this."

"I'm interested in more than cause of death," said Agnes. "I want to know how she spent her last hours."

"If she were poisoned to the extent that she was vomiting, then I might expect to see continued distress at the site of her death."

"Outside, she would have been hunched over, crippled with pain?"

"You are speculating too far, Inspector."

Agnes turned to Carnet. "Robert, could you talk to the maid again and see if anything is out of place here? Something that would indicate a struggle, ask if the chairs have been moved or if something is missing." Then an idea occurred to her. "Doctor, could she be pregnant? I was deathly ill with my first child. All day. Never-ending."

"She didn't look pregnant," said Carnet.

Agnes shook her head. "I didn't think she was about to deliver, but she might have morning sickness."

Doctor Blanchard murmured agreement.

"More importantly," Agnes continued, "she might have known she was pregnant. I'm interested in her state of mind. You can draw urine even though she is . . . cold, can't you?"

"Urine has a great deal of salt and ammonia. It doesn't freeze at these temperatures. The trouble is getting at it. And she might not have any in her bladder. It will be an invasive test done this way."

"She's going to be autopsied, you can't get more invasive than that, and being pregnant might play into her mental condition." Agnes looked around, making sure Petit hadn't joined them. "Not every woman wants to be pregnant. Sometimes it's just the initial surprise or the timing. She may have been angry or depressed or scared. If she'd just found out, she might have been in an altered state of mind. It could have pushed her to behave inappropriately."

"I can try to get a sample but I still need a method to test it."

Agnes had a distinct memory of a familiar box among the toiletries in the cook's well-stocked storeroom. Either the pregnancy test was bought and never needed or was part of the cook's desire to provide for any eventuality. It didn't matter. It was exactly what the doctor needed. "Leave finding a means to test it to me."

"While you're working your miracles, I'll do my part." The doctor paused before leaving, nodding to Carnet. "Tell her about the knife."

"Did you know that a pear knife is not really pointed? It's got a nice blade for cutting the fruit skin but isn't long—"

"Or dangerous?"

"That's another way to put it. The doctor got a laugh out of the idea. Says our weapon looks like a weapon. Long and sharp. More like a dagger than a knife."

What kind of blade could cut through an entire body, creating these wounds? "We've ruled out no one," she said. "I need to speak to the cook again, then I'll take a quick look upstairs where you found her clothes before I talk to the little girl."

Carnet gave her a half salute before walking off in the other direction. Halfway up a flight of broad stairs she heard voices: Julien Vallotton and his sister-in-law. After climbing a few more steps she slowed. They didn't know she was listening.

"I count the pills, that's how I know he didn't take one. He was no more drugged yesterday afternoon than I was," Marie-Chantal said.

"Why would Daniel lie?" Vallotton asked.

"With your alibi, you forget that the rest of us aren't so lucky."

"I think it takes more than being here to make you a suspect. Motive is usually a consideration, and what possible motive could Daniel have for killing a woman he barely knew?"

"He doesn't think I know," Marie-Chantal sounded choked, "about the other women."

"You think Daniel was having an affair and she threatened to tell you so he killed her? Pretty fast work, two weeks to start an affair and get it to the point where she would have such a hold over him."

"Don't be a hypocrite. You thought the same thing when you arrived. I heard you ask Antoinette how well Daniel knew her. We're stuck here for weeks. She's beautiful and smart and he would be attracted. How could he help it?"

They were silent and Agnes stopped walking. She was near the top of the stairs and didn't want to disturb them yet.

"I don't know what made you dream this up," Vallotton said. "Although just being here is enough of an excuse. I know it drove my mother mad, but you need to listen to yourself.

Besides, Daniel can't walk, how can he have an affair, much less stab a woman in the back outside in a storm? You're being ridiculous."

Marie-Chantal gave a strangled cry. "Of course he can walk."

Agnes tiptoed halfway down the stairs then clumped her way up again. When she reached the top, Vallotton was alone. He looked perplexed, not worried.

"She doesn't mean half of what she says and didn't know you were here." He glanced up and Agnes noticed the large mirror. She hadn't been looking up, but it was clear that Vallotton had seen her reflection in it. She flushed. "People with secrets shouldn't stand in corridors and raise their voices," he said. "Besides, I don't think my brother had anything to do with Felicity Cowell's death."

"Pretty damning when his wife is suspicious," Agnes said, although she couldn't believe a man whose leg was riddled with thin metal rods had stabbed a woman outside in a storm. She looked in each direction before turning down the hall.

"I may not have the highest opinion of Daniel, but I'm honest enough to admit that most of what I pretend to believe is the result of jealousy."

"You, jealous of him?" Agnes gave Julien Vallotton a hard glance.

"Sure, I inherited the responsibility and he got the woman I wanted to marry. Cause enough for a good case of jealousy."

Agnes wondered how much of what Vallotton said was true; wouldn't he want to protect his family above all? "Why would his wife suspect him?" She turned a corner and headed up another flight of stairs, hoping she would end up at the fur vault. Vallotton followed.

"She doesn't," he said. "She's just tired. Probably wishes she hadn't married into the family at all, which is, sadly, our usual state of affairs. My father, handsome, affluent, and influential, managed to have four wives. My mother was the last. Daniel's only on number one. He has some misery to make or he'll never catch up."

It all sounded too flippant to have the weight of truth. On the other hand she would have to speak with Daniel Vallotton again and see if he could walk. Apart from his injuries he was a strong man.

She stopped in front of a door and Vallotton nodded. "Fur vault."

Leaving the problem of Daniel Vallotton for later, Agnes unlocked the door. Earlier she had looked inside the room where Felicity Cowell's clothes had been found; now the space was flooded with natural light. She frowned at the realization that Petit had opened the shutters, altering the scene, although it appeared that he had photographed everything else in place. Shelves lining the walls were filled with long boxes, all neatly labeled in faded script. There was an enormous mirror on castors and a few marble-topped tables strewn with lamps, but otherwise there was no furniture. A set of modern clothes lay crumpled on the floor.

There was a loud rumbling noise outside and Vallotton crossed the room to the window. It overlooked the spot where the body was found and, among the fallen trees, a man with a chain saw was gesticulating to Carnet.

"I think we may have a clash of opinions about starting the cleanup from the storm," he said, leaving.

Alone, Agnes pulled a pen from her handbag and used it to

lift an article of clothing from the floor. The skirt of a dark suit. Next to it lay a tailored jacket and simple white blouse. Nearby was a pair of shoes. Good leather with a high but sensible-enough heel. A far cry from the white silk dress embroidered with diamonds that Felicity Cowell had died wearing. Agnes rocked back on her heels and studied the clothes. Even if she had a reason to wear that dress, why had the woman left the room barefoot? She hadn't planned to be outside. Had she panicked? Agnes thought about the pregnancy, then decided that Doctor Blanchard was right. She was speculating far beyond the evidence.

She maneuvered between the boxes of clothing to the center of the room and used her pen to nudge the mobile phone that lay on the floor. No markings, though they assumed it was the dead woman's. Unfortunately the battery was discharged and there was no way to tell when she had last used it. Much more interesting for the moment was a heavy silver-backed hand mirror with the glass shattered out of the frame. She studied its placement, then turned and ran a hand down a row of boxes, randomly lifting a lid. Old dresses wrapped in tissue paper; likely worth a fortune. Turning slowly, taking in the details again, an idea formed in her mind.

Footsteps pounded in the corridor and Petit arrived out of breath. "Carnet said you wanted to see me."

She was pleased he had managed to push impending fatherhood from the forefront of his mind and even more thankful he hadn't broken a leg while walking off his anger. "You photographed these rooms: what did you think was important?"

"Just a mess of her things. Looked liked she knocked a table over."

"You didn't move anything?"

"Of course not."

"What do you think about the clothes?"

"Good quality. Businesslike if you're in a high-end business. But she doesn't take care of them. Probably has plenty and doesn't need to make them last."

Agnes was surprised. Petit had more imagination than she'd given him credit for.

"What about another possibility? Stand here, in the doorway. You can't see her clothes from here. Maybe they fell in a messy pile or maybe they were shoved underneath the table. Could she have been hiding them?"

Petit crouched to study the angle from a normal person's height. "She might have kicked them there on purpose but it's the same thing, careless with her belongings."

"What about the broken mirror? That's a little too careless. An antique silver mirror. Probably valuable, and in her work she deals with antiques every day. She should have more respect, don't you think?"

Agnes pulled a piece of tissue paper from one of the storage boxes and used it to pick up the mirror, leaving the handle visible. The monogram was so elaborate that it took a moment to work out the letter V. "It belongs to the Vallottons. I don't think she would drop it carelessly."

"The handle was a distance from the glass," Petit said, "like it scattered when it broke."

"Not like this?" Agnes indicated a straight drop. "The trajectory would be affected by the weight of the handle; it's solid whereas the glass oval is even heavier." She tried to work out the release in her mind, testing different positions. The mathematics were easy enough. Gravity and weight and velocity were precise elements. She moved a few feet closer to the door, looking carefully at the labels on the boxes as she went, finally locating the one she needed. White silk with diamonds. "Coronation. 1804," was written in spidery faded script.

"She starts here, at the door, and looks into the boxes." Agnes ran her hand lightly along the lids that were not quite put back in place and the few that were still open. "She's looking for something specific, or simply curious until she comes to this one. The gown worn to Napoleon's coronation." Agnes made as if she was opening the box lid and mimed removing the dress. "She lays it aside and takes off her clothes. Or maybe she had already taken off her clothes. Maybe she folds them neatly, maybe she drops them in a heap right away."

"Is she alone?" Petit asked.

"That is the question, isn't it? For now we don't know. Maybe someone was watching her."

"Maybe they picked out that dress?"

"Good point, but did they force her to take that dress, threaten her in some way, or was this fun and playful? A striptease. We know that her clothes came off and landed on the floor. Somehow they ended up under that table. She threw them there or kicked them. Or someone else did." Agnes stood back and looked again. "Look at the trajectory of the items. At the angle and the movement—of the clothing, of the glass breakage. It's in one direction. I think she started here, the clothing was disturbed—we don't know how—and the mirror was thrown or tossed, all as she moved from where I am standing to . . ." She looked across the room. "To the other door."

"She was running from someone?"

"Or with someone. A game of dress-up or a violent epi-sode." Agnes wondered if the broken hand mirror was the be-ginning of the killer's violent behavior. Perhaps Felicity Cowell kicked the clothing as she fled her attacker? He or she threw the mirror and it hit her, or missed and broke on the floor. Or she threw the mirror? No, that would put the assailant be-tween her and the other door. Agnes ran her hand through her hair. Who among the household wouldn't care that they broke something valuable? Not one of the staff, but the Vallottons. Or Mulholland? His godmother would forgive him almost anything. He was British and perhaps his visit to the château had less to do with seeing the marquise and more to do with following a young woman to Switzerland. Agnes studied the objects, willing them to speak in the same way that data from financial crimes had spoken to her for years. There were always patterns; it was a matter of finding them.

"Maybe fear or panic caused her nausea," she said.

"Question for the doctor," Petit said. "Questions I can't an-swer. No one can answer." He stepped near and folded his arms across his chest. "I think I can make it to the top of the hill and to the hospital. I've studied it and with a rope and some help . . . My wife needs me. She shouldn't be having this baby alone."

"André, I understand. I've delivered three sons and my hus-band was with me." Tears sprang to Agnes's eyes at the mem-ory of her first pregnancy. And their trip to the hospital. It was the middle of the night and George had been thrilled, and his excitement had countered her last-minute fears. Where had that happiness gone? The trickle of memory threatened to overwhelm her.

"What if something happens?" Petit said. "What if this one doesn't go right and she dies and I wasn't there?"

"There's nothing we can do. You know that truthfully you can't climb that hill. There's a good chance you would end up with a broken arm or leg, and what good would that do your new baby when you're all home together in a day or two? Your wife's not alone, she's in a hospital where they deliver babies every day."

He stepped close, towering over her. Menace in the set of his shoulders. Blood rushed, filling her eardrums.

"Even if you made it up the hill, what then?" she said. "Sitting in the *gendarmerie*? They'd put you to work helping people in distress. You still couldn't make the trip to the hospital. Focus on what we can accomplish here. Think of the dead woman. She is someone's daughter, perhaps someone's wife or mother, and we owe them answers. We owe her justice."

A long moment passed. Turning swiftly, Petit left without a word and she drew a deep breath, leaning down to rest her hands on her knees like an athlete at the end of a long race. Slowly she stood upright, her emotions under control. The past locked away again.

Absently, she rummaged in her handbag for the bottle of lotion she'd taken from George's emergency kit. The smell was soothing and distantly familiar. She leaned her face near the window, feeling sorry for Petit.

Far below, Julien Vallotton walked past the gaping patches of black earth where fallen trees had ripped roots and ice from the ground. He stopped near Carnet and sent the man with the chain saw to a distant corner of the property.

"Never trouble for him," she murmured.

"I suspect he has more trouble than you realize." Marie-

Chantal stood in the doorway, her straight nose and elegant jaw sculpted by the jagged streaks of sunlight. Her shoulder-length blond hair glinted and she appeared smaller and more petite than Agnes remembered.

Marie-Chantal joined Agnes at the window and they watched Vallotton walk alone toward the shore. For a moment Agnes had a glimmer of comprehension about the burden of living here, the responsibility for care of a national monument.

Marie-Chantal glanced at Agnes's wedding ring and sighed. "You're married. You must understand regret." She wiped the moisture caused by her breath from the cold glass. "Regret that leads to guilt so strong you hurt? Longing for what you can't have and wondering if you only want it because of that? Emotions so confused you don't believe them?"

Agnes gripped the edge of a shutter so hard her rings dug into her flesh. The pain kept her from crying out. How could this woman understand regret? Or longing? "No, I wanted what I had," she said evenly.

Marie-Chantal stepped away from the window and shook her shoulders as if she had a chill. "I'm sorry. You have larger concerns. The poor dead woman."

Just that quickly the mood in the room changed, and Agnes could believe that Julien Vallotton was jealous of his brother. Marie-Chantal had a quality that was unusual if not unique: an intersection of beauty and intensity of personality that could alternately electrify or calm the atmosphere around her. Whatever laws of physics or emotions that made it happen, Agnes was grateful.

"Last night you said you spoke to Felicity Cowell only a few times?" she asked, pleased that her voice was steady.

"Yes," Marie-Chantal replied, "although we are about the same age. I admit that I was fascinated. She was the main topic of dinner conversation for weeks before she arrived. What she would do here, her expertise. I was jealous. To be that needed must feel . . . well, special. To have work that was valued."

"Did she avoid the family?"

"That sounds sneaky. I'd just say she knew her place." Marie-Chantal smiled apologetically. "An employee. Antoinette lends a certain atmosphere of formality."

"No mixing with the staff?"

"It's not a rule, but meals are served separately and it's a large house. We don't have any reason to interact and we have a sort of schedule for when the maids clean and things like that. We stay clear of them, let them do their work. Felicity Cowell wasn't exactly staff, however, I wouldn't have dreamed of bothering her while she worked. She did have dinner with us once. The night after she arrived. We had other guests and she rounded out the table."

"Did she eat alone the other nights?"

Marie-Chantal looked surprised. "I don't know. I never thought about it. Maybe she ate in the village since she stayed there."

Agnes was reminded that the inhabitants of the château lived a very different life from anyone she knew. "You and your husband never met Felicity in London?"

"No, I would have said. Besides, I'm not often there. That's Julien's town. I prefer Paris and Berlin. Hong Kong." Marie-Chantal looked around the room as if taking in the details. "Antoinette told me that Mademoiselle Cowell was here before she died. Did she run outside from here? It's a long way down."

"Why is this room called the fur vault?"

"There are likely furs somewhere. It's just as likely that they stored fur pelts here a thousand years ago and the name never changed. Names tend to stick. Daniel and I share a suite of rooms called the nursery although no children have slept there since the French Revolution."

Agnes snorted a half laugh. Since George's death she and the boys had spent most nights at her parents-in-law's. She slept in their guest room, which they assured her was a leftover title and not a reflection on her status in the house. She wasn't convinced and thought Marie-Chantal might consider the suggestive notion of being made to sleep in the nursery. The marquise wasn't a young woman and likely wanted to meet the next generation.

Marie-Chantal trailed her fingers across the boxes. "Fabulous, aren't they? Better than most museum collections. I've been told there are even more in an attic somewhere. Probably two hundred years of the best clothing in the world packed away."

"Who uses this room?" Agnes asked.

"No one, not now. Years ago, Antoinette's couturier would come from Paris with the gowns basted together and finish them according to her specifications. Friends of my mother's say she was exacting, the kind of client a couturier adores and hates. Balenciaga dressed her until he retired." Marie-Chantal smiled and Agnes felt the room light up. "Have you seen the portrait of her in the blue salon? Painted just before her marriage. It was a different time and she was only fifteen, but the portrait is magnificent. She looks young and old. Fresh and lovely, yet already strong and determined. I'll show you sometime."

While listening, Agnes walked through the small side door to the adjoining room, following the trajectory of damage left by whatever had happened the day before. There were three tall mirrors on wheeled stands, a wire dressmaker's form, and a row of hooks on the wall. With only a few straight-backed chairs, and no rugs, the room looked and felt empty. Nothing appeared disturbed. There was an even smaller door in the corner; it opened to a twisting spiral staircase. She led the way and Marie-Chantal followed, carrying a yellow hat laden with feathers that she had removed from a box.

Agnes negotiated the stairs, bracing herself against the walls to prevent a nasty tumble. She asked a question over her shoulder. "Everyone has an opinion, but I would like to hear your thoughts: why was Felicity Cowell wearing *that* dress?"

"This is the psychological part of the mystery, isn't it?" Marie-Chantal turned the hat in her hand as she descended, accustomed to the tortuous stairs. "Vanity, a desire to connect with that particular dress—after all, it does have a special history— curiosity. Who knows? I've always wanted to try on one of the early Balenciagas. Legendary designs, but I didn't want to ask. Actually I'm afraid that they'll be too small, and I don't think I can face a corset." They reached the bottom of the flight.

"But why that dress?" Agnes looked up and down the corridor, sighting the spot where they had discovered the vomit and wondering if Felicity felt ill and came down the stairs for help. Was it as simple as that? Perhaps she wasn't running from someone, but was seeking help. That still didn't explain her going outdoors. It was as if there were two parts to her trajectory and this moment in the hall was the break between them.

"I don't know if it matters what she was wearing. Of course she might have been trying to impress someone. Maybe she was going to steal it." Marie-Chantal shook her head. "No, I don't mean that, although it might have been clear to her that we wouldn't have known." She rested the tiny hat on her head and studied her reflection in a nearby mirror. "Maybe she was just having fun and saw something by chance. Or someone. And had to go down. Or maybe she was running away from something."

"You mean someone," said Agnes. She raised her hand to smell the lotion. It reminded her of something. Not George, but something. Or someone.

Marie-Chantal removed the hat and shrugged. "It's all just guesswork. It really doesn't matter. She's dead."

Ten

Agnes asked a final time if there was anything else the little girl remembered or wanted to tell her. Mimi shook her head, and Agnes smoothed the girl's hair and scooted her off the sofa. Then she thanked the nurse for her time.

She took a moment to decide what to do next. She was tired and cold. It was only noon and already the day felt long. At the other end of the room Arsov's nurse settled a blanket around his shoulders and across his legs, speaking close to his ear. To delay the return trip to the château, Agnes joined them.

"Talk of being capable of killing someone is nonsense," Arsov said without preamble.

Agnes took her place on the same chair she had occupied the night before and Arsov angled his wheelchair to face her. Before she had a chance to greet him properly, a maid pulled a rolling cart nearby. With a practiced flourish the butler removed domed silver covers from the food. Arsov grinned. Agnes noticed that the staff now had outdoor clothes on over their uniforms. It made for a bizarre scene.

"Don't eat much anymore, but I still like to look at good food," Arsov said. Lunch was a delicate filet of perch, accompanied by small potatoes and asparagus. A light wine sauce was on the side.

"Impressive with the power out," Agnes said, touching her heated plate, slightly in awe of the attention to detail.

"Pay them enough and they'll figure out a way. Brought my cook from Paris. Got rid of my secretary and everyone else when I came here, but I nearly cried at the thought of never tasting Antoine's food again, so I bribed him to leave France. You would have thought I was asking him to move to the Ukraine. I promised that if he'd stay with me three more years I'd set him up in his own restaurant anywhere in the world. He'll filet his hand to keep food on the table so I don't have reason to back out of my promise."

The butler opened a bottle of white wine and poured three glasses, offering one to Frédéric Estanguet, who was slouched deep in a chair near the French doors, far from the fire. He had offered to accompany Agnes, saying that no one should be outdoors alone in the cold. She hoped the change of atmosphere would help him recover from the shock of seeing the dead woman's body the night before. Despite her hopes, during the walk she had grown irritated. Wasn't there a Good Samaritan code of behavior? Seeing him now, she was angry. They had all had a bad experience. She wanted to tell Estanguet to buck up. He'd seen a dead body, not had one fall on him.

Prodded by the butler, Estanguet moved to a chair near the

low table they were using as an alternative to relocating to the even colder dining room. His hand was unsteady and Agnes wondered if he needed the nurse. Then Estanguet took a sip of wine, closed his eyes, and appeared to relax.

"Monsieur Arsov," she said, "your butler asked me if we had made progress on the investigation. I'm afraid I don't have much to report. He's very conscientious. He said he'd rechecked all the doors and windows to make sure they are locked. I don't think your staff have any cause to worry, although I am surprised you don't have professional security."

"You think a hired thug would take more care with my life than I do? I take my precautions. Since Stalingrad I have been ready to defend my life at all times. That was a lesson I learned well."

Agnes wanted to ask exactly how Arsov planned to defend himself. The old man could barely draw a solid breath and was too weak to walk. She surveyed the wheelchair, half expecting to see high-tech weaponry attached to the sides. Or was it possible that Arsov planned to light his oxygen tank with a cigarette and let it explode in an enemy's face? The idea had a certain dramatic flair. She felt her mind wandering and knew that it was the result of fatigue.

"Anyone can kill," Arsov said, absently slipping his hand to the empty space between his thigh and the chair arm. He smoothed the blanket and Agnes stifled a grin. The old man had a gun. She bet it wasn't licensed.

"The marquise, St. Sebastian bless that woman, could kill as easily as my butler opens a bottle of wine, and do it with a steady hand and no remorse." He shot Agnes a dark look. "How is she? Who does she think did it? You won't speculate, but you should. Madame la marquise has good instincts. It's reason that motivates a killer. What reason would motivate you? Don't look so shocked. Take the kindest mother, threaten her child, and create a killer. Same thing with cannibalism. Hungry enough and you'll eat anything. I ate shoe leather once. Very unsatisfying; later I wished I had the shoe leather to wear."

Agnes wouldn't be drawn into speculating. She took a forkful of fish and understood why Arsov couldn't bear to lose his chef.

"What did Mimi tell you?" Arsov demanded.

"What we already knew. Nothing."

The butler appeared in the doorway. "Monsieur Ralph Mulholland."

Mulholland crossed the threshold swiftly, pausing to acknowledge Agnes and Estanguet with a curt nod. "I came to see if you needed anything," he said to Arsov. "Ridiculous, I see now. You've even got the police."

"Inspector Lüthi is not here for me, she was speaking with Mimi." Arsov motioned Mulholland forward and the butler hastened to set another place for lunch.

"She is a good child, Mimi," Arsov continued. "She reminds me of my sister, Anya. Too young to be alone in the world. She will be taken care of when I am gone."

"Has she lived with the Vallottons long?" Agnes asked. "You mentioned they're her guardians."

"Her parents died and old Monsieur Vallotton brought her to live with them. He died a year later." Agnes hid a smile at Arsov calling anyone old. "She is their legal responsibly but

I am leaving my estate to her. They look after her, but she's not one of them." He removed a hand-rolled cigarette from a silver box and sucked on it like it was the next course of his meal.

"Isn't that a little unusual if the Vallottons are her legal guardians?" she asked.

"No one objects to more money," said Mulholland. "Especially guardians."

Agnes recalled that his parents had died when he was young.

"You are right," Arsov said. "I'll make her independent, plus I'm giving my collection of Russian *objets d'art* to them, as a token. A thank-you." Vaguely, he waved a hand toward the collections strewn across the nearby tables and cabinets: Fabergé eggs, enameled and bejeweled frames, silver-faced icons. "It is the least I can do. Might even be known as the Arsov collection someday, but that's not necessary. I'm not prideful."

Agnes smothered another smile. In the light of day the room looked like someone had ransacked a Romanov palace prior to the revolution.

Arsov glanced around as if sizing up the real estate. "This is very special place to me and Mimi would be happy here. I have asked Julien Vallotton to deed use of the house to her, just for her lifetime." Arsov plucked a speck of tobacco from his lips. "It is a bond between us, this place."

Agnes listened to his account of their time together, noting that neither Estanguet nor Mulholland ate much, despite the excellent food. Judging from the expression on Estanguet's face he was as intrigued as she was at the inclinations of the truly rich. At Arsov's age it was likely Mimi would still be a young girl when he died. She wouldn't need her own mansion.

On the other hand Mulholland looked surly. Perhaps this was what she could expect from her own boys when they reached their midtwenties. Surly boy-men. Agnes changed the subject.

"I don't know who the marquise suspects, but I'm sure she is unhappy. Not only a murder but the dress worn by Mademoiselle Cowell was valuable and it's ruined now."

"My dragon nurse told me. A dress worn to Napoleon's coronation. The marquise will think it good riddance. Her husband was part of the old French nobility, not the upstart emperor's. The emperor may have created modern Switzerland but the Vallottons didn't need him. The dead woman couldn't have chosen better."

"The dress has value, a history," said Agnes.

"You don't see value the way they do. The marquise values honor and Napoleon is not her idea of honor." Arsov sucked on a cigarette. "I may collect history but the Vallottons don't, they live it."

Mulholland set his wineglass on the table with a thump and called to the butler for more. Agnes considered dragging him outside and giving him a short lesson in manners. A weekend with her mother-in-law would be good for him.

"You've surely lived your share of history," she directed at Arsov.

"You think being born in Russia means *Doctor Zhivago*. Your generation thinks that is war. Julie Christie and Omar Sharif in fur, with tales of love and ice palaces."

"I think *Doctor Zhivago* was an earlier generation than mine and an earlier war than yours."

"Zhivago should have left Russia. I did. No one cared who died there. My family, my friends, my comrades-in-arms were killed as fodder for the egos of our leaders. When I decided to abandon my home country it took me weeks traveling at night along the Volga to find a way out. And that was by accident. Literally I ran smack—you say smack—into a man during the worst snowstorm of my life. It is fortunate that after my family was killed I had traveled to Stalingrad. I told you my brothers were there? In Stalingrad?"

Agnes shook her head.

"Well, they were. In the Red Army. And I found them. They were killed a few months later in the siege. That is another reason I left. There was no one for me." He puffed a ring of smoke, watching it dissipate. "Before they died, my battle instincts were honed. In Stalingrad the enemy could be around any corner. We occupied sections of buildings, ran past each other in parallel tunnels, risked meeting a sniper at every opening, and lived because of our instincts. You will not believe me, you think I must have had a sign that night during the blizzard—a military emblem on his collar, the feel of his hat, his cologne, his stink, something that told me this man who had his back to me was a Nazi. This, like heroism, you cannot understand until you see it for yourself. I *know* that my subconscious acted before I had chance to think. I slipped my knife into his side and ripped up, lucky that I struck soft tissue, fortunate that I had done this before."

Estanguet moaned and Agnes turned toward him, fighting her own sense of revulsion.

"He fell," Arsov continued. "There were others and I struck again."

Estanguet turned gray and Agnes wondered if his health was failing. Seeing the body, twenty-four hours of cold, and now this violent story. She considered asking a servant to accompany him to the château.

Estanguet gulped the last of his wine and walked toward the windows, turning his back on the conversation.

"Two more died that night in the snow," continued Arsov, "and I was face-to-face with a fourth. This one had a gun in his hand. Just before I thrust my knife and he fired his weapon, I swore. In Russian. He swore at the same time in English and that is what saved us. A word in German and the next moment would have been my end."

Agnes shivered, remembering the storm the previous night. She could imagine the whiteout. A fight in blinding conditions. Killing blindly. She rose and walked to stand next to Estanguet. Checking his coloring in her peripheral vision. He looked better.

She breathed on a small glass pane to clear the ice, but it was too thick to melt that way. Although it was impossible to see out, she had walked the property enough to know it now. She could picture the cliff behind them, and the broad flat knuckle of land that gave the château and the mansion a panoramic view across the lake south toward France. Old trees, now bent by the weight of ice, trickled out from the base of the cliff, ending in the grove where Felicity Cowell had died. Apart from this grove there was a neatness to the plateau, with the various outbuildings blending in almost too well: summer pavilion, old stables now used as a garage, the ice house, and the Orangerie at the end of the formal gardens. Did Felicity's assailant cross the lawn from one of these hiding places or was he or she lying in wait? Using the state of the body, and the timing of the arrival of the storm, Blanchard had narrowed the time of death to within about an hour and a half. Agnes had asked Carnet and Petit to talk to everyone again and get a better sense of their activities and of the storm during that period of time. How visible was the grove? Could Felicity even see where she was going? Why didn't someone see her attacker from the dozens of windows?

"You ran into a regiment of Brits?" Mulholland said behind her. "In the Soviet Union in 1942? Bloody unlikely."

"Yet the man was British," said Arsov, "cut off from his company. It was not a fighting unit. Their task was information gathering—spying if caught out of uniform. I came upon him just after he ran into the Germans and he believed I saved him. He was right. He was scouting for information about the movements of the armies, and about supply possibilities of the Russian oil fields, for oil was important to all sides then as now."

"Shame they stayed allies. Could have ended a bunch of nonsense right then," Mulholland said.

"Ah, but you needed us as a fighting people just as he needed me that night. We took shelter in a barn, unwilling to risk walking farther in the storm. I had such detail about the situation in Stalingrad that he decided to bring me to their headquarters."

With a glance at Estanguet, Agnes returned to her seat, wondering why Mulholland was here. He didn't seem like the neighborly sort. On the other hand, they were all stir-crazy in the aftermath of the storm. She pulled a blanket over her legs, testing to see if she could see her breath. She could.

"Monsieur Mulholland, I am surprised you hadn't met Mademoiselle Cowell before. In London. Two young people out on the town. She seemed like someone you would know."

"What does that mean? Someone I would know?"

She looked at him carefully before changing the subject. "I always thought I wanted to live a hundred years ago," she addressed herself to Arsov, "but this weather makes me think I was wrong."

"A hundred years ago you would have dressed warmer." Arsov settled his own blanket higher under his arms. "Even fifty years ago you would have dressed warmer. When I left my village I was fortunate to have my father's bearskin coat. It is the little things that saved my life."

"Did you manage to bring money with you?" Mulholland asked, attentive again.

"Money? You think we walked around with our pockets full of coins? What do I tell you?" Arsov called over to his nurse.

"Sew my diamonds into my hems." She laughed. "As if I have diamonds."

"Later I wished I had money. That is what they would say after the war, the ones who lived. Carry your wealth with you. Those were the lessons many took away. What I took away was to keep my money in a numbered account in Switzerland." He laughed a hacking half cough.

"But that came later. I traveled with the British for some weeks. Men at war are strange. They want to hear any news of the outside. News of Stalingrad was of interest, for these soldiers had not seen siege warfare and already we were famous. Because of my father's work I spoke fluent French and once out of Russia I wanted to join the famous Resistance."

Agnes covered a laugh with a cough.

"You want to ask how my Russian accent grew back?" Arsov's

eyes closed and a faint smile appeared. "I found that after the war, as I started my business, it was better to be a Russian who escaped Stalin, who struggled through every day, than a man with a Russian name and no connections in France who spoke beautiful French. My father would have despaired as I unlearned my beautiful accent and forgot selected pieces of grammar." He coughed and motioned for a handkerchief.

"These Brits were a cavalier group despite their serious mission. I think that like many who have seen horror, they were happy to get me to the place I wanted, even if they thought I would probably last only a few days or weeks. After all, we would all probably last only a few weeks."

Agnes wished she'd met Arsov under better circumstances, wondering if she could introduce her boys to him when the investigation was over. She'd underestimated him, thinking he was born to wealth or had made his money under the harsh Russian regime and retired to Switzerland to enjoy his last days in pure capitalism.

The old man blew another ring of smoke. "After several weeks we reached the Mediterranean. There was a man going ashore; I never learned his name, but he agreed to take me on his dingy. He had only one question for me: if I had a weapon. It seems a stupid question to you, here we are at war, but the British had not armed me. There was a limit to their help. I was a civilian or maybe there were other reasons, maybe it was simple and no one thought to ask me. I showed him my knife and he was disgusted. He reached into his boot and pulled out real weapons. A pair of daggers. The blades were long, each with a razor-sharp edge and beautiful engraving on the blade. Lightweight steel, of craftsmanship I had never seen before."

Agnes felt the power of the blades he described. Had Felicity Cowell seen the weapon that killed her? The idea of a knife was more frightening than a gun.

Arsov stabbed his cigarette out and smiled at her. "He used one of the pair to slash the side of our dingy to deflate it and we stepped onto the sand in water up to our thighs. Then he handed me the other. The boat washed away and he walked into the darkness leaving me alone in the night.

"I started my new life knowing that France was my destiny with my new Sykes-Fairbairn blade in my grip."

Eleven

She wore a wool dress and tights colored to match and was unhappy about it, but the nurse had insisted, and Mimi had learned long ago that this was the one adult who couldn't be swayed by tears (as was the kitchen staff at the Vallottons'), or by mention of her dead mother (which moved anyone in the Vallotton family), or tantrums (which worked with anyone else she had ever met). Only the nurse and Monsieur Arsov were imperturbable in front of these tactics. She tried mentioning her dead mother to Monsieur Arsov when they first met, but he had told her that everyone he had ever loved was dead and she should stop crying about her one sad tale. She had decided right then to like him. He was her best friend here. Everyone else was nice to her—she made a face when she thought of the housekeeper who was too strict to be called nice—but Monsieur Arsov was her special friend. He liked to race her down the long gold corridor of his house, pitting his steel wheels against her short legs, and never letting her win unless she earned it. The nurse had caught them once and objected, but Monsieur Arsov stopped her with a word. Or two words: a raise. Mimi wasn't sure what it meant but she had remembered the words since they seemed to work well. She liked words.

The police lady with the ugly boots said Mimi was the same age as her youngest boy. The woman seemed to miss her little boy and Mimi had let her stroke her hair, tolerating the affection so she could learn what was happening. They had questions and more questions. The nurse sat beside her with the wings of her hat hiding her face, and Mimi fingered her starched skirt thinking it had to hurt when she sat. Still, Mimi was grateful for the nurse's presence, for she knew Monsieur Arsov had insisted on it and that he would always protect her.

She only remembered parts of what they wanted to hear. She was tempted to make up answers, but that seemed like a way to get more questions, so she kept it simple and true. She had fallen over the dead lady when she was walking to Monsieur Arsov's. Reluctantly, she admitted that she had not walked directly from the Vallottons' to Arsov's—like she was supposed to do if she walked alone. One of the many, many rules: don't go by the edge of the lake alone, don't go on the battlements alone, don't walk up to the village alone. Rules made to be broken.

Now that the lady with the boots had finished with her, Mimi peered around the door from the hall. She eyed the grown-ups and waited until Monsieur Arsov spoke. People paid attention when he talked, and she used that time to move across the room on tiptoes, clutching her stuffed elephant Elie to her chest, knowing that if she made it to the sofa they would never see her. She was supposed to be "traumatized," whatever that was, and recuperating with hot chocolate in the kitchen. However, she wanted to hear what the adults said.

They were talking about the dead lady again. Mimi rolled her eyes. Surely they had talked about this enough. She had recognized the dead lady in the ice from the time days and days ago when they ate dinner together. Well, the dead lady ate dinner with the grown-ups. Mimi had been sent to the kitchen to have her dinner under the supervision of Marie-José, and then up to her room to sleep. She had nearly thrown a tantrum, but decided it would be better to go along meekly, and then creep back down and watch. After all, she didn't actually want to sit with them. Boring. She just wanted to watch and listen.

The dead lady was pretty, of course not as pretty as her own mother: The most beautiful woman who lived. Her mother had said pretty is as pretty does. The dead lady would have never said anything so ridiculous. She had seemed delighted with the attention, smiling this way and that. Holding herself apart from the other women and talking to the men who couldn't keep their eyes off her.

Mimi remembered the beautiful dresses and the handsome men and the way the candlelight reflected against the tall mirrors. It had been a magical evening. Now she listened to the policewoman say how sad it was and everyone agreed. Mimi looked carefully over the back of the sofa. They didn't look sad. No one was crying, not like when her mother died and old Monsieur Vallotton had wiped his eyes and told her that she would always be taken care of. That day even Madame Puguet had cried.

The grown-ups talked on and on until she wished she had gone to the kitchen and had that hot chocolate. For the first time she wished the nurse would interrupt and tell everyone that Monsieur Arsov needed his rest. She did that enough when Mimi visited. Why not now? They sat around somberly but not sad, talking about what *she* had seen as if they had been there. She settled down into the soft sofa and waited and remembered that special night when the candles had burned so beautifully, recollecting the beautiful dresses one by one.

Twelve

Petit cornered Agnes in the main hall of the château. He was desperate to leave.

"If you have three boys," he said, "you ought to know that my wife needs me."

"You know the protocol. If there was anything I could do, I would. Rescue services won't make you a priority over everyone who needs assistance."

"Why isn't this an emergency?"

"Because in the eyes of those who make the rules your wife doesn't need you. You aren't a trained medical professional. I've been in her situation. Once she arrived at the hospital she was focused one hundred percent on the delivery. I don't mean this cruelly, but in the midst of labor she won't miss you. She'll have a dozen people helping her. My deliveries are a blur." This wasn't entirely true, in fact his wife was probably cursing him and his job, but Agnes knew from experience that once the baby arrived all she would remember was the joy.

"It's a tale to tell your little boy or girl: the storm of the century the day he arrived. Now, if you could take this to the doctor?" She handed him the package the cook had given her. It was small and wrapped in brown paper. Petit turned on his heel and left and she was thankful he didn't ask what was inside the package. A pregnancy test would have seemed like salt in a wound.

With her hand on the library door handle she paused to collect her thoughts. Inside the library, Nick Graves was seated at a long table surrounded by books and papers. She drew a chair up near him. He ignored her.

"When we spoke earlier you said Felicity Cowell looked like someone you would know. What did you mean by that?"

Graves didn't speak so she took the plunge.

"Most Americans lump England with the Continent. They make it all part of Europe. But you don't. You're well traveled. You know the difference. You haven't been to Europe; you didn't lie to me when I asked, but you have been to England. She looked like someone you 'would know.' An interesting phrase. A specific phrase. You knew her."

Graves shoved back from the table and walked to a window. Agnes followed him into the niche. The window was coated with ice and the niche was deeply shadowed. For a brief moment she was afraid. They were very much alone and he was a powerful young man. Powerful enough to stab a healthy young woman.

"Did you run in the same circles in London? Was that why you said she looked like someone you knew? Did she follow you here?"

He laughed. Really laughed. "Yeah, I knew her. Knew all

about her. Uppity bitch, coming here like she owned the place. Pretended she didn't recognize me. It's been what? Three years? But she knew who I was and I knew for damn sure she was the same person. Felicity Cowell she might call herself but when I met her she was Courtney Cowell. Stripping in a nightclub."

Agnes sucked an invisible stream of air through her lips. It whistled. "You're certain?"

"I'm not likely to forget. I was in London for junior year and we met just after Christmas at an art opening. Nothing fancy, a student show. We became friends, or at least I thought we were."

"Something happened?"

"We had a lot of laughs. She was great-looking, funny, smart, and I liked her. I was working hard during the day and partying at night but we could talk. We talked for hours. She told me she was in London on her own, wanting to break into the art world. I was there doing sort of the same thing. Except I'm more art history and she was auctions. Still, we had a lot in common." He shrugged. "I was wrong."

"Who broke it off?"

"Wasn't much to break off, just laughs and some drinks."

He started to walk away but Agnes blocked his path. "What happened?"

"Okay, so my dad's a frigging senator, it's not like I throw that around when I'm trying to make a life on my own in the one city where no one recognizes me. Some friends from home came to town and Dad sent me extra cash to take them out. Out to a proper place, a place he'd like to hear about, not a cheap student dive. He pulled some strings and we went to a club, a famous one. It's private. And there she was. Taking her clothes off. She was angry when she saw me."

"She was embarrassed."

"She could have pulled it off. When I first saw her there I figured she was doing it for a lark. Like she was some rich guy's kid who wanted to see what it was like to live underground. I knew she'd lied to me, but she was so cool and posh I would have believed she was a duke's daughter walking on the wild side. I know what's it like to want to be invisible, to not be my father's son all the time."

This was the first true expression of who Felicity Cowell was that Agnes had heard. She'd seen for herself that the young woman was beautiful, but she'd only a vague sense of her personality; just sporadic words and impressions. This was three-dimensional. Real.

"You learned that she wasn't rich, that she needed the job?"

"She left that night after she saw me. When I was sober I realized that if she wanted to step outside a rich family's world she'd strip in a dive where no one would recognize her."

"Maybe she wanted to be seen? If she wanted to hurt someone close to her she might have wanted them to see what lengths she'd go to. Work in a club where their friends would see. Embarrass the family."

"Occurred to me. Sounds like my sister. But I saw Courtney, I mean Felicity, one more time before I left the city. I knew where to find her and I had to know. She told me the whole story to get rid of me. She'd left home when she was a kid, moved around, finally made it south to London. Made money doing whatever she had to."

Agnes didn't want to think what "doing whatever she had to" meant.

"Funny thing is," said Graves, "she'd never gone to a friggin' university, but she was the smartest person I've met. She had an amazing memory for art, for artists, for everything really, and she'd learned it all on her own. There was something special about her, but she hated me. Hated that I'd seen both sides of her. Then she walks in here. I knew it was her and just wanted to say hello."

"And she ignored you?"

"She wouldn't admit we'd met. I mean, it was between the two of us, but she wouldn't admit to anything. Acted like I was a stranger."

"She was afraid. If you'd told anyone here that she wasn't university trained she would have been fired."

"Well, I didn't kill her."

There was the sound of a door opening and Agnes knew this conversation was over. "You should have told me you knew her when I first asked. We would take your passport, but the roads are closed, so that's not really a worry. And we'll let you have a chance to talk to your embassy. I should warn you that if they had to pick between you being guilty and a member of this family being implicated, they would probably throw you in the frozen lake wearing your boots. You may think you know what power and influence mean, but here the ties are deep and strong."

When she reached the end of the room she was surprised that no one had entered and decided she had imagined the door opening. She left Graves looking worried and wondered what had made her say such nonsense. He was probably telling the truth. The more likely scenario was for Felicity Cowell to kill him. She toyed with the idea. Felicity could have threatened him. Wasn't a knife, like poison, a woman's weapon? If they fought, he might have struck her when she turned. Maybe he killed her out of fear, or perhaps he slipped after he got the knife from her. Agnes rubbed her forehead and knew that, as unlikely as it was, the idea had to be considered.

"I liked the part about saving us versus him." Daniel Vallotton was waiting for her outside the door, hunched over on a crutch.

"Quick recovery," she said, eyeing his leg. It still looked terrible, with thin steel rods emerging from all sides.

"Julien says I've had my fun with you. I didn't mean to disrupt your investigation, and I do use the wheelchair. I can only use one crutch because of my arm, so I can't go too far easily. I hobble up and down stairs then sit in the chair to rest my arm. Can't talk big brother into putting in an elevator." They turned down the long corridor. Daniel hopped on one leg, balanced on a single crutch under his one good arm. Agnes doubted he could have managed a knife out in a storm. She glanced at the leg and shuddered.

"To make a clean slate I also wanted to talk to you about the painkillers. I haven't taken one in a few weeks." He stopped. Agnes was uncomfortable. Why had he stopped here, in the deepest shadows?

"I was hiding, and didn't want to admit it in front of my entire family. I knew Julien had arrived so I faked being asleep when MC came into our room."

Agnes moved closer to a window, away from the shadows. "I'm glad you sought me out. I've wanted to ask if you chanced to meet Felicity Cowell in London. Your wife says that you spend more time there than she does."

"What else did she say? Did she tell you how we married?"

"I'm more interested in your relationship with Felicity Cowell."

"Is that what Julien suggested? Well, there wasn't a relationship. No matter what they tell you, there wasn't one." Daniel leaned heavily on one crutch. "Marie-Chantal almost married him, you know, Julien I mean. The morning of the murder I didn't want to see her reaction when he arrived and wonder if she regretted her decision to marry the second son."

Agnes didn't reply.

"She doesn't paint anymore." He shrugged. "I think we've made a big mistake."

He limped away and Agnes felt oddly sorry for him. She would need to talk to him again, and press him on any previous relationship with Felicity or Courtney Cowell. He struck her as a man of the world and it was possible he met Courtney in a circumstance where he either wouldn't want to remember her or actually didn't. Thinking about Felicity/Courtney, Agnes felt slightly ill. She collapsed onto a cushioned bench. Staring at an unfamiliar stone wall, thinking about a young woman selling her body when she had a first-class mind, she felt a cold hollow inside. One that no fire would warm.

Thirteen

It was late afternoon and the sun was setting when Agnes joined Carnet on the ground floor of the château in a small room that had been set aside for their use. Not luxurious, it was comfortably furnished with two deep sofas and a large table where they could lay out their notes. The slit windows let in strips of cold north light, however several old-fashioned oil lamps were lit and the room was reasonably bright despite the lack of electricity. Agnes started to remove her outdoor coat, but changed her mind. Despite the blazing fire in every fireplace it seemed that each room was colder than the last.

"One last thing from me," Carnet said after hearing her account of the day. "You were right about the coat. She was wearing one of Mulholland's when she died. He confirmed it."

"And others have confirmed that it always hung there. Looks like she pulled it on in haste. Grabbed the first one, not caring if it fit."

"Points to panic."

"Panic or fear. Either way she didn't plan to go outside until she was by the door."

They sat in contemplative silence for a few minutes.

"Not much different from financial crimes," Carnet said.

Agnes nearly missed the irony but caught his smile in time. "Thank goodness I had a chance to tell Sybille I made it here, or my kids would be frantic with worry. Now they probably can't wait to hear all about the place. They've seen it from the lake often enough to be curious. Of course, that will only make Sybille more irritated." She smiled. "But not with them. She takes good care of them. We're lucky that way, I suppose."

"I'm only inside to pretend to warm up," Carnet said, pulling on a second scarf. "I'm going to do another walk along the perimeter of the property. Haven't found a weapon, and between the two of us, Petit and I have searched every inch of the lawn and the outbuildings."

"Won't the plants in the Orangerie die in the cold?" Agnes asked.

"A solar-charged system keeps it above freezing. We'd probably do well to sleep there tonight." He held his hands to the blaze.

"Robert, I doubt you'll find anything more outside. Of course we aren't finding anything inside either. It's frustrating, all of these little lies. Nick Graves is only the most obvious. Reminds me of my oldest. He can look you right in the eye and lie, but you know it's a lie because when he's telling the truth he glances around, interested in everything else that's happening. The lie makes him think about how his actions are perceived. Wish they'd tell the truth and let us ignore the lies we don't care about."

"Which are those?" Carnet turned to warm his backside.

"Right now, I suppose all the ones that don't lead me to find who killed Felicity Cowell. I really don't care if they are trafficking heroin, I just want to bring the victim's murderer to justice."

"Actually, I think you would care if they were trafficking heroin."

Agnes rubbed her face and started to laugh. "Okay, so heroin or child pornography, arms trafficking maybe, but nothing else. I have the feeling that everyone tells these small lies, protecting things that aren't important given what we are trying to do, and if they told the truth we would make some progress. It's like my kids. The little lies take up so much energy that when they tell the truth it doesn't seem so important anymore, all those days of concealing and fretting."

"Keep whittling away. We've not found evidence of an outsider. Not that there was much chance of finding that after the storm."

"That's the trouble, it will be very easy to have to write this off as the work of a mysterious outsider, particularly now that Felicity Cowell's background may be a bit unsavory. Part of the time I know that's what they want. Who wouldn't?"

"Most people want a crime solved. Otherwise it leaves a long shadow," said Carnet.

"Julien Vallotton told me he doubted it was the first time someone had been killed here. He's right, of course, given the long history of the place, but they're not afraid of gossip. They don't care what outsiders think, ever. Why should this be any different? They aren't doing anything to pretend it has to be an outsider. They tell lies that keep the story close." Agnes looked at Carnet. "Marie-Chantal Vallotton can't decide whether to punish her husband by pretending he might be the killer or protect him in case . . . oh, I don't know from what. I don't think she really suspects him, but she's angry."

"You said you wondered if Daniel Vallotton knew the victim before, from a club in London. A place he wouldn't want his wife to know he visits."

"She might be angry at him, but it takes more than anger to kill someone."

"If Felicity Cowell surprised Daniel, showing up here with a different name from what she uses for her other work, it might be a trigger. She sees an opportunity. Maybe this was her chance to use that job for real money."

"Blackmail?" Agnes asked, hating the idea.

"She had a chance to talk to his wife, maybe to judge Marie-Chantal's reaction."

"That would be easy enough," said Agnes. "Woman-to-woman chat about an imaginary friend whose husband goes to strip clubs. It could be worse than a club. There is latitude with her doing 'whatever it took' to survive. Outright prostitution? She could tailor the story to fit hers perfectly."

"If Felicity Cowell gets the right answer—an incensed wife—then she threatens Daniel Vallotton. Blackmail is a powerful force. He strikes. You've seen him walk with crutches and he's in incredible physical shape apart from his broken arm and leg." Carnet turned to warm his front again. "Strong emotion can give people the strength they need to push through pain."

"Daniel Vallotton definitely could have met Felicity as Courtney. He impresses me as someone who probably frequents clubs. However, he wouldn't care who knows. If they met at a club I guarantee he's a card-carrying founding member."

"Maybe his wife doesn't like it. Maybe he promised to stop when they married. What a man does when he's single is not the same when he's got a wife. Plus he's a second son, and you've gathered that they live a very expensive lifestyle. Possibly more expensive than his older brother's. Yachts and race cars aren't cheap. Maybe she's the real money and he can't risk her leaving him."

Agnes ran a hand through her hair, ignoring Carnet's reaction to the result. "Marie-Chantal Vallotton is unhappy. How can anyone be unhappy when they look like her? She is beautiful, married to a handsome man, living in this incredible place, and she's unhappy. She wants to work, of all things."

"Do you need to work?"

"I don't see how that matters."

"When George died, did your family want you to return to work?"

"Of course not, they wanted me to stay home with the boys. They still want me to stay home."

"And you didn't. You love those boys and I know you miss them, so why did you return?"

Agnes rubbed her face and frowned. "I like my work."

"Why? It's not that pleasant. In financial crimes you often worked in drafty storage rooms with files, the office was always noisy and now, here, it's cold and we don't know if we'll be successful. All very unsatisfactory. Why do it? Why not go home once and for all?"

Agnes frowned. "My mother-in-law and I don't cohabit so well. And, it's not much of a comparison. Look at Marie-Chantal and then look at me. Not exactly a parallel."

Carnet smiled.

"If we were a parallel George would still be alive."

"You can't say that."

"It's true. Something with me, something with us, made him take his life. It wasn't the boys or work. If I were Marie-Chantal Vallotton he wouldn't have ended his life. Trust a woman's judgment on this."

"You're wrong."

"When he died they went through all of his work, reviewed all of his accounts for years in the past. Nothing was out of order, not one thing. He was the perfect employee with no mysteries lurking, ready to ruin him. He was healthy. His parents and I imagined he had a terminal cancer and didn't want to tell us or endure treatment. Can you believe we actually hoped that? Before they completed the autopsy, we actually prayed that he had a nasty terminal disease because we could understand fear of a lingering death. We speculated through the night, settling on pancreatic cancer as our choice."

"Normal responses. Of course you look for a reason, but think how irrational most were, and the rest were disproved. He didn't have a terminal disease, so you are left with an equally irrational one that can't be disproved now that he is dead."

"No, it was not normal. Sybille knows it, George's father knows it, and I know it. He didn't love me anymore and took . . . took that horrible way out. I will always wonder if it was because I don't quite fit in."

"That's absurd, as absurd as anything we've heard during this investigation."

"You should spend time with my mother-in-law. She'll give you plenty of details. I try, but I'm always just a little bit wrong. I still don't like to eat rabbit and every Easter she acts like I've committed sacrilege."

"Not everyone has rabbit at Easter."

"In our village they do." Agnes smiled. "When I think about the expense my parents went to arranging for a turkey to be delivered for our holidays. And yams and marshmallows and cranberry sauce. My mother did it because she had her own childhood memories from America and wanted to share them, but it didn't help. I was always pretending at school. Pretending I did what everyone else did. Not wanting anyone to know we celebrated the American Thanksgiving the fourth Thursday of November."

"George didn't die because you don't like rabbit."

"That's only a tiny example. He wouldn't want to admit his mistake to anyone. He wouldn't want to divorce me and upset the boys. Or hurt his parents."

"Divorce is hardly the end of the world."

"To my in-laws it is. Laws may change and times march on but they live in a small village and hold to the old ways. They'd prefer I came from a family who had lived in a neighboring village for the last thousand years. George loved them and knew this. He wouldn't have wanted to embarrass them with a divorce. Standards have to be upheld. The illusion maintained."

"Agnes, listen to yourself. His death upset the boys and brought more negative attention than a divorce would have. He had to have known that."

"Everyone has an opinion but no one, definitely not you, knows why."

She lifted her hands to cover her face and smelled the tang of hand lotion. George's lotion.

Fourteen

Agnes started at the sound of footsteps approaching Felicity Cowell's workroom. She dropped her hand from Winston's muzzle, embarrassed to be caught talking to him.

"My father's dog," Julien Vallotton said from the doorway, "has probably heard more confessions than some priests."

Winston shifted away from Agnes and looked from one human to the other. This section of the château was so isolated she hadn't expected anyone to join her. Perhaps that was because she had taken care to follow the route Felicity Cowell favored. That meant exiting through a heavy paneled door directly to the outside. From there, under the covered passageway between the menacing iron portcullis and the courtyard, she had taken a narrow door leading to an equally narrow stairway. It led up to Felicity Cowell's workroom. Winston had followed her. At first his size was intimidating, but he looked well fed and she decided it wasn't on guests. After that she appreciated his presence.

Similarly, Vallotton's appearance wasn't exactly unwelcome but he had startled her. In fact, more than startled her. She was starting to see menace around every corner. There were too many dark and unexplored places.

"What is it you do exactly?" she asked to cover her discomfiture.

"I'm a collector."

"Art? Antiques?"

"Buildings. Houses mainly. They're an art form of sorts."

She sighed. Most people she knew collected hotel soaps or postcards.

The workroom was nearly dark and Vallotton stepped into the hall and returned with a bundle of candles. He stuck them in a brass candelabra and lit them. Shadows sprang onto the walls, illuminating corners not visible with Agnes's flashlight beam. She was reminded of her initial impression: this room was not large or attractive when compared to the others in the château. In the center was a plain wooden desk and on it were stacks of unbound pages from the working auction catalogue. A digital camera, notebook, row of neatly aligned pencils, and a teacup—used and not empty—were arranged beside a small stack of books. The ceiling was high enough to give a sense of scale not seen in modern life, and normally the room would be illuminated from a bank of clerestory windows. Today ice blocked most of the light, and the sun was already low. The only heat source was a small fireplace. It was unlit and the room was bitterly cold.

"What were these rooms originally? They're isolated," said Agnes.

"Originally? Sleeping quarters for the guards," said Vallotton. "Easy access to the main gate and to a stair leading to the battlements."

"How did Felicity end up here?" Agnes asked.

"My story won't change, you know. That's the best part about telling the truth, it's consistent." When she didn't respond he continued, "I probably see or speak with Evelyn Leigh every month or so. He calls about something coming up for auction that we might want, or sometimes I ask him to keep an eye out for a particular item, a gift for my aunt, or my brother. I mentioned that we would have a formal sale to honor Father's wishes." He paused. "You might argue that Evelyn was able to use his very substantial powers of persuasion to convince me to stage a more public sale of many items. I think this was good business sense for him, and not part of a murder plot, but I will leave that to you. Evelyn suggested Mademoiselle Cowell should handle the preliminary onsite details. I looked at their website while we were on the telephone and glanced at her photograph—more out of idle curiosity than anything—but that was all I knew of her. I didn't have a reason to care, it was the firm we were hiring, not this one employee."

"Was she what you expected?"

Vallotton walked around the workroom. There were a dozen or so paintings leaning up against the walls and he surveyed them casually before turning to face Agnes. She felt it again, the subtle power he had over the space around him despite his reserve. By either his glance or his presence he defined the room as his, all of the possessions as his, and she nearly apologized for the question.

"I expected someone professional who would guide us to a successful conclusion. The rough catalogue you see here appears satisfactory. We had two phone conversations and she was articulate and knowledgeable. I did not expect her to end up dead on my lawn, so in that way she has defied expectations."

"What if I told you that she might not be as she appeared? What if I suspect she didn't have a university degree or a well-connected family or anything really?"

A flash of surprise crossed Vallotton's face and in that instant she was convinced he didn't know anything about Felicity Cowell's hidden life. He leaned against the wall and crossed his arms over his chest. "You must more than suspect this or you wouldn't mention it."

She relayed what Nick Graves had told her.

"And you believe him? Of course you do," Vallotton said slowly. "Why would he invent this? He knows you will be able to check the details in a few hours or days at the most. It's surprising, but not impossible. Evelyn told me he first hired Mademoiselle Cowell—"

He cocked an eye at Agnes who replied, "Same last name apparently, and I will still think of her as Felicity Cowell."

"Fair enough," Vallotton said. "Evelyn hired her as a summer intern, and he told me that she'd worked out so well he'd kept her on. Probably didn't inquire too carefully for the summer—likely didn't pay her—and once she was there he didn't think to go back and get references." He took a long slow breath. "Even her name isn't her real one? It never occurred to us."

He fingered the top of a painting, an abstract, Agnes noted. The artist's name was scrawled near the bottom of the canvas. Picasso. Of course.

"Graves said that it was three years ago when he was in London with her?" Vallotton asked.

"Three years ago exactly."

"When I glanced at her photograph online there was also a résumé. I remember that she graduated from the art program at the Sorbonne three years ago. Makes it more likely her credentials are fake. She couldn't have been in both places at the same time."

"She would have been fired if Graves told someone," Agnes said. "She would have been unhireable in the art world."

"You don't know the art world very well," Vallotton said. "But I get your point."

"She created this path out of a much harder life and now, in an instant, it's all over. She would lose her job, who knows what else, and—"

"What, stabs herself in despair?"

"No, but she and Graves could have had an altercation. Maybe she knew something about him that he's not telling us. We have a point of provocation. It escalates. Imagine you've worked hard—transformed your life—and now all will be lost. She would have been fired from this job, regardless of how the art world operates."

"Fired? Not by me. You won't believe me when I say that I don't care about her past. I have some sympathy for Mademoiselle Cowell. Yes, Evelyn would have dismissed her for this falsifying of her curriculum vitae, lying about her studies, claiming certificates and courses at prestigious institutions she had never visited, but I understand. I know what it's like to want to create a new past. I've lied about myself. Leaving off

Le Rosay and Georgetown, saying 'attended some college.' Letting the bosses think I was ashamed about the name. I can appreciate that she might not have gotten her position if she had told the truth. Did she have the right to show her worth? I think so."

"When have you lied about your résumé?"

"You really want to ask, when have I worked. For nearly a year at a ski resort in California. Squaw Valley. I ran the lifts, taught a few classes, and enjoyed myself thoroughly as far away from people I knew as possible."

"I would think that your clothes, your voice, would give you away."

"Like Mademoiselle Cowell's?"

"Your aunt thought she was hiding something."

Vallotton paused in his study of the art. "My aunt has un-surpassed instincts. It could be that she pays more attention to people, despite her appearance of negligence, or possibly she has a sixth sense."

"You understand this makes our job harder."

"Our?"

She frowned at Vallotton. "Mine, Carnet's, and Petit's. We start an investigation with known contacts—friends and family—and hope to tease out the problems that lead to murder and now our victim appears to have a double life."

"Not necessarily a double one. More of a ruptured one? A double life implies she has a husband and twelve kids some-where back in Newcastle who call her Courtney and like her stripping act. I doubt that. I think she found a way to move beyond her past. I'd like to think that's admirable."

"Still, she lied."

Agnes could imagine the horror and confusion on the girl's parents' faces when they were told: their daughter was dead so far from home and at a place so different than where they were from. She wondered if they already thought she was dead. If Nick Graves was telling the truth then Courtney Cowell had started her life far from where her life ended as Felicity.

"We're not making progress," Agnes said suddenly, deciding it might not be "our" investigation. Based on Bardy's recommendation, she had trusted Julien Vallotton this far, she might as well trust him all the way. "We may never know who did this. The chances of trace evidence are almost nonexistent, given the storm."

"One of us might confess. There's still time."

"And now we have a victim who was not who she pretended to be and for days we are stuck here with no access to her life in London. Every hour means evidence is eroding. And there can be jealousies and guilt that follow someone missing for ten years. There can be petty office troubles or evidence of mind-boggling deceit that is uncovered and I'm stuck here, maybe for another day or two, with no more information to go on." She rubbed her forehead and half laughed. "That may be the best news in fact, because when things return to normal, someone, Bardy in particular, will want to know what direction to take this investigation and I won't have any idea."

Vallotton opened a book that lay on the desk. It was filled with glossy photos of country houses of England. "Strange book for her to bring here."

"It's not yours?"

"Ours are stamped on the flyleaf." He flipped through a page or two. "I remember when this property came up at auction.

Nearly bought the place. Beautiful nineteenth-century topiary gardens."

Agnes read the caption. She didn't know where Cumbria was in England, but it looked cold and dark. For a moment she dreamed of sunny Florida, a place she usually hated but sounded good right now. "Why would you buy a house there?"

"A developer planned to purchase the property and destroy it to make room for a row of execrable cheap modern houses. Fortunately someone turned up and bought the house to live in." He thumped the book shut, but Agnes opened it again. She turned the pages one by one. Near the back there were words penciled in the margin next to a photograph of a Tudor-era mansion. The façade was flat gray stone punctuated by leaded windows. It was impressive in an austere, cold way.

"'My house,'" Agnes read the penciled note.

Vallotton looked over her shoulder. "You think Mademoiselle Cowell wrote this? If she's from a modest background then this isn't her family home, and it's certainly not where she lives in London. Do you have her address in the city?"

"Yes, from her handbag." Agnes gave him the address and he thought for a moment. "Nice neighborhood, the kind of place you want a younger sister to live if she is trying to escape the posh family home; could be expensive, but wouldn't have to be. Definitely flats or a townhouse and not what is in this photograph."

"A good address to aid her pretense of an affluent background?"

"Certainly. Someone on Evelyn's staff would have noted it when she started work and it would have sent a subtle signal of 'she's one of us.'"

Agnes opened the auction catalogue and glanced at the hand-written notes. "Looks like the same handwriting; mind you, I'm not an expert."

Vallotton studied the two samples side by side, then read the printed caption next to the photograph. "'Ancestral home of the Smythson-Markums.' Name doesn't mean anything to me, and you're right that it wasn't Mademoiselle Cowell's home unless she has a triple secret life as a Smythson-Markum. From what Graves said she has been true to her last name through-out. Maybe she just liked the house. Marked it as a goal. A con-crete manifestation of her dreams. No different than saying one day I will live in New York City or exhibit work at the Pompi-dou Centre."

Agnes was about to agree when Winston rose, giving a few seconds' warning before Marie-Chantal arrived. She was flushed and out of breath.

"I've been looking everywhere." She glanced accusingly from one to the other. "I wish mobile phones would work again. Felicity Cowell had a fiancé." She paused deliberately. "He's here and he's upset."

As they followed Marie-Chantal down the stairs, Vallotton leaned close to Agnes. "About Squaw Valley, let's not tell my brother. He thinks I was at Stanford, doing post-bac studies, not trying out his lifestyle for the winter."

"You didn't like it?"

"I loved it, but in the end we are who we are, and for me that life could only be one season."

Fifteen

Harry Thomason was in his late twenties, handsome in a boy-ish sort of way, the kind of man who would never look old. His dark hair was cut so it fell long over his brow and he looked fit without the build of an athlete. Despite winter gear, he appeared tired and cold.

"It's taken me most of the day to get here," he said, adding that he was currently a guest at the Beau-Rivage Palace hotel on the lake in Ouchy and was worn-out with worry that he hadn't heard from Felicity in days. He peeled off his outer garments and, without hesitating, handed them to the house-keeper.

"The blasted storm ended any hope of a phone call. Clearly couldn't fly back to London, so I decided to see her. Roads are closed even if I had a car. The hotel had some cross-country skis left by a guest, but they don't work on the ice, so I dumped them after a bit, kept the poles, and walked." They all glanced to his boots as if assessing the difficulty of the task. "Kept to the lake edge. Thank goodness it's flat because it was slick as hell and hard going. Where's Felicity?"

He looked around expectantly and Agnes glanced quickly from Julien Vallotton to Marie-Chantal, then the housekeeper. Her heart sank. No one had told Thomason his fiancée was dead. She asked him to accompany her out of the entrance hall, too many weapons there for this kind of news. He was at ease, turning to ask Madame Puguet if he could have a cup of tea.

"Now that I'm inside I can feel the cold, Earl Grey if you have it, with lemon, no sugar. Thank you."

Madame Puguet walked very slowly from the room, as if reluctant to leave. Marie-Chantal and Vallotton stood near, too near, as if they were waiting to catch the young man when he collapsed.

Agnes delivered the news quickly and with little detail, realizing as she did that there was little to relate. His fiancée had been found the afternoon before, stabbed outside the château just after the storm struck. A brief end to a brief life.

Thomason shook his head slightly and looked at Agnes stupidly. She repeated the words, then said them again in English to make sure he understood. As she spoke, a pit formed in her stomach and she knew it was too soon, she should not be here dealing with death when it was so close to her own heart. She saw what Carnet had seen when he told her about George— Thomason's eyes widened and his face froze, the expression blank. His skin was red from cold and wind, but beneath that he paled. Tears welled in his eyes and Agnes felt him remind himself to breathe. He swallowed, struggling to control emotions, then clenched his jaw. The others in the room did not speak or move.

Finally Thomason mastered himself and took the first step of many toward understanding. Even before he spoke, Agnes knew what he would ask, for they were a version of the same words she had used: where is she, can I see her, how did it happen? The words tumbled out, then there was nothing; he swayed. The perfect servant, Madame Puguet anticipated what he needed and moved fastest, leading him to a chair before he crumpled. Vallotton handed him a glass of something that Agnes assumed was alcohol.

"Impossible," Thomason said. "She didn't like the outdoors. Felicity would never be outdoors in a storm. You must be mistaken." He drank what was given him in a gulp, sputtered, then nearly dropped the glass. Madame Puguet refilled it.

Petit walked in holding the ancient radio to his ear, yelling into it. When he saw the group he stopped. "My wife had a boy!" He turned in a big circle, eyeing each of them with a grin on his face. When he got to Thomason he stopped. "How'd he get here? You found a way for someone to come down and didn't get me out?" Marie-Chantal pulled him away, whispering into his ear.

Thomason looked around wide-eyed as if accustomed to malicious pranks that could be righted through perseverance. Agnes wanted to congratulate Petit but didn't move. She paced her breathing to Thomason's, wondering if he would faint. She had.

His words didn't string together in sentences, they were snippets of remembrances, of questions, and of denial. Finally Vallotton interrupted. Thomason seemed to believe a man's voice more than a woman's, although Agnes thought it might be the tone of the man's voice, for she had recognized Thomason's accent and clothing and manner and knew that he was at home among these people.

Madame Puguet interceded and escorted Thomason from the room before he succumbed to an exhausted emotional collapse.

"Finally, someone who really knew her," Vallotton said quietly.

Agnes didn't respond. She mumbled an excuse and left the room, knowing where she needed to go. Sitting again in the dead woman's workroom, surrounded by paintings and little else, she wondered if it was possible for a room to feel emptier than empty. Only a half hour before, she had felt Felicity Cowell's presence. It had spoken of her personality: orderly, efficient, and confident about her business. Someone who had worked to achieve everything she had. Now the room felt abandoned like a stage set with props not yet used. The woman was a kaleidoscope of fiction: lower-class dropout with a brilliant mind; a stripper with a posh fiancé. She was everything and nothing.

They had doused the candles earlier and Agnes didn't want the light now. Blowing on her fingers to stimulate circulation, she flipped through the book of English manor houses. Despite everything she had learned, she wanted Felicity Cowell to be an innocent victim. A good girl, not from a wealthy family, but one who worked hard and made a life for herself with a loving fiancé. She wanted the murderer to have committed the crime, not in reaction to something Felicity had done, but in reaction to something in his or her own life. Agnes wanted her to be an innocent victim who would never have the chance to live in her English manor house.

Sitting in the dead woman's desk chair, Agnes admitted the picture she painted was most likely fiction. She knew that except in rare cases of random violence the victim was usually involved, somehow. Not culpable, but involved: domestic violence, jealousy or rage between work colleagues, a party to a love triangle. In this one case she hoped for a difference; she didn't want Felicity Cowell, outsider among the château's inhabitants, to be linked to the cause of the violence.

Thomason would need time before she could question him. This she knew from her own experience. She closed her eyes and tried to picture her husband, but the image was difficult to conjure. He was a memory, not a corpus.

"Am I disturbing you?"

Agnes rose, startled to see the marquise in the door frame, a candle in her hand.

"No, I'm just—"

"Remembering?"

"Yes," Agnes said, surprised. "More accurately, trying not to forget." Long shadows flickered between them.

"Be careful what you struggle to recall. In my experience the result is suspect. A filter across the truth and the haze of time. The desire to remember plays tricks."

"It's my husband, I have trouble recalling his face."

The marquise blew her candle out, plunging the room back into near darkness. "Be thankful. That is all I remember of mine. His face the last time I saw him."

Agnes waited for her to continue but the woman was gone. She sat in silence, listening. Then heels tapped. They were brisk, not those of the elderly marquise. A moment later Marie-Chantal hesitated at the threshold, framed by the reflection of her flashlight beam.

"I stayed here once—in the bedroom next door I mean,"

she said. "Years ago. A house party Julien organized when we were all at Le Rosay. I was sorry she didn't sleep there. It's such a pretty room. I didn't think to ask why she didn't." Marie-Chantal was beautifully dressed in a dark knee-length cashmere sweater dress over tall high-heeled boots. Agnes wondered how it was possible that such a woman could be unhappy.

Marie-Chantal started to remove her scarf, then stopped as if realizing that the room was exceptionally cold. "It seems neglectful now that I didn't even know she was engaged. She didn't wear a ring." Unconsciously Marie-Chantal glanced to her own left hand and enormous diamond.

"Apparently they were waiting to get the ring from his family." That much Harry had mumbled to Agnes.

Marie-Chantal moved to the front of the desk and flipped the catalogue open, aiming her light across the pages. "The few times we spoke, she talked about her work. The art here, and the sale. She loved what she did."

She moved toward the paintings and leaned against the wall, aiming her flashlight beam over them. "Wonderful pieces, but here they are the leftovers. Have they told you I paint?" She stepped back as if studying the canvases carefully. "Are you familiar with Morandi? There is one here. Or maybe Julien has it with him in London. Morandi painted only one thing his entire life. Bottles. He was a great favorite of my studio instructor in Paris. One thing, he would say. Paint one thing over and over and you have to infuse it with yourself, you can't simply go through the motions." She stepped away from the canvases. "I painted Julien. Sketches, careful studies in oil. Extravagant period pieces. Over and over. Interest. Infatuation. Obsession. You heard us earlier?"

Agnes nodded carefully. Wondering why it had never occurred to her that George might be having an affair. This beautiful woman suspected her husband, and yet that had never
been her fear. Perhaps it should have been. Something about
the smell of lotion jogged her memory. Had she simply not
suspected?

"Then you might guess that we were once a couple," Marie-
Chantal continued. "Call it what you will. In the end I wanted
to paint him but not marry him. Perhaps on some level I wanted
to be him. Daniel needs me. Julien doesn't. He's not selfish, it's
simply that he can stand alone." She smiled sorrowfully at
Agnes then, with a last look around the room, left.

Immediately Agnes felt the best piece of art had left the
room. Then she wondered which part of the conversation was
the most important. She had a suspicion that Marie-Chantal
knew the impact she had on people; she would have to. Pulling
her notebook from her handbag, Agnes checked her notes in
the dim light. Marie-Chantal had left the marquise for some
time during the afternoon of the murder to let Winston out
into the courtyard. But he wasn't a child. One couldn't ask a
Great Dane if she'd left him alone for a few minutes. Who
would know? Was it possible Marie-Chantal was jealous of
Felicity Cowell? Jealous of more than her professional life?
Either a long-standing association or a spur-of-the-moment
attraction between the dead woman and Daniel Vallotton that
escalated into spousal rage? A flirtation gone too far? Marie-
Chantal admitted to a strange kind of obsession with Julien,
but possibly that was covering for her other obsession—an obsession with her husband.

Felicity Cowell had been attractive even in death. Beautiful in life. Just as Marie-Chantal was beautiful. Agnes tapped her pen on the desk's edge. She took one last look around the workroom before blowing out the candle. She was left with a different sense of their victim and liked it. She hoped that put her in the right frame of mind to speak to Harry Thomason again. He might be suffering heartbreak, but her first concern had to be for the dead woman, no matter her real name.

Sixteen

Yet another beautiful room, was the first thought that occurred to Agnes when the housekeeper led her to Harry Thomason. In the past hour he had changed out of his heavy outdoor clothes into wool trousers, a linen shirt, and a cashmere sweater provided by the family. Incongruously, his feet were still in slippers, of the type Agnes associated with old men. Thomason looked tired and pale, but otherwise at ease in his surroundings. She knew from experience of death that words didn't help so she skipped elaborate condolences.

Petit was already there, notebook in hand, waiting. Eager to avoid the appearance of a police inquisition she had asked Julien Vallotton to join her as well. At first he carried the conversation and Agnes was not surprised that his social skills were up to the awkwardness. He easily led the discussion toward the questions that had to be asked.

"You'll meet my brother at dinner if you decide to join us. He's walked that path you took by the lake, but I haven't. Quite a distance, but nice enough in good weather; a feat after the storm."

"I'm from a family of walkers," Thomason replied. "We traipse around the moors near our home year-round; my mother is convinced a trek on rugged terrain is necessary before holiday dinners. From the hotel it was mostly flat. The ice was a challenge, but I was eager to see—" His eyes clouded and he struggled to maintain control of his emotions. "We hadn't talked in a few days and I really wanted to see her."

Vallotton rose and opened a cabinet then poured a beautiful golden brown liquid into two glasses. He inclined his head toward Agnes and she frowned a no, hoping Petit had the sense to decline. Her mind drifted to Marie-Chantal and the Vallotton brothers. How much jealousy lingered after she chose one over the other? Suspicions could easily turn into anger, then rage. On the other hand, they seemed to accept the strong undercurrents as part of life and relationships and she wondered: Had she missed the same between herself and George? Was there space in their lives for someone else?

After Thomason and Julien Vallotton had each taken a sip and commented favorably on the whiskey Vallotton continued, "You came down from the village? I'm curious to see how their recovery is proceeding. I can see some of the damage from our battlements."

"I haven't been to the village. I walked along the lake all the way from the hotel and then around the base of the cliff face."

Petit stood in alarm. All remnants of color faded from Thomason's face when the policeman explained that there was no path at the base of the cliff and Thomason must have walked on an ice shelf. Agnes shuddered and hoped that no one else had tried the same; the lake was deep and it would be a cold, watery grave. She caught Vallotton's eye. This was a new problem: if Felicity Cowell's killer left the property along the lake, he or she might already be dead. Petit would have to check the shoreline again. A fall through ice, a fall from a bridge. Both horrible ends.

"Dashed stupid, all week a disaster and then this end." Thomason took another deep drink and steadied himself. "Maybe best if I had plunged through."

Agnes knew that they would have to check Thomason's story. They would also have to determine if the lake had frozen over early enough for someone to leave the property the day before. Petit and Blanchard could put their heads together over weather patterns and travel. For the moment, though, Thomason's grief seemed real, but a killer could also feel or simulate emotion.

"This is painful, I know," she said. "You knew her better than anyone and we need your assistance. Did she mention knowing anyone here? Had she been here before?"

"She hadn't been to this part of Switzerland, and I told her to stay at the Beau-Rivage—that's where the firm puts me up when I travel to the region—but she wanted to stay nearer her work. Couldn't really blame her, what with the drive, and of course she would be just as comfortable onsite. For auctions of collections of this scale we often stay on the property, so it wasn't out of the ordinary."

Agnes felt sorry for the young man. He seemed to forget his fiancée's death at the start of each sentence and remember it a second later. She wanted to tell him the feeling wouldn't go away soon. Perhaps never. She lifted her hand to sniff George's lotion. There it was again. A memory, stronger than anything a photograph or words could call to mind.

"I wonder if I could see her room, just to see where she was last," Thomason said.

Focusing on Thomason required an effort. There was something important at the edge of her mind. "That's another point we would like to ask you about. She decided to stay at a small hotel in the village. It's not a bad place, but we were surprised by her decision. Any idea why she made this choice?"

For the first time Thomason seemed unsettled. He shrugged and swallowed a few times.

"Perhaps you have a sense of what she liked in a hotel," Agnes said. "Maybe she thought the village inn was quaint or she liked her privacy." Ridiculous, but she couldn't stop talking. She wanted to comfort this young man and at the same time something didn't seem right, she just couldn't put her finger on the reason for her concern. He swallowed again and rubbed his palms on his pants' legs.

"How did you two meet?" Agnes asked when he didn't reply.

Thomason brightened. "At work. I've been with the firm for eight years, straight out of university, and we met the first week she joined, two years ago. I'm in philately. I do other things, but that's my specialty, so we were fortunate to meet straight off." He launched into a lengthy explanation of his work and the internal organization of the firm, how their offices were on different floors, and Agnes let him talk. Now she could identify her concern. There was authenticity in his answer, which meant that what he said previously wasn't exactly the truth. She leaned forward and caught Vallotton's glance. She needed a cigarette and he knew it. She met his raised eyebrow with a fixed smile and sat back on the sofa, fingers stilled under the edge of her skirt.

"When did you speak with her last?"

Thomason looked around the room. "Can I see her body? I want it to be buried at my family's place. I think that's what she'd want."

"We can arrange for you to see her later. Right now I need to know more about the days before she died. We should be able to retrieve a record of her mobile phone calls tomorrow or the day after, but you may be able to help us now. Had her mood changed while she was here, or was she upset or worried about anything?"

"Why would she be upset? This job was an honor for her." He nodded to Vallotton. "You're important clients and for her to come here was exciting. Felicity worked hard. Harder than any of us and she was brilliant. You can't imagine her memory. She never forgot a painting or face or name. I'm good at what I do, I'm industrious and enjoy it, but she was different. She was special."

Agnes resisted the temptation to probe him about Felicity's earlier life and other name. He might know, or Graves could have lied. Although she doubted it. As Vallotton said, Graves would know that they could verify his story soon. If she asked Thomason she couldn't take the words back and he was so fragile. She remembered her own struggle with the details of George's death. Questions about Felicity's character could wait. Or could they? She glanced at Petit, sucking on the end of his pen, diligently taking notes. She wished Bardy was here.

Thomason smiled wanly. "We were both London outsiders.

It's a hard world to break into and that was part of what bound us together. London was our adopted home and we loved it and swore we would never leave."

Carnet entered the room, stretching his hand out to greet Thomason. Agnes tried to stand, but her knees buckled. George, was all she could think.

"Monsieur Vallotton." Madame Puguet appeared in the doorway. "Dinner is served."

Agnes knew that Julien Vallotton expected her to postpone the meal in order to finish questioning Thomason, but she couldn't speak. With a backward glance he led the younger man out of the room. Her heart was pounding so loudly she was certain it was audible. How had she not guessed? Nausea threatened. She placed a hand on Carnet's arm to stop him. With her other hand she pulled George's small bottle of hand lotion from her pocket.

"Must have dropped it," Carnet said, taking it from her. "My sister sends it from Australia. Some special concoction she pretends I need."

Again she tried to stand but couldn't. She couldn't find her balance. Her legs wouldn't bear her weight. "It was in my car. George put it there." Silence stretched between them. "You didn't even know George."

She felt him go still, like an animal judging the risk of flight.

"I told you I met him once, at the shooting competition."

"That was only a few minutes," she said. "And this is yours. I smelled it just now on your hand when you reached for Thomason's. It's a distinctive aroma. Unique. You knew George much better than that, didn't you?"

She raised her eyes to his and saw in them horror intermingled with truth. His mouth was open as if he was torn between speech and silence. He didn't move until she finally stood.

"You told me the first night here that George loved me and the boys, as if you knew."

"We met at the shooting match."

"A few minutes doesn't—"

His words overrode hers, tumbling out as if unstoppable. "We met there. It was the beginning."

She wanted to tell him to stop, but couldn't.

"I'd never felt that way before. We only spoke for a few minutes but he called me later and we met. Love at first sight, if you can believe it. And he felt the same. It only lasted a few weeks."

Agnes calculated rapidly. Her skin was cold and clammy and she steadied herself against the edge of the table. Her mouth went dry and she felt her heart accelerate. She couldn't breathe. "Three months," she heard herself say.

"No, six weeks until I ended it. I couldn't face what we were doing. I couldn't live with myself. He was married. We had to hide every emotion. At work, I could see your face when he called, and I knew he was telling you he had to work late. And I would leave right after you and meet—"

Agnes felt the room tilt and her chest constrict. She held out a hand as if to stop him, half wondering if she was dreaming, but his mouth continued to move, saying these terrible things. These treacherous things. She had had so many strange dreams after George's death that there was an element of repetition. She tried to speak but couldn't. Her throat had closed.

"He called me, texted me, emailed," Carnet continued, "but

I wouldn't see him. I thought this was the right thing to do. An abrupt break was necessary. I didn't think about what he was going through. I didn't let him reach out to me once I had made up my mind. I loved him but didn't want him to ruin his life, ruin the way his boys thought of him, destroy you, and so I ended it." His expression was one of total despair. "I never once, you have to believe me, never thought he would—"

"Kill himself over you."

They looked at each other, mirror images of horror. Agnes broke the gaze first. Then she ran from the room.

Seventeen

"Nausea. No more nausea," Agnes said, wiping her hand across her lips, feeling residual pain from the dry heaves flash across her ribs. She pressed a tissue to her eyes and dried her tears. For the first time she looked around. She had wandered far from where she started and it took a moment to orient herself. The furnishings came into focus and she leaned heavily against the open door. It was twice her height and intricately carved. The door swung back, striking the wall. She straightened and moved farther into the room, trying to not think. Shoving images from her mind as fast as they appeared. George. Carnet. George and the boys. George at the shooting match with Carnet. That final day under the Pont Bessières.

Herself with Robert Carnet. Working together. His deception. Her ignorance.

She pressed the tissue to her eyes again, staunching the flow of liquid, choking back another wave of bile, focusing on what was real right now. Trying to take in every detail, any detail, to think about something other than the unthinkable.

Carnet.

The end of her marriage. The end of George's life.

The room was long, the length familiar. She was directly above the library. Overhead was a beautifully carved and painted ceiling. Beneath her feet was an elaborate parquet floor scattered with large Oriental rugs. She put a fist to her eyes and took a deep breath. Her mind was a whirl. An unproductive whirl. She had to stop thinking about him. About them. Her chest hurt and her heart ached. Literally ached.

There were five windows overlooking the lake. She picked the nearest and studied the view from it. The glass was partially coated with ice, and she used that to concentrate on the storm and its aftermath until that train of thought led to here . . . and to her discovery. If she hadn't been trapped for two days with Carnet would he have told her about his affair with her husband or would she have continued in ignorance?

Despite the ice, moonlight streamed in and Agnes studied the outlines of the furnishings around her. A myriad of chairs and tables. She registered that they were completely draped in white cloth. It occurred to her that this was the condition of most of the rooms she had wandered through on this highest level of the château. Little used, but always ready for the family in case they needed another sitting room, or writing room or whatever room. Hidden knowledge, she thought, hardly knowing if she meant what was beneath the dust cloths or what had happened between her husband and her former boss. She rubbed her cheeks and looked for a mirror, certain her face was red and swollen.

Nearby a piece of cloth was draped over what looked like a large mirror. She pulled the fabric off with a hard yank. It slipped to the floor and she sighed. Not a mirror but an enormous oil painting of a seventeenth-century Vallotton in hunting garb. She tried another one, then another, not caring that someone would have to replace the covers. When all of the paintings were laid bare she paused. Still no mirror. She started on the tables. Obsessed now. Flinging cloth cover after cover to the floor. Abandoning the heaps of fabric as soon as they fell.

She uncovered tables laden with precious objects, chairs with deep silk cushions, and sofas with heavy tassels that brushed the floor. Sets of tapestried chairs. Two leather-covered writing desks and a half dozen delicate tables that held porcelain figurines and ivory carvings and every imaginable curiosity.

Finally there was nothing left to expose. She looked down the length of the space. She was focused. The light was dim, but it was enough. She clicked on her flashlight and aimed it across the surface of the nearest table, leaning down to survey the polished wood at eye level. Then she glanced at the other tables and opened the nearest glass-fronted cabinet. She angled down to study the shelves. It was very faint, but despite the cloth covers there was a microscopic coating of dust. More important, under the focus of a beam of light there were barely discernible places with no dust. Neat circles and precise oblongs. Each the mark of a missing object.

She stood and corrected herself. Not necessarily missing, but not here. Moved? Taken to another room? Carried to a place where the pieces could be observed and appreciated? She retraced her path through the adjacent rooms. Each was filled with furniture similarly covered in dust cloths. Working quickly but more carefully now, she pulled the covers away and shone her light on the surfaces, looking for the telltale spots of absolute cleanliness. She counted thirty places before she stopped and considered her discovery.

She had noticed that the Vallottons liked to group their collections: five porcelain shepherdesses, twelve pocket watches under glass, a trio of alabaster vases. From what she could tell about the missing objects, they were unrelated in type. Usually one of a group was missing. Since groups or collections would have been removed together for display elsewhere it was unlikely the individual pieces were taken to another location in the château. And the thin film of dust. The staff seemed thorough. If the housekeeper or a maid removed an object they would dust the surface of the table at the same time.

Turning to leave the last of the rooms, she caught sight of herself in the glass of a cabinet and started. Even in a poor reflection her eyes looked irritated and swollen. A memory of George slipped through her mind. A Saturday early in their marriage when they had taken the train to Zürich and wandered the Bahnhofstrasse, window-shopping at the finest stores in the world. Stores that sold jewelry and the sort of *objets d'art* that the Vallottons would own. She remembered how George insisted they go inside and look at a miniature globe. How carefully he had handled the carved wood and how reverently he had set it down after learning the price—several years of his salary. She smiled. They had been honored to even hold the piece and see it in person. Now she wondered if he had walked that same street with someone else. Not Carnet, she was sure they hadn't gone out in public together. But were there others? Other lovers. The idea chilled her. Then she remembered where she was. The Vallottons had likely been robbed, and rich or not, they wouldn't be happy about it. She had a job to do.

Agnes found the housekeeper hovering outside the dining room, monitoring dinner service for the family and their guests. Madame Puguet sniffed delicately and Agnes hoped she didn't smell like vomit. She resisted covering her mouth. Quickly she conveyed her concerns about the missing objects.

"Dust?" Madame Puguet said, as if Agnes had said there were rats chewing the upholstery.

"Only the very faintest trace. Mere particles, but using a strong light it was possible to see that several objects had been removed."

Madame Puguet took a step back as if she'd been struck. Then, shoulders stiff, she led the way to investigate herself.

One glance at the first tabletop and her eyes widened. She covered her mouth briefly, then seemed to gather her wits. "This should not have been taken away," she said, moving her hand toward an empty area between a series of gem-encrusted silver cups.

"Maybe a family member picked it up—" Agnes was silenced with a cold glance.

"The family doesn't pick objects up and carry them around." Madame Puguet walked through the room, studying each table and cabinet as she passed. "I will make a list of the items for Monsieur Vallotton. He must be informed at once."

Eighteen

Agnes paced the length of the sitting room, blowing into her hands and sniffing. She had gargled soap in a powder room, an action that had nearly made her sick again, but at least her breath was freshened. Insult to injury.

Julien Vallotton arrived from the dinner table. Agnes glanced down at her wrinkled skirt and compared her disheveled appearance to his immaculate garb.

"You should have joined us, or at least eaten," he said, gesturing to the platter of salmon, tomato, and shrimp canapés thoughtfully provided by the kitchen. "The others enjoyed themselves. Officer Petit is awash with enthusiasm about his new son."

"You've been burglarized," she said.

Vallotton waited for her to continue and for a moment she wanted someone different opposite her, someone who would jump up and start waving his hands in anger. Or show any emotion. She needed a distraction. Any reminder of George and her stomach threatened to heave.

"It's a lot of things," she added.

Madame Puguet entered the room, clearing her throat delicately. "The list is hasty, but I think it conveys the scope." She handed a piece of paper covered in her precise handwriting to Vallotton. The housekeeper looked pale and grim and Agnes realized she was taking the discovery hard. Madame Puguet started to speak, hesitated, and silently left the room.

Vallotton glanced at the paper. "You discovered this now?"

"I'm here to work. I spent dinner checking the rooms again. I was curious."

"You were curious the first time you walked through the property."

"I was looking for something different then." No need to tell him she was looking for evidence of violence the first time and for a distraction the second.

He read the list again.

"Nothing looks disturbed. I had to look carefully." She leaned forward. "There was dust under the cloths. Just a trace, but that's how I noticed the items were missing."

Vallotton tapped his leg absently.

"We will find out who did this," Agnes said.

"You think the theft is linked to Felicity Cowell's death?"

"I don't know. Madame Puguet said the items might have disappeared long ago."

"An inventory was made when my father died. Everything. That was two years ago. But since then, she's correct. There are rooms we never venture into and the furnishings remain covered to protect them."

"I don't think it's been two years. Weeks or months I'd believe, but not years. Someone in the lab could tell us how long it takes dust to settle through fabric, or drift up along the edges, but I'm sure it happens." Agnes looked around the luxurious furnishings of the room they were seated in. "The protection is mainly from light, isn't it? You know some dust will gather. The furniture isn't sealed, it's simply hidden."

Vallotton set the list on the table between them. "Before this, were you still hoping I would turn up guilty?"

She ignored him. "Tonight changes things, or at least it might." She scanned the list of stolen objects. "They're all portable."

"Not just portable, small," Vallotton added. "Nothing larger than fifty centimeters in length. Easy to quickly put everything into a few duffel bags and off you go."

"You think this was the work of one night . . . or day?"

"You think differently?"

"I don't want to make an assumption and forget the alternatives. How easy would it be for someone to come in and leave with these things?"

"If you had asked me two days ago I would have reminded you we live in a fortress. My entire childhood was spent preoccupied by the safety and boredom of this place. We used to walk on the outer edge of the battlements for a thrill; of course they are nearly a meter wide so it's not exactly tightrope walking. Clearly my perception has changed. As you know, we don't have a security system, but there are limited points of entry and you can't come in through a window or the roof without some trouble. Besides that, you would be visible for miles. You can't tell with the power out, but we illuminate the lakeside façade at night, special request of the bureau of tourism. Made my father sick, but he did it anyway. Come over the roof or down the walls to the windows at night and half of France would notice you in silhouette."

"I'll assume you haven't stolen from yourself to collect the insurance, but what about the people who live here and work here?"

"You might say we are self-insured, but to your other point, someone we know stealing from us, I really don't think—"

"You didn't think anyone would be murdered here either. Strip away what you want to believe and tell me who might steal. Now is the time to admit that a dear relative is a kleptomaniac."

"That would be a relief," Vallotton said. "Discovering Aunt Antoinette has an Achilles' heel." He stood and walked around the room, occasionally touching something. Agnes was reminded that every table was filled with precious objects: a small Corot on a stand with postcards tilted in front, a sketch by Henri de Toulouse-Lautrec in a sterling silver frame. Things so valuable even she recognized their worth. She smiled at what she would have to describe to her boys when she saw them. Then George sprang to mind and tears welled.

Vallotton looked at her sharply. "Surely I should be more upset than you?"

She swallowed. "I know you don't want to think someone in the household stole from you, but we need to consider everyone. Starting with the staff."

"I would start with family and friends, easier for us to sell the pieces."

"Then family first."

"You think of everything here as mine, and I suppose technically you are correct, but we don't see it that way. I may be the steward, but the château and its furnishings are ours collectively. Since the death of my father, that means me, my brother, my aunt, and MC. If any one of us wanted something—particularly these small things—all they need to do is take it. We keep good records, so it would be nice to know that it was moved or sold, but no one would care."

"How is that possible? These objects are valuable. You have to care if someone took them."

Vallotton stopped and opened a drawer. Agnes stood to see what he indicated. "You have to be joking," she said. The drawer was fitted with felt to hold coins. Heavy antique coins. Vallotton lifted the covering and held one out to her. It was a dull rich gold.

"My father loved his coins and stamps. We played with them as boys, not carelessly, but with an interest. Handle the pieces, learn about them, enjoy them. That's why we collect, to give the things life. I would rather a piece be broken—or stolen—if that's the exchange for living amongst them."

She took a different coin and held it up to the candlelight. "A crass question, but how much is this worth?"

Vallotton leaned near to examine it. "Good selection. Priceless."

Agnes dropped the coin back into its tray. "A meaningless sentiment."

"No, a literal word. If there is one known example of something that cannot be re-created then how can you assess a value? If it is lost, then no price can bring it back. Like the loss of a person, each one unique. Priceless."

Agnes rubbed her forehead. "Ralph Mulholland, Madame Puguet, and the rest of the staff. They aren't your family. They might take something."

He laughed. "Have you spent any time with Josette Puguet? She is devoted to us. My father left her a legacy. Enough for her to retire to the South of France and hire her own housekeeper. But she wouldn't dream of leaving."

"And Mulholland?"

"That's a question for my aunt, but I doubt he would insult her with such behavior. Besides, his parents left him an orphan and he's old enough to have control of his inheritance. And I don't think any of the staff would steal from us. What would they do with the things? Hard to dispose of if you don't have a connection with an auction house and proof of ownership for whatever you are selling. The items on your list are no ordinary trinkets. Someone needs a connection to the black market. A professional."

"Then we're left with someone—a professional—walking in the front door and leaving undetected." Agnes didn't say that she could easily have pocketed a few valuables. She remembered what the marquise had said about Estanguet that first night. Strangers wandering her halls like a hotel. "Or someone who took the pieces for another reason. Sentiment maybe? No interest in selling, but they like the looks of them and want to own them?"

Vallotton frowned. "Possible. And it's also possible someone wandered in. We no longer have the large staff that my father kept. His butler retired when he died. The man kept an eagle eye on the comings and goings and there was more live-in help. My aunt manages things differently. Although to walk in brazenly would suggest someone who knew they could move about freely with little chance of detection, and they would have to know their way around or risk running into someone."

They sat in silence for a moment. Agnes looked again at the list. "How much do you think the things on this list are worth?"

"Hard to tell. Several pieces could go for a good sum to the right buyer or at auction. But fenced on the black market the amount would be lower. Maybe you're right and they were taken for how they looked, or sentimental reasons. It is a bit odd that the pieces are valuable but not excessively so."

"There is another answer: Felicity Cowell." At his sharp look Agnes hesitated and pulled at the hem of her skirt. "Hear me out. She is the victim no matter what else we learn, but she was knowledgeable. Her employers say this, you agree, and her fiancé says she had an incredible breadth of knowledge. A breadth that stretched beyond the paintings and sculpture you are considering selling. Add to this we now know she didn't come from money. What if she arrived and the lure of such disposable wealth tempted her? Maybe this explains why she didn't want to sleep at the château."

"A premeditated crime?"

"I wondered if she didn't stay here because the room she was shown was so isolated. Then when we met Thomason, I thought she wanted somewhere private so he could join her at night. He might have been embarrassed to tell us. Now I wonder if there was a different reason. She recognized the possibilities. Madame Puguet told me she gave Felicity a complete tour the day of her arrival. To orient her, I suppose."

"More likely to size her up. Josette is very proprietorial about us."

"Either way she had a chance straightaway to see that many rooms were unoccupied, and that might have planted the seed and caused her to change her mind and stay in the village. She could take a few things each day in a briefcase or purse."

"And hide them in her hotel room?"

"We will look into it but she wouldn't have kept them there. No one disputes that she was very clever. She would have stashed the objects somewhere else."

Vallotton wound a clock absently. "This is becoming a bit farfetched. She's unfamiliar with the village, with the entire area, yet comes up with a place to store valuables not in her hotel room or workplace. Someplace safe where she has access without a car. I'm not sure I could do that and I've lived here my entire life."

"Maybe it was premeditated. She could have an accomplice who took the goods."

"Unfortunately, this makes more sense."

"And they have an argument and she dies." They sat back and looked at each other. "It's a strong hypothesis," Agnes admitted reluctantly. "When Graves told me the woman he knew admitted to doing whatever it took to survive I assumed prostitution."

"Makes sense; you knew she was taking her clothes off for money."

"But maybe she also stole? Harry Thomason could be her accomplice and we only have his word for their relationship. She never mentioned a fiancé and didn't wear a ring."

"A classic return to the scene of the crime?" Vallotton half laughed. "Doubtful."

"Maybe this is how he is leaving the crime scene. How do

we know he spent last night at the Beau-Rivage? That's a long way from here. He could have met her yesterday afternoon and they had an argument. She dies and he panics. The theft was a perfect crime, years spent looking at valuables and not having them yourself. Needing just a bit more to buy a first flat as a married couple. Something goes wrong at the end. Maybe she gets cold feet. Something triggers an argument and he strikes in the heat of anger or he has planned it all along and lures her outside. He starts to leave but the storm catches him."

"He didn't spend the night outdoors," Vallotton said. "It was bitter and he'd be near dead dressed like he was. That was cold weather gear, but not suited for sustained low temperatures."

"Not outside but somewhere close. The garage? Pick a big old sedan and you'd be quite comfortable, he might even turn on a car for extra warmth. Or the Orangerie? Warm enough to save the plants. More ice falls and the next day he pretends he's just arrived."

"Another suspect, and this time you have a motive."

"Yes, and it isn't as satisfying as I thought it would be."

Nineteen

It took the butler three minutes to open the door but it felt like three hours.

"Could have waited until morning," Petit said, teeth still chattering as they followed the man deeper into the mansion. Agnes wasn't about to tell him that the theft was only an excuse to escape the château. It was claustrophobic with Carnet somewhere within the walls. He couldn't leave, though she was certain he wanted to, and she was worried that he would seek her out; try to talk about George and what had happened. Try to explain. She shuddered at the thought.

"You think he'll let us look around?" Petit whispered. Agnes wished she'd told him to find a bottle of champagne and take it to bed to celebrate fatherhood alone. She hadn't been thinking clearly when he offered to accompany her.

Vladimir Arsov received them like a potentate welcoming foreign ambassadors, dismissing any notion of theft with a negligent wave of one hand and offering wine and food with a second wave toward the butler. When they refused refreshments, he suggested a tour of the formal rooms of the mansion. Petit took the handles of the wheelchair from Nurse Brighton and Agnes lit the way with her flashlight, deciding that this qualified as a distraction.

The doors of the lakeside ground-floor rooms were aligned along a single axis, an enfilade that ran the length of the mansion providing a vista through each room. As they walked, Petit asked a hundred questions while Arsov pointed out details of interest, waving a bony finger in vague directions. Agnes wished the light was stronger. Much of the detail was obscured by the darkness: an amber screen belonging to the Romanovs, Marie Antoinette's writing desk, Ming vases. Occasionally a servant crossed their path, a pale face illuminated by a flashlight or candle, but mostly they walked alone through the vast gilded rooms.

"The marquise," Arsov said, motioning to the large portrait of a young woman next to an even larger portrait of a man draped in a lion skin.

"Beautiful," Agnes murmured, aiming her flashlight in the direction indicated. The painting was a duplicate of the one Marie-Chantal had shown her in the château. Here the frame was as impressive as the art. She estimated the weight of the frame and canvas and wondered how they held it to the wall. She could barely keep a lightweight photo from falling to the floor in her house.

They returned to the main salon to find several hundred candles had been lit and placed on every available surface. "I was tired of the dark," Arsov remarked. When they were seated near the fireplace he looked from Agnes to Petit. "You didn't come here on a cold night to tell me I may have been robbed."

"Yes, we did," Petit said.

"Young man, I have never said such stupid things. Oh, maybe when I was very young. And you"—Arsov waved toward Agnes—"if he is too eager, you are too worried. Maybe you will make a good team. It is possible." He shrugged and adjusted the tube leading to his oxygen tank, snorting in air.

"We're not a te—" Agnes stopped Petit with a glance.

"I know what you came here to say, Inspector," Arsov said, fingers gripping the armrests of his wheelchair like talons. "If there was a burglary at the château and also here, maybe you change your focus of investigation. Trust me. I have not been robbed since I was eighteen. You know that I have security that the Vallottons don't. We lock our doors."

A bottle of wine had been decanted. Arsov took a drink, sucking the ruby liquid in between his teeth and rolling it in his mouth.

"The Rothschilds know how to make wine," he said after swallowing. "I used to visit their vineyard every year and buy cases and cases. Oh, the pleasure of talking wine with Philippe de Rothschild. It was the culmination of a dream I didn't even know I had."

Agnes took a small sip. "This is good."

"Good? It is the nectar of the gods."

Flames in the fireplace crackled and Agnes let her mind drift across the frozen lawn. She was tired to the point that each individual muscle ached. The wine and Arsov's confidence relaxed her. First her muscles, then her mind. The strands of her thoughts untangled, making them easier to compartmentalize. Arsov was right, she hadn't needed to come tonight to tell him about the theft, but she was glad she had. The old man reached for his silver box of cigarettes, seeming content, for he smiled at some private thought. The room was silent for some time. Petit shifted uncomfortably.

"Tell me why you are here," Arsov said.

"About the burglary." Agnes jolted out of a near doze.

"You are as bad as the young man. We have discussed this and for the Vallottons it is nothing. You tell me what they are missing and I say it is like losing the coins from your pocket."

"I think Monsieur Vallotton is worried."

"He will always worry, that one. What of the marquise?" Arsov flicked a piece of tobacco from his lip.

"I didn't speak with her this evening. She spends most of her time alone, in her rooms."

Arsov sucked on his cigarette, exhaling deliberately. "Officer Petit, you are restless, and this disturbs me. Have Nurse Brighton resume our tour. There is much else to see."

Petit nearly objected, but the nurse emerged from the shadows and took him by the elbow, urging him into the next room. Agnes stood as if to follow but Arsov motioned her to a closer chair.

"You are looking for something—something beyond your murderer. You are at the end of your capacity."

She straightened, but he waved her down. "You remind me of my American friends. You think I speak of your capacity as an officer of the law. Of your work. I do not think of that, I think of you as a person. You came tonight here to escape."

To object was meaningless. The old man could *see*.

"Few have confronted their limits, but you have. I recognize this. You are unsure. Was it the worst life will give you or is there something more? I have known the same feeling. First, when my mother and sisters died. Then when my brothers died in the battle for Stalingrad. What I saw there made me flee the armies, barely human at the time in my filth and hunger and fatigue. Later I heard the stories of cannibalism and I could not cast judgment, even though it may have been my brother or friend who was eaten. We were at the end of salvation, pushed beyond human capacity."

Agnes took another drink of her wine. Arsov smoked and stared toward the black reflection in the windows overlooking the lake.

"I do not know your troubles, but I do know it is possible to survive this low point in your life. I know because I did. Because I still am. Surviving."

"I lost my husband," she said without thinking. "He killed himself." She had never volunteered this information before; had avoided it, leaving the news to official channels or gossip.

Arsov peered at her. "And you were witness." It was not a question. "Like her," he said softly. "You will need to be strong like her."

"Who?"

"I tell you why I open this wine tonight. This fine bottle. It was not for you who have no taste for it, it was for the past. This storm has put my mind in the past. The distant past." He looped the oxygen tube onto his head before shoving the entire apparatus off the side of his chair.

"France was very different from Russia. For one thing it was warmer. I was young and, despite what I had suffered, I was still a naïve peasant. I had the buoyancy of youth. I didn't think or plan. I didn't think that no one would trust me. Why would you trust someone you do not know when neighbors, even family, were turning one another in? I had never lived in a place where I knew absolutely no one. It shook me. I should have been even more worried, however, like your Officer Petit, youth is stupid and I was in a mood that could be called euphoric. That is what kept me alive. Compared to Russia the air felt free from death. Compared to Russia, the land was green and easy and I was happy to be there."

Agnes could picture the Mediterranean landscape of France. There were similarities to Switzerland: the hills verdant slopes leading to mountainous crags and isolated villages. She leaned back on the soft cushion and let his voice float through her.

"I made my way north, through Vichy toward occupied France, with no plan, only a need for action. I slept out of doors, stealing small bits of food from gardens and eating nuts from the forest. I needed to destroy the Germans. I needed revenge for the way my mother and sisters had died. I saw people on the road and we exchanged stiff greetings from a careful distance. I didn't know how to say: I want to help you rid yourselves of the Germans, are you loyal to France or do you support the invaders? This is not a question easily broached. I have told you that evil does not rest on a man's face when he walks a country lane on a Sunday afternoon."

Agnes poured herself another glass of wine, feeling slightly drunk. The candlelight flickered and for the first time in days she was warm. She registered the idea of George and Carnet deep in her mind but at the same time it seemed a distant problem. The image of war, and of a young Russian man wandering the French countryside, occupied her. War and the millions who died. How could her trouble compare when this man had lost so much more and at such a young age? She took another mouthful of wine and enjoyed the rawness on her tongue.

"My mission found me. I had been watching a farmhouse for a week. Men came and went in the middle of the night. They weren't in uniform and Germans wouldn't behave this way. I sat and waited and pondered. I was a boy who understood the life of a small place, and I tried to imagine what my family would do if a stranger approached them. I tried to decide what to say."

"Even a perfect accent wouldn't hide that you were a foreigner."

"You know this, but I didn't."

"I was born here, my French is as good as anyone's, but they know." Agnes waved her hand, encompassing the room. "They know I'm different, somehow. They know my parents weren't Swiss, so I'm not really Swiss. Not like they want me to be."

Arsov blew a series of perfect smoke rings. Agnes inhaled.

"I was concealed at the edge of a wood," he said. "This night I would approach. They had to be working against the Germans. I could help them."

Agnes felt her eyes close and shook her head to wake. The warmth, the wine, the smoke, and his voice were lulling her into a stupor. She picked up the trail of his words.

"Foolish idea. At the very moment I thought it was time to approach, I heard voices, then men running and the noise of a car. There were gunshots, *rat-a-tat-tat*. The noise was close enough that for a moment I thought I had been hit. Not five meters from me heavy cars careened around the final bend in the road

to the farmhouse and men clambered out; they were in uniform and I held my breath. Were they friends of the household,
these Germans? If so, then I had a near escape." He turned to
look directly at her. "What do you think, Inspector Lüthi?"

She nearly dropped her wineglass on the table. "I think the
men you were watching—the household—they weren't friends
of the Germans. I think they were in danger and you were
right to be frightened."

"You are correct, and if I had gone to the farmhouse earlier
I would have been rounded up and shot, for they died right
there. The Germans left the bodies and drove off." He shifted
the blanket covering his chest, gripping the trim in his thin
hands. "I was lying there, wishing I had a cigarette, when I
heard a sound. A scrape. Then a moan, very faint, but something human. I replayed the events in my mind. Had a man
fallen from one of the cars? The Germans would not leave any
of their kind behind. Then I remembered those first shots,
when they had fired into the night before they arrived. The
night sounds of the forest were loud and it took me some time
to pinpoint the human ones. I had not lived through Stalingrad
by luck alone and I was suspicious. I crept up to the man as if
he was a threat. When I neared, I saw that he was dressed as a
peasant and that he was bleeding badly. He looked at me and
raised his gun."

Agnes gasped and Arsov gave a hacking laugh.

"You are afraid for wrong reason. This man raised his gun
to his own head. Like I say, I have a great deal of experience,
and we Russians would have done the same to escape the war
camps of the Germans. I was healthy and strong and fast and
held his hand. As we struggled, I identified myself. I was

strong enough to take the gun and he had to listen. It was my clothing that convinced him. I would have been a terrible spy in those days. My shirt and pants and coat weren't French. The cut was close enough to pass at a distance in the country, but to a man whose life depended on detail I looked foreign. In those first moments that helped him believe my story. I helped him bind his wounds and together we made our way north. When I returned his gun, he invited me to join his band of the Resistance. I had arrived."

"Amazing luck," Agnes said.

"In the balance of my experiences this was nothing. The great fortune was in who he was. The modern generation, your Officer Petit, you want your heroes. Well, this is one. I was a boy with nothing to lose. I was an adventurer who went from experience to experience, always coming out alive and having learned something; this man could have chosen the path of diplomacy, or the regular army, or simply escaped the war entirely, but he had selected his path deliberately. I hated the war and what it did to my family and my country; this man was a one-man army determined to stop the Nazis. It is for him that I made use of what I had learned at Stalingrad. My skills with munitions. It is for him that I wired cars to explode and train engines to melt. We were together for over two years."

"You were fortunate to have found a friend," said Agnes.

"Friend?" Arsov scoffed. "This man had no friends. I was still very young. I turned eighteen when I arrived in France and that is young, even in war. He was twice my age."

"Then a mentor."

"You are not listening. You do not understand him or the

work we did. Many, perhaps most, who worked for the Resistance lived in the town they had grown up in, where their family had lived for generations. They formed networks of old friends and connections and literally resisted by stirring up minor annoyances, destroying the rail lines, helping downed airmen find aid. He operated at a different level. He made the connection between towns, between regions, and even back to England and the Allies. This man, who we called Citoyen, knew people across the country and how they could help. This is why he was prepared to shoot himself when I found him. He would never be taken prisoner because he knew too much. I was not local and had no connections or network of my own, yet he kept me with him, using my skills to teach others and to do specific jobs. He said it was because he didn't know how or where to integrate me into society. He had a way of speaking that wavered between teasing and seriousness, and said that if I were German or English or even American he might have trusted me to assimilate, but a Russian—he would roll his eyes when he said it—could never imitate a Frenchman in everyday life. I liked to think that he enjoyed my company, and that he was pleased to have someone with him." Arsov motioned for another cigarette. He closed his eyes. "I was proud that he had selected me. Meeting him changed my life."

A cart rattled into the room. The butler pushed it near, followed by the nurse and Petit. He pulled small plates from a drawer and arranged them on the low table. Agnes was hungry now. The twist in her gut had unclenched and she regretted skipping the evening meal.

"Tournedos stuffed with truffle, breast of ducking with pear flavored with honey, lobster bisque, and mousse with winter berries," the butler said, pointing at the dishes before picking up utensils to serve. Petit sat close to the nurse and in a low voice peppered her with questions about the care of a newborn infant. Arsov took one small bite of each dish, closing his eyes to savor the flavors. Agnes lifted a forkful of duck. Exquisite.

Arsov stirred. "Citoyen taught me skills to live, but she taught me how to survive."

"She?" Agnes asked.

Arsov ignored her. "Citoyen's home was not like the Vallottons' or anything in Switzerland. It was a masterpiece of craftsmanship, of carved stone. A Renaissance palace rising from the river, all towers and gables and fairy tale. And she was there. It all started there."

Agnes could picture the setting from vacations in the Loire Valley. She sampled the tournedos.

"It was Citoyen's home but it was also perfect for our needs. The château's foundations were built across the broad shallow river and the water flowed under it; under the high stone arches. Along the riverbank we could enter through a hidden door into a room where we could conceal those we were bringing to safety: refugees, Jews, downed Allied fliers, they all passed through. It was well situated, the road was not much used, and there were places to turn off into the woods. Plus the river was shallow and, if necessary, we could walk in its bed."

Petit and the nurse set their napkins aside and walked toward the row of doors, their low voices engaged in animated discussion. Agnes felt Petit's happiness roll off his shoulders like a wave. She was pleased that he could feel such joy.

"It was a night like any other when my life changed again,"

Arsov continued. "You cannot anticipate this. You understand? Good or bad you do not predict. For me it will always be the best day of my life. It was the day that would keep me alive for all of the rest until this very moment." He smiled to himself. "You do not believe me? But it is truth. The first time I saw Anne-Marie was the middle of the night. We had run out of supplies and I risked going into the château to talk to Madame, Citoyen's wife, and there she was. I was so entranced, I was rude. I barely spoke to her. She waited silently in the kitchen while I spoke with Madame and I almost left without a word to her, but at the last moment I remembered that I might die that night and would have never touched her hand."

"But you did?" Agnes remembered the start of love, when all things are possible. The rush of blood to the face, the trembling hands, the lightness of an unsettled stomach.

"Anne-Marie had emerged from the darkness of the château like a tigress, hiding a knife behind her as if that would protect Madame from me, a hardened fighter. A young boy, her brother Frédéric, cowered behind her. She didn't know who I was and I had never heard Madame laugh as she did at the sight of us eyeing each other. She introduced us very formally, and I did not know what to say. I know I scowled, frightening the boy. Then I said Madame had told me that her guest was a nuisance. Were those words to say to the one you would love more than your own life?" He tapped cigarette ash into a bowl, eyes fixed in the distance.

"When I left, I walked right up to her where she cowered in the corner with her knife, and brushed my lips on her hand. It was an electric shock."

Agnes wondered what it would have been like to fall in

love and stay together for the long decades of life. How long had Arsov lived with Anne-Marie? He was very old. The dark recesses of her mind squirmed and she remembered Carnet's confession. That was what he felt when meeting George. An electric shock. A feeling reciprocated. They had not ended happily.

"Although it was dangerous, now many times I found reasons to return to the château. Anne-Marie and her brother— he was much younger, maybe four years old—had taken refuge with Madame and Anne-Marie stayed even when Frédéric was sent deeper into the countryside for safety. I was young and vain and knew that she stayed for me. It was heart-wrenching, her tears and his cries the day he left. I was young and full of idealism. The boy would be safer, and she and I would not be separated. For me she was my heart, the one who would come to know all of my secrets. They knew my true name, what my life had been before. With her I began to dream of life again."

The flood wall had broken and, unbidden, her dreams, hers and George's, flowed. What had they dreamt of? Was their dream ever truly his dream?

"I had found someone to live for. We were the same, Anne-Marie and me. Madame was of another world, yet for the duration of these years she was our partner in a strange way. She guarded Citoyen's secrets carefully. We used the château and he hated that it put her in danger, but she insisted. Anne-Marie and Madame lived in that great place all alone and it was silent and forbidding and they were always waiting, not knowing when we would need their help; Madame afraid someone would realize her husband had not fled the country at the start of the war and use her to get to him. She lived a dangerous double life, always balancing a need to keep the villagers suspicious and aloof, mixing disdain and chilly acceptance of the Germans, and her real work for the Resistance."

"She is the one who showed you how to survive?"

Arsov started, as if dragged from a dream. "Yes, she showed me how to survive the worst that can happen." He motioned for a cigarette and Agnes held out the silver box. "I remember the beginning of the end so clearly. On this particular trip Citoyen and I were in the region to meet a man important to the war effort. He is dead now, this man, but I will call him Monsieur X for his role in the war remains a great secret. We were ambushed on our way to the rendezvous. Citoyen was injured, badly, bullets in his abdomen and his thigh, and we were separated. There was another hiding place that we occasionally used and I took Monsieur X there, then left to find Citoyen. Because of his injuries, I knew he would have to make his way to the château, for there we had medicine. He traveled slowly and, despite my detour, I arrived just after him. From the bank of the river I heard the shots, then saw Anne-Marie run screaming from the château into the arms of the Germans who were jumping from their automobiles. She was hysterical—that was not acting—screaming that an injured man had broken in and that Madame had shot him. She sobbed and fell on the ground and the German captain ordered a search for more partisans. I knew what had happened without the explanation that came later. Citoyen hadn't time to hide; the Germans were too close and he had shot himself, standing in the kitchen of his home in front of his wife rather than be taken or implicate her. Anne-Marie was sent out to sell the story to the Germans when they arrived only a few minutes later. Her hysteria was real and they believed that she was frightened of the man. They searched the château. I could see lights flickering through the normally darkened windows, but they were looking for others like Citoyen, men who had crept in under darkness to steal. They did not look, really search, for secret hideaways and those who were in the room under the bridge were not discovered."

"Didn't someone recognize Citoyen and realize he was Madame's husband?" Agnes asked. "Of course the Germans weren't locals. They wouldn't have known him."

"He should not have been recognizable by the local platoon, but Madame knew that the Germans were thorough. They document and we knew that." Arsov paused. "That is why there were two shots. The first, his, instant death. The second was Madame's into his face. She destroyed his features." His fingers curled until his hands were tight fists. "I have never met a woman like Madame before or since. I was at first deceived by her elegance and manner, but beneath this calm disinterest was a woman who was deeply interested and unafraid to act. She would never have let him die in vain."

Agnes was afraid to breathe, to do anything to disturb the quiet of the room. Some ways off Petit laughed loudly and, although the nurse shushed him, the spell was broken.

"Who are Citoyen and Madame?" asked Agnes. "Their real names."

"Have you ever had a secret, Inspector, a real life-and-death secret? I have had these secrets, secrets between two people, and the release does not necessarily come with death. Le Citoyen and Madame separately gave me a chance at life. He gave me France and she introduced me to my love. I will never forget this or stop serving them."

Agnes waited silently for a few minutes. Arsov was asleep. The nurse approached and nodded. He was old and needed his rest. They would go.

Twenty

Agnes jolted awake at the sound of footsteps. She was seated in the dark shadows of the château's library. Most of the candles had long since guttered and the fires were banked for the night.

"I couldn't sleep," she said, embarrassed when she saw the figure in front of her. "I wanted a book to read," she added inconsequently.

Marie-Chantal held her finger to her lips and motioned toward Mimi, who was nestled deep into the seat of a wing-backed chair. "She was put to bed hours ago and when I checked she'd gotten up again. She is incorrigible." She studied the sleeping figure. "It's almost a shame to wake her, though."

A shadow flickered across the fireplace and Estanguet emerged from the dark. He lifted his hand from the candle he was shielding and the glow extended across Mimi. "I can carry her for you," he said. Sleepily, Agnes decided that he could retake his title of Good Samaritan.

While he gathered the girl, Marie-Chantal looked at Agnes doubtfully. "If you were looking for a book there are better ones, to read I mean, in the blue sitting room. That's where we keep the ordinary books."

Agnes stretched and stood, wishing them goodnight. She had come here for a book. She must have fallen asleep the moment she sat in the deeply cushioned chair. Running her flashlight beam down the shelves she wondered if she should take one now. It wasn't clear how the volumes were organized. By language? Or subject? There was a section in Latin, another in Greek. She knew that she was too tired to read, yet now she wasn't sure she could fall asleep again. The sense of peace she had felt at Arsov's had vanished during the cold return to the château, and she was further unsettled by Petit's prattling happiness, his boundless joy at the newness of fatherhood.

She walked the length of the library, delaying the inevitable return to her room and the numbing loneliness that visited her most nights. She'd read about spouses committing suicide after their partners died and had thought that was only for the old and the weak. But this—this despair was rooted so firmly she finally understood how the mind closed options until there was only one. The numbness was as painful as the aching of her heart.

Her light flashed across a bronze bust and the craggy features reminded her of Arsov. She studied the man's deep-set eyes and wondered why Arsov's story hadn't filled her with the sense of longing and despair that Petit's mindless jabbering had. As she walked toward the doors she wondered if it was because even in Arsov's happiness there was a shadow of despair. Just as his despair was filled with the joy of living. She was sure he would have said it was his Russian soul, but there was something more. Some balance that she hadn't yet grasped. Perhaps the tragedy he had known during the war had colored his happiness as her own tragedy would certainly color her future. Was it about acknowledging the worst that could happen? Was that enough? Arsov and Madame had lived through the worst that a human could endure and woke the next day and the next. Was that all it took?

Inside her bedroom she closed the door and leaned against it. Unbidden, a sob erupted. She wept for herself and for George until she was wrung dry of any feeling. She felt the hours pass, half-awake and half-asleep. Somewhere in the distance a clock chimed and she counted the bells. It was late, or early, depending on one's perspective. Wiping her eyes, she looked around and relit a candle. She had difficulty focusing: Had she heard a noise or was she dreaming? What had she dreamt? A tapping sound? She couldn't remember, and that made her think she had heard something.

The curtains were closed against the cold and only a thin sliver of moonlight darted through the folds, but it was enough to see by. She sat up in bed with the blanket clutched to her throat, wishing she had checked the walls for hidden entrances. The cold air stimulated her senses and she leapt up, angry with herself. Swiftly she walked to the window and threw back the heavy curtains, scanning the lawn for signs of someone causing mischief, but the moonlit acres were empty. Trying to visualize what was above and below her room she heard a noise, a slow *thump, thump* right outside her door. She crossed the room in five long steps and flung the door open. The marquise stood in the middle of the corridor, her expression severe. She hesitated slightly when she saw Agnes.

"I wanted to check the fire in Mimi's room. There's always danger with a fire at night."

Agnes wanted to add, yes but it keeps you warm. There certainly wasn't a fire lit in her room.

"She has a *Kachelofen*."

Agnes nearly smiled. She had forgotten the marquise's ability to read minds. She had seen a few of the ceramic stoves over the years. Tall structures, wonderfully warm by all accounts. And not dangerous to leave lit unattended. She started to ask the marquise if she knew anything of Arsov's past when the other woman spoke.

"Does Mademoiselle Cowell have any siblings?"

"None that her fiancé knew of. Or Nick Graves."

"The American student," the marquise said, the tone in her voice causing Agnes to believe what Julien Vallotton said about the woman not meeting anyone new, ever. "This evening Julien told me that Mademoiselle Cowell had another name."

"Courtney Cowell, we believe," said Agnes.

The marquise stood as silent as a statue, so still she didn't appear to breathe. "Interesting to keep a surname but change the Christian name."

"Easier to get new paperwork, you can call yourself by almost any nickname you want and make it semi-official, but a surname is harder to fix."

"Unless you are adopted or married."

"She's a bit old for adoption, but she could have formally petitioned to change her name if she'd wanted. Maybe she had."

"Is Monsieur Estanguet still here? I do not know that name. He is not from the village, is he?"

"We're all still here, I'm afraid. Impossible for anyone to be evacuated. And Monsieur Estanguet is from Estavayer-le-Lac. He's got the farthest to go. Probably wishes he'd not bothered to help us down the hill now."

The marquise glanced toward Mimi's room.

"She's handling this well. Better than some adults might," Agnes said, thinking about Estanguet.

"The mind of a child is difficult to understand," said the marquise. "Their fears. Their concerns. Adults lie, conceal, pretend, but they do it for reasons that can be deduced through logic. Children have imaginations that cannot separate fantasy from reality. To them a fairy story is real. Just as real as a story about something that happened outside their door. They lose that as they mature, but for a time their mind is open. As adults we close ours."

"Perhaps that's why Mimi isn't traumatized."

"You are very concrete, whereas I was speaking in larger terms." Without another word the marquise walked silently toward the stairs.

A bit affronted, Agnes stepped back into her room. She settled in bed and listened. Nothing. She glanced at the walls and wondered if there was a concealed door, trying to summon the will to search. She closed her eyes, too tired to get up. Unbidden, an image crept into her consciousness: Carnet and George. She shuddered slightly then she laughed, a sound tinged with hysteria. Their relationship defied imagination, and if it weren't for the naked emotion she had seen on Carnet's face, she would have believed it more likely to be a story he concocted to alleviate her self-blame. The idea that George had fallen in love with Carnet, enough in love that he couldn't live without him, would have sounded ridiculous only a few hours earlier, but in the depths of the night, after exhausting herself of any other emotion, she knew that it was possible. And that she could accept it. Her husband had not died because of her, but because of himself. She took a deep breath. When did the sequence of events start or stop? Did it start with that fateful day at the shooting match? She had cajoled George into going, even though he had promised to take their youngest son fishing. Was this sequence of events punishment for her selfishness? What would have changed if he hadn't met Carnet? Would it have been merely another man on another day? And what if Carnet hadn't cared who was hurt by their actions: she and George would have divorced, their boys and his parents not understanding. Her parents-in-law were too much a part of the old customs of their village and way of life to have accepted homosexuality, even if the law did. Their instinct would have been to cut George from their lives, and then what of her, of the boys? Reminders. Still to blame, surely.

Rubbing her eyes to stop the tears, Agnes understood that at some deep level she was thankful that George had chosen to die because of what he couldn't have, and not because of what she couldn't give him. Now she could see the impossible situation he faced. He knew what his parents would think if they found out about Carnet, but to have found love and lost it was equally heart-wrenching. He must have felt that he was in a dark hole with no way out. The Lüthis would never have accepted that their son was gay. And he had already lost the man he loved. Imperceptibly a burden lifted from her heart. She rolled over, wrapping herself in the down cover, embracing the weight of sleep.

DAY THREE

Twenty-one

The sun was well over the horizon, although Agnes wouldn't have guessed it from the temperature outside. Squinting against the sun, she focused on keeping her footing. The lane between the château and the mansion was coated with a layer of thick ice partially covered by a more recent crust of snow. It required steady nerves and luck to traverse. To keep her mind off falling, she silently debated gloved hands in-pockets or out-of-pockets. Out-of-pockets won as more conducive to catching herself during a tumble.

Much of the focus was an effort to ignore André Petit sliding along beside her. Now that he was a father, he was a squirting fountain of questions on parenting. If parenting hadn't reminded her of George she wouldn't have minded. Today that was a topic she had to avoid. Anything that reminded her of George or her children would take her down the dark path of questions and regret. Therefore she tuned Petit out. Thankfully, he didn't seem to notice. Rhetorical questions, apparently.

They'd chosen to walk to Arsov's on the lane rather than cross the lawn. A plan better in theory than in practice since it was quickly apparent that ice coating a hard surface was slicker than ice on grass. Only forty-eight hours after the storm began and she wanted to banish winter forever.

"Do you think Monsieur Carnet is safe on his own?"

Petit's question jolted Agnes back to attention.

"Of course he is." She toned down her annoyance midsentence, replaying breakfast in her mind. Afraid that Carnet would seek her out, she had latched onto Petit as a natural buffer. Unfortunately she had told him that they shouldn't be alone because of the murderer. She should have told him he had to stick by her side so she could evaluate him before sending a recommendation to the cantonal police with his application. It was too late to change her story now.

"Carnet's experienced and capable," she said. "He'll be fine."

"I understand. I'll stay close to protect you."

Not what she had in mind, the image of the weak inspector. Perhaps not too late to change her story.

"What's that?" Petit halted, slamming his arm out across her chest. She stumbled and nearly fell, holding on to him for support. Only when she was steady did she hear the noise. Pounding? A man shouting?

"The ice house," they said together, veering off the drive toward the low building set halfway into the earth beneath them. Petit fell, sliding down the gentle slope to land in front of the façade. Agnes careened inelegantly into the side of the structure where it emerged from the hill, grasping the corner in a final attempt to stay upright. When her feet were firmly placed under her, she could hear the noise clearly.

"Someone's locked in," she said.

"The evidence," Petit said.

"The body," she echoed, moving forward. Petit blocked her.

"This could be the murderer."

"No, it's Ralph Mulholland." She didn't add: who could be the murderer. Mulholland wasn't an armed maniac. Or was he?

"Monsieur Mulholland," she called out over his screams.

Petit rapped a fist on the locked door a couple times. The shouting stopped.

"Monsieur Mulholland?" Agnes repeated loudly.

"About fucking time."

Definitely Mulholland. She wished she could leave him. Instead, she searched through her pockets for the key Doctor Blanchard had turned over to her. The lock opened easily and Mulholland fell out of the doorway, gasping like a fish on a hook. He was wrapped in a dozen old flour sacks topped by a large canvas tarp. He was shaking violently.

"Oh my god, I thought I was going to die in there," he said.

Petit briskly rubbed the other man's arms but Mulholland shoved him away. Agnes wondered if he'd been attacked. She pulled her flashlight from her coat pocket and stepped cautiously into the squat wood building, running the beam from corner to corner. No one there. However, the door leading to the actual ice storage room was open. She glanced inside. No one.

Once she was certain she was alone, she swung her light to the table. What she had observed peripherally now horrified her. The canvas covering Felicity Cowell's body was missing—claimed by Mulholland. The Mylar blanket was askew, and a startling white leg was exposed. Agnes hurried back to the entrance to give Mulholland a piece of her mind, stopping only when she took another look at him. Accusations would have to wait. He was in distress.

She grabbed the spare Mylar blanket from the floor and handed it to Petit to wrap around the other man. Hesitating, she handed over her borrowed hat as well.

"Fucking cold, nobody around. Dark as pitch." Mulholland turned his face to the sun as if there was warmth to be captured. "Trapped in there with . . . that." He waved his hand toward the room.

If he could speak he wasn't in immediate danger although he was clearly cold, tired, and angry. Agnes wanted answers now.

"You've disturbed our evidence, the body—"

"You think I was there on purpose? Oh my god, I think I've got frostbite. I can't feel my fingers. My nose."

His hands were scraped and shredded from pounding on the doorway. Beneath the flour sacks and Mylar blanket he was wearing a suit and tie. Dressed for dinner? His voice was hoarse, his eyes were hollow, and he looked exhausted.

"How did you get locked in there?" she asked.

Mulholland tightened the Mylar blanket around his chest, eyes closed and mouth open, taking long deep breaths. "Kitchen pantry. Door shut behind me and I knew no one would hear me shout. I had to keep going. Finally there was a slope up and I came out into this room. Pitch-dark. There wasn't anywhere else to go. This was the end. Knew I'd walked a long way but I'd lost track of direction and I could have been anywhere. Under the château, in the château. At Arsov's. Then I felt her. It was cold. I kept screaming but no one came. I knew you'd check on her eventually and had to stay if I wanted to be found."

"What door shut behind you?"

"Under the kitchen. The pantry."

"Inspector Lüthi!" Marie-Chantal Vallotton walked briskly across the lawn, dressed as if for a *Vogue* photo shoot: thigh-high outdoor boots, blond knee-length coat of curly lamb with matching hat. Enormous sunglasses. Agnes glanced down to her own rumpled clothes, wondering if she should remind everyone she'd been wearing the same skirt, blouse, and jacket for three days.

"Have you seen Mimi?" Marie-Chantal asked.

"Not this morning," Agnes said, eyeing the cuts on Mulholland's hands. They would need to be treated.

"She's missing."

Agnes turned toward Marie-Chantal. She felt sick. She'd told Petit they were in danger without really believing it.

"Hiding, at Arsov's most likely." Marie-Chantal looked at Mulholland. "Ralph, what are you wearing? You look ill. Is that why we didn't see you after dinner?"

"You've been here since last night?" Agnes asked.

He nodded, shivering, teeth chattering.

"André, get him inside," she said, motioning toward Petit. "He needs medical attention."

Petit gave her a deliberate look, his eyes nearly popping out of their sockets. "Maybe we should stick together. You could come back with me."

She tried to hide her exasperation. "Go. Madame Vallotton will walk with me to Monsieur Arsov's. And ask Doctor Blanchard to come out here and make sure everything is . . . in order. Return the key to him."

Petit glanced up and down Marie-Chantal and apparently

decided she wasn't a murderess. He took Mulholland's arm and steered him to the château.

Marie-Chantal removed her sunglasses and peered through the doorway into the ice house. "Ralph spent the night out here? He always seemed reckless, but he must be mad."

Agnes crossed to the inner room. There was a wide walkway leading around a pit and she peered down. She shone her light in, estimating it was five meters deep. At the bottom was a rotting wooden ladder lying on traces of straw. Clearly this was where the blocks of ice were stored before modern refrigeration. A quarter way around the pit a door led off the walkway. Carefully, she eased her way toward it, questioning the wisdom of allowing Petit to leave. She heard the click of heels behind her and drew a sharp breath. Then she exhaled calmly.

There wasn't any danger here.

"Mulholland came up through this tunnel," she said over her shoulder, glad her voice didn't shake. "One we didn't know about." She allowed a little anger to creep in.

The door was sturdy. She opened it and peered inside. A long hallway sloped downward, disappearing into inky darkness. She thought through the trajectory. A straight line would lead to the château. A point in Mulholland's favor. Still, someone would have to go down and inspect the length of it. But not now. And not alone.

The implications were serious. Was the ice house locked before they used it to store Felicity Cowell's body? If not, then it was a perfect point of access and escape for their killer. She stood back from the door, studying it. It was built of rough timber, as were the walls of the room. She swung the door closed. There was no visible handle or hinges and it bolted from the tunnel side, which made sense to keep intruders out. Surveying the wall she admitted that the door was only evident when open. Blanchard and Petit wouldn't have seen it when they checked the room before leaving the body.

"The tunnel runs to the kitchen," Marie-Chantal said, her voice echoing in the enclosed space.

Agnes shone her flashlight beam directly into the other woman's face. Marie-Chantal blocked the light with her hand and her diamond engagement ring reflected thousands of points of light across the walls. Agnes moved the beam.

"For staff to bring ice inside," Marie-Chantal continued. "The small door to the lawn that you've been using is new. They have been carving ice sculpture here for over a hundred years." She stopped. "You're not interested in that."

Agnes shook her head pointedly and motioned Marie-Chantal out. "Why didn't someone tell us about this way in?"

"I didn't know about it. But now that I see it, I know what it is. There's a similar pathway at my parents' place in France."

Agnes resisted a tart comment. In the outer room she hazarded a glance at Felicity Cowell, thankful only a leg was visible. She would leave re-covering the body to the doctor. He could determine if anything important had been disturbed. At a glance it looked like Mulholland had stumbled past the table, searching for a way out. He had grappled for something to warm himself, then likely stayed as far from the corpse as possible once he realized where he was. If he was telling the truth and was in the room by accident, then he'd spent a bad night. Cold, dark, and in the company of a dead body. If he'd come in on purpose to tamper with evidence and had gotten locked inside, then too bad.

Agnes closed the door behind them, making sure the lock caught.

"Mimi?" she asked, temporarily leaving the question of Mulholland aside.

"Hiding," Marie-Chantal said. "She's sweet, but likes to hide. Not always hiding exactly, but she likes the empty rooms, the attics, the cupboards. We have to search her out. One time I counted nineteen staircases while I was looking. Who knew? I was exhausted."

"You're sure she's only hiding? She hasn't—" Agnes didn't want to voice her fears.

"It's a constant battle. Not really a battle, we humor her. Every once in a while she stays hidden for a long time— overnight even—and it is annoying."

"Why are you out here looking for her?"

"She's at Monsieur Arsov's half the time. More than half actually, and with the cold she shouldn't have walked over alone. Leaving the château on her own has to be stopped. Nanny Egger usually keeps her in line, but since she's frozen in some-where else, it falls to me. Inconvenient that most of the staff had the day off when the ice arrived."

Agnes turned toward the mansion and Marie-Chantal fol-lowed her. "It is okay if I accompany you, isn't it? You seemed so serious, Inspector. I thought perhaps I was interfering in police business. Of course with Ralph trapped in that place . . ."

"I had a note from Monsieur Arsov this morning, asking me to pay him a visit. One of his servants brought it over. I suspect he wants to be updated."

"Not used to waiting," Marie-Chantal agreed, picking her way elegantly across the ice.

Agnes studied the other woman's technique but it looked impossible, although perhaps the high heels helped, spiking into the ice with each step.

"I shouldn't say that," Marie-Chantal continued. "Monsieur Arsov is lovely. Now my father, there's a man unused to waiting. With Monsieur Arsov there is something charming."

"Do you know him well?"

"No, I'm embarrassed to admit. I should visit more than I do. He comes to tea or dinner about once a month—Antoinette makes a big production occasionally—but there are other guests and we don't talk about personal matters. He's very private."

Agnes shot Marie-Chantal a glance. She would have described Arsov as gregarious, in the manner of an old man used to getting his way and controlling the conversation. He'd talked easily enough the day before.

"He told me a little about his time in the Second World War," she said.

"Really?" said Marie-Chantal. "He's never said a word about his past to me, or to anyone as far as I know. It's all business, business. Not as emphatically as others; that's what makes him charming. But still, business. The dollar versus the franc, the pound versus the yen. Boring, but there's something in how he talks. As if he really doesn't care about the money." She turned to Agnes. "That's it. He can out-think the others but I wonder if he isn't laughing at them." She smiled. "No matter, let's hope Mimi is driving him mad this morning. He gives her hot chocolate until she's sick. We pretend we don't know. You have to feel sorry for her, an orphan living with us in this big lonely place. I knew her parents and I suppose they knew what was best when they named Daniel's father her guardian in their will. Of course, they didn't think they'd die before him. Mimi needs some fun. She needs to be spoiled."

When they reached the mansion, Arsov's butler hadn't seen Mimi. However, he admitted that one of the other servants had attended the door for some time that morning. Marie-Chantal kept up a stream of chatter. "We wouldn't normally call this early but with Mimi vanished—"

"What's this about Mimi?" Arsov demanded as they crossed the threshold into the large salon. His wheelchair was pulled near a table laden with breakfast foods. Agnes smelled hot scones and eyed the silver coffeepot wishfully. Her own breakfast seemed hours ago.

"Madame Puguet is convinced Mimi was stolen from her bed last night," Marie-Chantal said, pulling off her gloves. "She disappeared, vanished, and no one knows what happened. I'm here to ask if she wandered—"

"Stop," Agnes said, moving swiftly past her.

Arsov was pale, his expression vacant, and he seemed to no longer hear them. They reached him together and Marie-Chantal knelt and patted his face lightly. Agnes looked over her shoulder for the butler but the man had disappeared.

"He didn't faint," she said, pushing Marie-Chantal away. She put her ear to the old man's chest. "He's breathing naturally, but his color's worsening. I think he's had a stroke." Arsov slipped forward, a small leather book tumbling from his lap. Agnes caught the book and shoved it into her pocket, supporting Arsov on her shoulder. He felt as frail as a baby bird. His breath on her neck was a faint trickle of air.

Marie-Chantal called out and within seconds Nurse Brighton arrived. One glance at the scene in front of her and she ran swiftly toward them, wings of her hat flapping. Agnes moved out of the way, telling herself that it was irrational to be surprised. Arsov was old and ill.

"We can get an air ambulance," she said. "They'll send one for an emergency. I think our radio is working reliably—"

The nurse stopped her with a wave of the hand, her attention focused on her patient. "No ambulance. He doesn't want to spend his last days in a hospital or hooked up to machines."

She yanked a tapestry bellpull multiple times and the butler and several male servants arrived at a run. Her orders were calm and professional and two of the men gently held Arsov upright in his wheelchair and propelled him toward his bedroom, leaving the other servants to wander off looking bewildered and upset. The nurse gave Agnes and Marie-Chantal a doubtful look, then swept from the room.

"This is my fault," Marie-Chantal cried, when she and Agnes were alone. "I should have thought about how it would sound just two days after—" She covered her face with her hands. "I can't even remember what I said, but it was bad, wasn't it? Madame Puguet doesn't think Mimi was stolen away. She's hiding, like always. I made it sound dramatic and now he's had a stroke and will die and it's all my fault."

Agnes tried to console her. Marie-Chantal pushed away. "I have to know. Antoinette will never forgive me." She headed from the room.

Agnes thought Marie-Chantal was too upset to charge into a sickroom. "Let me ask. I can make sure Nurse Brighton doesn't want to call an air ambulance."

Marie-Chantal glanced around the room. "Take the oxygen. They'll need that. Please take it and find out. I have to know if I killed him."

Agnes picked up the small container and, after straightening her skirt, walked the long enfilade along the façade, through open door after open door, for once immune to the grandeur of the spaces. At the opposite end of the mansion, nearest Château Vallotton, the wheelchair was parked in a doorway. Arsov's bedroom. The sight of the discarded blanket on the empty leather seat was heart-wrenching and she prepared herself for the worst. The door to the room was open, but the interior was mostly hidden by a large trifold tapestry screen. She took a step in and the nurse turned from her task, frowning. Reluctantly she waved Agnes forward.

"This is why I guard him so closely. He's more frail than he lets on."

Agnes handed the nurse the oxygen container then noticed another, larger one, in the corner. "Madame Vallotton is worried and wanted me to see—"

"Save your breath. It doesn't do any good to worry once something has happened." Nurse Brighton led Agnes around the screen into the room, giving a satisfied smile when she gawked. "The bed is supposed to have belonged to Napoleon, or maybe a Prussian king. I didn't pay much attention to what he told me about it."

The bed was narrow and not long, but it was impressive with a tall headboard enclosing three sides. High overhead a carved coronet was surmounted by white plumes and draped with purple velvet that extended to brackets on the headboard, resulting in a tentlike effect. Arsov lay covered by a blanket amidst the splendor. Overwhelmed by emotion, Agnes drew near. Thin and frail, his glasses had been removed and with them some of his dignity. He looked so old he resembled a helpless infant.

The size and scale of the room further diminished him. The space was filled with framed photographs and small art objects, and in the center three deep-cushioned chairs surrounded a small table. The room was clearly filled with carefully selected mementos and Agnes thought it should be called a memory chamber. She stood quietly while the nurse continued her examination: taking Arsov's pulse and making notations about other vital signs.

"Can you tell me your name?" the nurse asked, bending over the bed.

Agnes heard the mumbled response, but the words were too slurred and low to understand. The nurse placed her hands in her patient's and asked him to squeeze. Agnes watched closely for an indication of Arsov's health. He gripped the nurse's right hand, while his left one remained limp. Nurse Brighton made a few more notations, then added another blanket to the one already tucked in around him. When finished, she poured herself a glass of water from a carafe and drank it down. Agnes realized that the nurse was more upset than she let on.

"I was a nurse at a private clinic in London," Nurse Brighton said, studying Arsov. "Monsieur was in for treatment and we met and he liked me. I'd never thought to leave my job there, but he pays well and this was my chance to retire early with some earnings put aside." She took another long swallow of water.

"What would they do for him at the hospital?"

"There's no need for a hospital. He didn't have a stroke; he had a transient ischemic attack. He's having trouble seeing and speaking, similar to a stroke. And he's confused. But it will pass. We'll keep him warm and comfortable and he should recover."

She walked to the far side of the room and opened the heavy drapes all the way, letting daylight flood the space. "Anyway, it was part of my contract that I agree to attend him here regardless of his medical condition."

The bedroom occupied a corner of the mansion and in one direction the view to the lake was magnificent. In the other, the view gave onto the grove separating the property from the château.

"In the event of a decline in his health—like today—he insisted that he be treated here," Nurse Brighton said. "In this room, and that I keep the drapes open." She shrugged her shoulders as if the details weren't of interest, although she would follow the instructions faithfully.

They looked at the man in the bed. His skin was gray and his breathing shallow.

"He is weaker than he looks," she said. "All this talk of the past, then the idea that the girl is missing, it was too much for him. He's old and shouldn't be bothered."

Twenty-two

Agnes stood in the cold marble entrance hall of the mansion and reread the note in her hand. The handwriting was shaky and fatigue made the words blur even more. She rubbed the bridge of her nose and resisted the temptation to interrupt Arsov's butler, who was clearly upset. She wondered how much was worry that the old man's illness would mean lost jobs here, and how much was genuine concern.

"I'm sorry," she interrupted, "but I actually came to ask Monsieur Arsov about the message he sent me this morning."

"The note, yes." The butler regained his composure. Then he paled. "It was evidence? Now he can't speak and it will hurt your investigation and that poor woman's killer will go free."

"I'm not sure his message had anything to do with the investigation. Unless you know something about it?" He looked aghast at the suggestion.

She expressed her sympathy one more time and drew a distressed Marie-Chantal Vallotton out the front door. A few steps down the drive they stood in silence, Agnes reflecting on the old man's health.

"He can't be that ill," she said. "No matter what Nurse Brighton says, they would have called for a helicopter if he was in danger of dying. The lawn is broad enough for an air ambulance to land. She must know what she's doing."

Marie-Chantal pressed a hand to her face. "I think I need to be alone." She darted down the drive as quickly as she could in her heels.

Agnes watched her leave, also pleased to be alone for a moment. She reread the note Arsov had sent and tried to understand the meaning: *I have been too strict. Please come see me.*

She was flummoxed. Strict with who, with what? And what did this have to do with her? When the maid set the note by her plate at breakfast she had assumed it was related to the murder investigation; there was no other reason for Arsov to want to see her. Now she wasn't certain. What if he wasn't thinking clearly in the hours leading up to his collapse? "Too strict" sounded more like something to do with the little girl, Mimi. Perhaps the note wasn't even intended for her.

Slipping the note into her coat pocket, she turned toward the edge of the lake, foregoing the treacherous drive. Here the light snow provided traction and she walked more confidently, thinking about the problems facing them. Unfortunate as Arsov's condition was, he was not her worry. Felicity Cowell was.

Although there was no real evidence, Harry Thomason remained at the forefront of her list of suspects, with Nick Graves less and less likely as a murderer. Insensitive lout, perhaps, but murderer, no. Thomason's relationship to the victim combined with the theft made him a possible candidate, but there wasn't more to go on than suspicion. Had he and Felicity schemed to rob the Vallottons and then fought and he killed her? Or had he planned the murder all along to rid himself of an accomplice? Perhaps he had discovered she was a thief and struck in anger and surprise. There were various scenarios, and the only one she could rule out was accidental death. The knife didn't slip into Felicity Cowell. It was driven very purposefully into her back. Brutally, even. She wished for the hundredth time that they had the knife. Was it an object of value that triggered an argument? Or was it brought intentionally to kill her?

She walked all the way to the lake's edge before turning to study the château. The impact of the storm was enormous. The entire façade near the lake was sheeted with ice: glass, stone, and wood all sealed by nature. She smiled. To her boys these days would be a wonderful memory of afternoons outside in the winter weather. Her oldest would expect stories from her time away, convinced that being a police inspector was thrilling. None of them, sitting in their grandparents' house warmed by blazing fireplaces, would know about the stranded cars and cold homes. For this, she was grateful.

She shoved her hands in her pockets and turned to look out over the frozen gray lake. Broken and ice-encased trees edged the shore; otherwise it was impossible to tell precisely where the water ended. Dangerous. She studied the shoreline intently, as if it held the solution to all of her questions, trying to drown out memories with concentration. Home still meant George. Memories were Pandora's box.

She couldn't stop herself. George was too present in everything she did and thought and said. She needed to re-contextualize her memories. He wasn't solid, plodding George, but someone different—no longer devoted son, husband, and father. Instead, a different man, one she didn't know.

Unfortunately, forever, remembering George meant thinking of Carnet. He was a different kind of memory—flat—for the range of their shared experiences was thinner, despite seeing each other for hours every day at work. At the same time, the memory was crisp, and she steeled herself and then let the images slip across her mind's eye. She needed to look at him differently, an image without preconception. Stripping away her feelings, she conceded that although not handsome, he was charismatic. She swallowed bile. Desirable even.

Wind whipped across her face and stinging tears formed at the corners of her eyes. She closed them. Melancholy was an emotion she had grown familiar with; it was a comfort. The cold burned her cheeks and she pictured George, only this time he wasn't alone, he was standing next to Carnet at the shooting match, laughing and gesticulating widely as he explained something, a broad smile on his animated face. She tried to wallow in her darkening emotions, but a nudge of a smile tilted the corner of her mouth. How had she not seen it? She was a police inspector, for god's sake. Were her eyes clouded because it was another man? Or because it was too close to her? Pressing a gloved hand to her heart, she took a deep breath. Every day had been a struggle, every day she had examined herself and her failings and never had she blamed that terrible day on George. She took another deep breath, feeling that she was on a precipice. She looked out over the water. There was no blame; life would move on. At the edge of her mind there was another voice: Sybille's. Morning had redoubled her conviction that his parents could not know. Let someone else lead the way for equality and acceptance; her boys had been through enough to not suffer renewed pity from the villagers. She frowned, realizing it was unfair to George to hide his true self from his sons. She was wondering about telling them when they were older and able to understand and be accepting of the powerful struggle he had faced, when a shouted "good morning" made her turn.

Julien Vallotton appeared from behind a tangle of limbs, dressed for outdoor work and carrying a bundle of orange strips. Taking a deep breath to clear her mind, Agnes met him halfway across the lawn, but not before wondering again exactly where the shore began. Harry Thomason's story about walking around the point of the cliff was more believable now that she had seen the edge for herself. She sighed. She needed someone to be guilty. A day and a half had passed and they were no closer to a solution than when she arrived. For a moment she was glad Bardy was trapped at home without a telephone. He couldn't know of her failure.

"Marking trees," Vallotton said, when he was near enough to be heard. "More will have to come down than fell, too many limbs have been stripped away. Carnet came by earlier offering to help." He looked at Agnes closely. "He seemed distressed. Have you discovered something?"

"He's probably tired. Monsieur Arsov has had a stroke—or something like a stroke." *Transient ischemic attack* didn't roll off the tongue easily. "Nurse Brighton insists he will recover, and that he doesn't want to go to the hospital."

Vallotton looked toward the mansion, then studied his own residence. "Stubborn. Like my father. In his last months he knew it was the end and had his bed moved to the tower there."

Agnes followed his eye to the original tower nearest the lake. The top floor was marked by a series of tall narrow slits with slightly shorter openings running horizontally through them, creating stunted crosses. Openings for bows and arrows now in-filled with glass.

"He wanted to die in command of the surroundings, just as he'd lived." Vallotton turned to Agnes. "He'd lived through a century of change and probably thought willpower would get him through another one. He and Arsov are like-minded."

Ice crunched and they both turned. Petit arrived at a near run, slipping with every other step but managing to keep his balance. "Carnet sent me to find you, Inspector. I got the radio working regular and he talked to my chief. I wrote it out for you." He thrust a piece of paper into Agnes's hand. "And the doctor gave me this for you." He extracted an envelope from his pocket.

Agnes pulled the doctor's note from the envelope first. Skimming it, she wasn't surprised. She handed it to Vallotton.

"The family has to know," he said after reading. "Sad, really, better if they didn't."

Petit looked from one to the other. Agnes took the note and handed it to him. She watched the expression on his face when he read the words. Joy, surprise, then comprehension.

"This affects Thomason and his story," she said to Vallotton. "He certainly didn't mention it and I think he would have." She slipped her hand inside her coat and ran her thumb along the inside of her waistband, biting her lip. "Maybe she told him and he was angry and killed her."

"Because she was pregnant?" Vallotton asked.

Petit sucked in a shock of air.

Agnes gave Vallotton an exasperated look, turning to Petit. "Take Doctor Blanchard's note to Carnet if he hasn't seen it. He needs to know."

Petit walked off silently, reading the note again.

Vallotton waited until the other man was out of earshot. "You think Thomason might not be the father?"

They studied each other then turned to view the landscape.

"We shouldn't think the worst, not yet," Agnes said, scanning Carnet's note. "This will probably be terrible news for him."

"Either way," Vallotton added, which earned him another sharp look.

Winston ambled up, crossing the ice with an expression of fixed dignity, as if he was entirely comfortable with his paws slithering out from under him every fifth step. Agnes smiled. He had a long bone in his mouth, which reminded her that he usually managed to convey an attitude more human than canine. He drew near and Vallotton started to take and throw it when she gave a startled shout. She grabbed Winston's collar and wrenched the bone from between his teeth.

Vallotton arched an eyebrow. "Is that what I think—"

"Oh, yes," she said. "This is a human femur."

Twenty-three

It wasn't difficult to retrace Winston's path across the crust of new snow. It was perfect for retaining paw prints.

"Maybe he picked the bone up in the village," Agnes said.

"A human bone? What, from the butcher?" Julien Vallotton asked, dubiously.

"The local cemetery."

Passing a member of the household staff who was vigorously attacking a fallen tree with an ax, Agnes and Vallotton exchanged a look. "Maybe it's the result of an early morning accident," she said.

"I've seen that in a movie. Person killed, then boiled."

"I think I've seen that one, too." Agnes turned the bone over in her hands. "It's cracked and dirty. Clearly old and I think it's safe to say it's been exposed to the elements or in the earth for some time. Is there a cemetery in the village?"

"Yes, it's small but adequate since we don't have a big demand for plots here."

Meaning they didn't practice the recycling of gravesites common elsewhere in the region. Also meaning there was absolutely no reason a human bone would have been unearthed.

Closer to the château, the ground was more heavily trafficked. Agnes studied the mess of footprints and broken ice. Off to the side, Winston watched as they looked for evidence of his path. Then, with a bored sigh and wagging tail, he turned and trotted in the direction of the grove. Without comment, the humans followed and Agnes felt a shiver of apprehension as she neared the place where they had found Felicity Cowell two days ago.

"It's not hers," Vallotton mumbled.

Agnes gave him a scathing look as they rounded the final branches. She hadn't walked this deep into the grove since the previous morning and the change was shocking. More trees had fallen, including one enormous old chestnut. The trunk had been a few meters from the bench where they found the body; its branches forming part of the canopy that had protected the corpse from the worst of the storm. Now, the strength of the branches that had held against the weight of the ice was the reason for the tree's demise. Instead of the branches shearing off, leaving a bare trunk, the tree had been weighted with ice until the roots sheared and the entire structure fell. When that happened, an enormous clod of earth was excavated along with the roots. The soaring structure loomed three meters high, dangling roots and soil. The black hole of frozen ground where the earth had been ripped up stretched almost to the bench and it was there, very near the stone seat, that a skeleton lay at the bottom of the dirt pit. Only the bones of one foot and leg were clearly visible. The remainder was covered by a layer of earth and something that appeared man-made.

"A shroud," Vallotton said, before jumping into the hole. It was obvious this was a human skeleton. He held out his hand to her and Agnes clambered down, slightly unsettled to be nearly waist deep in the earth.

"There was a family cemetery on the property," Vallotton said, "from the earliest days, but I was always told it was at the other end, near the cliff, and all of the bodies were moved about three hundred years ago to the new churchyard in the village."

"I don't think these bones are that old," Agnes said. "That looks like remains of fabric." She pointed to strands extending from the frozen ground.

"The bones aren't new." Vallotton brushed dirt away with a gloved hand.

"No, they're not recently buried; however, I also don't think this was part of a cemetery. There would be some evidence of even a simple wood coffin. Nails or something." She hesitated to touch anything, although she wasn't sure if it was out of respect for the dead or in anticipation of the investigation that would have to occur. "We can hardly get assistance to the living right now, so I don't think anyone's going to come see about this for some time. We should cover the bones again."

"I'll get a tarp and hold it down with stones. Keep the animals away," Vallotton said.

Agnes glanced at Winston, who was studying her with equal interest. Suddenly she wanted to know more immediately. "Let's ask Doctor Blanchard to look first, maybe he can tell us something."

Taking the dog with them as a preventative measure, Agnes and Julien Vallotton entered the château.

"When was this door put in?" Agnes asked, remembering Marie-Chantal's comment that it was recent.

"I don't know. A hundred years ago? Hundred twenty-five?"

Agnes decided the family had a different idea of time than she did. They climbed the stairs to the main level where Winston shook himself and trotted off in search of other adventures. Agnes remembered a more important architectural question.

"I found Ralph Mulholland locked in the ice house this morning. He used an underground tunnel. A tunnel no one told us about."

Vallotton looked surprised.

"It led from the pantry?" she added. "Or someplace in the kitchen."

Julien Vallotton frowned, rubbing his forehead. Finally he nodded slowly. "I'd forgotten about it. Hasn't been used in my lifetime if it's really there." He led the way toward the kitchen, sending the startled cook into a flurry of confusion.

"It's here, monsieur. I've never seen the door open, but I know where it is," the cook said, wiping her hands on her apron and leading them to the secondary corridor. They went deeper into the service part of the château than Agnes had gone the day before. The corridor turned before dead-ending.

"When was the last time you were in the kitchen?" Agnes whispered to Vallotton.

"My aunt frowns on it."

"Never?" Agnes was aghast.

He grinned at her. "When I was a boy, I used to sneak down for treats."

"Greedy little beggars, you and Monsieur Daniel were," the cook called over her shoulder, making Agnes laugh. "Here's the door." She pointed into a small room. "The old cook told me it was all ramps out to the ice house, no stairs. Built that way to carry the ice sculptures. Must have been lovely. Well, I'm back at my work now."

The cook left and Agnes flicked on her flashlight. The storeroom had glass panes at the top of the interior wall, borrowing some light from the hall lamps. Not overly large, it was empty with a sturdy door set in the back wall. A canvas curtain was pushed into the corner. If Mulholland had pulled the curtain back then that was the reason neither Carnet nor Petit had noticed the door themselves. The door was slightly open, the heavy latch not fastened.

"This doesn't make sense," said Agnes. "Mulholland said he couldn't get back in."

"Hand me your light," Vallotton said, opening the door all the way.

"I'm going with you."

She followed Vallotton into the darkness. The corridor was lined with rough lumber. It was fairly wide and the stone floor sloped down gradually. There were slight grooves in the surface.

"Marks from a rolling table, I'd say. Must have used a hand cart to bring ice up." Vallotton ran his beam along the floor before moving it ahead of them. They'd gone ten or fifteen meters when they reached another door. Vallotton tried to open it, shoving with his shoulder. It didn't move.

"Look," Agnes said. There was a long iron bolt at both the top and bottom of the door. "The one on the bottom must have slipped down and closed."

Vallotton fiddled with it. "Moves easily enough. Bad luck on Mulholland's part. Door must have swung shut and the bolt was perfectly aligned. It dropped." He thumped the door. "It's too thick to hear through, plus we're well underground now. He was right, no one would have heard him here. Should we go on?"

"No, Petit and Carnet will walk the length in case—" she didn't complete the sentence.

"I understand. Evidence about Mademoiselle Cowell's death. I've told you I didn't do it and don't know who did. I certainly am not concealing knowledge of the tunnel to hide evidence."

Agnes hoped not. That would end her career as fast as it put him in custody. She led the way back to the kitchen.

"Why was Mulholland down here at all?" she wondered.

He arched a skeptical eyebrow. "Bored? Maybe he likes architecture and was curious?"

"You like architecture and barely remembered it, and this is your house. Besides, your cook never saw him. If he is interested in architecture I'd think he'd ask her to reveal the secrets of the kitchen, or ask you. You could give a tour. There's something not right about him."

"He's a bit of an odd one, but I know a lot of people who are far more off. He probably is bored. Maybe he was hungry in the night. Mysterious door looks interesting and he gives it a try."

"I think the mysterious door was concealed when he found it." Agnes thanked the cook as they retraced their steps through her domain. "Mulholland roaming around at night is, I suppose, no stranger than you working outside just now. I thought you had people to do that sort of thing for you."

"It is my property," Vallotton said. "Surely I don't look that feeble?"

"Everyone else seems to be safely inside."

"I think my brother is chomping at the bit. He'd be ice fishing or skating or something dangerous if he could walk properly. Mulholland is likely bored with the storm keeping him in. Even Mimi has outdone herself with this latest round of hide-and-seek. At least MC is entertained looking for her. Only my aunt's routine isn't changed by man or ice."

They entered a sitting room near the main hall and a maid took Agnes's coat and handed her a heavy sweater to ward off the indoor chill; it was easy to become accustomed to such thoughtfulness. Vallotton stepped into another room and reemerged minutes later having exchanged outdoor boots and sweater for his usual elegant attire. They held their hands out to the fireplace to warm them. Vallotton asked the maid if Harry Thomason was still in the breakfast room, while Agnes asked her to find Petit and the doctor.

When she heard Petit approach, Agnes motioned Vallotton to the breakfast room. They found Thomason sitting alone at the cleared table, looking worse than he had the day before after his long, cold walk. Agnes was tempted to believe that this was how grief looked, then she remembered why she was here and took a seat a few chairs down from him. He had to be treated as a possible suspect. Vallotton joined them, pouring himself a cup of coffee from a silver pot before choosing a chair opposite Thomason. Petit selected a chair against the wall where he could take notes unobtrusively.

"The others ate earlier," Thomason said, as if they were expecting a party.

"I've news," Agnes began. "About Felicity. The doctor is fairly certain she was killed by a knife or long blade. It punctured her heart and she—" She caught herself before completing the sentence with: had bled out into her chest cavity. "She died nearly instantly. Within a few minutes. Probably without time to understand what was happening." She hesitated. "It would have been painless."

The image of George flashed through her mind. Carnet appearing from nowhere, kneeling beside her on the street, saying it happened fast and that George hadn't felt anything. One minute he was alive and the next, nothing. Agnes swallowed. She had known it was not that simple. There was a moment in between. Did it matter that he had done this to himself? Had he regretted his decision in the seconds it took to fall from the Pont Bessières? Had he seen the end coming—the hard pavement at the center of the Rue Centrale—and at the last moment cried *No!*

"He assured me that she would have only felt a slap on her back. No pain. Death came rapidly." Agnes swallowed, remembering that long day. Shock, despair, and anger in quick succession, all overloading her emotions. Then Carnet driving her home and the final horror, in some ways worse than telling the boys, of telling George's parents. They understood the finality of death.

She focused on the task at hand, and on the information in

Carnet's note. He had spoken on the radio with the *gendarmerie*. They had communicated with their counterparts in London. Most of Nick Graves's revelations about Felicity Cowell were now confirmed.

"You won't be the one to tell her parents," she began. "The police in the United Kingdom sent an officer to them with the details and by the time you're back in London they will be through the first stage of grief, and you can be a comfort." She fought rising panic. She had not been a comfort to Sybille. She was a reminder.

Thomason looked up bleary-eyed. "Her parents aren't living. They died years ago and she lived with distant relatives until she was old enough to be on her own. They treated her well enough, but she felt she was a burden; they were much older and had their own lives and suddenly she was dumped on them. They'll be sorry, and may miss her but won't grieve. I am her family now."

Petit looked up sharply and Agnes willed him to silence. She felt Julien Vallotton's subtle reaction and she shifted uncomfortably, wanting to look at him but also unwilling to show Thomason her confusion. The message Carnet had relayed to her from the *gendarmerie* was simple but clear. The police in the United Kingdom had done their part and confirmed that Felicity Cowell was Courtney Cowell. Her parents were very much alive and well and they had shared details about their daughter's life, including her real name and education. Or lack thereof. Agnes was thankful Vallotton had the gift of silence and tried to remember what Thomason had said the day before. Something that made her think he understood that Felicity was trying to make it in a world much different than her background. Something was wrong, but she wanted him to show his hand first.

"You said she had a strong sense of being an outsider."

"We both do . . . did. My parents never come to London, they'd left the townhouse closed for years, and when I moved to the city you'd have thought I was going to a foreign war. We're strictly gentleman farmers and my father takes it seriously. My sisters ride to hounds and will marry other farmers and all will continue as it has forever. I think my going to work for Mother's cousin about caused a divorce. I offered not to be paid—'course that woke the old man up. He's no objection to money, and an auction house isn't 'trade.'" Thomason laughed bitterly. "We're practically on the border of Scotland and as isolated as we were a hundred years ago. That's what I meant by being an outsider. Felicity came to London after she was on her own. Her guardians took care of her and she had every advantage growing up—in terms of school and traveling and all the usual stuff. They don't like England, but felt an obligation to rear her there. She felt they resented her tying them down when she was young. It was the feeling of affection that she said she missed by not having her parents. That was important to her. That was what we had together." His voice cracked with emotion.

Agnes glanced at Vallotton, who raised an eyebrow but didn't speak. Over his shoulder Petit's eyes were wide with interest. Agnes hesitated to share more of what she knew. If Thomason didn't know Felicity's parents were alive, what else didn't he know? Using a different name was one thing. After all, many people dropped or added nicknames, but clearly he didn't know that her education was more of the street-smart variety than of a girl carefully chaperoned through museums by her cold but very proper relatives. Agnes marveled that Felicity had been able to pull it off. How had she created a new person, correct in all the details, out of her past? Agnes knew how hard it was to assimilate. She had been born in Switzerland yet didn't feel Swiss. There were too many deeply ingrained customs that weren't part of her parents' household. Somehow Felicity Cowell had broken into what was by all accounts one of the most insular clubs in the world: the British landed gentry.

"Had you set a date for the wedding?" she asked before Petit could blurt out what he knew. She wanted to learn from Thomason, not tell him what they knew. Not yet. Thomason gulped slightly and didn't reply. "Had she met your parents?" She hated herself for thinking that his parents might have suspected Felicity's background. He had painted their picture very effectively and she sensed they might suspect something was odd about their potential daughter-in-law.

"No, we were planning to, but they live so far north, and it was difficult."

Particularly if one of you has so much to hide. "If she wasn't close to her guardians, your mother would have filled that void, the interest in the details of the wedding. I imagine your family, steeped in so much tradition, would have wanted something special." She didn't know exactly what she was probing for, but she wanted to draw him out about their plans and his relationship to the dead woman. Had his parents suspected something even before they met her?

"We hadn't set one." Thomason fiddled with an empty coffee cup, his thumb looped through the handle. Agnes was afraid the delicate china might break, he was so tense. He took a few short, deep breaths and seemed near to tears, then he spoke in a burst. "Sod it. We weren't absolutely engaged. I asked her and she wanted time to decide. She was worried about my parents. I think I'd made them sound too cold, and told her too many stories about my sisters locked up there in the north, ready to marry men just like my father. Maybe she thought I would change once we were married. She knew that I would eventually inherit Harley House, but I promised that we could always live in London. I swore to her we would stay there, but maybe she was right, maybe I would have changed my mind and wanted to live on the estate once it was mine." He turned to Vallotton, his voice shaky. "You understand. Why can't it be both ways? Who wouldn't want to live there? I would go back and make my mark and I wouldn't have to be like my father. She and I could have put our own stamp on the place. But she was worried, she wanted time, and I gave her that time and now she's dead and I know we would have been married. I know she would have said yes."

Anguish aged his face and for a moment it appeared that he would lose control, but he placed the tips of his fingers on the edge of the dining table and focused on them. He took a deep breath and blinked several times then looked at Agnes. She hesitated and felt Vallotton shift in his chair. She knew what he wanted; they had to tell Thomason the rest, they couldn't justify keeping these details from him. Thomason had to be near thirty, but she could tell that he had lived a sheltered life and for him love was simple and sweet. This would be the final blow to his innocence. This would in some ways be worse than death. She drew a deep steadying breath.

"The local police in Britain have spoken with Felicity's parents and her sister." Agnes spoke forcefully, but was careful to keep her voice emotionless. "I'm sure the family will want to meet you once you return. They had been estranged from Courtney—that was her birth name—for years, at least a decade. They don't know anything about her life in London. The news of the promise of a happy future with you will be a double-edged sword. Sorrow for what is lost, tempered by the thought that their daughter had the chance at happiness." She doubted Courtney's family and the young man in front of her would find anything in common, but it wasn't for her to decide.

Thomason's face drained to white with shock. Petit shifted in his chair as if preparing to catch the other man if he collapsed. Agnes knew she had to ask Thomason about the baby.

"How . . . who . . ." Thomason's words were choked and barely audible. He shoved away from the table, his chair falling backward. Some deeply ingrained reflex made him apologize to Vallotton, then he abruptly fled the room. Vallotton glanced at Agnes, then walked after the young man.

Agnes watched Petit close his notebook carefully.

"I'll go check the tunnel now if you don't need me anymore," he said.

She nodded, wondering if he was getting too strong a lesson in the possible pitfalls of parenting. Alone she picked up a heavy silver knife and balanced it in her hand, thinking that her heart was so heavy she could understand how an end to suffering was appealing.

Twenty-four

"This trip gets more and more interesting," Doctor Blanchard said, pulling on his outdoor gear. "What you need is a forensic pathologist, but you also needed a regular pathologist so I'm as good at standing in for one as for the other. Actually, I'm a bit more interested in this problem. Occasionally people find bones in the woods or in a field in my village and they need to know the story. Usually animal bones." Coat, hat, and gloves in place, he decided he needed a last sip of hot coffee. Agnes didn't blame him and tried to stem her impatience. She was so tired she thought she would fall asleep if she sat down, but more coffee was out of the question. Her hands were nearly shaking with caffeine.

" 'Course then they have a question because there's only one or two specimens. I think anyone would recognize a whole cow if they found it." Blanchard snorted a laugh. "Bones are interesting when you start to compare the diets and other factors that—"

Before he could get too far into his lecture, Agnes asked what he proposed they do with their skeleton.

"Julien Vallotton told me he has a good camera so we start with that, and then I'll plan to remove the remains before they are overly exposed to the elements or an animal hauls them away. Who can help?"

Twenty minutes later, Agnes watched from an upper window of the château. Carnet and Doctor Blanchard walked to the damaged grove carrying a camera, small shovel, broom, and plastic tarp. She was thankful she was seeing Carnet again for the first time at a distance. She leaned closer to the window and something moved against her leg. Patting her coat pocket, she remembered the small book she had taken from Arsov when he collapsed. She pulled it out, noting the age and condition of the delicate leather cover, careful not to damage it. The front pages of the book were stuck together and she opened it near the middle. The pages were covered with handwriting. It wasn't Arsov's; that was clear. The old-fashioned script was a woman's. A young woman's or girl's, she amended, studying the careful rounded flourishes. She skimmed a few pages, excerpting only bits and pieces, when something made her stop. Dates. This was a diary. She was reading in February of an unknown year during the Second World War.

I've counted the days since my last period and there are too many days and I know that my health is poor. Madame already worries too much about me and there is nothing to be done. There is too little food, and I worry constantly. When I am in bed, alone in my room and cannot sleep, I think of her strength and try to emulate it, but I always fail when morning comes. The only thing that can distract me when my cough erupts is thinking of him.

Agnes smiled, remembering her own early crushes. This sounded like a young woman.

Today is six months since we met and I cannot speak to him or even write to tell him how I feel, how he has changed my life. I had hoped to find a way to send a letter, but Madame says it is too dangerous, even if we knew where to send it, and she is right, the last thing I can do is risk his life. I have decided that I will write to him here, and when we next meet I will give it to him.

Agnes leaned against the wall, unsteady. Young love. Full of promise. And agony. She turned the page and was surprised that it was in the form of a letter. A letter intended for Arsov. That was why Arsov had the diary. This was Anne-Marie's.

Mon Amour, One day when we are old and gray and sit along the Seine enjoying baguettes like we have not eaten now in many in year . . .

Agnes skimmed ahead.

. . . I will remember this war and think not of the bad days, but only that it brought us together. Isn't that enough? We will forget everything that happened to us, we will make our love cancel all the death, the death of our loved ones.

Thinking of Arsov, Agnes smiled. Their love had canceled all other tragedy.

You have my answer, we will marry and it cannot happen quickly enough. Come back to me and we will be united the moment you walk through the door. Then you will be mine forever. I miss you. Return to me dear heart.

She prepared to turn the page when Julien Vallotton appeared at her shoulder. She slipped the book back into her pocket. Vallotton looked out the window briefly.

"You recognized the name of Thomason's home," he said. "Once he calmed a little, I asked him about it. They inherited the property from his mother's family, Harley House, home of the Smythson-Markums."

"'My house,'" Agnes said, remembering the words penciled in Felicity's book beside the photograph of the tall gray house in the north of England.

"At least we know she was trying out the idea," he said, "and it confirms that she and Thomason had a relationship. Hadn't you wondered? You had proof of what Graves said—her name, her other life—but still wondered if Thomason was telling the truth about the two of them."

"He'd have to be a good actor."

"Not entirely. The relationship could have been in his mind only. Now I think there's enough to agree that she was thinking of his house as possibly hers."

"True. What else did Thomason say to you?"

"I barely asked about Harley House when he broke down again. I offered him a sedative and left him in his bedroom. It was cruel to ask more. I think he's not inventing his connection to her."

"You're right, I believe that he had asked her to marry him, but I still need to talk to him; we need to know what he knew about her pregnancy. He's not in the clear yet." She turned to face Vallotton. "We'll give Thomason a little time; until then, what about the missing items? I haven't forgotten about the theft."

"Maybe I'll care next week, but today, knowing a woman died violently I can't feel that it matters. They were simply things. I have many others."

Through the ice-frosted window Agnes watched Carnet and Blanchard glance from the site where they found Felicity Cowell to the newly uncovered grave only a few meters away. With so many trees destroyed, the area was now visible from the château's windows.

"I'm afraid I have to care today," she said. "Maybe Felicity thought Thomason expected her to have money of her own? He certainly thought she came from money. Who knows how far the lie had gone before she realized that Thomason was interested in her romantically. Maybe she introduced herself as having a trust fund, isn't that what you people usually have?"

Vallotton frowned as Blanchard knelt. "How old do you think the bones are, really?" he asked. "I realize they're not new, but ten years? Fifty? A hundred? That piece of fabric, or whatever it was, makes me think they're newer than I would like."

"Any missing relatives in the family tree?"

"You should also ask about friends of relatives, servants, who knows where this will lead. I have a bad feeling."

Suddenly, Agnes did as well.

Twenty-five

No one had a right to put her here. That was her first thought when she woke. Then she realized that her elephant, Elie, was not with her and she wanted to cry. She had dozens of hiding places in the château, most where she could see and hear what others were doing without being observed. There were cozy warm places and dusty uncomfortable places, but this was different. This place was cold and damp and scary. She hadn't seen a face when the hands covered her mouth and nose and she had tried every trick she could think of: struggling, kicking, then pretending to go limp. That's when the nasty person hit her. Or at least that's what she thought had happened. Now, lying on a cold damp floor, her head hurt and she wished above all things that Elie was with her.

Twenty-six

Ralph Mulholland walked through the room pulling on an outdoor coat.

"You recovered quickly," Agnes said. He was startled to see her and she took advantage of his hesitation and asked him to be seated, pointing out the fire in the hearth and saying that it was small but put out a surprising amount of heat.

"I'm surprised you are going back outside after your overnight ordeal. I thought you'd be sleeping."

"Madame Puguet gave me a concoction to drink, set me right up again."

"You should have seen the doctor. Let him look at your hands."

He scowled. "She knows what to do."

Agnes wondered at the household's distrust of outsiders. Surely an unknown doctor was better than a housekeeper if you have suffered a shock.

"But outside so soon?" she said. "Is that a good idea?"

"Probably have nightmares if I sleep. Besides, I'm not a child. I can do on a few hours' nap. I'm going to talk to Monsieur Arsov. A neighborly chat. That's allowed."

He was so defiant it gave her a second of pleasure to tell him that Arsov was not receiving callers, and for what reason. Her pleasure was short-lived as Mulholland's haughty expression swiftly altered to despair. He pulled a cigarette from a heavy gold case and lit it with shaking fingers. "It's not possible. The old man is a horse."

"His nurse says he'll recover; it's only been a few hours and he's resting comfortably." She took pity on him. "You should visit; they'll want him to know his friends came by."

"Friends?" Mulholland stood abruptly. "He wouldn't even—" He stopped midsentence. "You make me nervous."

"You mentioned that before and I asked your godmother." Agnes smiled briefly. "Petit was in uniform the night we arrived and I thought that was what bothered you." She held his gaze, something she had learned to do with her oldest son. "But your parents died in Africa, didn't they? And, according to the marquise, you were told by the headmaster while at school, so you have no painful association with the police. Maybe your nerves are caused by another incident, another reason?"

Silence stretched for a long minute.

"Hard for either of you to know what associations the mind makes, isn't it?" Mulholland said. "War refugees can't stand the slamming of a door, but the sound of a gun doesn't bother them. Maybe I do fear the sight of you. Maybe there is an unconscious association." He nibbled the edge of a fingernail. Agnes winced at the sight of his damaged hands. They were a reminder of his terror in the ice house. Before she could question him further, there were footsteps and the marquise entered the room followed by Julien Vallotton. Mulholland took advantage of the distraction and fled, leaving Agnes determined to talk to him again very soon.

The marquise was dressed in wool trousers and a jacket with a fox stole around her shoulders for added warmth. Despite the simplicity of the clothing, Agnes knew these were expensive garments. She also thought Vallotton looked slightly amused at his aunt's sudden interest in what was happening outside her suite of rooms. Agnes stood and greeted them both.

"Inspector Lüthi, we must apologize for embroiling you in another little mystery," the marquise said.

"All of the valuables should be traceable eventually," Agnes replied. "Once the power is on we will contact major auction houses."

The marquise stopped her. "You may keep my nephew informed; it is of no interest to me if these trifles are found. I was speaking of the discovery of bones in our garden. Have you learned anything about them? Julien had very little to say other than that you brought an expert"—she made it sound like a very bad word—"to inspect them."

"I don't know about an expert, however, Doctor Blanchard is knowledgeable and thinks they are a few decades old. He took photographs and—" Agnes stopped, realizing that the details might be disconcerting.

"I would like to meet this doctor—I believe I remember him as a small boy, his mother used to have a shop in the village—and see where the discovery was made." The marquise led the way down the long hall to the door. A maid trailed them, dispensing coats and scarves.

"I am familiar with the boundaries of the old cemetery," the marquise said. "We played there as children, imagining the forgotten dead would rise up and claim us." She allowed herself to be draped in a fur while Agnes shrugged on her coat.

"Julien," the marquise continued, "I think that was your father's way of terrorizing me. I always assumed—even hoped— that one day we would discover older remains on the property, predating our family's time here. As a girl I was quite enthralled with archaeology. Of course, I hoped it would convince my father to take me somewhere exotic. Persia was my dream, but I would have settled for Egypt. I ended up in France."

When they reached the stair to the outside door, Madame Puguet stepped from the kitchen and asked if anyone had seen Mimi. No one had seen her since she was put to bed the night before. Agnes sympathized. Her oldest son had spent a good part of one summer hiding. It was hard to make children understand why their parents were desperate with worry. She and George had spent more hours than she liked to recall searching across roads and creek beds, every time finding their son holed up safe and sound, often thrilled with the search he had watched from a high perch. Not knowing enough about the girl's favorite hiding places to be of help, she ignored the family discussion and studied the lawn. She knew these were not ancient bones, but the marquise would see that for herself quickly enough.

Once outside, it was clear that the temperature hadn't risen and the air, though still, was bitter. Agnes shivered despite her coat, but the marquise was well bundled in furs and Vallotton appeared oblivious. They made their way in near silence. Doctor Blanchard was standing at the edge of the gaping hole, stomping his feet to warm them. Agnes thought he was lucky he'd been in his outdoor farm clothes when he arrived at the château. Personally, she didn't think she'd ever be warm again, but perhaps that was only the feeling in her heart. At the last minute she saw Carnet standing waist deep in the hole. She stopped, unable to speak, barely able to see through a mist of emotion.

Through the haze she heard Blanchard chatter, clearly delighted that the marquise was interested in the skeleton. He launched into an explanation of his process. After photographing the area, he and Carnet had used a small broom to expose the parts of the skeleton that were on the surface. Tattered fragments of fabric covered a small portion of the remains. He had brushed the dirt from the hips, part of one arm, and the skull as well as a leg. The femur Winston had removed lay in place again. The rest of the bones were trapped in the frozen earth.

"This was not a proper grave," the marquise said when the doctor paused.

He agreed. "It's hard to know how deep the body was when buried. A grave may have been dug. I know the village well, but not this landscape. Does anyone remember details of the terrain before the tree fell and dislodged the ground?"

"Flat, or nearly, out from the bench to the tree," said Vallotton.

"There is a continuous low slope up to the château," Agnes said, rousing herself. Vallotton and the marquise studied the area as if it was new to them, and Agnes added, "The bones might have started out nearer the surface. A small mound might have blended with the slope, then add irregularities expected at the base of the tree and you might overlook it, thinking it was roots near the surface. Leaves pile up in a grove and the ground thickens over time." She felt Carnet studying her and avoided his eyes. Was it possible that two days ago she was so ashamed about her imagined role in George's death that she didn't want to see him? Where was his shame?

"For most of my life this grove was a dense wood," said the marquise. "It was planted when the mansion was built in the 1840s. That particular Madame Vallotton thought herself a very modern woman and she hated the sight of the château and intended for the wood to block the view. It did, growing up over time and thickening into a dense miniature forest. My brother was of the opposite mind-set. He liked the view between the two residences and thinned the trees about fifteen years ago. Before that it would have been possible for a shallow grave to go undetected."

"The grove would also have concealed someone digging a deeper one," added Agnes, imagining the hate or fear that would fuel the digging of a secret grave. For a second she allowed herself to bury Carnet. To cut him from their lives. To backtrack and stop the forward motion leading to disaster.

"When I was a boy, Daniel and I would pretend to hunt wild boar here," said Vallotton. "It was a dense wood then."

"With the damage to the area around the bones I can't fully evaluate the grave site," said the doctor, "but she appears to have been deliberately wrapped in a covering. I hesitate to qualify it as anything more than material or fabric and can't tell yet if it was a simple cloth or formed into a shroud or clothing or designed for some other use. I'll collect everything, taking photographs as I do, and we'll see if there are other clues as it is uncovered. The ground is frozen solid and I risk damaging anything we find if we dig more. Best to do some preliminary investigations—what's available at the surface—and preserve the rest of her until the temperature rises."

"Her?" asked the marquise.

The doctor said a few words about the condition of the bones and the evidence from the pelvis that they were those of a relatively young woman. The group stood in silence for a moment.

"Is it possible she fell asleep by the tree and died of cold or an injury or illness?" asked Vallotton.

Agnes shot him a look. Why did they always retreat to intellectual discussions and peaceful solutions? This woman had been buried in a lonely grave. Not even a grave. A hole in the ground. She didn't drift off into a peaceful sleep. When was it enough: murder, theft, a skeleton? When would one of the Vallottons show a crack in the façade of acceptance? She caught a glimpse of Carnet's expression and knew that he was thinking the same thing.

Doctor Blanchard was speaking. "Doubtful," he said. "Look at these fragments of fabric under her skull and how they appear to come up and over the face; and here in the arm area you have the same thing. She may have been wrapped head to foot in the material in a way that means she didn't do it herself. I postulate it must have been different from normal cloth and for that reason fragments still remain whereas the other clothing, if there was any, has long disintegrated. Possibly it was oilcloth. That might explain the resistance."

"How did she die?" the marquise asked, drawing closer. "You say that she was young."

"Age based on her teeth and her pelvic bones." Blanchard stepped into the hole and used the broom to clear a bit more earth from the skull. "Other evidence suggests that she is beyond adolescence, but the teeth look young. As we age, the teeth grind down. Hers are still rounded." He brushed the forehead of the skull gently, then cleared away some more loose dirt down her shoulder and arm.

"Of course, I've not done a complete study," he continued, "but there is no suggestion yet of the cause of death, although a bullet or knife could pierce an organ with no damage to the bone." He cleared more earth from the woman's other hand and looked closer. "There's a piece of jewelry." He loosened a finger bone and slid a ring off, rubbing it on his pant leg. "A signet ring."

The marquise stepped to the edge of the hole and took it from him. After a cursory glance, she handed it to back to the doctor. "It is not one of ours."

Blanchard turned it over for inspection. "Large enough to be a man's. Clearly not ancient. No date or engraving. I'll keep it with the bones. Turn them all in together."

The marquise sat down suddenly on the bench. She clutched her fur to her throat, and a flicker of concern crossed Vallotton's face. Agnes hoped the older woman wasn't having an attack of some sort. The memory of Arsov's weak body still bothered her and they were nearly the same age. She glanced toward Arsov's and the marquise followed her gaze.

"How is he?"

"Nurse Brighton is confident he'll recover."

"He shouldn't be told about this," the marquise said. "Very unsettling to hear of another corpse, no matter its age, when one is ill." She clutched her fur closer to her throat and slipped her hand through the crook of Vallotton's arm, standing. "Although it is fascinating what one can learn from bones. I suppose this is even more intriguing than the death of poor Mademoiselle Cowell."

Agnes felt the accusation.

They were only a few steps away when the marquise stopped. "Doctor Blanchard, when you are finished, please have the bones reinterred in the cemetery at Ville-sur-Lac. Once we are able to communicate, I will give instruction that the remains be buried in the Vallotton plot. She has been one of us for this long and we take care of our own."

Agnes started to follow the Vallottons indoors when movement caught her eye. She peered toward Arsov's, studying the nearest window. The old man's bedroom, she now knew. There was a figure behind the glass. The figure moved and she recognized the broad flaps of Nurse Brighton's cap. Hesitating, Agnes turned toward the mansion. It would be better to tell the nurse what they had discovered. She could keep the story from the sick man. Otherwise the servants were likely to gossip and who knows what tales would emerge.

With a feeling near to waking, Agnes had a revelation about the theft. Walking from the open grave, she reminded herself that she also needed to lay Felicity Cowell to rest.

Twenty-seven

The nurse swept an appraising look around the room. "He thinks he's stronger than he is, don't tire him."

Agnes took a step nearer Arsov's bed. "He can hear me?"

The nurse, never eager to praise, had informed her that this was what she had expected. Arsov had regained consciousness and would recover. To Agnes, the recovery seemed like a miracle. The old man was propped against pillows, his eyes half-opened.

"I've been dreaming," he said.

Agnes glanced out the large window to the open grave where they found the skeleton and was thankful he couldn't see the place from bed. Despite what the nurse said, Arsov looked weak. The marquise was right: he didn't need news of death. Even a death decades old.

"I came to return your book," she said, extracting the diary from her coat. "I didn't mean to take it . . ." She stopped herself before mentioning the reason she had accidentally slipped it into her pocket.

"Hers," he said, stretching out a hand. "Her story. I was dreaming of her."

Agnes held the book out but he motioned her away. "Read to me," he said.

She hesitated before taking a chair. These were very personal writings. With a glance at the old man she flipped the diary open and selected a page at random. "The date is April and this is what is written." She looked up to see if he was serious, then began:

"I have had so many moments of panic and terror and then, today, the worst happened."

She stopped. This was not a soothing story. However, there was a faint smile on Arsov's lips, so she continued.

"I stepped from the bakery with the boys holding my hands and a tall German ordered me to halt. You cannot imagine what those words sound like in his foul tongue. He did not even bother to speak French! I tried to squeeze the boys' hands reassuringly, but I felt my knees knock together and I was afraid I would blurt out either an obvious lie or refuse to answer a routine question."

Agnes turned the fragile page carefully.

"I don't remember what he asked or how I answered. All I could see were the trucks taking us away to the work camps."

Agnes drew in a sharp breath. Arsov tapped his hand impatiently on the bedcover. She continued reading.

"I would have failed my brother and Anthony and his parents and everyone I love. Then, just when I thought we were lost, a long black car pulled up and the door opened and She stepped out. She wore high heels and a long black skirt with a fur around her shoulders and I think she is the most elegant person I have ever seen."

Agnes smiled. This had to be Madame. Clearly Arsov and Anne-Marie shared an admiration for her. She kept reading.

"Her hat was at a perfect angle with a long feather running off the brim and everyone on the street stopped to watch. The stupid German didn't notice her coming behind him until she spoke. It was in his nasty Boche language; however, I can't describe it, when she spoke it almost sounded beautiful."

Arsov stretched his hand to the edge of his bed, running his fingers carefully as if searching for something. "Is she gone?" he murmured. "Dragon nurse? Is she gone?"

"I can get her." Agnes rose.

"No, in drawer. A cigarette."

"Oh, I don't think so."

"You think I worry about health at my age? Give me cigarette."

Agnes reached forward and opened the drawer, spying the hand-rolled cigarettes cradled in a silver box. She held one for him and lit it after removing his oxygen tube and shoving the tank away. She felt like a schoolgirl again: positive she would get in trouble with the headmistress but unable to stop herself. Hopefully Nurse Brighton would stay away until he finished. Hopefully he wouldn't die without the oxygen.

"Read," Arsov said, eyes closed and fingers clutched around the rolled white paper. A small hazy ring hovered above him. "Read. This is one of my favorite parts. I can hear her voice in the words. I can feel our paths coming together. This is what led her to me. The moment that changed my life."

Agnes opened the diary and found her place. "'*I still don't know what she said to le Boche,*'" she continued reading,

> "*but he gave me a look that should have pushed me into the curb, then he turned and walked away. I thought I would faint with fear, and she said to me in a low voice: Get in the car. And, like that, I knew we were saved. The boys were so overwhelmed they sat holding hands in the backseat, ogling the fine furnishings of the interior. Madame didn't speak or ask me any questions; it was as if she already knew the answers, and we drove to the apartment where I was living and she told me what to do in a few short sentences. She kept the boys in the car while I ran through our tiny rooms, collecting things to take with me.*"

Agnes held the place with her finger. "Madame is the woman you told me about. Who taught you to survive?"

"Read."

> "*It seems silly that I trusted her so quickly; after all, she spoke German and could have been in collusion with them. Wouldn't*

that be like a fairy tale: the beautiful woman who bewitches the children and takes them away? But that is not what happened. We had so few things of value, only a few changes of clothes and a toy or two, photographs. I ran back out to the big black car, threw our cases in the back and sat on the seat beside her while she drove us out of town. Not toward the château, which is where I now know Madame lives, but in the other direction, south toward the next village. The boys had fallen asleep, and Madame had me cover them with a blanket from head to toe.

"In the village I waited with them while she inquired at the market about eggs, but I think that was not all she was doing, for when she returned she told me that there was a family who would take the boys. They were in Vichy and it would be safer. She said that it was my decision. Can you imagine what I thought? She was so confident and had taken everything into her own hands and now she asked for my decision. I told her I couldn't let them go, and she smiled and called me a fool. I had misunderstood. She was asking if I wanted to go with them, or send them on and stay with her. I started to explain that they were not really my nephews, and that Anthony's parents were missing and I had been brought here to safety with my brother, in hopes that together we would escape whatever was coming. She laughed again, a short brittle laugh and said 'Who do you think arranged for you to come? You and your brother and the little Schawinskie who is now called Rieux?' and I nearly choked, for that was Anthony's true name and suddenly I felt that she had had her eye on us from a distance the entire time, and that was why *she had arrived at just the moment when we were to be discovered."*

The next pages were stuck together, damaged by water long ago. Agnes turned to the next legible section. "This is later," she said. "Maybe months later? I don't see a date.

"Last night after I was in bed I heard soft noises and I listened carefully, but couldn't hear more and so I crept quietly into the kitchen. I had not heard a car or even footsteps and les Boches always arrived with lots of noise, but I was curious and worried. Creeping out of the hall what did I find? A man! When I walked into the kitchen, he turned so fast I thought he was going to strike me. Madame stopped his arm and laughed at the expressions on our faces. I don't think I have ever heard her laugh before, and my heart rose. She introduced us very formally, and he scowled and said to her: I thought you said she wasn't a nuisance. And what did Madame say? That, far from a nuisance, I am a protector. She was right! I had concealed behind my back a long knife, its blade honed to a sharp edge. They talked in low voices, ignoring me, but I didn't want to go back to bed. I couldn't with him there. His face was smeared with something to make it black, but his teeth flashed white when he spoke, and once he smiled directly at me I didn't care what he said, I just wanted to hear him. He was not handsome like movie stars in the magazines, but there was something strong and confident in the way he carried himself, every move seemed controlled . . . like a panther outside a zoo. I think he has charisma."

Arsov snorted and Agnes shot him a look.

"He stayed for some time, and when he left he bowed low over Madame's hand and said something to her, then he walked right up to me and brushed his lips on my hand. I felt him like an electric shock, then he was gone, out the door and into the night. I stood looking at the door after it closed behind him until Madame laughed. I think I must have blushed to the roots of my hair, then I realized that this was the second time that night she had laughed and it felt good. Before I turned for my room she said to me: 'I think Marcel will return much sooner than usual now.'"

Agnes looked at Arsov. He had his eyes closed and motioned with his hand for her to continue. "She writes,

"It is now the middle of the night but I am unable to sleep. I have said his name into my pillow and I had to bring my book out of hiding—although I am crouched at the hiding place in case the Germans return—to write about this day. He has to return! He kissed my hand and I have to see him again. (I think I must wash my hair and see if Madame has a pair of combs I may borrow. This roll I usually wear is ugly!)"

"I remember those combs," Arsov whispered. "And her hair, when it was down on her shoulders, was the most beautiful sight in the world."

"You were called Marcel," Agnes said.

"Living in France, speaking my perfect French before I

took care to forget it, you did not expect me to be called Vladimir? Many people used false names for our work; I used a false name always. Except with Anne-Marie and her brother. They knew my true name. I liked Marcel; to me it rang of France. It made me belong. It is strange to hear these words of hers spoken. I have read them many times in these last years but when you read them . . . they come to life for me. When you speak I can hear her."

Footsteps sounded in the corridor and Agnes looked up as Petit entered. He gaped in every direction at the objects in the bedroom. She motioned for him to be quiet, rising to meet him at the door.

"The girl, Mimi, she's still not been found," he said.

Agnes glanced at Arsov but the old man's eyes were closed. She maneuvered Petit behind the screen nearer the door. "You checked the tunnel?"

"Carnet and I did. The entire length. Nothing. Monsieur Mulholland is probably the only person to walk that tunnel in a half century. In a few places his footsteps were clear enough in the dust."

The nurse entered and motioned for them to step out of the room. "Monsieur needs his rest. Come back later if you want to visit. He will be better by the hour."

Agnes followed Petit. "I think it is time we worried about Mimi."

They were halfway across the lawn before she remembered that she still had Arsov's book. There was time later to return it.

Twenty-eight

Everyone in the household had their assignment. Carnet and Madame Puguet were in charge and the château and the grounds had been divided into areas to search, vast dark areas. Cabinets were to be opened, shelves studied, no inch overlooked in their attempt to find Mimi's hiding place. This time she couldn't stay one step ahead of them even if she tried. They would flush her out. The sense of worry was pervasive, although they were still divided about the seriousness of her disappearance.

"Is this the longest she has been missing?" Agnes asked, wishing she'd not been lost in her own preoccupation earlier. They should have explored every nook and cranny hours ago, in broad daylight.

"No, she hid in a trunk in the attic for a day and a half one time. Nanny almost threatened to quit," said Madame Puguet. "Should have been fired."

Agnes glanced around the assembled group; their faces

were serious and, she admitted, tired. Three days of cold, and now it was already growing dark. The lack of electric light made their task more difficult.

Only Daniel Vallotton was staying behind. The marquise was teamed with Marie-Chantal. Carnet and Petit volunteered to check the outbuildings again. The household staff partnered amongst themselves and with Doctor Blanchard, Nick Graves, Ralph Mulholland, and Frédéric Estanguet. Julien Vallotton had offered to accompany Agnes.

The groups broke off and she followed Vallotton. They didn't speak until he stopped at the top of a stairway. "Our assignment," he said, motioning to the dark hall and handing her a flashlight. Slowly and methodically they started going room to room.

"Remember, she's tiny," Vallotton said, looking behind and under an enormous Spanish chest, before opening it to look inside. "She hid in my aunt's bed one time. Right there in plain sight under a thick blanket so it appeared wrinkled from a distance. I think sometimes she doesn't hide on purpose, but we pass by her and she likes the idea and stays until she's noticed. When her parents first died no one wanted to upset her. Bad habits caught hold."

Agnes turned toward the next room. "How many more?"

"Five on this level, upstairs is the same, then downstairs."

Agnes checked behind long drapes, then ran her light under the bed, marveling that even bedrooms no one occupied were kept in a state of perfect readiness. "Downstairs? We are downstairs."

"Euphemism for *dungeon*." She started and Vallotton laughed. "Mostly a wine cellar now."

They finished the last room on that floor and Vallotton pointed up then down with a questioning look.

"Down first," she said, thinking a dungeon sounded more appealing as a hiding place to a little girl. Besides, she was curious to see what it looked like.

Vallotton led her to a door that looked heavy but swung aside on well-oiled hinges. Agnes could imagine a little girl doing the same, then sneaking into the forbidden depths. She had a suspicion that her boys would mark a dungeon high on their list of places to visit and claim as a private getaway. She wasn't certain little girls felt the same; however, by all accounts Mimi was adventurous.

The stairs were steep and narrow. At the bottom of the flight was a wide arched opening through a thick stone wall. She paused as Vallotton changed the angle of his flashlight.

"It's not a real dungeon," Vallotton repeated. Before she could respond he flicked his light forward. The room was a marvel. Arches sprang from fat pillars and created domes that supported the enormous weight of the structure above. The floor was covered with fine white stones that Agnes knew would crunch pleasantly underfoot. But that wasn't what was most impressive.

"Wine cellar," she said matter-of-factly. She aimed her light alongside Vallotton's, peering into the depths of the space, making a rough calculation. There had to be thousands of wine bottles. Maybe ten thousand. Or more. The long central corridor fed between rows of wooden shelves stacked with bottles.

"It's been a wine cellar for two hundred years," Vallotton commented. He started down the central aisle and Agnes joined him, then she realized that this was a waste of time since the bottles were too closely packed to allow anyone to hide, even a small girl.

"If Mimi climbed on the shelving she would have caused an avalanche of glass and wine," she said. "Is there anywhere else she could hide down here?"

"There's an older section through a door at the end of the room."

"I'll start there." Agnes marched down the middle aisle, enjoying the crunch of gravel beneath her shoes. At the far end of the room a thick wood door was nestled in a recess. She pushed it aside with one shoulder and immediately felt the air change. Behind her might be a wine cellar but this was a dungeon. Even the air smelled of despair; thick with damp and earth. She stepped into the darkness and a second wall forced her to turn sharply to the right. She flicked the beam of her flashlight, orienting herself. The ceiling lowered until she felt she might touch it with her hands. The walls were not made from well-cut and aligned stone, as they were in the wine cellar. They were rough-hewn, darkened with age. Her arm brushed against a wall and came away moist. She stumbled over the uneven ground, thinking it was not merely constructed, but was actually carved out of the rock. The surface sloped down and she walked carefully, wishing she had a wider beam of light, only able to see directly in front of her feet. Everything else was pitch darkness.

She paused but heard nothing. She called out. Still nothing. She had the sense that there was another barrier ahead.

The corridor had transformed into a tunnel and it switched back and forth three times, each direction descending slightly farther into the cut rock, each turn cutting off more fresh air from the outer room. Finally she reached another door. This one was metal. Iron, she suspected, and for a moment she considered turning back. Surely a child wouldn't wander this far alone? Nothing about this path was charming or intriguing. It was frightening. She pushed the door, testing it. There was a loud screech of metal on metal but it swung open and Agnes continued. If Mimi came this far she might easily pass through the opening and become too frightened to find her way back out. All the more reason to look.

Agnes swept her light into the room. "Mimi?" she called. The beam glowed against the far wall. Here, the stone was more than moist, it was damp and dotted with moss. Iron rings were fixed at intervals, the metal glistening with orange rust. She shivered.

"Mimi?" she called out again, louder this time, running her light across the floor and over the walls, trying to ignore the piles of chains lumped at intervals. This was what her boys would imagine and it was more frightening than she wanted to admit. People came to sad and lonely ends down here.

She was nearly finished with her survey of the long room when she realized that the fourth wall wasn't original. It was more like what she remembered in the wine cellar. The stones were well cut and nearly smooth. More modern than their surroundings. She ran her light along the entire surface, looking for a door, or any indication of a passage or hiding place. Nothing. She wondered if they had considered extending the wine cellar into this chamber, started the work, then changed their minds.

It didn't matter. This was a dead end and there was no Mimi.

Quickly and carefully she retraced her steps. Vallotton met

her by the door. He shook his head. Desperate to be above-ground, Agnes turned toward the stairs and led the way up. On the main floor of the château they crossed to other stairs and started up another level. She felt calmer now. It was somewhat of a relief that the little girl hadn't been trapped in such a terrible place. She had slowed to catch her breath, hoping Vallotton wouldn't remark on what smoking did to lungs, when his light flickered. He tapped it hard. The light dimmed then doused.

"I'll get batteries. Wait here and I'll be right back," he said.

For a few moments Agnes waited in the semidarkness, then, unwilling to stand in one place in the cold, she continued up the flight of stairs and headed for the other end of the corridor, hoping to get a view out across the lake and rid herself of memories of the dungeon. She was nearly at the end when she saw a shadow. The figure moved. It was Ralph Mulholland. She lifted her flashlight to illuminate his face and he pulled a cigarette from his gold case and offered her one. Reluctantly she shook her head no.

"I thought you were helping with the search?" she asked.

"I needed a minute alone."

"You had enough strength to go for a walk after spending the night with a corpse and now you can't help find a little girl?"

"I needed a minute to think. To get my head straight. I haven't slept and my eyes hurt and we were looking everywhere. The maid, what's her name? Marie-José, she thinks Mimi was kidnapped and there will be a ransom note."

"I think we would have already had a ransom note if that was the case." Agnes didn't mention the real reason she had agreed Mimi must be hiding: it was impossible to leave the

Vallottons' grounds. The little girl had to be here. Hiding. Because of her sons she knew firsthand how easily children could hide if they wanted to, and how much they enjoyed knowing the adults were searching. It was possible the little girl hid because of the furor she created. Children her age didn't understand the repercussions and the real fears of adults.

Mulholland shuddered and Agnes didn't think it was because of the cold.

"Something may have gone wrong," he said. "Maybe they didn't mean to kill her and now that she's dead they won't send a note. Like in America with the Lindbergh baby. We'll never know what happened."

"You're letting your imagination run away. It's the atmosphere here and you're tired. Doctor Blanchard may have something to help you sleep."

"There are bad people in the world. They wouldn't hesitate to hurt a girl."

He pulled out a gold lighter and lit his cigarette. Agnes wanted to pluck it from his lips and inhale; she breathed in deeply, catching a little of the scent. His panic was palpable and she touched the note in her pocket. Remembering what had occurred to her earlier about his coat.

"You know Monsieur Arsov," she said.

He hesitated. "Of course, we all know him."

"But you were cultivating a special relationship. You were planning to visit him the day Felicity Cowell died. He's not very understanding, is he? He sent me a note this morning. It said he'd been too strict, not helpful enough."

Mulholland narrowed his eyes at her.

"I thought he meant too strict with Mimi," Agnes continued. "I wondered if he'd been uncharacteristically strict and that was what caused this hiding episode. But I don't think that was it at all." She looked carefully at the young man in front of her. His eyes were deeply shadowed and he didn't look well. "Why are you stealing from the Vallottons?"

Mulholland placed his hand to his chest. He stepped back, into the darkness away from her light, and she followed him. His shoulders collapsed forward and he appeared to shrink into himself, trembling. She waited and watched.

"They wouldn't wait." He stumbled over his words. "I think they meant to kill me and got Felicity Cowell instead; she was wearing my coat and the storm was so dense it could have been me." That was what Agnes remembered. His panic the night she arrived.

"And now Mimi is missing," he continued. "I never thought they would hurt someone else, I thought it was only me they would come after. I thought I was safe here."

She felt his fear, a wave of palpable emotion that spread like an airborne disease, and almost stepped away from him. "Who are they?"

"Russians, a Russian."

"Arsov? He threatened you?" She raised her light to see his face. This made no sense. Arsov was too old and feeble to threaten a strong young man. And there were no Russians on his staff.

Mulholland shook his head, all bravado finished. Even his voice changed. "No, not him. The ones I borrowed money from. They want it now. All of it."

Clarity came in a flood, as did memories of stories she had heard while working in financial crimes. Arsov's note also now made sense. He was wealthy enough to help and perhaps less judgmental than the Vallottons.

"Monsieur Arsov knew of your trouble?"

"I'd hinted. I'd hoped he would volunteer to help. Maybe ask if he could help. He knew what I needed." Mulholland wiped his brow. "The day she was killed I knew time was running out." The words tumbled from Mulholland's lips. "That's why I was outside. Trying to work up my nerve to see that—well, to see him. Then his butler turned me away. Said the old man didn't have time for me. For me! The godson of—" He stopped abruptly. "I was waiting, sitting in the summer pavilion, about to freeze to death, when I saw the policeman."

"I think Monsieur Arsov changed his mind. That's what he meant in his note. He had been too strict. When I told him about the thefts, he may have wondered if it was you. That's why he wanted to talk to me. He wanted to help you."

"That's brilliant. Too bloody late now."

She wondered if Mulholland was right and it was possible that someone looking for him had killed Felicity, mistaking her for the man. However, she'd had some experience with the Russian mafia—at the points where they intersected with financial crimes—and didn't think this was their style, at least not in Switzerland. They were more likely to either wait for Mulholland to leave the country and make a spectacle of his death, or lure him away and dump the body somewhere. They wanted to be able to bank in Switzerland and would keep a low profile in the country. At the same time, a clean kill with no grand gesture wasn't their style either.

"You don't know what it's been like." Mulholland placed a palm flat on his chest and pressed. "I swore that once this was over I would get a job in a bank, or an insurance company, working nine to five, or whatever people do. But it never ends." He closed his eyes and breathed through his mouth. "I'll never set foot on a yacht again, or ski, or borrow money."

Agnes watched him fumble for another cigarette and was moved to pity. He inhaled deeply, his hand no longer shaking.

"That day was one dismal failure after another. Every minute I was one step farther down the path of no return. Jesus, I was starting to have dreams that the police would arrest me. Bad dreams that ended with a cold dark jail cell. And that day, the day she was murdered, was the worst. That fucking, filthy recluse of a man could save me with a word as easily as most people ordered water in a restaurant, but wouldn't take the time to see me. Driving me to ruin. Fucking foreigner."

Agnes didn't point out that Mulholland was also a foreigner in Switzerland. The young man spat out a fleck of tobacco, weighing the hand-rolled cigarette on his palm. Agnes saw his eyes dart to his gold case. For a moment he weighed the case in his hand, delaying. She could sense him estimating.

"Who else could I ask?" he continued. "Someone who wasn't a fucking Slav. Someone who understood what a gentleman needed and how hard it was to have a name like mine. Fucking Norman conquerors and our legacy, name and land but no *money* and now not even land. Still, a chap has to order champagne— vintage stuff, not California sparkling wine, and send flowers and fly first class."

"Your parents didn't leave you with any funds?"

"The last time I saw my mother she was exclaiming about

their new airplane. That it was simply *darling*, perfect for *skimming* over the plains. Her new Leica camera in its custom leather case, film hanging in canisters from the woven strap. She thought she was a modern-day Isak Dinesen . . . without the trouble of having to actually live in the country for years or write anything more than a postcard.

"When the headmaster called me to chapel and told me they'd crashed their second day in Africa, he forgot to mention that I wouldn't be back after winter break; there was no money to pay the fees and my parents already owed the school for two years. Like the fucking Duke of Edinburgh: proud name, no money, and too many rich connections. Someone should have said sorry old boy but you're poor and you will have to go to the local comprehensive. Tough luck. Instead, I was sent to my new guardian's school, expensive but they paid the bills, vacationed on yachts, learned to ski, and maintained my birthright." He slumped. "At the least the Duke of Edinburgh had the sense to marry a rich woman."

"Am I interrupting?" Vallotton asked from the darkness.

Mulholland pressed back against the wall and Agnes thought he would run if he could only push past them. She explained quickly, sparing none of the details.

"How much?" Vallotton asked.

Mulholland mentioned a sum that made Agnes queasy, but Vallotton only looked thoughtful, then repeated his question. Mulholland's hands shook so hard he couldn't hold his cigarette to his lips. He tripled the figure, faltering as he spoke. Vallotton raised an eyebrow and looked satisfied this time.

"You had a long way to go raising the money at that rate."

"I only took a few things, enough to show them I intended to pay."

"Enough to pay the interest, maybe," Vallotton said. "How were you selling them?"

"I didn't have to, I would hand over whatever I had and they would credit me for it."

"Why didn't you say something to Daniel?"

"Not bloody likely he'd be able to help."

"But a good problem for him to tackle. Might have thought of something. At least he'd understand. My father bailed him out enough times. He'd be sympathetic."

"I was going to ask Arsov. That's where I was the day she was killed. I asked to see him, but he didn't have time for me and I waited around, thinking I'd catch him outside. I had to do it then, I had my nerve up and couldn't wait; they'd been threatening for weeks, well months, but lately they seemed serious." Mulholland sat and placed his head in his hands. "I thought it was me they were after, then I saw the police and found out she died, and saw the coat she was wearing. It was mine. With the storm I thought they were aiming for me and got her instead."

"Good lord, at least Daniel borrowed from a bank or friends." Vallotton stood silently for a moment. "I'll take care of it."

Mulholland looked like he would faint with relief. "They're desperate men. Russian mafia, and they've threatened to kill me."

"I'm sure that somewhere in our past we've dealt with worse." Vallotton nodded to Agnes. "We need to get back to the search."

For a split second Agnes saw fear in Mulholland's eyes. She thought of Mimi and her stomach clenched. They needed to find the girl. Thomason had arrived across the frozen ice, perhaps someone else had as well. For the first time she realized that kidnapping was a possibility.

Twenty-nine

They had finished their assigned area of the château and Julien Vallotton left to report to Madame Puguet. No Mimi. Agnes reconsidered the idea of someone crossing the ice and kidnapping her. Thomason making it across was unlikely enough. Two people doing it defied the odds. Besides, the Russian mafia didn't operate that way in Switzerland. Frustrated with waiting, she pulled the diary from her pocket. The corridor was dark but she had a flashlight and several oil lamps burned at intervals. It was enough to read by. It was strange to think of Arsov as young and in love. Moreover, it warmed her to know that he had found someone to love his entire life.

She flipped past where she had read earlier. The ink was faded and difficult to read, but she was more familiar with the young woman's handwriting now. She tilted the book toward the light.

Tonight is my last night here, and I'm filled with joy that I will see Marcel soon. He and Madame have decided that I must go to Switzerland and I know that I can be strong for the journey. I must be; although some days I feel more tired than I admit. Everyone does so much. They help so many people, while I am only a burden. Marcel will not let me say this, but I feel it. I have promised him that in Switzerland I will go into the mountains for good clean air to defeat this horrible sickness and thinking about our future gives me strength. When next I write I will be in another country, reunited with him, and all will be well! My only sadness is that I cannot take Frédéric. He is safe with his new family, and I would put everyone in danger by contacting him. Madame is right that he is too young to be worried by news of my illness. He was terrified when he left us, and hearing that I am ill would only frighten him again. He is surely happy with new brothers to play with. Safe and happy. When this war is over, he will join me and Marcel and we will start our new life together.

Agnes smiled. To think that the diary had survived a war. She was reminded of her mother's advice to keep a journal. Perhaps there was merit in the idea. On the other hand her mother wanted her to record her feelings in the wake of George's death. Those were days she didn't want to remember in detail.

Footsteps sounded at the far end of the corridor and she raced to finish reading the section.

She has given me a ring to show them when I arrive, as a token. It is a kind of code between us all and I must not lose it.

"Inspector, I need to talk to you."

The young maid, Marie-José, stepped near and Agnes slipped the diary in her pocket, annoyed by the interruption. "Did you find Mimi?" she asked.

"No. That's why I'm here."

Agnes tamped down the dull panic in her gut. The château was enormous. Dozens of people could hide if they wanted to. It was more and more likely that Mimi had gotten trapped or had fallen through the floor in some unused part of an attic. A thousand scenarios were possible, each preventing her from coming out of hiding. They needed daylight to search again.

"What will happen when you find out who killed the woman?" Marie-José asked, nervously twisting the strings of her apron.

Agnes shifted mental gears. "Jail, trial, and then prison if we've done our job right."

"I wouldn't have thought it of anyone I know."

"Not all killers are the same: some enjoy the act of the crime, others strike in the anger of the moment. Our job is to find justice for the victim." Agnes hesitated, remembering the first night, when Marie-José recounted Nick Graves leaving the library. The girl had the same nervousness about her to-night. "That's why we keep asking questions."

"I'm engaged," Marie-José said.

Agnes waited patiently.

"He's nice enough, and will inherit his father's butcher shop, which is a nice living. We're planning to stay with my parents for a bit, then move somewhere nearer Lausanne for a few years. I'd like to be nearer the city; more things to do."

"Was your fiancé here the afternoon Mademoiselle Cowell died?"

"No, he doesn't come down here." Marie-José looked horrified. "Madame Puguet is strict about visitors, says if we want visitors we should work in a tearoom. It's not Alfred at all, it's me."

Agnes didn't move, afraid to startle the girl. A confession? She desperately hoped for one, at the same time she desperately wanted it to not be this plain young girl.

"I shouldn't have thought it, what with Alfred loving me like he does, but he was so handsome and has this spirit about him and Alfred is so predictable." Marie-José pressed her palms to her eyes and stood that way for a minute, then she seemed to work through her agony. "With Mimi missing and everything so serious I need to tell you what I didn't before. I wanted him to notice me and he did, he asked my name and told me I looked nice and followed me down to the kitchen one day."

"Who?"

"Nick Graves. Him following me that time made me feel good. Special. When he left the room the other afternoon I made up a question to ask him."

"And saw him with Mademoiselle Cowell?" Agnes hardly dared breathe. This could be it. The evidence they needed.

"No, he'd left, like I told you. But I also left. I went to his room and he wasn't there. I took his cuff links, the ones he only wears at dinner, with his family crest, and when he came through the blue room next to the library I pretended I'd found them when cleaning. I asked if they were his. He knew I'd invented the story. I could see it in his eyes and I was ashamed and said I'd put them in his bedroom right away and did he want to come with me. I sort of meant to be sure I returned them, but he knew it was an invitation." She wrapped her arms around herself. "Like something out of a bad movie."

"Did you go to his room together?"

"No, he laughed at me. I threw the cuff links down on the carpet and ran out the other way. The blue room is connected to the east wing with a narrow corridor that we use when we do the cleaning, and I ran that way, thinking to have a few minutes alone, but I heard Madame Puguet and knew that if she saw me there I'd catch it. She knows our schedule, and I wasn't supposed to be anywhere near the east wing that time of day. I couldn't explain to her; I would have been so ashamed and she might have dismissed me. I went down the hall, and thought to go through the fur vault and down the other stairs. Not likely anyone would see me there. I grabbed the doorknob but it didn't turn and I thought it was stuck. I yanked it and realized it was locked. Then I heard a noise. Like something dropped or shattered."

"Like a hand mirror?"

"Could have been. That's when I panicked. Whoever was in the room had heard me tugging on a locked door where I shouldn't be, so I ran for the stairs and back to my work. I came to your room the other night to tell you, but you didn't come to the door, and the marquise came up the stairs. I had to leave."

Agnes wanted to tell the girl that she was the reason for a bad night's sleep, but she tempered her voice. "This all occurred the day Mademoiselle Cowell was murdered?"

"Yes, Madame, I mean Inspector. When you questioned Monsieur Graves I should have said that I left him by the library in the blue room and that he couldn't have gotten to the fur vault before me. I suppose I wanted him to be in a bit of trouble for how he treated me. I don't know if there was more than one person in the room or if it was even Mademoiselle Cowell, but it wasn't me, or Monsieur Graves." She paused and added grudgingly, "Or Madame Puguet."

She started and Agnes turned to see Vallotton approach.

"I'll go now," Marie-José said.

"Thank you," Agnes said, "and I will want Officer Petit to speak with you. He'll get a signed statement."

Marie-José nodded to Julien Vallotton and fled down the hall. Agnes hoped Vallotton brought good news. It didn't look like it from his expression.

"They are checking the outbuildings again," he said.

"I don't believe Mimi could have left the château," Agnes said.

"That's what Carnet said. That there aren't any footprints he and Petit can't explain. None made by a small girl. Mimi would have had to literally walk in someone's footprints without leaving an impression and either go up the hill—which is impossible without the right footgear, and even then it is rough going—or to Arsov's."

"Did someone check there again?" Agnes asked.

"Yes, when they checked the outbuildings the first time. And at Arsov's there aren't hidden rooms and abandoned dungeons. They would have found her. Besides, they keep the doors locked. She couldn't have entered without being noticed." Vallotton moved to stare out the window onto the lake. "Maybe there are Russian kidnappers."

"Unlikely, although I think you should let Mulholland sweat it out for a few more hours."

"He'll sweat regardless. He's lucky to be alive; although they probably thought he was likely to find a way to pay, and they want their money."

"You'll give it to them?"

"It's theirs. He wasn't being blackmailed. They made a loan and gave him terms. He owed them."

"That's a lot of money."

"What's a human life worth?"

Agnes drew in a breath.

"He's a boy—" Vallotton started.

"He's nearly thirty."

"Age doesn't make a man. It doesn't matter. He's my aunt's godson, I have to keep him safe, for her."

"From thugs."

Vallotton grinned. "I'll talk to Daniel and see what he can come up with. He'll probably think of a way to pay back the money and give the impression that they've been serviced by the devil. Be good for him. Give him something to think about and speed up his recovery."

"It must be nice to have enough money to buy your way out of trouble."

Vallotton looked at her. There was a strange calm in his eyes and she regretted her words. "I mean most people wouldn't be able to extricate themselves from the mess Mulholland has created."

"I would think you of all people would understand that money can't solve all problems."

A tsunami of thought swept through her and she wondered how he knew about George, her boys, and her mother-in-law.

These were her troubles, and all the money in the world wouldn't have made it right. A strange expression flitted across his face, she thought it was comprehension, then sorrow. Swiftly it was gone and she doubted herself.

Men's voices reverberated against the halls, breaking the solitude. Shouts. Bodies hitting furniture.

"Your lies. You fu—"

"Uh-oh," Agnes said, moving swiftly toward the voices. Vallotton followed close on her heels. They recognized the voices. Thomason and Graves. Fiancé and former lover.

Thomason had Graves in a headlock, momentarily startling Agnes, who assumed the stocky American would be a match for the slimmer Brit. She wedged herself between them but they either didn't notice her or didn't care.

"Bastard. Lying . . ." Thomason's words ended in a grunt as Graves slammed him into Agnes and both of them into the wall.

She tried to make herself heard above their shouts, elbowing Thomason to move aside. The men were too locked in combat to hear, speak, or see.

"This will stop." Julien Vallotton's words were low and cut like a knife through the air. Thomason and Graves froze, released their holds, and stepped away from each other. No longer trapped, Agnes sagged against the wall, breathing heavily. Vallotton stood a few feet away, his posture, tone, and gaze conveying the kind of disdain that made regiments cower. Agnes struggled to catch her breath, wondering if there was a training course for this kind of command. When she regained her composure, she looked at Vallotton again and decided it took about a thousand years of absolute certitude.

Vallotton took Thomason by the elbow and guided him down the hall. Agnes held out a hand to stop Graves from walking away.

"Time to tell the truth," she said. "What happened the day Felicity Cowell died?"

"I didn't kill her."

"No, but you haven't told us everything. Now is the time."

Graves massaged his knuckles as if he'd hurt them in his brawl with Thomason.

"You confronted her, didn't you?" Agnes said.

"No." He plunged his hands in his pockets. "Yes. But she was alive when I left her."

"Why didn't you tell us this before?"

"And admit that I was the last person to see her alive?"

"The last person before her killer."

"That's too close for comfort."

Agnes took a step back, stifling a sigh. He was just a big kid. Tall and muscular, but still a kid at heart. "Marie-José was in the library cleaning and you left." She held out a hand to stop him from speaking. "She doesn't know where you went but when you returned she met you in the blue sitting room. The two of you spoke, and you walked away. Toward the library. She was upset and went in the other direction. Toward the fur vault where she heard movement. Mademoiselle Cowell was alive when you returned to the library. Marie-José is your alibi for the time of Felicity Cowell's death."

Graves relaxed perceptibly.

"I want to hear your version of what happened when you saw her last."

Graves removed his hands from his pockets like a school-boy preparing to recite a lesson. "I'd had enough of her ignoring me. Like I wasn't good enough for her. Me, not good enough. I was telling the truth about the ice hitting the library windows and driving me nuts. I had to get out of there, but it was storming and I didn't want to go outside. I didn't go after her on purpose but I wandered around a little, into rooms I normally don't go into. Closed-up rooms, just curious. There she was, trying on dresses. Wearing a fancy old-fashioned gown. Acting like she was the lady of the manor."

"You spoke?"

"Hell, yes. I told her she was a deceitful tramp and would never fit in here. I could tell that's what she was thinking." His lips tightened into a grim line. "I said things that weren't true. She would have fit in. She was like water on fire, a smooth perfect surface that made everything else fade by comparison. But I was angry. The way she treated me. Ignoring me. I told her I was going to tell them all. I was going to tell her nasty secret."

Agnes knew there was an array of secrets to choose from: Felicity's real name, her lack of education. Was the pregnancy a secret? "Tell me everything you remember about the room."

"There were a lot of boxes. Couple of chairs—"

"No. What was she wearing? Were there other clothes around?"

"She was wearing some sort of evening dress. Stones, probably diamonds, on it. Sounds like what you found her in." He ran a hand through his hair. "Look, I was worked up. Angry. Her own clothes were draped on the back of a chair and I may have thrown them at her. That's all I remember. Then she yelled at me to leave. I'd never seen her like that before. Even in London, when she told me everything, her anger was cold. This time was different." He shrugged. "I didn't care. I'd had my say. She slammed the door behind me and locked it. That was the last time I saw her. I headed downstairs."

Agnes imagined those minutes when Felicity Cowell was interrupted while trying on the coronation gown. Likely she was thinking about Thomason and his proposal, wondering if she would fit in with his family. Already worried about her past. Then Graves threatens to tell the Vallottons. He throws her clothes to the ground where they land halfway concealed under the table. Felicity is panicked now. Angry, she tells him to leave. When alone she replays his threat in her mind and hurls the mirror to the floor, beyond caring what she breaks. When Marie-José turns the doorknob Felicity's state of mind is precarious. She doesn't know who it is: Graves returned? A member of the family? Even the marquise. It doesn't matter. She can't risk being seen in the dress and the family and servants have the door key. Before anyone can enter she runs from the room, down the small spiral stairs. Reaching the lower corridor, she vomits.

Agnes remembered her own pregnancies. How nausea would come on suddenly, then pass as quickly. Felicity was already distressed, perhaps questioning her entire future. Pregnant and unsure about marrying Thomason—feeling trapped—and her secret past about to be exposed. Her options were closing in. Agnes recalled where other members of the household were at that time. The housekeeper had joined Marie-Chantal in the corridor off the entrance hall to discuss Julien Vallotton's arrival. The cook had sought them out to finalize the menu. Agnes visualized their paths. Dressed as she was, Felicity could not have risked a member of the household seeing her. She was trapped. Footsteps nearing from two directions. The only way she could avoid being caught was to descend the steps by the kitchen. When the voices drew nearer she would have worried they might descend the stairs and find her, and . . . she what? Agnes asked herself. Had she used the coat and boots to stay warm while waiting for everyone to leave, then panicked and gone outside? What went through her mind in those final moments?

André Petit arrived at a trot, startling Agnes from her reverie. "Thought I heard shouts," he said, looking from Agnes to Graves, grasping the atmosphere but not the reason.

"Officer Petit," Agnes said. "Please take Monsieur Graves to his room and ask him to repeat to you what he told me. The more detail the better. Then find the maid, Marie-José, and ask her to tell you what she told me this evening. She'll know what I mean."

Petit's eyes bulged with excitement and he grabbed Graves's arm, manhandling him down the stairs. Agnes didn't object, returning her mind to Felicity on that last day. Embarrassed by what Graves knew, unsure if she could deceive Thomason. Trapped by others approaching. Had she, in that moment of despair, run outside? A need to hide, to be alone, to think. Agnes shook her head. A momentary lack of regard for her health in the cold of the storm? Even a desire to take the quick way out. To kill herself. With a sense of surety Agnes touched her own forehead as if to check a fever. She knew that feeling. Just the smallest fleeting sense of despair where the idea of an end to suffering seems like the only alternative. But Felicity took a coat and shoes, something in her mind still rational.

She wasn't George. She sat on the bench, she didn't walk into the lake. Agnes wondered if Felicity would have stood up and walked back into the château if she hadn't been killed.

"What were you thinking?" Julien Vallotton's words brought her back to the present. He was speaking to Thomason while rummaging through a cabinet. He located a couple glasses and a bottle and poured. "Fist-fighting like schoolboys."

Agnes approached. Was alcohol always the answer here? Both men took a swig while Agnes waved off the offer, although she wouldn't have turned down a cigarette. She caught Vallotton's eye and wondered if he read her mind. She decided to not frown so about the alcohol. Everyone could have their own vice.

She turned her mind to Thomason. Upon closer inspection he had dark circles under his eyes. She knew all too well what he was experiencing, and wondered if Vallotton was worried about the other man's state of mind, just as she was worried about Felicity Cowell's. People did strange things in the midst of grief. The young man was surely struggling between maintaining a façade of imperturbability and the need to grieve. She let the shade of suspicion cross her mind, torn between regretting even the thought and reminding herself that he would need to be watched. Watched and questioned again. It was possible he had met Felicity outside in the storm. And killed her.

"The things he said about her—"

Julien Vallotton stopped Thomason with a raised palm. "Enough of what was said. Inspector Lüthi has questions. There are still serious matters to discuss."

Agnes watched the transformation. Thomason slipped his

gentlemanly façade back on like it was a shirt. There would be no more outbursts tonight.

"I thought the Swiss police would have solved this over-night," he said politely. "Have you learned more about Felicity?" He stumbled over her name.

"It's okay," said Agnes. "We all knew her as Felicity and should respect her choice."

She wished Thomason had taken the sleeping pills Doctor Blanchard suggested. He would have avoided the fight with Graves and, more important, she could ignore him for a few more hours. She needed to sleep and then think. She indicated a grouping of chairs in an alcove.

"Let's go back to when you arrived in Switzerland. This might give me some insight into Felicity's mind-set. How did she sound before she left London? And while she was here, could you sense she was concerned? Or troubled?"

Thomason paced, and for a moment Agnes thought he was going to run to a door and leave. Instead, he walked the ten meters to the end of the corridor and drew back a heavy cur-tain. The gray-on-black silhouette of the French Alps domi-nated the landscape under the sliver of moon.

"She left London earlier than planned and I tried to call her and got voicemail. Not unusual. If she was working she wouldn't have answered her phone."

"Probably endeared her to your employers," Agnes said. "A serious young woman. Hardworking. She didn't know you were in Switzerland?"

Thomason twisted the drapery in his hand and let it sling loose. "Yes, she knew I was here."

"At the Beau-Rivage. Nice hotel."

"Like I said, it's where my family . . . and the firm always stay."

"Would you have expected Felicity to stay there? It's what, an easy half hour by automobile? A beautiful drive." Met with silence, Agnes persisted. "This is one of the most important unanswered questions and I know you were asked before. Wouldn't you have expected her to stay there?"

"Yes, until I thought that she was staying at the château. Who wouldn't choose to stay here? But I couldn't come and knock on the door after—" he paused. "She was working and we hadn't spoken since she arrived. We were both busy."

Thomason returned to the table and Vallotton refilled the other man's glass.

"You were in a state of great distress when you arrived yesterday," Agnes said gently.

"I was worried, I hadn't spoken with her in days."

"But you said it wasn't unusual for her to ignore phone calls when she was working. Did you have a reason to be worried for her? Here, in Switzerland?"

Thomason looked astounded, a flash of total honesty. He laughed. "No, I wasn't worried about her, although I should have been. I was worried that she might forget me, not need me. And I was right. She did need me, here with her, protecting her."

"You called her Wednesday? The day she died?"

"Of course I did. No, I called Tuesday night, by Wednesday my phone battery had died. That's when I realized I hadn't packed my charger. I meant to get one, but I was so upset and she hadn't answered any of my other calls, so it didn't matter. Then the power went out."

"Why were you upset? Had you fought?"

"No," Thomason sounded weary. "No fight. It was just her way. She had a way of keeping me unsettled. She could have married anyone; I know that she had boyfriends before we met. People more successful than me. What if she decided she had made the wrong decision? What if she changed her mind?" He turned to them suddenly. "She said she didn't have a family. Why did she lie to me?"

He closed his eyes and for a moment Agnes thought he was praying. Then Thomason gripped his hands into fists. "I wanted to marry her. She was perfect. The most beautiful, smartest, funniest person I knew and we were going to have a great life together."

Vallotton spoke, "She promised you a decision at the end of this trip, didn't she? It would either be yes or no."

The look of devastation on Thomason's face was genuine. "She wasn't like most girls. When they hear your voice and learn your name and who your people are and where you live, they are ready to marry you no matter if you have a chimpanzee for a brother. Felicity was different; she didn't care. She loved me, but she wanted to give it consideration. I gave her a bloody book with our house in it, I was so desperate to impress her. She just laughed and said, 'Who lives in places like this?' She didn't care about any of that; she had her own ideas." He lowered his head to his hands. "She said she would answer when she returned from the trip. Then I ended up in Switzerland at the same time and had to know. I knew that she wasn't answering her phone, because we had agreed on a timeline: I was going to her flat to have dinner when I returned. She was a stickler for keeping to arrangements. But we were just a few kilometers apart and that changed everything. I had to know."

Agnes wanted to turn away from the pain on the young man's face while at the same time she wondered if Felicity had turned him down and he had killed her.

"I think now I know why I hadn't met her family. I think you know why." Thomason buried his face in his hands for a moment, then he turned to Vallotton. "Are you married?"

"No." He paused. "I'm a widower. My wife died in a car accident a year ago."

Agnes looked at him carefully, searching for a lie. Something invented to placate Thomason, but his eyes had the look of truth.

Thomason turned to him; their knees touched they were so close. "You do understand."

"Yes, I do."

"How did you meet your wife?"

Agnes expected Vallotton to brush the question aside, but he didn't.

"Meet Amélie? We didn't meet; we were born knowing each other. My family doesn't meet people, we just see those whom we know, acquaintances renewed, strengthened, let go. It was always a matter of finding the link, the brother or mother or common distant cousin. I had . . . lost someone dear to me, someone I thought to form a life with, and Amélie dared me to marry her, saying who else would tolerate all of my relatives. She didn't need me, didn't need anyone, and was funny and beautiful and swept me off my feet. She was the most daring woman I'd ever known."

Agnes suddenly wished she'd taken that drink.

"Felicity was afraid I would leave her if I met her family," Thomason said. "She lied because she didn't trust me enough to tell the truth."

Agnes felt the anxiety of a young woman running through the château, hiding her past, unable to confide in anyone. About to be exposed. Pushed outdoors into a killing cold.

"But you now know the truth," said Vallotton, "and that's the truth she would have learned if she lived. You wouldn't have cared about her family. That's what you have to take away with you. Your truth." Vallotton started to stand, but Thomason gripped his knee.

"But I think I would have cared."

DAY FOUR

Thirty

She was tired and cold. She had waited and waited for her eyes to adjust to the dark, but they hadn't. It was pitch-black. Her stomach grumbled and that made her angry. She had nothing to eat or drink. Tears formed in the corners of her eyes and she squeezed them shut. Crying wouldn't help; it never did. She thought of Monsieur Arsov and what he would do. He wouldn't cry.

He would do something; he would find a way out. She pushed her lips together and concentrated on stopping the tears, but it was difficult. She had never been alone like this; even when she hid there were always people around, walking by but not noticing, looking, calling her name. When she hid she was in control.

She bit her lip. Monsieur Arsov. What would he do? She remembered the stories he told her about when he was young and first came to Switzerland, and earlier, when he lived in France. In the stories he was always hungry and there was mud and loud noises, but in the end he always made it home safely. Not luck he would say, but per-something. She sounded the word out: "perseverance."

She lay curled into a ball with her hands over her face. Slowly she moved, stretching out her legs, then her arms. The floor beneath her was hard, cold, and slightly damp. Like rock. She rubbed it and realized that it was exactly like rock. She was in a cave. Bats! she nearly screamed.

Mimi sat up and wrapped her arms around her bent knees. It took several minutes to stop shaking, she was so frightened, but she drew a few deep breaths and decided to try another experiment. She spoke out loud. Nothing. She called out again, this time louder. Her voice echoed, but it wasn't a long echo. She remembered an outing with Madame Puguet. They drove into the mountains. There they had picnicked and walked into a cave that had gone on and on. When they were so far away they couldn't see the entrance, they had called out and their voices echoed back and forth and back again. This was different. This place didn't sound very big.

Her stomach growled and tears overflowed her eyes and fell onto her cheeks. If only she had Elie. She gulped and strained to see, but there was nothing. It was black, black, black. What would Monsieur Arsov do? Something. That's what he said, that he never gave up and he always did something. Keep moving forward, he said. She inched forward, sliding on the rock. Nothing changed and she moved a little more. There was a scuttling noise nearby and she froze, then she understood what it was and started to cry in earnest.

Thirty-one

Agnes stopped at the door to a room she had not seen before, as surprised by its interior as she was to see Doctor Blanchard hunched over a microscope in the middle of the night. A row of oil lamps cast overlapping shadows across the table in front of him.

"Couldn't sleep thinking about the girl," he said when she entered. "Settled for this." He waved a hand over the instruments.

"I agree." Agnes had the same problem sleeping. She was exhausted, but couldn't rest thinking of Mimi not in her bed. She suspected others were wandering the corridors of the château, unable to sleep, waiting for daybreak so they could continue to look for the girl. After they officially called off the search for the night she had asked Petit to radio up the hill and alert the *gendarmerie*. The transmission was an admission that there was real cause for concern. At the same time, Agnes knew that alerting the village police was giving false hope to everyone around her. Mimi hadn't climbed the cliff. Perhaps it would be better if she had.

Madame Puguet had whispered the idea to her: could Mimi have wandered out to the edge of the lake and fallen through? The frozen edge was deceiving. Even if Mimi knew that there was no land under the far end of the cliff she might have been tempted to edge her way onto the seemingly solid surface. Every winter otherwise intelligent adults fell through ice-coated lakes and ponds and died. A full day after Mimi disappeared there was no chance she would have survived a plunge into the lake. This would be a search for her remains.

Keeping the darkest of her thoughts to herself, Agnes had assured the distraught housekeeper that they would search the lake's edge at first light. Carnet and Petit had seen no child-sized footprints during their searches; however, they couldn't guarantee she hadn't ventured outside. Some patches of ice had little or no snow. Agnes didn't know what she would do if they found the girl frozen in the lake.

For now, for another hour, she had to content herself with waiting. Returning her attention to Blanchard, she looked around the room with renewed interest. The four walls contained a kind of mad scientist's chamber, with weights, scales, glass beakers, and, in pride of place, a double row of sleek microscopes with gleaming brass and nickel fittings arrayed across two tables. Agnes lifted her light to the walls. Glass-fronted boxes displayed pinned butterflies in perpetual flight. She scanned past an arachnid display, hoping the eight-legged creatures were well and truly dead, before landing on a fully articulated skeleton hanging on a wire.

"Daniel Vallotton told me his uncle was a scientist," said the doctor. "Died young. An experiment gone awry. He left behind quite a collection of instruments and specimens." Blanchard shifted a box of bones onto the table. "Officer Petit took me out again late last night to see our body. Mademoiselle Cowell, I mean. Nothing to be done right now, but I wanted to check on her."

Agnes could imagine the doctor tucking the corpse in for the night, telling her to be patient, they would get her to a morgue soon enough. Mulholland's time in the ice house had offended the doctor's sensibilities. A corpse should at least have privacy.

"These bones I could do something with," Blanchard said, tapping the box. "The microscopes are high quality even if they are antiques."

Agnes waited patiently through the technical jargon about the difference between the capability of the antique lenses and those in a modern lab. Surreptitiously she checked her watch. The hour they had agreed upon to start the search was approaching. If only dawn would break.

She moved to study the scrap of rotted fabric that the doctor had placed under a different microscope. Her middle son had the makings of scientist. He would be impressed by this home laboratory. Near the microscope the doctor had placed the clear plastic bag containing the ring found with the skeleton. Agnes knew fingerprints weren't a concern and removed it, curious about the design. The metal was dull gold, and it was heavier than she expected. But then, it was a man's. The signet portion of the ring was deep green. Bloodstone, she recalled. The crest was elaborate and difficult to make out. She tilted it toward a candle then picked up a small lens brush and used it to dislodge some dirt. When fully revealed, it was a pretty design, a coronet of alternating leaves and pearls in trefoil surmounting a shield surrounded by draping plumes. Her heart beat faster; she rubbed her eyes to clear them.

"I had a suspicion and was able to take a look at our bones," the doctor finally concluded.

Agnes ignored him, holding the ring almost in the flame of a candle. The carving on even a large signet ring was tiny. She was tired—perhaps imaging things, and needed to be sure. She looked again. She knew this crest. It was at the top right-hand corner of the painting of the marquise that Marie-Chantal had shown her. The painting done on the occasion of the marriage of Antoinette Vallotton to the Marquise de Tornay. The painting decorated by the artist with the crests of both families.

"—had TB," the doctor said.

Agnes jerked her head up. "Tuberculosis? These bones? The bones of the young woman we found today . . . I mean yesterday? With this ring?"

"Yes, as I was saying, once I cleaned the bones up a bit I could tell that the surface was pitted. I think it is consistent with what we would find with an advanced case of tuberculosis. Very advanced."

She slipped the ring back in the plastic bag and fished the diary from her pocket. It was all in here. The young woman ill, tuberculosis. The ring she took as *laissez-passer*. The ring that would identify her as friend of Madame's upon arrival in Switzerland. The ring given to her by Madame. Madame la marquise Antoinette Vallotton de Tornay. Citoyen's wife and Arsov's friend during the war. A chill swept through Agnes. Why had the marquise said nothing? And why was the love of Arsov's life buried in unconsecrated ground?

With a hasty word to the doctor she went in search of the person who could answer her questions.

The marquise was seated on her silver chair just as she had been when Agnes first met her. There was a tray of tea and toast on a nearby table. Clearly no one in the household was able to sleep.

"You know whose skeleton we found under that tree." It wasn't a question and Agnes didn't pause for social niceties.

"I wondered how long it would take for you to understand. Only a few hours apparently." The marquise waved her hand toward the opposite chair but Agnes remained standing. She had little time. She had allowed herself to be distracted by the thefts and wouldn't be again. Light was breaking and they needed to find Mimi. And she needed to find Felicity Cowell's murderer. The woman buried under the tree, no matter who she was, could wait. The marquise appeared to read her mood.

"Yes, I believe I know who lays under that tree."

"She was wearing your ring. She had tuberculosis."

"The disease was more common in those days." The marquise smiled softly. "And it was not my ring. It was my late husband's."

"She was in love with Monsieur Arsov." Agnes remembered the young girl writing about Marcel. Writing about Arsov. A young girl who was given a ring before traveling.

"Until yesterday I did not know where she rested. Unbelievable, really, after all these years to find her here." The marquise shook herself slightly as if waking. "Anne-Marie lived with me during the war. But you clearly know this. And yes, she was ill. Her health failed quickly and we decided to risk the journey to Switzerland. There was some access to medicines even with the borders closed and the population living on subsistence. At a minimum she would be spared the constant fear that we lived with."

"Someone abandoned her here?"

"Marcel, Monsieur Arsov, was in Italy and it would have taken two more weeks for him to come for her. I was afraid to wait that long; that is how weak Anne-Marie had become." The marquise glanced to the book in Agnes's hand. "You have read her diary. You have heard her spirit in the words she wrote. She would not believe she was ill, just tired, yet she was frail and already slipping from us. Marcel—that is who he shall always be for me in those days—arranged for a colleague to take her. They were to cross into Switzerland together and arrive here, on the shore beside my family home. We had loyal servants who would have taken care of her." The marquise studied her hand as if searching for something. "That is why I gave Anne-Marie my husband's ring. I needed something to give her as proof of our connection. We did not dare write anything."

"I don't understand. You must have known who she was when we uncovered the skeleton?"

The marquise lifted a hand to stop Agnes speaking. "You will not believe that I was stunned. Old habits die hard. I believe you know who my husband was. What we did during the war." Agnes nodded hesitantly, remembering the story from the diary. The story of how the marquise's husband died. What had the marquise said to her that night in the workroom? That she should be thankful that her memories could fade, that all she remembered of her husband was his face the last time she saw him: the night she destroyed his face so the Germans couldn't identify him. It was the marquise who taught Arsov how to survive.

"These things have been secret for so long I could not speak of them immediately." The marquise pulled her fox stole closer. "You cannot imagine what Europe was like after the war. You think that peace means a return to normalcy, when in fact it is another stage of desolation. My brother had seen more of the war than me, and we were united in our desire to live in the present. I did not seek out answers. I lost my husband, many other family members. Friends. I did not try to find Marcel. Or Anne-Marie. If you had asked me then if I thought they survived the war I don't know what I would have answered. I was beyond thinking anyone would survive. Life and death were capricious. It was not something to examine."

Agnes felt she was watching the woman age before her eyes. She adjusted the wick in an oil lamp to have something to do. The pain in the marquise's voice was difficult to bear.

"Anne-Marie left with her guide and two others," the marquise continued. "Important men with scientific secrets who needed to reach Zürich. I knew nothing of the details of their journey. We were very careful to compartmentalize information. I did learn later that they went by boat across the lake. Risky, but I did not question why."

"She made it," Agnes said.

"Based on what was found in that grave, yes and no."

"I thought they had years together. That they married and had a whole life of happiness. To hear Monsieur Arsov speak of her, it was like she'd been dead only a few years. Not over fifty.

And why didn't he marry someone else? He must have met someone." Her voice faltered. Was it a guarantee to meet someone
else?

The marquise reached out to hold Agnes's arm. "I do not
know what happened on that trip."

"You must have spoken of it later, now. Monsieur Arsov is
your neighbor."

"What is there to speak of? Two years ago he contacted me
and asked if he could visit. After so many years I was delighted
when he mentioned a desire to live here. He did not mention
her directly and I did not ask. I did glimpse her diary in his
hand once. I recognized it. Now I suppose the men she traveled with gave it to him. They were not cruel men. I understood without a direct reference that Marcel wanted to be here,
on the shore of this lake, in old age. This was where they were
to embark upon a new, freer life together. Seeing her bones I
understand that this is where his heart broke. Do you understand? That the heart can literally break?" The marquise relaxed
her grip and dropped her hand away.

"Yes, I understand the heart breaking." Arsov and Anne-
Marie, herself and George. She added George and Carnet.
Julien Vallotton's spouse who had died tragically, as had the
marquise's. And there was Thomason. Heartbroken and deceived. She wondered if Marie-Chantal and Daniel, with their
difficult beginning, would end up the happiest of all.

"I do not think Marcel, Monsieur Arsov, knows she died
here," said the marquise suddenly. "He would not have left her
unattended. Even if he had to leave her during the war—to
save someone else's life, to do his duty to others—he would
have returned and given her a proper burial. And later, he and

I knew each other well enough that he could have made this request of me."

"Then how did she end up here, abandoned? Why?"

"I have had nearly a day to ponder this question. She was weak. It is not unreasonable that she died during the journey. We knew it was a risk. The men she was with had other responsibilities. I trusted them, I still do. They probably did the best they could for her without abandoning their mission. They couldn't travel with a dead woman, nor could they ask for help that might result in being turned over to the authorities. They likely dug a hasty grave and left her. Understand how we felt. The world was at war. One more death made little difference. We saw death every day. I thought every day would be my last."

"But Arsov knew she didn't arrive."

"What do you tell a man—that his fiancée died and you had to leave her hidden among brush in a grove of trees? No, you invent a nicer story. After all, she is dead, there is no changing the fact. You say that she died in France, that a nice widow woman nursed her last moments and promised to bury her in the village. You give him her diary as a memento." The marquise shifted slightly in her silver chair. "I don't know what they told him, but it was not the truth. We teach our children not to lie, but in war lies are necessities. My entire life during those years was a lie. I have to forgive others for doing the same."

Agnes blinked back tears. She nodded. "I do understand. And I'll make sure Arsov's household doesn't mention to him what we found. He's very frail." She couldn't bear the thought of Arsov finding out that his true love had lain in a hastily dug grave for over fifty years. The passages of the diary echoed through her mind, the voice of a young woman in love. Perhaps she was fortunate, this young woman who would never know the sting of the loss of love.

She had one last question. "You asked about Felicity Cowell's siblings the other night. Why?"

"Perhaps I was thinking of my brother and his death and how it impacted me. He was the last of my generation."

Agnes replayed the moment. "No." They were talking about Felicity Cowell's false name. How she changed her name. "Something else triggered your thoughts." She paged through the diary. "Her brother. Anne-Marie's brother."

"A tiny child. We sent him to live with a family deeper in the countryside. It was difficult to part them, but a safer place for him. Anywhere near me was unsafe by this time. I was under constant surveillance. And, whereas a grown person is difficult to explain, children blend in easier. The family had lost a child of the same age and would pass him off as their own to the authorities."

"What was his name? What was his and Anne-Marie's surname?"

"Faivre."

"What was his first name?"

The marquise hesitated.

"It was Frédéric," Agnes said, finding the page in the diary. "Anne-Marie's much younger brother was Frédéric Faivre. And you can change your name. What was the family called he went to live with?"

"I don't recall, I didn't know them personally."

"Estanguet?" asked Agnes. There was a long pause. When the marquise nodded, she ran.

Thirty-two

Julien Vallotton was at the door when Agnes ran into the room.

"We're waiting for daylight to start the search," he said.

She pushed past him wordlessly, stopping only when she reached Ralph Mulholland. She grasped his arm, ignoring the stunned expressions of the three Vallottons.

"Monsieur Arsov wouldn't see you on Wednesday, yet you waited for him. You said that you waited outside. Why did you wait outside on a cold day to see a very old man?"

Daniel Vallotton hoisted himself up on crutches and his brother drew near but Agnes ignored them. "Why outside during a storm?"

"He goes out every day," Mulholland replied. "Sits on that bloody bench and stares out over the lake. Someone—a servant or a visitor—pushes him there and leaves him for a while. I wanted him alone. Where he couldn't walk away from me, or call for someone to haul me off. I needed to explain to him how serious my situation was. He'd have to listen."

"Frédéric," Agnes whispered, turning to the group. "Where is Estanguet? Frédéric Estanguet?"

They looked around the shadows of the room as if expecting the man to jump out at them.

"Is *he* missing now?" Julien Vallotton asked.

"It was all about revenge. Revenge on Monsieur Arsov. Estanguet thought Arsov was sitting on the bench and because of the storm didn't realize that he stabbed Felicity Cowell by mistake. They are both slight in build, and she was wearing a man's coat. That first night he was stunned. We thought it was the sight of the body or the cold. He was stunned because he thought he'd killed a man, not a woman. And since then Monsieur Arsov hasn't been unattended or outside, there hasn't been another chance to get near him." Agnes grabbed the stuffed elephant from a chair and waved it under their noses as if that were proof. "Estanguet knows how Arsov feels about Mimi and he took her. I don't know what he has done with her, but her took her because she is what Arsov loves best in the world."

Winston paced nearby, his head and shoulders brushing her skirt. Julien Vallotton nudged the dog away.

"Let's hope he only hid her," Agnes said. "He can't have taken her far. She must be here, somewhere on this property. They couldn't have made it up the cliff without our knowing."

"Why revenge on Arsov?" Daniel Vallotton slumped back into his wheelchair, rolling it backward and forward rapidly. Marie-Chantal put down her coffee cup and joined him.

"If Estanguet's sister hadn't died in the last year of the war Arsov would have married her. But Frédéric Estanguet was very young, little more than a toddler. He was separated from her and he blames Arsov." Agnes took a deep breath. "She's the skeleton we found yesterday."

"This makes no sense," said Marie-Chantal. "Many children were orphaned."

"I don't think we can understand his mental state, but I know whose bones are on your lawn, and I know that she is the woman Arsov was in love with, and that Frédéric Estanguet is her brother."

Julien Vallotton stepped forward. "Mimi is our prime concern, the details don't matter now."

"Did someone check the ice house tunnel?" said Marie-Chantal.

"We looked there," said Agnes. "And in all of the other buildings: the summer pavilion, the old stables, the Orangerie. They aren't complicated structures. They don't have secrets. Plus, they're not heated. A few hours in one of them and she would freeze to death. I don't think that's what Estanguet wants. At least not yet or he would have made sure we found her body. He has a plan for revenge." She looked around desperately. "She has to be here. Somewhere in the château."

"We'll call for help—" Julien interjected.

"Call who?" Agnes asked.

"Inspector Lüthi is the police," Marie-Chantal added.

Officer Petit walked through the door, bundled for the worst outdoor weather from his boots to his cap. Carnet was close on his heels, pulling on his puffy coat.

"All ready to start," Petit said. "Carnet has a plan and if we could get a couple of people to help—"

"Not now," Agnes interrupted. Quickly she explained the

situation to them. "When was the last time anyone saw Monsieur Estanguet?"

Carnet turned on his heel. "I'll check the man's bedroom to see if he's there. If he's not, I'll start searching for him. I'll get Madame Puguet to assist."

"André," Agnes said. "Go to Arsov's, quickly. Wake them up. Put the butler and Nurse Brighton on alert but say nothing to the old man. There's nothing to be gained by frightening him. Stay close. I believe Estanguet has already killed once."

Petit sprinted away, leaving the rest of the room frozen in a tableau of concern.

"We have to do something more to find her. Can we get dogs?" said Daniel. "What did mother's family raise, bloodhounds?"

Winston walked the length of the room. Agnes glanced at the animal, then at Julien Vallotton. Together they looked at the dog.

"He's not a bloodhound," Agnes said speculatively.

"I've taken him hunting," Daniel said. "He's got a good nose."

"MC, call him," Vallotton said.

Agnes held the stuffed animal out to Winston, wondering if the Great Dane even noticed the toy, his eyes were so focused on hers, like he was thinking. The humans stood transfixed for a moment. Everyone stilled, as if waiting for magic, then Winston turned away, his large form moving at the languid pace he usually took through the household. They let out a collective sigh. Nothing.

Mulholland crashed a coffee cup onto a table, cursing.

"I can't believe Monsieur Estanguet would kill," Marie-

Chantal said. "Madame Puguet knows him, he's been using the library for months. Are we positive? He seemed like such a kind old man. I can't believe he would hurt Mimi."

"He used his time here to plan his attack on Monsieur Arsov," said Agnes, keeping her eyes trained on Winston. The dog was at the door, as if waiting on her. He swept his head forward and caught her eye before taking off at a rapid clip. "He's going," she said.

Winston pricked his ears. He lunged forward at a lope. Agnes and Julien sprinted to catch up. Marie-Chantal grabbed the handles of Daniel's wheelchair and Mulholland brought up the rear.

Winston led them down a long corridor to the opposite wing of the château. They burst through the door of a large room, rarely used. Agnes stopped when she was across the threshold. Her heart was pounding and she experienced a rapid sense of disappointment. No Mimi. And Marie-Chantal was correct, maybe Estanguet hadn't taken the girl. Maybe she had created this out of whole cloth based on a painting, a ring, and the idea that someone could change their name.

The room resembled a medieval banquet hall. In the center stood a long table surrounded by forty high-backed wood chairs. Large Flemish tapestries covered three of the walls. Two complete suits of armor guarded the opposite door. Despite this, the space felt empty.

Winston walked the perimeter, nose down. Agnes caught her breath and wondered if they were all crazy, following a dog. She held Mimi's stuffed toy out to him. He ignored her.

"Who searched this room last night?" she asked.

"I did," said Mulholland. He was pale. "With Monsieur Estanguet."

They glanced around.

"There's nowhere to hide," Marie-Chantal said. "Under the table. I suppose around the suits of armor. There's nowhere else."

"We pulled out the chairs," Mulholland said. "Estanguet suggested we see if she was lying on top of them." He shrugged. "And he thumped the tapestries, but they're too close to the wall to conceal even a small child. This can't be where she is. We looked."

Agnes did a quick circuit of the room, glancing behind the suits of armor, under the table. She fingered her pocket, wishing for a cigarette. They had to be close. Mimi was in the château, she was sure of it.

"Do you remember getting lost for a few days when you were small?" Julien asked Daniel. "I was already at boarding school, but the old cook talked about it for years."

"I was three? Maybe four?" Daniel replied. "I don't remember anything other than what they told me later. There was a door open and I wandered in and someone shut it and didn't know to look for me there."

"How would Estanguet know where to hide her?" Marie-Chantal asked. "How could he find someplace we don't know about?"

"He's been in the library for months," said Agnes, eyes trained on Winston. "Maybe he learned something there. Documents that show the château's evolution. Hidden passages, places built over. I keep finding concealed stairs. There are tunnels you had forgotten about. Maybe we didn't search everywhere."

"The American might have helped him," Mulholland said.

"What do you know about him?" Agnes asked.

"*Unwittingly* helped him. Nick Graves is doing research on the construction of the château." The Vallottons looked at Mulholland, startled. "I can read," he said. "And sometimes when I can't sleep I wander the library. His notes are laid out on one of the tables."

Winston rubbed his head along the largest of the tapestries. Six meters long and four tall, it covered the length of one wall. Agnes noticed that the woven hunting scene was complete with mounted horses, running dogs, and fearsome wild beasts, and she hoped that wasn't what attracted Winston. He walked up and down the length of the fabric, nose down, inhaling huge drafts of air. Under the pressure from his head the entire scene rippled. Suddenly he stopped, drawing in a torrent of oxygen through his nose. He held his breath for a second, then moaned, sitting.

"There," Agnes pointed. "He's found something."

Julien ran to the end of the tapestry and hauled the edge away from the wall. It was heavy and he could only move it a hand's width from the stone. "Hand me a light," he called.

Agnes knelt to peer beneath his outstretched arm, attempting to help hold the fabric. Her flashlight beam caught the outline of a slight recess in the wall several meters away. Winston pushed underneath and Agnes followed. The fabric's weight pressed against her head and shoulder, and she had difficulty edging forward. In front of her, the dog's nose was pressed to the ground and his back end quivered.

"He's got the scent," Agnes called out, her voice muffled. "There's a door. It doesn't run all the way to the ground, that's why no one saw it beneath the bottom of the tapestry. What's behind this wall?"

"A billiard room is on the other side," said Daniel, "but between this room and that, the wall is more of a thickness. There's a spiral stair up and a small water closet, some built-in cabinets further along."

"There's room in the thickness then, for concealment," Agnes said.

Julien Vallotton slipped behind her and held the light while she ran her hands along the wood surface. She found a ring latch flush with the wood. She pulled and turned the ring, but it was locked. She pulled again and tried to rattle it loose, but the door was solid and the lock held.

"There's no key. Mimi?" she called out, pressing her mouth to the juncture of door and wall. Nothing. She called out again.

Vallotton joined her. "Mimi!"

"She can't hear us even if she's there," said Agnes, ducking from beneath the tapestry. She motioned to Marie-Chantal.

"Watch your head," Daniel Vallotton hollered to his brother.

Mulholland joined the women and together they yanked. The rod holding the tapestry pulled from the wall and a thousand pounds of cloth crashed to the ground in a thunder of dust. The iron rod and brackets slipped past Julien Vallotton's head and landed on top of the heap of fabric. They stood still for a moment, stunned.

"More notice next time," Julien Vallotton said before turning to pound on the door.

Agnes grabbed an iron fire poker from a cold hearth, then leapt over the pile of cloth. Julien stepped sideways. She judged the heft of the poker then swung. It crashed into the metal fitting of the old lock. She struck again but the iron pieces wouldn't dislodge.

"Mimi?" she called out again, swinging violently. Winston waited until the poker was lowered, then pressed his nose to the door and sniffed loudly.

"Wait," said Julien. "Listen."

They held their ears to the wood. There was a muffled cry.

"It's her," he said.

"Someone get the doctor," Agnes called over her shoulder.

Marie-Chantal and Mulholland ran for help and Agnes wiped perspiration from her brow. Julien took the poker. On the third strike, the lock dislodged and he wrenched it from the casing. The door fell open. Agnes swung her flashlight beam into the darkness and followed him down the steep irregular stairs, nearly pushing him over in her hurry. It was a small slice of dungeon, unchanged since ancient times, isolated from the larger sections by modifications long forgotten. It was very dark and the air was moist and stale. It felt like fear.

Agnes moved her light back and forth and cried out when she saw Mimi's slight form lying on the bare rock. The little girl looked up, her face swollen with tears. Winston reached her first, leaping down the stairs in his excitement. Mimi clutched his furry sides and Agnes ran her light up and down them both, hoping the girl wasn't injured.

"Where's Elie?" were Mimi's first coherent words and Agnes wanted to cry with relief.

Marie-Chantal and Doctor Blanchard arrived at a run and Julien held Winston back; the animal clearly felt that a thorough licking was all that Mimi needed. Agnes trusted the dog's instincts and felt a great lightness. The girl would recover.

They draped a blanket over Mimi and Julien gathered her in his arms and carefully climbed the steep stone stairs.

"He shouldn't have put me there. I was hungry and cold."

Agnes backed away. The girl was safe but the man was still out there. Angry. Desperate. And if she was right about this, she was right about everything.

Thirty-three

Agnes didn't pause to ring the doorbell. She shoved the heavy double doors of the mansion open, surprised they were unlocked. The household was strangely silent. She wondered if Petit had them corralled together in the salon, his idea of a subtle guard. Pausing in the marble entry hall, she reminded herself not to frighten a sick old man with her concern. Mimi was safe and there was no reason to think anything had happened at the Arsov mansion.

A glance down the long corridor confirmed she was wrong. Arsov's butler lay partially concealed behind one of the tall porcelain urns, legs askew, head tilted unnaturally against the marble baseboard, a smear of blood on the cream-colored surface. His chest rose and fell evenly and Agnes ran past him, afraid for Petit, now certain that she was right and that there was no more time. Veering toward Arsov's bedroom she broke into a sprint, scanning each room as she passed, hoping to find an ally. But dawn was just breaking and the household was asleep.

She reached the open door to the bedroom and stopped to listen. Silence. She crept forward, hidden by the large tri-fold screen, not wanting to lose the advantage of surprise. Across the room, in her line of sight, André Petit lay on his back, skin scraped off the side of his head. She nearly cried out. A small marble bust lay nearby on the floor. She narrowed her eyes and studied his chest. He was breathing. She thought of his two-day-old son and hoped beyond all hope that he was not critically injured.

Beyond her line of sight, she heard a man's voice followed by a faint cry.

"Murderer," Estanguet said.

Agnes darted around the tapestry screen. At the far end of the room, Frédéric Estanguet pinned Arsov against the deep bed. The old man's face was pale gray and his eyes were closed. Agnes saw the glint of a long knife in Estanguet's hand and she leapt forward. He saw her and flicked the blade toward Arsov's throat. She halted, the element of surprise lost.

"He killed my sister," Estanguet said. "Took the last family I had."

The tiniest thread of blood appeared on the pale blue silk of Arsov's pajamas. Agnes watched in horror as it blossomed across his chest. Agnes knew there was no time to reason with Estanguet. Arsov was too weak. She grabbed an antique bronze inkwell, took aim, and threw it. The metal struck Estanguet's head, knocking him to the floor. The dagger flew from his hand. Seizing the opportunity, she lunged, but Estanguet scrambled to find his weapon and Agnes felt his hand come in contact with her ankle. Pain seared her leg and she was thrown off balance. Blood sprayed the floor and she realized he had sliced her calf. With her other foot, she stepped on his wrist, but he was strong despite his age and pulled free, throwing her against a table. Glass shattered.

Lying on her back, scrambling to avoid Estanguet, she searched for a weapon. Anything heavy or sharp. Estanguet laughed, a sickening sound of hysteria, and slashed at her chest with the dagger. She kicked him away and pain shot up her injured leg like fire. She clambered to her feet, her head reeling. "Your sister wouldn't want you to do this. This doesn't honor Anne-Marie's memory."

"You don't know what he did to me. Sent me to live with those terrible people. I heard my sister cry, she didn't want to send me away and he took me. Then he made me an orphan."

"War is terrible. Many children lost their parents. No one wanted this to happen to you. Anne-Marie cried because she knew she would miss you, but she knew it was for the best. A new family. A safe family. You were safer away from Resistance operations."

She sensed that Estanguet was torn between targets. His eyes darted between her and Arsov. She gripped the side of a table for balance.

"He sent me away to be a slave. Those people. The Estanguets," he spat, "they made me work for every scrap of food. I slept in an attic, did the hardest farm chores. The other kids beat me up. He did this to me."

The red stain on Arsov's chest expanded, no longer a blossoming flower but a river. "Your sister loved Monsieur Arsov," Agnes said. "They tried to do what was right for you. It was wartime, there were no perfect solutions, particularly for innocent children. They thought the family would take care of you. Treat you like the son they had lost."

Estanguet lunged for her. She moved quickly, dodging his blade and sidestepping the table, practically falling onto Arsov's bed. The old man's eyes fluttered.

"Anne-Marie?" he said weakly. "Frédéric?"

"Yes, me," Estanguet said. "The little boy you sent away. The little boy who had to change his name—"

"Frédéric?" Arsov repeated.

Agnes pulled her scarf off and pressed it to Arsov's side, trying to staunch the blood that now dripped from his chest to his legs. "He thought he was saving you," she said. "The invasion threatened."

"What do you know?" Estanguet raged. "Those people were not my parents and they never let me forget it. Their oldest son threatened to hand me over to the Nazis and they didn't stop him taunting me. Every day I lived in fear. I knew what the monster Nazis were and every day I thought I would be sent to them. To be tortured and killed. Even after the war, when the boys at school mocked me for being circumcised, they did nothing to protect me. And when my false parents died, they left me with nothing. A teenage boy with no name of his own and no family. They made me take their name and I had nothing left. I was no longer Frédéric Faivre. What boy understands this? Why should this be forgiven? Why should this man live to be old, rich, doing whatever pleases him, when she is dead and I am alone? I was alone my entire life. He took everything from me. My name, my family. The life that should have been mine."

Agnes felt woozy and understood that blood was pooling in her shoe. The cut to her leg was deep. Estanguet had lost touch with reality overnight. His eyes were no longer those of an elderly villager, they were crazed.

"I took what he loves," he said. "Let's see how he feels when Mimi is never found. I was never found. No one ever came for me. No family claimed me after the war. She will die and he will always know that he killed her. He won't know where she is but he will know she is dead. This is my revenge. He came here with his trucks of antiques and here, in Switzerland, I will have revenge for what happened all those years ago."

"But we have found her," Agnes cried. "She is safe and unharmed."

"You lie. You've searched. I helped, and no one knows where she is."

"In the dungeon. We found the door behind the tapestry. She is safe."

Estanguet howled like a wounded animal. He stalked toward the bed and flicked the tip of his knife toward her.

Agnes kept her body between him and Arsov to protect the older man, pressing her shoulder into Estanguet's chest, grappling for his knife, knowing Arsov was losing consciousness and couldn't sustain another injury.

Estanguet stopped aiming his knife at the other man and turned on her. The movement caught her off guard and she lost her hold on him. The blade sliced into her and she spun away. Falling. On her hands and knees she looked over her shoulder and saw Estanguet lean over Arsov. She struggled to breathe, wondering what was wrong. Everything seemed heavy. Gripping the handles of Arsov's wheelchair, she pulled herself up. First to her knees. She heaved with pain.

Estanguet pulled Arsov to a sitting position, holding the old man, whispering into his ear. Tears rolled down Arsov's face and Estanguet dropped him to the bed and ran for the door. Agnes tried to follow him, to pull herself up, to stand, but she couldn't. She felt something sticky under her shirt.

Estanguet reached the tapestry screen at the entrance to the bedroom and stopped to take one last look at the man he had hated for so many decades. The blanket on Arsov's wheelchair slipped and Agnes lost her grip. Her head hit the seat. It hurt. She opened her eyes, then she smiled.

Nurse Brighton walked through the door carrying a tray of the morning's medicines and Agnes tried to call out a warning, but the nurse saw Petit on the floor and screamed, dropping the tray. Estanguet twisted to grab her, his knife at the ready.

Agnes watched him turn, watched the arc of his arm, the direction his shoulder tilted. She judged the distance, the movement of air, her own nerves, and found her kneeling stance.

The shot reverberated. The gun she had found in Arsov's chair dropped from her hand. Estanguet fell backward, an ugly patch of red flowering high on his chest, near his shoulder. She watched him release his knife and go still. Then she passed out.

When she opened her eyes, Julien Vallotton was kneeling over her. In her line of sight blood had pooled on the beautiful parquet floor. Somewhere in the background a woman, one of the maids, she decided, was crying. She turned her head to watch Nurse Brighton lean over Arsov.

"Is he dead?" she murmured.

Julien Vallotton took her hand and followed her gaze. They watched Nurse Brighton pull a clean blanket over Arsov's face, her eyes brimming with tears.

Agnes tried to pull herself up to a sitting position and failed. "I took a first at Bienne. George was proud." Her thoughts were disconnected, but she remembered that was the day George met Carnet. In her mind that was also the day she had practiced for, and was the reason she had handled so many weapons, but it was too late to save anyone.

She started to shake. Vallotton removed his coat and laid it over her. She tried to object but her hand struck the floor and she felt the warm stickiness dripping from her side and closed her eyes thinking that now she knew how George had felt. Unafraid. At peace.

Thirty-four

The doorbell rang and Agnes called out to say she would answer it, but her eldest son ran to the door before she could move. She sighed deeply and sat back, not knowing whether to be grateful or worried. The boys hadn't been allowed to see her the first days in intensive care, and afterward in the hospital she hadn't wanted them to worry. Now, at home, they had missed the worst of the bandages and the medicines streaming in through tubes, but she knew that their father's death was on their minds, and now they had nearly lost their mother. It was too great a burden for children.

She heard the murmur of voices from the front hall and adjusted the blanket across her legs, thankful for the fire blazing on the hearth of George's parents' home. Even though the air in the weeks following the storm was spring-like, she still couldn't get warm. The voices got louder and she hoped it wasn't another neighbor coming to visit. There had been an interminable stream of guests, each one saying they knew she needed rest but that they had to bring something to cheer her up. The visits were always followed by low-voiced arguments with Sybille, who said Agnes wasn't grateful enough for their interest. An argument that alternated with how reckless she was. How little she cared for her boys.

She closed her eyes and swallowed hard as the scent of a winter stew wafted into the room. The thought of food made her ill. Weak tea and clear broth were all she could stomach. She tried to breathe without smelling, but the effort was too great. She gave up and swallowed again to stifle what came next: the bitter taste of adrenaline. It lingered along with the cold. The taste and feel of fear.

The voices in the hall grew louder and she sat up abruptly, wincing.

"Don't get up on our account," Julien Vallotton said.

Agnes tried to anyway, and he crossed the room and put a hand on her shoulder to stop her.

"They wouldn't let me out of the hospital for the funeral," she said, instantly regretting her words. She sounded so impolite. Why did he unsettle her so? "No one told me about it until it was too late, or I might have left anyway."

"Hello to you as well." Vallotton smiled. "You were missed, but we knew you couldn't make it. They said a special prayer for you at the service."

She squirmed at the thought. Was there an appropriate prayer for someone who arrived too late to save a life?

"We reinterred Anne-Marie Faivre when we buried Monsieur Arsov. That was her name. Faivre. And of course Frédéric Estanguet's last name when he was a child. Anne-Marie and Arsov are now in our family plot. The monument hasn't been placed yet, but Marie-Chantal designed it and I think Arsov would approve."

Agnes closed her eyes for a moment and shifted to a more comfortable position. There was a *clack-clack* of high heels.

"Madame Lüthi has offered tea and I came to see if Julien would also like a slice of cake. Daniel says he can't manage the steps. He'll wait in the car." Marie-Chantal Vallotton walked in and Agnes grinned despite the pain. Marie-Chantal's outfit would no doubt impress Sybille. She wore a very chic wool suit with extremely high-heeled leather boots and a concoction of wool and feathers angled on her head. An ensemble at home on a Paris runway. She stole a glance at Julien Vallotton and realized that he was also extremely well dressed, beyond his usual tailored suit. She knew they did this as a tribute to her and tears came to her eyes.

A few steps behind Marie-Chantal, Sybille arrived wearing a fresh apron, smoothing her hair back into a bun.

"Your friends are very nice to stop by and check on you." She smiled across the group as if expecting—hoping? Agnes wondered—one of the Vallottons would counter her suggestion that they were friends.

"It wasn't necessary," Agnes said. "Bardy sent me a full report."

"Of course it wasn't necessary," Marie-Chantal said, turning the full force of her smile on first Agnes, then Sybille. "But we were anxious to see you. We peeked in at the CHUV when you were in intensive care but you were sleeping and wouldn't have known. Poor Mimi was nearly sick with jealousy when the medical helicopter landed to evacuate you to the hospital. If she hadn't already convinced Doctor Blanchard that she was merely dehydrated and exhausted, she might have joined you and Officer Petit on the ride."

Agnes smiled. Her boys had asked her about the journey to the hospital, clearly disappointed that she didn't remember anything about the dramatic flight. She had later learned that a second helicopter had taken Arsov and his butler, along with Felicity Cowell's body and Estanguet, to the hospital. Petit had recovered quickly, and was in good enough spirits to remark that finally he'd gotten his evacuation. He had brought his son from the maternity ward to see her.

"Julien's aunt," Marie-Chantal said in Sybille's direction, "Madame la marquise, wanted to come today, but we wouldn't let her. You aren't well enough to have a crowd and we stopped by unannounced. Terrible manners."

Agnes stifled another smile, now positive this performance was for her mother-in-law's benefit. The marquise wasn't likely to leave the château for anyone.

"When you are ready, walking, and feeling better, you have to come stay with us." Marie-Chantal clapped her hands together as if an idea just struck her. "You could come now. Madame Lüthi can have a respite from her role as nurse and you will be very comfortable—"

"I couldn't dream of Agnes leaving us. I am devoted to her care," Sybille interrupted as if she hadn't wanted exactly this only a few minutes before they arrived.

"We wouldn't have come today," Julien said, "but Étienne Bardy phoned to tell me that you are receiving a special commendation. For heroism and bravery. He will give you all the details but there will be a formal presentation ceremony and he wanted us to know. I insisted on coming here and telling you myself." He crossed the room to shake Sybille's hand. "You must be very proud of her. A hero in the family."

Agnes thought Sybille would choke.

"Maybe I can help you with tea and cake," Marie-Chantal interrupted, escorting Sybille from the room. "The cake smells so good. Vanilla-flavored with orange, is it?"

"Thank you," Agnes said to Vallotton with a nod after her mother-in-law, wondering for a moment what the Vallottons thought of her home. The atmosphere rolling off Sybille was cold, but the home itself was warm, full of dark wood and relics of distant ancestors.

"My aunt would visit, you know." At Agnes's expression, Vallotton shrugged. "She offered."

"Knowing I would politely refuse and come to her instead."

"'Old habits die hard' is the saying."

"I was glad I didn't kill him."

"Bardy told me that if you'd meant to kill him, Estanguet would be dead. He knew you shot to disable. Nurse Brighton would have been a good hostage, or maybe he would have killed her immediately. From her account Estanguet was spiraling out of control. Of course you know that Arsov's butler and Officer Petit recovered from their injuries, but something happened between the time Estanguet attacked them and when you arrived. Estanguet was in a rage. Honestly, it was a miracle you could aim at all. You'd lost a lot of blood."

Agnes remembered thinking she couldn't stand because her leg was badly cut. She thought the blood on her chest was from Arsov's wounds, not realizing that Estanguet's knife had found its mark, sliding into her abdomen. Later, at the hospital, they had explained that adrenaline conceals pain.

"He stabbed me and Monsieur Arsov with the same blade he used on Felicity Cowell," she said. "To think she died because of mistaken identity. She was wearing that borrowed coat, sitting on the bench where he sat every day, and with the storm raging Estanguet couldn't tell that she was a woman and not an old man. He'd been planning it for months. Ever since he heard the name Vladimir Arsov. He had the day picked and even the storm didn't deter him."

Agnes paused to catch her breath, wondering if she would ever fully recover from her wounds. "That storm," she said. "It will be called the storm of the century, but people won't realize that beyond the road accidents it killed in other ways. If there hadn't been a storm Arsov would have been outside. Maybe Estanguet would have killed him there, or maybe Felicity Cowell's presence would have saved his life. And her own."

"Estanguet would have found another opportunity," said Vallotton. "He was determined to have his revenge."

Agnes shifted the blanket that covered her legs. "When we found Felicity Cowell's body Doctor Blanchard told me she wouldn't have felt any pain and I didn't believe him. Now, I guess he was right. The blade was sharp." She thought about George. Maybe he hadn't felt anything, just a great sense of approaching emptiness. Vallotton moved to touch her arm and she shook herself.

"Just thinking about that day," she said. "Hard to believe so much harm came from what Estanguet cobbled together as a child. If only he had known the truth. At least he might have realized that they really did what they thought was best for him. If he had, then when he found Arsov the two men might have bonded over their love for Anne-Marie and not turned it into a tragedy."

"It's hard to give up on the notions we have of people that come out of childhood."

"If the Estanguets had treated him well things would have been different. Or if he had confronted Arsov. Questioned him."

Vallotton stood to look out the front window of the chalet. "I wonder if the serendipity of the meeting made it worse. Imagine sitting in a café and hearing a name that you have harbored a grudge against your entire life. A secret name you were warned not to share. The notion of secrecy ensured a small boy would remember the name Vladimir Arsov. The man who stole his sister away."

"It may have been serendipity at the start, but it was premeditated in the end," said Agnes. "He spent months planning how to slip down the hill and strike. Did you know that Estanguet is a mountain climber? Bardy told me. Estanguet was careful to cover his proficiency and tell me that he was a guide on gentle walks. Instead, he'd climbed some impressive sites recently despite his age. When the storm came he knew that it would be the perfect cover. He had picked the day and made his preparations and suddenly the conditions are even better. No one would see him and he had the skills to climb back up and hide among the others in the village. Any trace was erased and no one suspected that he came from anywhere other than his car. He was enough of a regular by then to blend in. Premeditated."

"If he'd resisted the need to find out what happened he would have gotten away with killing her. His offer to help

Carnet down the hill was the only reason he was on the property. The only reason you had any reason to suspect him."

Agnes pondered this. She wondered if she would have made the connection if they hadn't found Anne-Marie's bones.

Vallotton slipped his hands in his pockets. "My aunt feels responsible. She thinks she should have recognized him."

"She almost did. I think it was on her mind, which is why she mentioned seeing Estanguet the first night I was there. We spoke about children and changes that happen over time, and loss. I think that too many thoughts were in her head, and she didn't pinpoint that it was literally seeing Estanguet that triggered her memories. He was a mere child when she knew him. She had no reason to recognize him. I associated her thoughts with Felicity Cowell's other name and her parents learning what had happened."

"I think he was often on her mind, perhaps subconsciously, but there. When Mimi's parents died she encouraged my father to adopt her. We didn't question her reasons, but I understand better now. She had always wondered what happened to the two boys who were with her during the war. After what happened with Estanguet she told me that she had been assured that both boys were well settled; now she realizes that for at least one of them that was not true."

"No one but Frédéric Faivre-Estanguet is responsible, not you, not the marquise. Not me, even though if I'd arrived minutes earlier Arsov would have lived."

"He'd nearly died the day before."

"That's my point. We did the best we could." She thought about George. Could she have saved him if she'd understood his struggles, or would any acknowledgment of what had already transpired have moved him toward the same end for a different reason? "Estanguet took that knife from its case at Arsov's when he toured during the Fête Nationale. I suspect he hoped to kill Arsov that day but for whatever reason was unable to. He decided to wait. Plan. Perhaps if he had confronted him that first day Estanguet would have gotten the truth he needed."

"*Mère*, have you seen—" A small blond boy stopped a few feet inside the living room, surprised by the sight of a stranger.

Julien Vallotton stepped forward to introduce himself and motioned toward the window. Daniel saw them and tapped the horn. "You like it?"

"Like it? A 1907 Rolls-Royce Silver Ghost? It has a seven-liter engine that's naturally aspirated, a side valve, and a four-speed manual gearbox."

"You know your cars," Julien said.

"Is it yours? Wow!"

"This is Peter, my youngest," Agnes said, smiling.

"I thought you and your brothers might want to go for a ride. When your mom is completely healed we can bring her out in it."

Peter's eyes widened and he nodded.

"Go get your brothers," Agnes said. "Nice of you," she said to Vallotton after her son ran into the kitchen, hollering for his siblings.

"A ploy to get on their good side after we nearly killed their mother."

Agnes noticed the package leaning against the door frame. It was the size and shape of a small painting.

"The auction is going ahead? I'm sure you'll have a great deal of interest after all . . ." She wasn't sure how to characterize what had happened.

"The notoriety?" Vallotton laughed. "I'm sending one painting to London by courier and they have promised to bury it in the back of a sale catalogue. My duty will be done for the attorneys. I'll send a large check to charity to satisfy everyone else, and we will hope that the outside world forgets us again. This one is for you. Something to say thank you . . . A little better than a ride in a car."

Over his shoulder Agnes caught sight of the woods that stretched down the hill and eventually over the small mountain and toward Château Vallotton and Lac Léman. She squinted into the cold sun. In her mind's eye she could picture a small girl running across the lawn, shrieking with delight as Winston chased her. The lawn would still be dotted with great piles of branches gathered from damaged trees. It would be some time before the landscape recovered and she wondered if humans should model their recovery on Mother Nature; she knew it took years.

"How is Mimi?" she asked.

"She talks about those days often, but the doctors say that's good. Now she's staying with us as our guest."

"Guest? Where else would she go?"

He half laughed. "Technically she now lives next door. Arsov made the request and we've honored it. We've deeded the villa to her for her lifetime. Right now, while she is so young, she stays as our guest at the château." He smiled at Agnes. "She likes that word—*guest*—and has tried to use it against Madame Puguet and Nanny with only some effect.

Something along the lines that guests don't have to do home-work, or eat their dinner. I think it will take some time to re-solve."

"Likely until she is eighteen."

"Twenty-one."

"I didn't have a chance to thank you that day," Agnes said.

"Once I knew Mimi was more scared than hurt I followed you. I should have run." He leveled his gaze on her. "How are you healing?"

Agnes touched her side involuntarily. "Well enough. No wonder that dagger was famous. Cut straight though the mus-cle, but I'll be fine, didn't lose any organs, which I gather was a possibility. Leg nerves a bit damaged and the scar is quite nasty, but they say it will fade. It was the knot on my head that gave them fits in the hospital. Stitches I can handle, but MRIs every day for a week wore me out. I think they like the idea that they haven't discovered the injury that will kill you, but they still might."

Marie-Chantal was laughing as she entered the room, three adoring boys in tow. "Julien, I think we should go for that drive now. Daniel is waiting." The boys were pulling on out-door coats and gloves and Sybille Lüthi opened the door, her eyes drawn straight to the gleaming automobile in the drive.

"It was worth it in the end, I hope?" Vallotton said. "All the trouble we put you through?"

Agnes looked from him to her mother-in-law's astounded expression and smiled. "Looks like it might be."